I0628832

Shudder

A very dark fairy tale

By

A A Prideaux

Text Copyright © 2013 Ann Agnes Prideaux
The right of A A Prideaux to be identified as author of this
work has been asserted by her in accordance with the
Copyright, Designs and Patents Act 1988

All Rights Reserved

No reproduction, copy or transmission of this publication
may be made without written permission. No paragraph of
this publication may be reproduced, copied or transmitted
save with the written permission of the publisher, or in
accordance with the provisions of the Copyright Act 1956
(as amended)
Any person who commits any unauthorised act in relation
to this publication may be liable to criminal prosecution
and civil claims for damages.

A CIP catalogue record for this title is
Available from the British Library.
ISBN 978-0-9930676-3-1

www.paganuspublishing.co.uk
First published in 2013 as Shudder
Edited Second Edition published in 2015

Paganus Publishing
Ruthin
Wales.

Paganus Publishing

Cover Designed by

Richard Fulke Paganus Prideaux © 2015

Dedication

For my son, Richard Fulke Paganus
Prideaux.
He knows why.

Who or what is Shudder?

The Old Mill was the place in Mill Town where most people worked. Years passed and the mill closed, but something remained inside.

The townspeople had ignored the missing children and the frightening stories of devils and ghosts for as long as they could remember. It was easier to carry on and accept the money the Snooty family provided in return for working at the mill. Everyone allowed the Council members to run their lives and control their ideas without question. Questions were always ignored and the questioner punished.

When Lydia Prix returned to the town after her marriage failed, she had no choice but to face the demons of the past and ultimately face the truth. The town would never be the same again.

If you go down to the woods today, you may end up being frightened of more than you think...

Contents

Shudder is based on a creepy family member of mine, who was not a blood relation. I am pleased to confirm that he is now very dead...

PROLOGUE

When Lydia left Mill Town, she did so with no intention of returning.

It didn't matter that her parents, grandparents and siblings and all the generations prior had lived there. That meant nothing to her.

Escaping with the hope of saving herself and her family from the threat of harm had been the only sensible move at the time. Lydia had been told often enough that if she mentioned to anyone what had happened to her, her loved ones would be hurt. Lydia believed and feared those threats.

By the time she left, her spirit had been so exhausted that she couldn't care less whether he hurt other people or not. Her thoughts had turned so far inwards that the outside world had become to mean very little. She could be easily led anywhere.

That could be the only explanation for marrying that old idiot Mr Wrinkles Pollack. He was more than happy to take home a pretty young bride from Mill Town to clean and cook for him. But soon after they arrived at Seaside, he was back sailing across the bay to catch fish to sell in the surrounding market towns. Mr Pollack didn't mind leaving Lydia to her own devices so long as food and tidy clothes were available on his return.

Nothing else was demanded of her and for that she was eternally grateful, if a little bored.

Lydia loved the harbour side cottage they lived in. Inside she felt safe and warm, cuddled by the old stone walls. Although the place had been untidy and dark when she arrived as the latest possession of her husband, it had taken her exactly one week...

One week, to clean and decorate the cottage. She chose pale blue, white and green, mirroring the colours of the sea which she quickly grew to love. She painted an old rowing boat white and propped it on it's stern against the wall. It acted as a bench seat with the bow providing a roof under which Lydia spent many hours meditating. She faced out to sea and watched the ships and listened to the seabirds and the waves.

Baskets of samphire and sea aster hung from brackets at the front of the house and it was possible to see the harbour from every room. All the furniture was made from carved driftwood and her style was envied and copied by her neighbours.

When Mr Pollack returned from long voyages he told her tales of monsters and mermaids and dragons in the sky. The fish he brought back were huge and tasty and in great demand. On his short trips he brought back small fish and crabs and then sailed out again on the same tide.

One evening Mr Pollack announced that he thought it was time for them to become keepers and ordered her to come with him and collect a child from Finders Hospital. He hadn't known about Lydia's vow made the day after their marriage, never to become a keeper with him. She instead dreamt of the day she would find children with a nicer man.

Lydia hardly had a relationship with her husband. He was not interested in decorating or gardens, or tales of her walks along the cliff. When he left on the tide, he usually did so without a wave.

But the coastguard was a different matter. He visited Lydia in the evening and filled the time available before sleep. He accompanied her on cliff walks where they planned how to increase her savings using his side line of profitable smuggling. He needed a hiding place and Lydia's harbour side cottage with it's cellar leading to an underground cave, suited both parties well.

And now, after years of planning and smuggling she was returning home. Ready to face her demons. Time had dulled the memories of her youth and she wondered whether perhaps she had imagined some of it. Sometimes she wasn't sure what her reality was.

It was true that no one else had ever talked about similar happenings. So it could be possible that she had mixed up horror stories told by her friends and exaggerated the content and included it in her own childhood memories.

She stared out of the coach window at the mist covered moors. Noting the few trees painted like black sticks against rocky outcrops, she felt a familiar childhood shiver.

"Do I recognise you dear?" asked the old lady sitting opposite. This lady had boarded at the beginning of the moor over which they now travelled.

"I don't know," replied Lydia honestly. "I am travelling from Seaside back to Mill Town."

"Back to Mill Town?" The old lady seemed interested. "I thought there weren't many who left Mill Town unless it's back to you know where…" she tailed off, a little embarrassed.

"Yes, back to Mill Town." Lydia wasn't going to get irritated. She didn't remember this old lady and to be frank didn't care what she thought. Since marrying and moving to Seaside, Lydia had been told that she was arrogant.

So her husband informed her.

Lydia preferred to see herself as confident. After those early experiences, she had vowed never to let anyone make decisions of any kind on her behalf. She let no one into her secret thoughts and memories. They belonged to her alone.

"Did you used to live there then dear?" The old lady was as interested in gossip as anyone in Mill Town.

Lydia looked at her travelling companion and tried to remember to keep a smile on her face. She knew that her face fell into a natural position of sternness and either scared or angered the person in whose direction her face was pointing. So here it was, the smiley face arriving in response to her thoughts.

"I did live there, but I left to get married and have lived at Seaside with my husband for years now."

"Couldn't you find a husband amongst your own kind? There are plenty of nice young men here. Your family must have been so disappointed that you chose a mixed marriage. No children? Mind you, Finders would have difficulty with a mule baby. I don't think there are any about these days."

Lydia dropped her smiley face pretence and retorted, "I would prefer that you didn't talk to me like that. I find it disgusting."

"Please yourself dear. But perhaps you should have thought about your poor family's feelings before you married a foreigner." The old lady triumphantly folded her arms across her chest, content in the knowledge she had upset new adversary.

Lydia stopped pretending to be sociable and looked out of the window at the moor again. Her mind went back to the day she left Mill Town and she shivered involuntarily at the recollection. She continued to stare out of the window, wanting no further contact with the odious woman with whom she shared the carriage.

Lydia relaxed against the background noise of the trotting goats which pulled their carriage. She had recently heard that some people were starting to use ponies instead of goats, as they were apparently far more versatile.

Lydia had always hated living in Mill Town. To be honest she had always hated living.

It hadn't been that much fun trying to find interesting ways to get through the days of her girlhood. The lovely blackness of sleep and loneliness had often been preferable to the frightening brightness of the day.

Her keepers, though harmless enough, appeared to have had little idea of how to raise their brood of six. Finders Hospital, from where everyone came, had no problems with sending baby after baby to the Prix household. There were no reports of ill treatment and the children were all clean and polite and healthy.

On the surface at least.

Lydia closed her eyes and immediately saw a picture of Uncle Cal. She opened her eyes again quickly and sat forward, feeling sick and anxious. The old woman looked at her with interest, a smug expression arriving upon her face when she saw how unsettled the young woman now was.

Lydia breathed rapidly, surprised that Cal could make her feel so bad after so long. She hadn't thought about him much since leaving Mill Town. Perhaps her mind was going a bit addled now she was coming home.

Home.

Shouldn't Seaside be home? She had been married for - how many years was it? It seemed a long time. But it was soon all to be over. Finished. As soon as she arrived in Mill Town, she would see the Lawyer and get a divorce.

Then she intended to finally face her past and make Cal pay for the evil things he had done. It was the only way to move on with the rest of her life. She had no idea how she was going to achieve this, but she had a definite faith that a solution would turn up at the right time. Her Grandfather Treen had promised her that it was so.

She hadn't told Treen about her Uncle. That part of her life was kept secret, sometimes even from herself. No one else would be interested anyway. The one time she had complained, she was forced to endure a prolonged stay at the Doctor's hospital, ensuring that she didn't complain again.

But it wasn't just Cal, there was something else. Lydia leaned back in her seat, closed her eyes and allowed her mind to wander back to the first time she had encountered the creature.

CHAPTER ONE *THE OLD MILL*

"Why do you always cheat when you play ball with us, David?"

Lydia was good at taking charge, even though she was only eleven years old. Her father said that she was bossy, but she did not care. She was a girl who needed to be in control. It was imperative.

"I don't cheat. I am the only one playing by the rules. You lot don't understand rules," he answered petulantly.

"That's because no one cares about rules, there's only six of us playing!" Lydia answered, not to be outdone.

The other children remained quiet during arguments such as this. The arguments happened a lot.

Lydia's two youngest sisters, who had arrived from Finders on the same day often tagged along with Lydia and her best friend David. The other two children Betty and Jimmy lived next door but one to Lydia and had been encouraged to come along to make up numbers for the game. They hadn't really wanted to come, but did as they were told.

"Is someone shouting you?"

The children looked over to the row of houses which separated the field from the road, but could not see anyone.

It was usual about this time of the evening for at least one of their keepers to shout them to come in. The group stared at the cottages and remained silent. They were used to being suddenly summoned back home. Tonight there was no one shouting, so the children carried on with their game.

The field was on a steep slope and gave a spectacular view across a valley to the moors beyond. It was part of the once sparsely populated moors on this side of the valley. But more cottages had been built during recent years and the houses at the top of the hill were now almost touching the houses by the river.

The playing field remained safe from the builders, because it belonged to the mill next door. This huge building had been producing beautiful cloth and employment for the town since the middle of the last century. Occupants of the cottages, young and old had been employed there since it opened.

The mill, now called the old mill, stood grey and silent on the horizon. Grey building next to grey building, each a separate unit joined only by steps and alleys. There was a huge chimney in the middle, soaring to the sky. Where does the sky go and does the chimney reach it? Lydia had asked her parents. She never received a satisfactory answer.

The noise inside the mill was almost too loud and all the workers soon learned the art of lip reading. The heat was unbearable and the air thick with fibres and dust. No worker cared, because the money they earned at the mill was better than could be earned working in one of the town shops. And everyone who worked at the old mill knew each other. It was a home away from home.

Breakfast, lunch and tea was served by a team of little ladies scurrying from floor to floor, pushing trolleys full to the brim with tea, cakes and toast. One day it all stopped. The red cheeked, smiley tea ladies lost their jobs. The hard working girls, experts with the looms which made cloth for the City ladies, were told not to come into work again. No more were they able to sneak out pieces of gold cloth and coloured weaves. They returned to their cottages and houses and boiled cabbage and rhubarb only so that they could feed their families.

The wonderfully moustachioed men who ran from grey building to grey building, fixing looms and mending machinery had to go home and persuade the donkeys and goats to work the land so they could grow the cabbage and rhubarb.

The mill owner, Mr Snooty, had decided to invest in the City banks. He wanted to make money in a tidy way and shop for clothes in the City. The Snootys still lived at the big house in full view of the old mill and they often discussed knocking it down or turning it into a zoo.

This mattered not to the group of children playing ball in the field. They could not remember the mill being open and had become used to the high-wired fences with notices informing them in huge writing:

'KEEP OUT'

So they did. No one entered the mill or the grounds and if a ball was inadvertently kicked over the fencing, the children stood silent and looked at the ball. When it did not hurl itself back over the fence, they would return home and fetch another ball during a telling off from one of the keepers as they searched in the sheds amongst cages and discarded toys.

"What is that?" asked a little sister, pointing at the buildings.

They all looked up at the mill and saw a light moving. The light was dim at first as if it were deep inside the building. Then it brightened as it came towards the window and moved along slowly, lighting first one window then the next.

"Who is in there, do you think?" asked another sister.

"I don't know," answered her twin.

"Let's go in and see," said David, still feeling bruised from the cheating accusation. He needed to show his dominance of the group.

"Are you mental?" Lydia had no intention of letting the pressure drop on her friend.

"Probably, I play with you often enough." Nerves were getting the better of him.

The rest of the group looked scared and the two neighbours' children announced they would be returning home. The afternoon had taken a turn they could not cope with. They scampered across the field, over the fence and disappeared into a cottage. The little cloud of dust which followed each child as they ran, met a slammed door and not knowing what to do next, disintegrated.

Now there were four.

"Come on, let's go and see what is going on. My mother said she used to work there when she was a girl and they used to have cake," said David.

This information brightened the mood of the others and they agreed that they would at least go and look through the gate.

Evening was descending upon them and although the sky had darkened and closed in, the children had not yet noticed. They made their way up the field and towards the gate of the old mill grounds. The track they met originated from the side of the cottages and came to a halt outside the mill, stopping suddenly at the gates. These metal gates possessed the beauty the craftsman intended.

Gold and black metal entwined to form the word **'Mill'**. But the sign telling all onlookers to **'Keep Out, Move Away and Don't Come Back'** rather spoilt the effect.

The gate opened with a push from Lydia and the group crept in. The light in the sky faded and the sun fell down behind the chimney. Still the children moved towards the main door as if in a trance. The light inside the building had stopped in front of one window, casting flickering shadows against the coloured glass.

"I have changed my mind," said Alice, the youngest twin.

"Me too, I am going home," said Janey the oldest twin. If you are a twin you know how important this distinction is.

"No you are not. You are both coming in with us," David informed them, "and you will be in more danger if you try and go back now. The yard and field are in darkness, so you will have to wait for us to take you back. Anything could happen to you there."

The two little ones thought about the problem for a moment, put thumbs in their mouths and held hands. They followed the elder two children to the door.

The big wooden doors opened against the combined weight of the children and swung noisily to one side revealing a large reception area. This had been the entrance used by all the workers back in the days of exciting business. A little office to the right had been the home of the caretaker doorman for many years. It was his decision whether a visitor would be allowed in or not. Now, the little office with its trumpet telephone and notice board housed only mice and spiders and bats.

Even David and Lydia were feeling nervous, but neither wanted to show the other how scared they were. They had come too far now to back down. After all what was the worst that could happen?

Chances were that the light was being held by someone they knew, another child perhaps who was camping out in the mill or someone looking for something to steal.

"I think the light has gone." David offered this information hopefully. Perhaps Lydia would rise to the bait and agree that they may as well go home now after all.

Nothing doing.

She marched forward, emboldened by the weakness shown by her friend and reached the door to the main factory floor. Inside they heard a shuffling sound and one of the smaller children screamed. They all jumped in fear and anticipation and ran back to the main door.

"Stop it!" Lydia was breathing heavily, almost tempted to leave and drag the others with her.

"I can't help it," cried Janey. "What was that noise?"

"Probably a bat or something, I expect. Are we going to do this?" Lydia looked across at David. They had come too far really. Why had they not just gone straight home? Why come into the mill at all?

"Yes let's go in. We shall have something to tell the others at school tomorrow. No one else has done this, we will be heroes." The thought made David pull back his shoulders and stand straight, in contrast to his previous crouching stance.

As one, they moved back towards the inner door and carefully opened it.

The factory floor had a different feel to the reception hall. Although it was now almost completely dark outside, the moon was reflecting on the gold and silver machinery and created a gloomy glow to the area. The space was huge and the children felt very tiny. Even the four of them together hardly filled half the space of the doormat on which they stood. They huddled together for warmth and comfort.

The light was now at the other side of the floor and only visible as a glow. It was impossible to see who or what was holding it and apart from some flickering from the flame, nothing else was obvious. Lydia strained her eyes against the semi darkness and hoped for a realisation that the light was merely a firefly or a reflection of the moon. But they weren't to be appeased so easily. The light came from some sort of lamp with an unusually large flame and was being held by someone. Or something. And this something made no noise.

"I think we have proved that we are not scared. We can leave now," Lydia informed her companions.

"I agree," David answered. "We can leave now, I should say."

The little ones looked up at the older two with grateful expressions. They wanted to go now. They wanted to go home to their keepers.

Suddenly David decided to give it another shot.

"Hello!" he shouted. "Who are you?"

There was no answer and so David tried again.

"We are not scared of you. Make yourself known to us or you will be in serious trouble."

"What sort of serious trouble?" asked Lydia.

"I don't know," he answered with a shrug of his shoulders.

They both giggled at the silliness of the statement. They felt close at that moment, good friends again.

Suddenly, there was a loud scurrying noise and looking back, they saw that the light was now in the middle of the room. Still no one was visible and Lydia was conscious that the outside door was a long way away. There was no movement from the direction of the lamp, just a glow and a flickering flame. Lydia was afraid.

"Why did we do this?" she asked David.

"I don't know really, but I am never doing it again," he answered.

The door banged shut behind them and they screamed in unison. Lydia noticed that the light was now only a few feet away from them. This horror was too much for the little ones and they turned on their heels and tried to open the door, pulling in vain on the brass handle which held the door shut. David and Lydia tried to help them with the handle and keep an eye on the trouble which was coming their way. There was an increased amount of energy amongst the group now and they were perilously close to panic.

The handle freed and the two youngest ran out into the hall, when suddenly the door slammed shut. Only now they had their backs to the lamp. They tried in vain to open the door, uttering little whimpers of terror. The door was firmly jammed shut.

"Run and fetch help!" Lydia shouted through the door to the little girls.

David and Lydia reached for each other's hand and held on tightly. They were as scared as it was possible to be. Time seemed to slow and then almost stop. Their senses heightened and their breath came in short gasps. The two friends turned slowly around to face the demon.

They were not quick enough. Long bony fingers grabbed the children by the shoulders and swiftly turned them around to face the door again. They could see a reflection of a tall figure standing behind them in the glass above the doors.

Looking down to her shoulder, Lydia saw the pale hand which held her in a vice like grip. She noted the long fingers which ended in long nails. These nails were blue and sharply pointed. Lydia knew that she must remember every detail so that she could tell her father and Policeman Glees as soon they could get out of the place. She tried to look a bit further up and noticed that his arm was thin and bony and spiky. She shook involuntarily because she was vaguely reminded of something. A memory which came into her mind briefly and then floated away just out of reach. It was not a nice memory and she was not entirely sure that she wanted to remember it.

David gripped her hand tightly and she stopped looking at the creature's arm and turned to her friend. He smiled tensely at her and she felt moved as she noticed the tears on his cheeks.

"Don't be frightened," she said. "You will be alright."

"Let go of her!" David said to the creature. It was not a shout, he had tried to make it a command. But there was no response.

24

Where was that vibrating coming from? Lydia thought that she could feel shaking passing from his arm to her shoulder. One of the fingers rose slowly. The hand was rigid, but it managed to stroke the side of her face.

The upward stroke was not soft or gentle, it was like sticky leather against her young skin. As he moved his finger downwards there was resistance, as though his skin was covered in scales. Lydia heard a moaning coming from the thing, man, whatever it was. She was so frightened and knew that this was a precursor to something even more terrible and she could not quite remember what it was. If she could remember it now, it must have happened to her before, mustn't it?

"Are you alright David?" she said quietly. Her eyes had been tightly clenched but now she opened them again. There was a smell coming from the creature which she thought she recognised from somewhere else. A hot room, an old man. Trapped.

"I think so," he said. They were talking as though the man thing was not there. If only it would talk or let them know what it intended to do.

"What are you going to do to us?" asked David. "You must let us go. Our keepers will be looking for us."

The vibrating began again and David was rewarded for his question with stroking on his face too.

"Why are you shaking? Are you laughing at us?" David was conscious of his tears and although he was not crying out loud, he knew that Lydia had seen his tears and he felt a little ashamed. Lydia would never mention the tears to anyone else, not ever.

"He isn't laughing David. He's shuddering."

Lydia raised her eyes to the door which led to the outside hall and safety. In the bulls-eye pane of glass, she could see the distorted reflection of her tormentor. She screamed long and loud.

The two little sisters ran out in to the entrance hall and as they did, the door slammed loudly behind them. They stood frozen to the spot in the middle of the floor. They felt far more vulnerable than if they had been standing at the edge of the room. Standing in the middle was terrifying. They felt very alone and sick with fear and they could no longer see David and Lydia.

Suddenly there was a crash of falling glass to their left and a jar fell to the floor. It had been thrown but no one was there. The little girls screamed and the energy of the scream gave feeling to their legs and they scrabbled their way out of the main door.

Half falling, half running down the stone steps, they arrived in the dark yard and felt the same terrible sensation of being in the centre of a deserted space, too scared to go forward and petrified of going back. Anything could be waiting for them in the shadows.

"What are we going to do now?" asked Alice.

"Should we go back and see what is happening to David and Lydia? They must be in terrible danger."

"We can't do anything for them except fetch a keeper or the policeman."

They looked back at the windows of the old mill and saw the glow of the lamp against the glass. Then they heard a scream.

"That was Lydia!" Alice said, alarm in her voice.

26

"Let's go now and fetch help!" Janey pulled at her sister's arm and as she did so, she noticed that the light in the mill had gone out.

They ran out of the gates, down the lane and past the old air raid shelters.

These shelters had been used for protection by the mill workers during the bombings from the other Country. Now they were overgrown with brambles and nettles and creepers of all sorts. Foxes and badgers and rabbits and weasels lived amongst the undergrowth. As a general rule the girls would have been worried about going past the buildings, especially in the dark, but tonight was different. There was no old weasel which could match the scariness of all they had just seen.

The narrow lane met the main road and the girls stopped again. The road was deserted except for the old couple from up the road, who were making their way back from the shops. It was no good asking them for help, they would be useless.

They turned left and ran to the second gate, the gate to their home. The gate was already open and the girls ran through it gratefully and up the path. They crashed through the door and tumbled into the kitchen.

"Mother, father, come quickly, we need help!" they shouted. But no one was there to hear, the kitchen was empty. The flames in the fire grate created dancing shadows on the wall. The kettle was whistling merrily upon the fire. The girls ran into the sitting room, but no one was there. They ran upstairs and still no one there.

"Where is everyone?" asked Alice.

"I don't know. You don't think anything has happened to them do you?"

"Don't be ridiculous!" Alice felt braver now that she was on familiar ground.

"Perhaps they are outside. Perhaps they are looking for us," she added hopefully. Their keepers were not as a rule bothered unduly whether the girls were at home or not.

There was a note on the table and Janey read it:

Girls, we have gone out. Feed yourselves.

The instructions were clear and succinct. There was bread and cheese and some rhubarb pie on the table next to the note. Janey began to eat some bread.

"What are you doing?" asked Alice incredulously.

"Eating, what does it look like?" Janey answered tetchily.

"We are supposed to be getting help."

Janey had the decency to look ashamed. In her hunger, she had forgotten the immediate problem.

"Who shall we ask then?"

"Follow me," said Alice, for she had an idea.

They were not to speak to the people next door, or the people next door but one. The girls did not know why that was, but their training had been thorough so they did not entertain that prospect. That left them to choose between the last cottage on the row and the house over the road.

The end cottage housed their mother's sister, Auntie Cal and her husband. The house opposite was the home of the Doctor and his sisters. The driver of a goat cart shouted at them as he swerved to avoid the pair. The lamps he had hanging from brackets on the front of the cart swung violently from side to side, but they all managed to pass each other without mishap. The girls ran through the entrance gates of the grand old stone house. The winding drive led them to the yellow front door of Doctor Catapult, a lovely friendly man who gave them sweets and lollipops whenever they visited. Children never needed to make an appointment to see him. Lots of young children came here and played in the woods and the summerhouse.

"Sad he never had children of his own," the townspeople said. "Never mind, he looks after everyone else's."

The twins had great faith that Doctor Catapult would help them. They hammered on the familiar yellow door, but there was no answer. They tried the big bell pull on the wall next to the door. They did not usually have to use the bell because the door was thrown wide open when the Doctor saw children coming down the drive.

"How long should we knock for?" asked Alice.

"One more knock and then we must go somewhere else."

One more knock produced only sore knuckles and the children turned and walked back down the drive. Alice looked back briefly because she thought she saw the curtains moving. But she was mistaken and the girls went back to the road.

They stood on the pavement.

"There is no alternative Janey."

"I know. But I really don't want to."

"We have to help them. It may be too late already."

There was nothing else to be done. The two girls held hands and crossed the road towards the end cottage. This cottage had been built at the same time as the other cottages, but looked different. It was darker and colder and had a wobbly path. Well, not really a wobbly path, it was just that whenever the girls walked down the path, their legs wobbled. Lydia told their mother about the wobbly path, but she would not listen.

"You just go down and visit your uncle, you know how much he looks forward to seeing you," Mother would say.

Tonight, the girls walked up the wobbly path and climbed the steps to the door. The cottages were built upon the steep hill which led down to the river and backed onto the field in front of the old mill. Because of the slope this was the not the only cottage that needed steps.

They knocked at the back door and it was opened swiftly by their aunt.

"What do you two want at this time of night? You should be at home, your mother will be worried." She spat the words at them.

"Mother is not at home," began Janey.

"Get off home anyway. She won't be long, she's only gone to the inn with your dad and the other kids. Go on clear off." She started to close the door.

"No auntie, we need your help. Lydia and David are in trouble!"

"What sort of trouble?" She was suspicious now.

Auntie Cal was a fat, unsavoury woman with a big round red face. Her husband, their uncle, was tall and as skinny as she was fat. They hated each other.

"There is a monster in the mill and it tried to get us and we ran away and it's still got Lydia and David and we think it is going to kill them both." The girls pleaded.

Their aunt looked at the two of them, shivering on the steps, white faced and frightened in the dark night.

"Get off home you bad girls," she said and slammed the door shut.

The girls sat down on the top step and looked over the valley to the little cottages on the other side. Twinkling lights shone from the windows and it was easy to imagine the normal life going on behind the walls. They thought about the children happily eating supper with their keepers and talking about their day. Janey and Alice felt very lonely.

"What now?" asked Alice.

"We are going to have to go back and help them. I don't know what we can do though."

"We have got to do something."

Janey led her sister, younger by ten minutes, out onto the road and back to their own house.

"We will get father's gun and go and shoot it. That is all we can do."

"No, we are not allowed!" said Alice.

As they arrived at the gate of their house they noticed some people walking towards them down Mill Lane.

"Who are you?" Janey said quietly, afraid of the answer.

There was no answer.

"Who is that?" Alice was getting fed up of this, although she still held tightly on to her sister's hand.

"It's me stupid. It's me." Lydia ran towards her sisters and began to cry. She was shaking uncontrollably. David stood next to her and did not speak. He seemed unable to.

"We were trying to get help, but no one was in and the Cals wouldn't come and help and we tried so hard." Janey was crying too.

"We were just coming back to get father's gun and we were coming to the mill again. I am so sorry it took us so long, but no one would help you see." Alice felt the urgent need to let her big sister know that they had not forgotten her.

"It's alright, it's all over now." Lydia hugged her little sisters, but she looked over their shoulders into the face of her friend David and her face froze into an expression of sadness that she thought would never leave her again.

By the time the keepers arrived home, the drama appeared to have passed. David went home and the sisters ate the food Mother had left out for them. The keepers were in a very good mood, humming and singing and did not notice the tense atmosphere in the little kitchen. Mother pottered about getting things ready for school the next day and smoked her pipe. It was the same as every other evening.

Much to the surprise of the little girls, David and Lydia had made them agree to say nothing.

"It turned out to be not much in the end," said Lydia.

"Yea, it was just a tramp that used to work there years ago and wanted a place to stay," added David.

"Why didn't he say anything then?" asked Alice.

"He couldn't talk," Lydia answered quickly.

"How did you find out that he used to work there then?" asked Janey.

"He wrote it down," David said quickly.

"He wrote it down!" Alice said. "I might be only eight, but I am not an idiot."

Lydia looked at David as though he was an idiot.

"Look, it will be easier not to tell anyone else about what happened," Lydia said reasonably. "We will just keep it to ourselves and say no more about it. They won't let us play out again if they think there is going to be trouble."

The girls reluctantly agreed.

Lydia went with David to the door.

"We can't keep quiet for ever Lydia," he said.

"We can," she answered. "We have to."

The night was extra cold now, winter would be upon them soon. The eleven-year-olds hugged each other.

Nothing would be the same again.

CHAPTER TWO *LAWYERS*

The cart stopped and there was a knock on the roof.

"Mill Town!" shouted the driver.

Lydia stretched and gathered her possessions together. The old woman was nowhere to be seen and Lydia assumed that she must have got out of the cart as soon as they stopped.

A few moments later, she stood on the pavement on the high street of Mill Town. This was the place she had gone to dances, school and shopped. Mill Village on the outskirts of the town was where she had lived and where the old mill was located. The town became bigger at the expense of the village after the mill closed.

There were few people about, most having finished their work for the day and gone home. Shoppers never hung around much when dusk began to fall, there being too many jobs to do at home.

Lydia picked up the large case, which the cart driver had thrown onto the ground and made her way over to the inn.

She pushed open the front door of the 'Rat and Handbag' and went in. Lydia had no intention of going to her parents, as she still felt a good deal of resentment towards them. There had been few letters passing between them since her marriage and no visits.

Lydia was appalled at the way they had been so pleased to see the back of her and almost thrown her into the marriage. It was difficult to forget.

She pushed open the door and was met with the pungent smell of pipe smoke mixed with smoke from the lamps and the fire. She blinked, but refrained from rubbing her eyes so that she didn't spoil her face. Lydia had forgotten how clean the air was at Seaside compared to her home town. There, everyone who smoked did so in front of their harbour side cottages and the smoke from that hobby blew straight up the steep road which ran from the harbour to the cliffs behind, then up and over the moors beyond.

Struggling with her bags, she made her way to the bar.

After booking a room for two nights, she gratefully accepted assistance with her luggage and followed the young man out of the bar and up the narrow winding staircases and corridors, until her room was reached. It was a small room, but the view was of the main street and she could see all the shops and offices.

"Thank you. Please bring my meal up to me here would you?" she said to the young man who had brought in the cases for her. He left the room with raised eyebrows, not being used to orders from strangers. Lydia looked outside.

The familiar sights made her smile. The shops had lamps in the windows, the better to view inside. Some parts of Mill Town she had missed.

Because her journey had been so tiring and she had an appointment with the Lawyer tomorrow afternoon she decided to remain in her room and go straight to sleep after eating. She unpacked her belongings and made ready for sleep.

The following day, Lydia stood at the lawyer's window, looking out at the park on the opposite side of the road. Autumn in the town was a miserable affair, grey and boring. Today was market day and usually would offer some colour from the canopies which covered the stalls and the wide array of fruit and vegetables and foods and clothes.

Everyone from the surrounding villages would descend on the town and meet for coffee and gossip. They would dress in their best clothes in order to impress their neighbours and speak in voices that would not be recognised at home. That was the way of it, everyone did it and no one minded.

On every other Wednesday in the history of the town, the streets were busy and the scurrying of shoppers caused the pigeons to stay on their roosts up high on the roofs of the shops. To scamper about on the streets as they usually did, was very dangerous and they only came down when the stalls had been cleared up. Then they enjoyed sharing the leavings, sometimes after fighting with weasels and rats. Happy times.

Today was different, for there had been a murder. Yes, a murder and there had never been a murder known of in the history of the Mill Town, way back in the days of their great-great-grand-keepers. Inspector Glees had told everyone that they must not meet in large groups and had banned the market until Friday, which caused a great deal of trouble for everyone. For Friday was the day of the coffee morning for the ladies in the town, so what were they to do now? Have the coffee morning and then come to market?

Such a lot of trouble for the inn keepers too as they were now not going to enjoy sales of rhubarb wine and cabbage salads which went down so well on market day.

This was what the inn keeper's wife had been trying to tell Lydia earlier, but she had listened only half-heartedly.

"Mrs Pollack, I am afraid that Mr Scriber will be a little late. He has some unforeseen business to deal with, but should be with you in another ten minutes."

The secretary at the town lawyer's did not look unduly worried about the delay the client would have to endure.

The secretary was a needle-nosed woman with black hair piled high on her head and glasses which turned up at the corners. She dressed in a beige top and skirt and finished off the look with a large black belt around her middle. This style may suit a chic woman from City, but the secretary could not carry off the look, as she was the shape of an egg.

"Not to worry, I'll wait," Lydia said.

Lydia felt slow and tired today. After her meal last night she had slept like a dead thing. Perhaps she had expected the market noises to wake her but nothing had. It was as though she had been drugged. And when the inn keeper's wife had knocked on her door at lunchtime saying, "I was a bit worried about you dearie. Not waking up and coming down for your food. What with all the goings on..."

"Oh I'm fine, just very tired I think. I shall get dressed and come down for lunch now." Lydia wasn't in the mood for gossip, a favourite pastime of everyone it seemed. She was not going to ask about any goings on. After bathing and dressing she came downstairs in order to eat a light lunch before her appointment. She spoke to no one.

The walk from the inn had failed to clear her head and she wondered if she was sickening for something. Lydia turned again to the window and looked out at the park. The windows, small with leaded panes gave a good view of the street and its inhabitants. The shops and offices were built higgledy-piggledy next to each other. These shop fronts had the same leaded panes as the lawyer's office and front doors with bright colours of yellow, green, red and blue.

Signs above the doors gave such information as **MEAT, BREAD, GREEN THINGS** and so on. The sign outside this office stated, **LAWYER.**

Each business passed down a family line and so it was not necessary to write the name of the shopkeeper, for everyone already knew their name. Of course, they also knew what business was conducted within each establishment, but some Council official had passed a law which said that the nature of the business conducted within must be made clear to everyone. For, what if a stranger did not know where to go?

"A stranger? A stranger?" it was said. "What do we care about a stranger coming to Mill Town? We don't want any stranger to know what is going on here. It is none of his business!"

But the law was passed.

The Council was made up of members of the Snooty family and their peers. The ordinary folk held few positions of authority.

The one and only policeman, Inspector Glees, recently promoted, dealt with every problem that might happen. There was little evidence of crime, apart from some missing children and a few burglaries.

Goat carts carried people from the villages to the Town Street. There was talk that Archie Gribble was inventing some sort of machine which would carry many people from one place to another without using goats at all. He lit a fire under a bowl of water and made the resulting steam drive the wheels of the cart. He had set fire to three carts so far and it seemed unlikely that it would ever take off as a scheme.

Lydia noticed that it was becoming increasingly difficult to see the park due to the heavy rain which had begun to fall. The few people on the street were putting up umbrellas and bashing into each other, for it was difficult to see through them.

"I should invent a see through umbrella," said Lydia, apparently out loud, for she heard in reply.

"What's that my dear?"

"See through umbrellas," she repeated.

"I see. I think it is a good idea, and then I could see trouble coming."

A little old lady was sitting in the seat next to the window. Lydia had not heard her enter and wondered vaguely where she had seen her before. Then she thought she heard someone tapping at the window and looked outside. Dusk was falling and Lydia noticed how early that was happening just lately. Autumn seemed to come very quickly once it started.

Suddenly, over by the park gates she saw a figure, a shape, something horrible which brought back memories long battened down in a box in her mind.

Terror, terror!

Lydia was aware of the rapid beating of her heart and she felt sweaty and faint. The office and the window and all her senses seemed to fall over an edge in her mind. She staggered back and her hand went to her mouth. She thought she was going to be sick.

"Are you alright my dear?" asked the old lady. She had left her seat and was now standing next to Lydia, putting her hand around her waist. Even when standing the lady was only as tall as Lydia's breast, but her sweet little face was upturned and full of concern.

"Yes, no, oh I don't know. I thought I saw something, someone outside. I was frightened." She gabbled out the words.

"What did you see my dear? Did you see the murderer?"

"What? The murderer? What murderer?" Lydia looked at the old lady, confused. What a question to ask. What she had seen was not a murderer, he was worse than that.

"Mr Scriber will see you now, Mrs Pollack," announced the secretary. "You can go straight in."

Lydia picked up her bag and jacket and immediately dropped them both. Everything fell from her bag on to the carpet and the old lady helped her pick it all up. A clay pipe, a lid from a bottle, a purse full of gold coins, some notes and a large key.

"Thank you very much," she said to the lady. "You have been very kind."

"It was nothing my dear," she replied.

Lydia made her way towards the office door of the solicitor feeling weak and vulnerable. She knocked on the big cherry wood door and was invited in.

Mr Scriber was sitting at his desk and writing in a large red journal. Without looking up he asked Lydia to sit down. Lydia obeyed, although she felt that lawyers were as rude as doctors in the way they did not acknowledge the presence of another person.

She waited patiently until he had finished writing, glad in truth, for the few moments to get her thoughts together after the shock. She looked around the office, noticing the paintings of men who looked similar to the lawyer.

"Apologies for asking you to wait Mrs Pollack, but I have been dealing with the murder and that has rather taken priority over everything." He looked at her as though expecting a barrage of questions. Lydia asked none, feeling that the lawyer ought to be a little more discreet.

"What can I do for you?" he asked.

"I want to divorce my husband," she said quickly. There, it was out in the open and there would be no going back now. He had said that she would not dare to divorce him, but here she was arranging to do just that.

"I see," said the lawyer. "Why do you want to do that? You need to have a good reason."

Lydia was aware that a wife needed to have good reasons, but of course a husband did not. This was another wonderful rule from the Council people. She had a good reason however.

"He tries to steal my money. I earned it through honest work and he waits until I am asleep or away from the house and tries to find it and steal it. I want a divorce."

Theft of money from either party was indeed a good reason. People of this land were allowed to earn anything they could and were entitled to keep it and give it away to whomever they wished. Theft was punishable even within marriage. No one could take away your money or jewels, no one. The coastguard had helped her come up with this untruthful story.

"Well, that is a good reason. Do you have proof of this?"

Lydia handed over a signed document from the coastguard at Seaside. The lawyer read through it solemnly and returned it to her.

"We can get you a divorce within a month, if that suits."

"That suits me admirably," she said with gratitude.

As the lawyer began to fill in the necessary documents, Lydia thought of her marriage. She had not realised how boring life would be with the fisherman. He spent much of his time at sea and when he came home, he smelt of fish. He was rarely out of his fishing clothes and two years into the marriage had grown a beard, which now was very bushy. Mr Pollack's beard did not grow towards the ground, it grew outwards and was tightly curled. Sometimes, Lydia was sure that she could see seahorses and barnacles in it. He had also become rounder and rounder as the years went on. In his yellow shiny coat, he looked like a beach ball.

"Now Mrs Pollack, just sign here and here and just here."

Lydia obeyed.

"Now we just have to send a messenger with this to Mr Pollack, have him sign and that will be that. Apart from the Town Hall Ceremony of course."

"Yes, the Town Hall Ceremony." That would be something to look forward to.

"Where shall you be staying from now on?" he asked.

"I hope to be staying here in Mill Town at my Gran's until I find a cottage of my own," she replied. Lydia hoped to find a house near Gran and start her own business and enjoy life for once. It had been a long time since she had enjoyed her life. About twenty years.

She sighed.

"Well, I shall send this off tomorrow and will contact you as soon as I get a reply. Then you must come straight back and finalise everything."

Lydia thanked him, got her belongings together and left the office. She went to the secretary's desk and waited for her to find a pen and a suitable form to fill in. She looked idly about the room.

"Oh, the nice old lady has gone then," she said, for the sake of something to say.

"What old lady?" replied the secretary, as she filled in details of Gran's cottage.

"The one who was in here with me, before," Lydia said crossly.

"I didn't see her." The secretary gave her a funny look. She had already decided that this Mrs Pollack was a bit foreign and odd, living at Seaside and being here in Mill Town getting divorced. She did not approve.

"Oh." Lydia thought that she had better say nothing more. She wanted to get back to her room and have some food and a sleep. Tomorrow was to be a busy day.

She went out into the street where the rain was still falling heavily. It was also quite dark and the street was deserted. As she looked right and left, in order to get her bearings, her eyes fell directly on the entrance of the park. No, no, no, don't look there Lydia, you must not look there.

But of course, she did look there and saw the stone pillars where the great park gates hung on huge hinges. They were black and made from iron and the metal had been bent into the word **'PARK'** at the top of the gates.

Well, in truth, one gate said **'PA'** and the other said **'RK'**.

What was that shadow against the pillar? No, don't be ridiculous, there was no shadow, just the flickering lights which hung from holders fixed into the stone.

Lydia shook with cold and as the rain began to fall faster, she walked quickly towards the inn. A tall man dressed in black walked towards her and said, "What are you doing Miss?"

It was Inspector Glees, the tallest man in Mill Town. This post did not pass from father to son, but was offered by the Council to the tallest man shortly after the last policeman died. Each policeman held the position to the end of his life, even if the last years meant that he could only travel in a sedan chair.

"I am going to the Rat and Handbag Inn," she told him.

"Well, you be careful Miss, there is a murderer about you know," he informed her unnecessarily. She had not thought about that and was now quite unnerved.

"Will you walk me to the inn?" she found herself asking him.

"Now then, you are funny. You must be a stranger! Off you go to the inn and don't you get yourself murdered!" he added helpfully.

Lydia pulled her coat tight around her body and marched more purposefully towards her goal. She knew she was the only one on the street now as she could hear her footsteps echoing against the shop fronts. Clip, clip, clip, clip, they went. Lydia felt cold again, as though ice was being thrown over her. It seemed to be taking far too long to get to the inn.

Clip, clip, clip, clip. Slap, slap, slap, slap. What was that? Someone else was walking behind her. She looked over her shoulder but saw nothing.

Clip, slap, clip, slap. She moved faster and then into a run. So did the other person. She stopped. So did the other person.

She turned around and saw someone dart into a shop doorway. He was very tall and very thin, a spiky sort of creature.

No! It couldn't be, not after all this time!

Lydia ran, heart pounding, tears running down her face, vision blurred. She turned into the door of the inn and arrived at the reception desk. The young man from last night looked at her as though she were mad and handed over her key. Lydia caught sight of her face in the mirror behind the reception desk and saw a frightened, pale woman, hair plastered to her head and wide frightened eyes.

"Are you alright Mrs Pollack? Do you need the doctor?" he asked.

"I'm fine," she answered and made her way upstairs. Her legs were wobbling and she felt ill. After fumbling with the lock on the door she went in to the room and threw up all over the carpet. She stood there for a moment panting and crying, knowing she would have to clean it up. What was happening?

She went over to the window and looked out. The lamp in her room was not yet lit and she was able to look onto the street from the darkened windows. Her imagination told her that something was standing at the entrance to the alleyway opposite. She quickly drew the curtains, lit the lamp and set about cleaning up the mess.

The thought of going downstairs again to eat filled her with dread and so she took the fish paste ships biscuits from her bag and ate those instead. They certainly settled her stomach and when she washed them down with a bottle of rhubarb juice, she almost felt like her old self. She stood up and went to the window again and looked out. There was no monster man on the street now, just a few people leaving their flats to go to the inn. They were missing the market meeting of today and so had come out to see if there was any gossip they could catch up with.

Lydia thought about going down to join them, but after leaving her room and standing in the tiny dark corridor outside the door, she changed her mind.

The old feelings overwhelmed her as the corridor floor began to move and the lamps on the wall blew out. She stood stock still, her senses on red alert, straining to make sense of the sounds on the stairs. She ran back into the room and slammed the door shut.

When Lydia woke the next morning, it took a moment or two before she realised that she was lying on the bed and still in her clothes from yesterday. She washed and made her way downstairs to breakfast. The innkeeper met her at the bottom of the stairs.

"We missed you last night Mrs Pollack, did you not feel well?"

"No, not really, I had a busy day yesterday, much to do."

The innkeeper showed her into the little dining room and Lydia sat down to enjoy hot nettle tea and toast. She was now set for the day.

Debating in her mind during breakfast whether or not to walk or take the cart down to Mill Village, she eventually decided to catch the ten o'clock cart.

Apart from another lady who was taking a piglet back to her cottage, there was only the driver for company. Lydia watched the piglet in its little harness sitting comfortably on its mistress's lap quite oblivious of the fact that his life would not be what he was expecting at the moment. Life never turns out how you expect it to.

The cart made its way down the very steep hill which led into Mill Village. The driver kept applying the brake, so that the cart did not hit the goat, for it did not like that. After a little while they stopped directly outside the entrance to the mill.

Lydia felt her chest tighten as they waited for the other lady to alight.

Looking to her left she could see the mill gates, but there were no air raid shelters to be seen, just heaps of bricks and wood. The sign at the end of the lane took her attention:

FOR SALE – MILL APARTMENTS.

"Excuse me driver, but what does that sign mean?" she asked.

"They have just about finished converting the old mill into flats and they are very expensive, hardly anyone around here can afford them."

"So did the old mill family sell them?"

"Oh no, they arranged all the building themselves and employed all sorts of villagers in the work, but now they have been sacked again. Just a few finishing off things, they say. They want City people here to bring more money, though I don't know what they would find to do here."

Lydia looked at the second cottage, the home of her keepers and the house in which she had grown up. She was not making the first stop here for she wanted to call on her Gran, where her little sisters now also lived. No one knew that she was coming; she wanted it to be a surprise. She hadn't mentioned it in the few letters sent via the post cart between them all. So they did not yet know that she was returning as a wealthy and independent young woman.

Lydia was surprised to see the curtains still drawn at her old home, but had no time to think about it as her attention was sought by the driver.

"Heard about the murder?" he said.

"Yes, they were talking about it in the inn, but I don't know who got murdered or where it happened, do you?"

"It was that young man, from around here I believe. In fact come to think of it, he used to live in this road somewhere, I don't know where though."

Lydia began to feel frightened again. A young man had been murdered, she may know him. The cart moved off and Lydia watched the cottages pass by on the left and the Doctor's stone house on the right.

"Is the Doctor still there?" she said to the driver.

"Oh, knew him did you? Yes Doctor Catapult is still there, but he is an old man now. Not the same as he was, that's for sure."

They passed the cottage of her Aunt and Uncle Cal. The place looked as grim as ever and Lydia shivered.

After this final cottage there were fields on both sides. Lydia had a good view of the old mill on her left hand side, tall and grey behind the field which still separated the cottages from the fence surrounding it.

They used to have some good games in that field, she remembered. Of course she remembered everything else too.

Her mind went back twenty years, to that first night. In a flash she recalled the feelings and the almost unbelievable things which occurred. She closed her eyes.

The things he had done to them and the things he made them do, was beyond comprehension. She remembered him saying that if they ever told anyone, he would find and kill them both. He would also kill their brothers and sisters if they ever breathed a word. He said that no matter how old they got, he would know what they were doing and thinking and he would make them pay, over and over again.

But everyone was safe, Lydia had never told anyone. She had written a diary when she was lonely and fed up at Seaside in order to keep hold of her sanity. She burnt the journal in the fire before she left on Tuesday. Then she took her case and left Seaside, intending never to return. The note she left Mr Pollack on the kitchen table would explain all. He wouldn't mind too greatly, she knew. He would soon find comfort with that fat, fair haired June woman from the quayside.

"I only left Mill Town to protect everyone," she said.

"Is that right Miss?" answered the driver.

Lydia blushed, she really must stop talking out loud. It was a dreadful habit she had picked up while spending so many lonely hours during her marriage.

The cart turned left at the bottom of the hill and trotted along Wide Lane passing in front of the old mill. It looked as dark and dreary as ever and it was to be hoped that the new apartments would give the place life. They arrived at a crossroads, where Bell Lane turned left back to Town Street and on the right was Wood Lane and led to, well, the woods.

Gran Prix lived on Wood Lane.

Lydia jumped off the cart at the crossroads and the driver passed down her cases. She intended to stay here for a few nights until she was fixed up in a cottage of her own. The cart went off in the direction of the countryside and Lydia walked towards the house on the edge of the woods. She could see the chimney smoking merrily away and she imagined her Gran busily sorting out lunch and drying washing and caring for the garden. Hopefully her little sisters would be there as well.

Her step quickened, it had been so long since she had seen her family and now she couldn't wait any longer. This time she would stay, she was grown up, nothing could happen now.

As she turned into the gateway, a woman was running out of the front door crying as if she would never stop. It was her sister Marjoram.

"Lydia, Lydia," she cried out. "How did you know?" she said in a startled tone. Her eyes were puffy and swollen.

"Know what, Marjoram?"

"About Michaelmas! He's been killed!"

For the umpteenth time in these past two days, Lydia felt her heart miss a beat. This time, her legs gave way and she   fell   to   the   ground.

CHAPTER THREE *IT'S MURDER!*

This was an unexpected turn of events. Their brother Michaelmas, the victim of a murderer. Nothing like this had ever happened in the recent history of the town, certainly not in the memory of anyone living.

"What happened?" asked Lydia, as soon as they were in the kitchen, holding cups of nettle tea and looking shocked, terribly shocked. Lydia had been helped into the cottage on the arm of someone, it may have been her father, but she could not quite remember.

She was finding it difficult to piece together what was going on. Her life was in turmoil enough without all of this. She had imagined her homecoming being a time of explanation and joy and new starts. She had a fleeting selfish thought that a swift journey back to Seaside and her little blue and white cottage would have been a relief.

She turned her attention back to the room because someone was speaking in answer to her question.

"Inspector Glees came and told us this morning. I mean we all knew that there had been a murder yesterday, but we did not know who it was. And then it turns out that it was our dear brother."

The kitchen of Gran Prix was filled to bursting point with their keepers, Gran, Janey, Alice, Marjoram and now Lydia. The kitchen was very small and with the people and the table and the fire and the cupboards, it seemed that nothing else could fit in.

Lydia wondered idly where her other sister Sadie was. Perhaps she didn't know yet, Lydia herself had not known twenty minutes ago, or was it ten minutes ago? She didn't really know what was going on. She looked around the room in which she sat, bewildered, all feelings exaggerated and her senses on edge.

She noted the yellow painted mantelpiece which topped the dark blue fireplace. It hadn't changed in all of her memory. Surrounded with hops intermingled with ivy, it provided perfect roosts for the little birds and butterflies who lived there. Pots and pans and dishes covered in flowers hung about the walls. An owl sitting on a carved log placed in one corner of the kitchen kept watch over the proceedings.

"So, what happened and why?" she repeated.

"Michaelmas was working in the woods," said Janey.

"He always worked in the woods," said Alice,

"He kept the paths clear and looked after the trees," said Mother.

"He loved his job and was very good at it," said father.

"There was no danger in the woods, he was never frightened of going in there," said Marjoram.

"But what happened?" Lydia said again.

"He was found dead in a clearing, as though he had just fallen asleep. There were no marks on him, he looked very peaceful. Apparently the log man found him when he was walking through and he went straight to the policeman." Gran Prix gave all information clearly.

It seemed that when the log man found Michaelmas, he could see no one else around. Knowing who the victim was, he did not want to be the one to let the family know and so left it to the Inspector. Glees then insisted upon secrecy until he was ready to speak. Apparently he had reached the conclusion of murder due to the fact that the word

Murder

had been written in the dirt next to the body. Inspector Glees was nothing if not thorough in the gathering of evidence.

"He thinks that Michaelmas wrote it before he died," Marjoram informed Lydia.

"He would have wanted us to know what had happened," said Mother.

Lydia could make no sense of what she was hearing. Even the knock at the back door seemed out of place.

Inspector Glees was calling to see the family. He squeezed his huge frame into the already cramped kitchen disturbing the birds in the ivy as he tried to move around the room and find a suitable area in which to stand. He found a place in front of the assembled family and put his hands behind his back before he cleared his throat and began to speak.

"Now, I have presented all the facts to the Council and we have reached the conclusion that Michaelmas Prix was murdered by someone yesterday. As yet we have no evidence as to who committed the crime and so until we have some evidence we shall keep an open mind," he announced grandly. He said no more, merely smiled and stood in front of the fireplace.

The family looked at him and nodded encouragingly waiting for the rest. But there was nothing.

"What are you going to do about catching the murderer Inspector?" asked Lydia, finding her voice.

"As soon as someone brings me some evidence I shall look at it and until then perhaps we can all get on with our lives."

The family looked at him, not quite sure what to say. After all, because there had never been a murder before in Mill Town, no one was sure what the form was.

Janey found her voice and asked, "There must be something you can do. You could ask around the place and find out if anyone saw anything."

"Mr Scriber the lawyer knows about it and he says that he will keep his ear to the ground. If you hear anything, then you can tell me and I will tell the Council and take it from there." The whole process seemed very unsatisfactory.

The kettle whistling on the range broke the tension and Gran busied herself with cups and plates and the like.

Inspector Glees had some tea and biscuits, smiled and chatted a good deal and left. He took some fresh rhubarb with him and a bunch of the cabbage roses Gran had growing in the front garden. It was all very nice. He waved as he walked up Wood Lane towards the crossroads.

"I don't understand all of this. Tell me exactly what happened," demanded Lydia of the family as they sat around the table.

She learned that Michaelmas had been working in the wood for the past two years and had a small house which went with the job. He had recently met a girl and they had been walking out and seemed to be getting on very nicely. There were no problems in his life, he seemed as happy as he could be. The family did not see him every day, but he would call on Gran and his sisters with his washing and take back some cooked food. He was not a good cook, what man was?

Yesterday he had been working as usual, although no one in the Prix family had seen him since the day before. He appeared to have spoken to no one until the log man found his body very early in the day and reported it as soon as he got to Town Street.

The Inspector immediately decided to stop the Town Market, in case someone else died, although the logic of that decision was beyond everyone in the room.

Michaelmas was lying on the large rock in the clearing with the writing on the ground next to him. He had no enemies and was a popular person. There were no strangers about and no sign of any violence.

Lydia drank some more of the offered tea and thought deeply.

"Why are you here anyway?" asked her mother. It had just dawned on her that her daughter was at home for the first time in several years.

"I am getting a divorce and shall be coming back to live in Mill Town or the Mill Village."

This announcement brought mixed reactions from the family. The keepers looked worried as they did not want a child back in their cottage. Her sisters and Gran looked very pleased as they had disliked Mr Pollack from the first and could never understand why Lydia had married him.

"You must move in here," said Gran and the twins smiled approvingly. Marjoram lived nearby and was glad also. She was married to a cart wirer called Mr Chariot and their son Bobby would soon be joined by a sister Dotty, who was to be picked up from the Finders Hospital this very week.

"You can help me with the new child Lydia, I should be glad of that," she said. "I cannot offer you a bed, but I can certainly offer you company."

"You will have company enough with us Lydia and you can help us with our new business. We are going to make a fortune and be on the Council like the Snooty lot. Then we can make a difference in this boring old town."

It turned out that Janey and Alice, encouraged by their Gran, had imported some ponies from Somewhere Else and were trying to convince the locals that the ponies would be better to have around than goats.

"We think everyone will have a pony before long," Janey said to Lydia.

"I've heard that somewhere," she answered.

They showed her the room which was to be hers. It was next to Gran's and Lydia remembered staying there during Christmas time years ago. It was small and pretty, with a mirror and table in front of the little window and a bed made from walnut with a goose down cover. The pictures around the wall were of family members and the walls painted to look like a garden. She remembered it exactly like this, and had thought of the room many times during her life at Seaside.

After putting her case on the floor and taking off her shoes, she decided to have a little lie down and get her bearings. She was giddy, not just the light headed sort, but her head was now spinning so badly that she was finding it difficult to focus her eyes. She decided to close them and wait for the spinning to stop.

She lay down on the white bedcover, and within a few moments found herself hugging the same teddy she had hugged as a frightened young girl in her scared childhood.

She began to remember, or dream, she was never quite sure what it was she did. This dream was about her schooldays. School was horrible, she could remember that easily enough. Although a bright girl, Lydia found it difficult to focus on lessons when Mrs Bark the teacher droned on for hours.

She would tell the class about the history of Mill Town and only referred in passing to the towns and places which existed outside their experience. There was no need to know what other people did, the Council decided. Just learn about how to stay happily here in Mill Town and make this the only future. That way no one would ever want to leave.

It was true, most people did not want to leave. This was a population that lived by such sayings as, 'Least said, soonest mended,' and 'Never let the sun set on an argument' and similar. It annoyed Lydia intensely. Everything was geared to causing as little trouble as possible, no matter what happened.

She had rebelled for a while, seeing how far she could push the teachers and the keepers with her questions and attitude, but it got her exactly nowhere. She was considered to be a troublemaker and her parents even took her to see Doctor Catapult.

"What is to be done with her?" they asked, very confused about the situation. "She isn't normal. Perhaps there was something that they knew about at the Finders

57

Hospital and they didn't tell us. What do you think Doctor?"

Doctor Catapult asked them to leave her with him and he examined her thoroughly over the next few days. Lydia could only vaguely remember that sleepover at the Doctor's house. He had given her some medicine which he told her would relax her and help her to forget about being so argumentative. She didn't bother to confront anyone after that because it wasn't worth the effort.

She remembered the two sisters who had lived with the Doctor and decided she would pay a visit now that she was back. Perhaps they would remember something about those days.

She fell into a fitful sleep, dreaming of home and her brother and then her cottage at Seaside. All her sisters were there, standing in front of the cottage and calling to her, 'Help us, you must help us.' 'I will,' she called out, 'I promise I will.'

She woke with a start and realised that she was sitting bolt upright in bed. She would help them, she would.

She got up and washed her face in the bowl of rose petal water which had been placed on a stand in the corner of the room. While changing into her flowery dress, Lydia remembered that her husband preferred her in her seagull dress and felt a surge of gratitude that she would never have to consider him again.

She brushed her hair and thought, for the first time in years, that she wasn't such a bad looking girl after all. She smiled at the image in the mirror and the image smiled back.

She went back downstairs and insisted that the girls take her into the woods to the exact spot where Michaelmas

58

had been found. They agreed to do so as soon as they all had something to eat.

"A shock has to be fed," said Gran, "otherwise there'll be fainting. We don't want fainting."

So they sat at the wooden table, which had been fashioned from an apple tree trunk by their grandfather. He made the table and other furniture after the mill closed and his skills were no longer required. Grandfather Treen Prix was an expert in making the small wooden parts required in the mill. The skill of carving and whittling had been passed down from father to son and once the mill closed, the skill was on its way to being lost.

Michaelmas had not found the need to learn such a time consuming and unrequired trade and had instead gone to work for the owners of the woods.

Treen spent his time making wonderful items which were now kept in his shed. This place had been locked after his death and had been rarely opened since. The furniture in the house was the only testament to his genius. The Snooty mill family had more to answer for than they realised.

"When they finally leave this town on the last cart, they must explain themselves to those who have gone before," said Gran solemnly. Treen had taken the final cart seven years previously.

Shortly after breakfast, the three of them left the cottage and made their way into the woods. In front of the cottage ran Wood Lane which passed straight through the middle of the woods by a well-defined track that carts and walkers used on a regular basis.

It continued to Moor Land and Moor Town but this was not the way the sisters travelled today. They went through Gran's garden, between the roses and the

59

vegetables, then through the briar hedge where they had to duck. Gran was much shorter than they and she could only reach just above her head when clipping it's branches. They arrived in the water area where the river had been used to great effect. Here it was damp and cool and the dark green plants fell lazily over the tiny waterfalls and crinkly streams, bobbing where the leaves touched the water. Anyone who looked closely could see fishes and creatures swimming quiet and elegant as they moved from one rock hiding place to the next.

The noise was like a tiny piano playing constantly in the undergrowth. Lydia had spent much of her childhood here hiding from the questions and company. Today walking through, she thought of her brother and was glad that he had at least passed quickly.

The three scrambled over the moss covered stone wall at the edge of the garden and were now firmly in the middle of the woods. They had seen little sunlight since entering the water garden and so the darkness of the woods did not come as a shock.

Here the experience was not one of peace and quiet. The woods were much noisier than might be expected. The birds were singing loudly, the undergrowth was experiencing permanent action and scurrying and there were eyes peeping and ears listening around every corner. Why was that?

"It is very noisy here today," said Lydia.

"I was thinking that myself." Janey was starting to get worried, but did not want to alarm the others.

"You know, Lydia, Michaelmas was not that happy." Alice broke the news that she had been keeping to herself for the past day.

They stopped and faced each other.

"Tell me," ordered Lydia, the bossiness returning. She may have been away for five years, but the same family dynamics accepted before, applied now. Her sister answered the question swiftly.

"He said that someone had been following him to work recently and he did not know who it was. It only started on Sunday and at first he was ignoring it, but then it happened on Monday too and was going on for the whole day. He thought he saw something behind the trees but, when he looked there was nothing there. He could hear crackling noises and a sort of swishing that made his hair stand on end. He spent his last two days looking behind him instead of doing his job."

"Why didn't anybody do anything about it?" asked Lydia.

"Because he said there was nothing really to worry about and he would handle it himself. He said he had a plan to trap whoever it was and teach them a lesson they would not forget. He said not to tell anyone because they would just make a fuss. I wish I had made more of a fuss," she added with feeling.

"Well, I intend to find out exactly what happened," Lydia informed them, "even if that stupid policeman does nothing, we shall. Are you ready to help?"

The girls agreed with their elder sister, although just at this moment did not feel quite as brave as she appeared to be.

They made their way through the woods and it had to be noted that today the woods had a special creepy feel. Before, the noises and scampering only added to the experience of family and familiarity, but now it was scary.

The trees appeared to bend in the breeze which had suddenly started up. As the branches bent and moved, the sun was visible and then gone. The effect of this meant that the girls had difficulty re-focusing their eyes in the brightness and the shadow.

"I wouldn't want to be here on my own in the dark," said Lydia.

"We didn't mind doing it too much when we were children."

"We were braver then."

"No, not braver. Innocent. We did not know the kind of things which could happen to a person," said Lydia, and the girls looked at her.

"Knowing that there is a murderer about suddenly seems real in here doesn't it? I mean out there," she pointed in the direction of the cottages, "it's unreal and unbelievable. But in here I can see how someone or something could get behind you and surprise you when you weren't expecting it. Like that night at the…" Alice did not finish, because the words would not come out.

The others said nothing but moved forwards to the clearing where their brother had been found. Alice and Janey had never really discovered what had happened that night after they ran away to get help from their neighbours. The story told to them by David and Lydia never had made sense, but despite many questions, they had not expanded on it. Their keepers asked nothing and noticed nothing, not ever.

"Will you tell us what really happened Lydia?" Alice asked.

"No," was the response.

They moved on in silence, the atmosphere tense between them. Lydia was quite aware of the tension, but what could she do? She must go and see David today.

"Do you know where David is?" she asked.

Janey felt unreasonably cross with her sister, so answered, "No."

They reached the clearing after saying nothing else to each other. As they entered the fern and rock strewn area, Alice pointed to the centrepiece, a huge flat rock patterned with fungi and moss.

"That's where he was found," Janey informed her.

They walked towards the rock and Lydia had the weird sensation that she could see their brother laid out flat on the rock, eyes peacefully closed, arms folded across his chest. They moved nearer and she felt her chest tighten and could not breathe. No, she was not imagining it, there he was, laid out on the rock just as she had imagined.

Only it wasn't Michaelmas. It was Sadie.

CHAPTER FOUR *THE CLEARING*

"No, no, no, no! This can't be true! What is going on here? Are we dreaming?" The loud screams from Alice and Janey should have been heard back at Gran's cottage.

Lydia put her hand to her mouth. She had not screamed out loud for almost twenty years, preferring to keep her feelings inside. Did it do her any good? Perhaps. She stopped caring about that a long time ago.

Back then she vowed never to show fear again. Fear weakens a person, makes compromise where there isn't a compromise. Fear was just an excuse for a quiet life and a way to avoid confrontation. No, that would not be happening again. She would keep the feeling to herself and live life in the moment. Experience what was actually happening and not what might.

"Come on you two. Let's think about all this in a logical fashion," she said to the others. "We have to get to the bottom of these murders, so we must take notice of everything that is around here now. That stupid Glees bloke is rubbish. As soon as we tell him what has happened, he will just take Sadie away and tell us that there is nothing more to be done."

"How can you act as if nothing has gone on here and behave like a cold fish?" Alice was angry with the whole situation, not really with her sister. It was now completely beyond her comprehension.

Lydia, however, had trained herself differently. She could keep her feelings hidden in little boxes in her mind and deal only with whatever needed dealing with.

"Because it is important we discover what happened to them both. Keep alert and remember everything that is lying around here, including footprints and broken branches. Things like that."

The girls looked at each other and began to walk around the area.

"We shall have to fetch help," said Alice.

"Not yet," answered Lydia coldly. "I am going to catch the twisted devil that is doing this."

"You can't do that on your own," Janey said.

"Help me then," said Lydia.

The twins looked at their sister and said, "Yes"

There was something else behind this story that they were not sure about, but they needed to find out what was happening. Lydia looked steely and determined. Although the girls had not seen her for several years, they recognised her single mindedness. After more discussion, the three of them stood around the body of Sadie and had a really good look.

She was smiling in her death and that seemed quite comforting. Her hands lay across her chest, forearms crossed over and palms flat. Her legs were stretched out and she looked quite comfortable lying on the large flat rock.

She was dressed in her daily clothes, hair tied neatly behind her head and her shopping bag placed carefully against the side of the rock. Now that was odd in itself. What had happened there?

The ground surrounding the rock was undamaged. The moss and the grass and small flowers sat prettily together, gazing up at the sun which was streaming down through the gap in the trees. The body and the rock were bathed in beautiful light, all the more amazing because the rest of the woods were in darkness.

"We have to take advantage of this light while the sun is out, it is the best chance we have of finding any clues," said Janey.

"You are right, as soon as the sun moves behind a cloud, we'll find nothing," agreed Alice.

The girls moved quickly about the clearing, taking mental note of all they saw. Which was not very revealing, Lydia thought.

She stood at the edge of the clearing and surveyed the scene in front of her. She knew that she must be clinical and detached about the process.

Sadie was lying flat on her back on the rock, although seemingly peaceful, she was most definitely dead. In fact, if there hadn't been a death in the same place yesterday, she could almost understand a verdict of normal death. Sadie looked as though she had laid her shopping bag against the stone, climbed on top and just died. But that can't have been what happened. For a start there was no valid reason Sadie would have been walking through the woods with her shopping bag. She would usually walk along the lane away from the shadows.

"Perhaps she came to look at the place where Michaelmas died," said Alice.

"I can understand that, but why come all alone when she knew there is a murderer about?" answered Janey. "It does not make sense at all."

"I am not so sure that she even knows about Michaelmas, she never gets to hear anything up where she lives," said Janey.

That was true.

Lydia continued looking and noticed that nothing was disturbed or appeared to be disturbed. She looked upwards to the branches of the trees and could see nothing unusual.

The dark woods surrounding the sunny clearing did not seem particularly menacing at the moment. Peace reigned everywhere.

"You have to go for help, I think now," she said to her sisters.

"Who should go?"

"You two go together, I am not scared to stay here," Lydia told them.

It was true, at the time she made this statement, she did not feel scared.

The girls left, holding hands and walking towards the lane. The journey would not be as simple as might be thought. The girls had to leave the sunny clearing and travel through the dark woods in order to make their way to the lane leading to the town.

Lydia was left on her own, guarding the body and left with her thoughts. The moment the girls left, she became aware of being totally alone. The feeling accompanied a slight shivering and then – she listened hard. Was that a noise? No, it must be her imagination. The noises were not out of the ordinary noises. She could hear birds and leaves and the odd scurrying about, but that was normal.

Crack!

That noise wasn't normal. Now her senses were on red alert again. Where had that come from? She could not work out whether it was in front or behind her. The atmosphere had changed and electricity seemed to fill the clearing. She had promised that she would not show fear, so she tried to relax and keep calm. That was difficult.

She looked around the clearing. Positioning herself at the edge, she waved goodbye to the girls and moved nearer the centre. That didn't help much because the thought of moving nearer to a dead body, even the dead body of her sister, was uncomfortable.

As she walked in a circle by the body on the rock, she could see nothing. The clearing was still bathed in sunlight and Lydia realised that if she stood in the centre, the light made it almost impossible for her see through dark trees. Putting her hand on the rock and feeling the ivy gripping the sides, Lydia pushed the flowers and bracken out of her way.

Wait a moment. There had been no ivy when they first arrived and the flowers were tiny, barely showing their faces to the world. Now they were standing proud and high adjacent to the tall bracken.

Crack!

She looked up and tried to pinpoint the direction of the sound. Her heart was beating wildly, then missing beats making her feel very light headed and wobbly. She knew that she could get into trouble if she lost her grip even for a moment.

She released slightly the death grip with which she held the rock and moved her hands until she came into contact with the body on top. The body was warm.

Lydia turned away from the trees and gave all her attention to her sister. How stupid she had been. All that talk about checking the clearing and looking for clues to see what had occurred and she never once had thought of touching the body. It was still warm!

That meant Sadie must have died just before they found her and the murderer must have been watching them the whole time. He was probably still here and now he knew that Lydia was alone. You stupid, stupid cow Lydia.

The hair on the back of her neck stood on end and as she realised that she was being watched. She whirled around and checked the edge of the clearing. There was a light shining through the trees. She wondered briefly whether her sisters had returned early, but that was not likely. Lydia could not see who was holding the lamp due to the fact she was still standing in bright sunlight.

She blinked and the light was gone.

"Is there anyone there?" she asked feebly. Did she want someone to answer or not?

She scanned the trees and noticed the light again in the opposite direction of the original sighting. How could it have got there so quickly? Perhaps there were two lights.

That was a helpful and relaxing thought, two people watching her from the woods while she stood there alone in the clearing.

"Hello! Who is there?" she tried again.

There was no answer.

The light vanished and reappeared in another part of the wood. Lydia felt her heart bump, bump, bump in her chest. The muscles around her chest were tightening and she was starting to have difficulty in breathing. This was getting bad – don't lose control Lydia. She felt sweat appearing around her hairline and her legs were feeling wobbly again.

"Don't be ridiculous, let me know who you are!" she demanded.

No answer.

Rustle.

Someone or something was standing behind her. She could feel a presence but could see nothing. Her back and arms were freezing cold and she could hear a familiar noise. Lydia was rooted to the spot in spite of her mind screaming – run!

A hand touched her back and moved slowly and carefully downwards to her thighs and then back up to her neck, before resting gently on her shoulder. This was almost unbearable. The fingers were long and Lydia knew that she had felt this hand on her back before.

But, this time the hand did not grip tightly and yet she still could not move. It was she who was frozen, immobilised by her own fear. Relax, relax, relax. She had practised what she would do if ever in this situation again and yet none of it worked. She was only conscious of her mind working overtime and had no connection to her body at all.

She could feel the large slippery hand on her shoulder and knew that terrible things were going to happen to her. In this moment, she remembered it all.

The fingers stretched out and stroked her face and then the other hand began to move carefully over her shoulders and down her chest. She could only wait until it was all over.

"Please let it be over quickly!" She said that out loud, because she heard her voice, only it sounded like someone else's voice.

The dreadful shuddering began.

"Lydia! Where are you?" She became vaguely aware of voices.

"Lydia! Where have you gone?" Lydia thought she recognised that voice. Then she saw a face looking directly at her.

"What has happened to you?"

Lydia couldn't speak, nor could she make sense about what was going on.

"Lydia, you should have come to see me first."

So, David had come to save her. It was a bit late now. He was always too late. He had scarcely got into trouble after that night when they lost their childhood innocence so many years ago. He always let her face the problems and do the protecting and then tell her how she must avoid confrontation. Thanks for that David.

"That's why I wouldn't marry you," she said to him.

He looked stung. He had come to help her and she wanted to start an argument. He decided not to respond.

Lydia noticed more faces surrounding her from above and surmised that she must be lying down on the ground.

"Did you see him?" she asked.

"Who?" said Alice. For she and her twin sister were there.

"That thing, man, whatever it was. It was here, again and he did things, again." She found the words came out haltingly.

David looked white and shocked and the girls looked puzzled.

"There is nothing here, Lydia, you must have fainted or something."

Inspector Glees was here too.

"I didn't faint, I don't faint," she told them. But, of course she must have fainted, for here she was lying down on the ground and could not remember how she came to be lying down on the ground. Her mind felt weird and still she had no control over her body. There was that stupid policeman, how on earth did he get to be in charge of people's lives?

Her two sisters, David and a couple of others who she could not identify just at the moment as she could only see the tops of their heads, were standing around the prostate body of a young woman.

Where was Sadie? The rock had no one lying on top, so Lydia surmised again that she must have been unconscious for far longer than she had originally thought. The place must have been cleared up and the body taken to – where? The same place as Michaelmas probably, but Lydia had no idea where that place was.

She looked beyond the clearing, over the trees and soon realised that her gaze could not penetrate through the blanket of green. Where was that thing? She wished that she hadn't fainted, because it would have been easier to work out how far away it had gone. She looked over at the old mill on the side of the hill. She saw some men beavering away, putting final touches to the renovation of the mill.

Her attention went back to the clearing and the group bending over the woman. What was the matter with her? Lydia looked closer. At the exact same moment Lydia realised who the woman was, she was staring back into the face of David. Only for a fleeting second of that moment did she think that she saw the creature again.

"I thought we had lost you!" David was saying to her.

"Where is Sadie?" asked Lydia. Her voice was so quiet it almost made her jump.

"We wanted to ask you the same thing," answered Janey. "What has happened to her?"

"She was there just a minute ago. I can't understand what is going on."

All sense of her known reality and its boundaries were lost on her. Warped boundaries they may have been, but at least she had understood them.

"I don't think that it is very amusing, making jokes about murder and dead bodies," said Glees, "pretending that you have fainted and can't remember anything will not to be allowed or tolerated. I shall inform the Council and they will decide how to deal with this."

The Inspector walked out of the clearing and through the woods towards the path. The group which remained in the clearing made no response.

There was no body and Lydia was still on the ground. The sun had carried on with its journey across the sky and now light was thrown only against the trees to one side of the clearing, casting the spot on which they stood into shadow. It was colder and there was a tense atmosphere among the group.

"So, where do you think this body has gone then?" asked Mr Chariot. He had been sent there by his wife who he had left crying and wailing in the kitchen. When the girls ran to their cottage after leaving the woods over an hour ago, the information given to the family was incoherent and bumbling. One spoke and then the other and none of it made real sense.

Once it was established that there was yet another dead body in the woods and in all likelihood a sister, Marjoram insisted that her husband accompany the girls to fetch help. They found the Inspector surprisingly close to the cottage walking down Wood Lane towards the town. He was with David.

"That was handy!" he said to them. "I didn't see anything happening. You Prix lot are attention seekers!"

What a peculiar thing to say Janey thought. Lydia was right about him, he was useless and horrible. She wondered why David was with him. They had been in deep conversation when the girls found them.

Along the way the group also collected Bill Riddle and Tom Pinewood. Bill was the log man who discovered the murdered Michaelmas and Tom was his assistant. Bill had been working at the edge of the wood all morning and insisted he had heard nothing. He said that he had not even seen the girls running out of the wood, they having used the far track while he was working nearer Wood Lane.

Bill and Tom stayed for a little while after the Inspector left.

"I would like to know why you said there was a body in the first place," said Bill. He was looking at the ground and kicking the dirt around his feet. Most of the dirt was kicked in the direction of Lydia, causing David to stand up and turn towards the log man.

"Don't do that," he threatened the man.

"Alright," Bill answered calmly, although he was sneering at him.

Lydia brushed away the mess from her body and said, "Come on. Let's go back home. I don't want to be in the woods when the dark comes proper."

It was true. As the sun fell rapidly out of the sky, the once sunny clearing felt intimidating and frightening.

"What about Sadie?" asked Alice.

"We can't do anything while it is dark. I will feel better in the morning and we can see what is going on," answered Lydia. The truth was that she needed to get her mind back together again. This was outside her control and that disturbed her greatly. Lydia liked to be in control.

She got to her feet in an unsteady fashion. David helped her and she noted how concerned he seemed to be. Lydia was not convinced that the concern was about her welfare. He was obviously not convinced that the girls had seen what they said they had seen.

"Why do you think I would make something like that up?"

"I haven't said that you did make it up."

"So why don't you believe me? The twins saw her too, you know."

"Where is she now then?" David sounded petulant.

"That creature thingy was here again, David." Lydia looked directly at her old friend, her eyes searching his face for signs of empathy. But there was none.

"I don't want to talk about that Lydia. All of that is history and we don't need to remember any of it."

"You clown," she said to him. "How can you say that? You and I both know what happened before and I think it all just happened again. I am not making it up, I wouldn't make it up. The whole thing is far too horrible to joke about and I am surprised you think it of me. It was here and I know it had something to do with Sadie vanishing."

He looked at her as though she was simple. Lydia assumed that his mind had decided to repress everything unpleasant and now he was a good compliant member of the town. Lydia hated him for that. It meant that she was even more alone with her memories, for the only person who knew what it felt like to have this burden was deciding to ignore it.

"There is no need to be hysterical Lydia. I hear you are getting a divorce from your husband, I expect you are feeling a bit emotional."

She pushed away his helping arm and swayed towards the rest of the group who had walked ahead of them and not been party to the conversations.

David followed more slowly and thought about what had just been said.

It was true that he shouldn't have been so unsympathetic towards his old friend, they had shared so much. But the shock of discovering Lydia was not only back in town, but also that she was in trouble, had hit him harder than he could admit. Since Lydia left, he had become involved in some things that would upset her. But it was necessary if he was ever to make the town safe again.

"David! Hurry up, you don't want to be left in the woods on your own, it's getting dark." So, even Bill was worried.

The group arrived at Gran's house, but only Lydia and the girls went in. It did not seem appropriate for the men to enter as well. After all, they had their own houses to go to and stories to tell.

Gran was white faced when they entered the kitchen, but in her old fashioned practical way she sat them around the table and fed them and gave them drinks while listening to everything they had to say. The girls knew that Gran would come up with a sensible solution.

"We must find out if Sadie has been at home lately," she said, "and take it from there. Sadie hasn't been here today, but that wouldn't be unusual, she may not have heard about Michaelmas yet. As soon as it is light one of us must go there and find out."

"We can do that Gran," said the girls.

"I am going to see the Inspector and find out what he knows. He must know more than he is saying. I want to find out everything that happened to Michaelmas. I am going to get to the bottom of this," Lydia said determinedly.

"Well, nothing more can be done tonight, you must all go to bed and we shall start early in the morning."

Lydia went up to her room and lay down on the bed. After recovering her senses she put her hand in her pocket and pulled out the handful of dirt which had been kicked at her while she lay on the ground in the clearing. She put the pile on the side table and picked out a shiny key.

This had something to do with everything, she thought. She put the key back in her pocket and went straight to sleep.

CHAPTER FIVE *TAKING CHARGE*

Lydia experienced the blissful moment of complete oblivion of the reality of her situation when she first woke. But the thoughts soon came crashing and tumbling to the forefront of her mind.

She sat bolt upright and immediately realised how dizzy she was again. When the room finally stopped spinning, she swung her legs to the floor. What was the dizziness about? She remembered reading somewhere, or was she told it? That dizziness meant your mind was trying to tell you something important and you really ought to listen.

"Come on then mind, tell me what it is. I can't be any more of a jangle than I am now."

But her mind was either not paying attention or just refusing to answer.

Lydia washed and dressed quickly and went downstairs into the warm kitchen. Outside it was still dark and probably cold. The temperature along the landing and down the stairwell was generally an accurate indicator of the conditions outside.

The kitchen though, felt and smelt lovely. Gran rose early every day of her life to ensure that there would be a friendly and comfortable welcome for whoever entered it and whatever time that happened.

As soon as Lydia lifted the latch on the little yellow door and entered the kitchen, Gran scuttled across the room and enveloped her granddaughter in a big hug.

"Oh I worry so much about you Lydia. You are always in some drama or other and not letting us know how you feel. I know you try and make decisions to look after the others, but you must remember to look after yourself."

This took Lydia by surprise and she felt tears coming to her eyes and blinked and managed to stop them before they started. No place for crying.

By the time her meal was on the table, the twins were downstairs and out the door in order to look after their ponies. And as soon as they had done that, Mr Chariot arrived.

It appeared that he had travelled over to Sadie's house the night before and discovered that no one had seen Sadie since she left for town on Thursday morning. Of course, this had been an unplanned journey as the market usually took place on the Wednesday, but provisions were needed. Apparently she had known about her brother dying, but had decided nevertheless to go shopping.

"Who will feed the family if I don't get some provisions?" she had said to her husband, Charlie Prince.

Some observers might have said that rather than being worried about the shopping, she was more interested in seeing Farmer Hornbeam. A single man and admirer of the buxom Sadie, they were often seen chatting for hours during market day. "Just good friends," she told anyone who asked. "We have lots in common," she would say.

Whatever the truth, she had left her house yesterday morning singing and swinging her shopping bag and had not returned home as of last night.

"Well she won't!" said Alice, the girls now having returned to eat.

Lydia was still a bit dizzy and decided to go out on her own to get her head sorted.

"If I walk for a while, I will work things out," she told the others in answer to their objections. "I will know where to go and what to do next."

She left the cottage by the front door and walked down the steps towards the gate which led to Wood Lane. To her left was a privet hedge and to her right an extravagant rose garden. All colours and sizes of roses bloomed there and the sight and scent of the place made her stop for a moment to take it all in. Grandfather Prix had planted the garden and she remembered as a child how she would help him weed and dig and clip. He told her how to kill slugs with beer, a process which both fascinated and upset her.

There was a second when Lydia thought she saw her Grandfather bending over his roses, wearing the beige hat, white shirt and brown trousers he wore every day that Lydia could remember seeing him. She smiled at his image and made her way to the gate.

She opened the white gate and went through it onto the lane. Opposite the cottage was a wall which surrounded the home of the Snooty family. Although the families had been near neighbours for all of their lives, they had nothing to do with each other. The stone wall surrounding their Manor was high and impossible to see over, unless climbed. This was a feat achieved often by the Prix children in earlier days. The large house was set back in the grounds beyond the wall and had never been seen on the inside by the Prixs.

Lydia didn't bother to cross the road. Instead she walked along the path which ran past the front of the Prix cottage and headed towards the crossroads. Standing there for a minute or two, she waited for inspiration as to which direction she should take. Straight on led directly to Town Street via Bell Lane. Turning left along Wide Lane would take her in front of the old mill and lead to the junction with Mill Lane. That in turn would join up with Town Street after passing her childhood home. Then a right turning off Town Street took her to the top of Bell Lane.

Lydia turned left.

The walk was pleasant and Lydia nodded and smiled at some neighbours she vaguely remembered from her childhood here. The wall of the Snooty property continued round from Wood Lane along Wide Lane, ensuring that no one could see inside.

They liked their privacy it was said by some, while others said it was because they did not want trouble after they closed down the mill and had thrown most of their neighbours out of work. As it was, most people ignored them.

Lydia arrived at the little shop which had been built into the fabric of the wall, a building which had originally been intended as a guard house. For years the lady who lived there sold sweeties and toys to the local children. Mrs Ladywoman had been living and working there for the memory of everyone who was alive to this day, and no one could work out her real age. Whatever it was, everyone agreed that she was old.

Lydia climbed the three steps which led to the shop doorway and entered. She loved the sound of the tinkling bell on the door which announced her presence to the owner.

The smells in the shop were wonderful and Lydia realised with a pang that she had not eaten sweets since she left Mill Village five years ago. That was a sad admission and soon she had in her bag a selection of all her old favourites.

She had chosen them from the many jars and boxes displayed on the shelves covering the shop interior. The shopkeeper counted out change on to the counter.

"I am very sorry to hear about your brother Miss Prix," Mrs Ladywoman said.

"Yes, thank you. Only I am Mrs Pollack, well not for long, soon I shall be divorced and then I will be Miss Prix again, I suppose..." Her voice tailed off and she realised how ridiculous she sounded. She felt as though she was trying to score points from the old lady. Well if that were true, she had failed miserably.

"I am sorry Mrs Ladywoman. It has been a very stressful few days," she said.

"Of course it has my dear. I understand. Things have never been the same for you since that night at the mill, have they?"

Lydia stared at her, shocked.

"I don't know what you mean." She wasn't so slow that would give the game away.

"Oh I think you do my dear. Anyway, now that you are grown up you can perhaps get to the bottom of that as well as these murders."

The old lady continued to smile at her customer throughout this conversation and gave nothing more away in her manner.

"Do you know something that I don't?" asked Lydia.

"I may do, but I don't know what you know, do I my dear?"

Was the old lady being weird or what?

"No, I don't suppose you do." Then as an afterthought, "If you do know anything, you ought to tell Inspector Glees."

"You think that Inspector Glees can help do you my dear? Has he helped you with anything so far?"

"Look, if you have something to say then just say it to me." Lydia was getting cross.

"I am only a sweet shop keeper my dear. What could I know that would help anyone? I do remember you when you were a small girl though. I know your family and especially Grandfather Treen. His father was sweet on me once you know!" She laughed merrily at this memory and continued. "I remember your aunt and your uncle, though I don't like those two very much. Something wrong with them. I don't like the Council people and I don't like the Doctor and I don't like that David that you always had an eye for."

"I didn't have an eye for David."

"Didn't you my dear? Well perhaps you didn't. I am quite old and I forget things. But I do see a lot from my shop window. When the mill was open there was business

83

all day from the workers and when it closed my business suffered.

"I had to stop selling most of the things I used to sell. Now the building work is going on and as soon as the places start selling then I shall have a good business again."

Lydia wondered how long the old lady would last in this new world she envisaged.

"Course all the new owners won't know about the history of the mill and what went on there, no not until they are settled." She stopped talking and looked again at her customer as if just remembering she was there.

"My sister said she saw you in the lawyer's the other day," said Mrs Ladywoman.

"I didn't realise that was your sister. I don't think I knew you had a sister living."

"Hard to believe there is more than one person my age isn't it?" she laughed.

Lydia made to leave the shop and once her hand was on the door knob, the old lady was by her side and grabbed hold of her arm.

"If you should ever need help or advice, you will come back to me won't you dear?"

She seemed truly worried.

"Err yes of course," answered Lydia, having no intention to do anything of the kind.

It was only when she was back outside on the pavement that Lydia realised how dark and claustrophobic the shop had seemed. She breathed in the fresh air and looked about her. The inn opposite was closed as it would be until lunchtime. Lydia seemed to remember her keepers spending a lot of time there and she vaguely wondered whether that was still the case. It probably was. This inn had been the frequent of the mill workers and Lydia remembered walking past this way holding the safe and warm hand of her Grandfather and seeing the men and women laughing and singing through the small windows of the inn. It had always looked very jolly in there, but Grandfather had discouraged her.

"Drinking and foolery is just a waste of time Lydia. Time is a precious thing and we can buy no more than we are given. Don't waste a moment of it on silliness, even if encouraged to do so."

Wow, she had not thought of that for a long time. Come on Lydia, make your time count.

She carried on, walking passing cottages on the right and left of the lane and reached the fish and chip shop which sat directly opposite the mill. She knew that this also had been built especially for the workers. Food from there had on odd occasions been allowed as a treat from Gran.

Auntie Cal worked there for a long time and Lydia thought that it was here that she had met her husband. She pulled a face at the thought of him. Cal was tall and skinny and white faced with blood red lips. He had a horrid smile which he saved for the children when they were alone. Lydia always knew instinctively to keep out of his way unless with an adult. Creepy, creepy man. Had he worked at the mill at one point? Maybe he had. She knew that during their childhood he had worked as an entertainer in an inn on Town Street, playing an instrument and singing. She did not think that he had made much money doing that.

She remembered the girls in the cottage opposite his own, the cottage which was next to the Doctor's house. They had once complained to Auntie Cal that Uncle Cal would stand and stare at them through the window without moving. Auntie Cal went round and said that they ought to find their own husbands and stop trying to steal hers or she would punch them. They never complained again.

It was also because of this shop that she had met Wrinkles Pollack and left Mill Town. She could not say that she lived to regret the decision, because the decision had been made by others and not by her.

She thought about him bringing the fish that one time. Usually old Mr Pollack brought the fish for the shop, but he had not been feeling well one day just over five years ago, so young Mr Pollack brought the fish alongside his father. Old Mr Pollack died after falling off the goat cart with a dizzy spell on the way up Mill Lane just outside Lydia's home. The old man was brought in and Doctor Catapult sent for and before long the old Mr Pollack died and young Mr Pollack was after Lydia and one thing led to another and she was off to Seaside.

Apart from feeling nostalgic, Lydia had not thought too much about her life in Mill Town and Village since she had been away. She had just hidden herself at Seaside thinking about nothing really. Had it been a waste of time? That she could never know. She reminded herself how rich she had become while away, so that was a bonus.

Make your time count Lydia.

With Treen's words ringing in her ears, she stepped up the pace. Passing the mill made her realise just how much was going on there. The Snooty mill family were obviously going to make a lot of money. The mill covered a huge area and was being converted into small houses and flats and some shops. Lydia wondered how much extra money would be made by Mill Town if the new people became self-sufficient.

At the entrance gates, she noticed a sales office and stopped to look in at the window. All the properties were being advertised there and some already had the words:

Sold
and
Let

written across the pictures.

A salesman beckoned from inside and Lydia went in. Before she knew what had happened she had arranged to meet him there the next day and have a look round some of the apartments.

Would she buy one of them? She had to live somewhere. But the old mill?

She carried on walking along Wide Lane until she came to the junction with Mill Lane where she turned right and began the steep walk up the hill. Now, the mill field was on her right and she thought again about the times she and her friends and family had played games there throughout their childhood. They had such fun.

Michaelmas loved to play ball and thinking of her little brother meant that Lydia was starting to cry as she walked. That would do no good to anyone. Without realising it, she was standing outside the gate of her aunt's house looking down the path.

The wobbly path, she thought. That brought back some wonderful memories.

"Hello, little Liddy. I heard you were back in town. Come to see me have you?"

Lydia gave an involuntary tremor, the sound of his voice made her feel quite nauseous.

"No. I haven't." She could hardly bear to look at him. He was no different from how she remembered him. Although, perhaps he had more wrinkles and greyer hair.

"That's a pretty dress Lydia, did you wear it to come and see me?" Lydia thought that she might be sick, right there in front of him. How dare he comment like that on the things she wore?

"What else are you wearing that's pretty Lydia?" She looked at him full in the face and saw his little eyes peering from behind his large dark glasses. She saw his spiky hair and pale pockmarked face and she shivered again.

"Come into the house little Liddy," he said in that dreadful voice of his.

She turned round smartly and began to cross the road, causing a goat cart to swerve violently as she did so. 'Stupid girl' she thought and chose to ignore the sniggering she could hear from her Uncle Cal.

She stood outside the Doctor's house. The cottage to the left of this gateway still housed the family who had complained all those years before. She could not see anyone in the windows, perhaps they never bothered to look out of the windows again.

The Doctor's house was the same as she remembered it. The lawns either side of the driveway looked immaculate and she could see the summerhouse under the trees. What was it they all used to play there? Hide and seek? The Doctor was always pleased to see the children. Were his sisters?

Perhaps.

By now Lydia was standing outside the front door and so she rang the bell. That bell is new she thought to herself. The door was always open when she was a girl. Didn't someone open it as soon as a child was seen running down the drive? Then the visitor could go directly into the hallway and through to the kitchen where there would be rhubarb cakes and tea. Lovely!

Lydia rang the bell again and waited patiently for an answer, but there was none. She wondered whether or not to look in through the front window, but resisted the temptation. What to do next?

She walked around the back of the house, the occupants never used to mind, so she didn't think they would now. She noticed almost immediately the lack of life in the house and garden.

Even when there had been no children visiting, there was always a gardener or maid or some such about the place. But today, the curtains were half drawn and inside seemed dark and unoccupied. She made her way around to the kitchen door and knocked there. There was definitely someone about, she could see movement.

"Hello, is anyone there?"

There was no answer, but Lydia was sure there was someone moving about. She bent down and looked in through the windows. She needed to bend down in order to see underneath the drawn curtains. She saw a kitchen table with nothing upon it and cupboards lining the walls. These were decorated beautifully with paintings of flowers and birds. Gran would like them. It was not very light in there but Lydia could still make out the chairs and the pegs on the wall next to the hall door. There was nothing out on any of the surfaces, which Lydia found incredibly odd. Everyone had stuff over kitchen tops, unless of course they were a bit obsessed.

A tap on her shoulder make her jump upright again with a start.

"Hello. Who do we have here then?" The male voice made her feel odd.

"Hello Doctor Catapult. I'm Lydia Prix, do you remember me?"

The Doctor with his kindly round face and twinkling eyes said, "Well naturally I remember you my dear. How perfectly lovely it is to see you. You must come inside and have some tea with us."

He ushered her inside the room into which she had just been looking and fussed and faffed around her while placing her in a chair. Then he called to his sisters and told them to come and see their visitor.

"Your sisters are still alive then?"

Why had she said that? The words were out there in front of her face and she was staring at them, floating about in the room. It was too late to bring them back.

The Doctor laughed and answered, "Yes Lydia, my sisters are still alive. They will be happy to see you I should think too!"

So they were. The two old ladies came into the kitchen. One was tall and skinny and the other short and well, quite chubby. They were both very jolly and happy. Dressed in black dresses and beads which dangled almost to the floor and hair which tried to reach the ceiling with curls and bows and bats and beads, they looked like salt and pepper pots.

"Well how lovely to see you my dear! So much has happened to you this past couple of days since you returned we hear. Such tragedies, such adventures!"

Lydia could not decide whether they were being kind or nosy. She chose kind because now was not really the time to fall out.

"How did you find out?" she asked as she could think of nothing else to say.

"Well your Uncle Cal was just here telling us all about it. Did you not see him on the way out?"

Lydia was surprised, no, shocked to hear that. Why should creepy Uncle Cal be round here telling them about her life?

"Don't be upset dear! We weren't gossiping about you! Only talking and being neighbourly, you know how it is!" The old women almost talked at the same time, like a pair of weird twins.

"Not really, I never gossip myself."

The atmosphere changed a little in the kitchen with that comment, but tea was made and biscuits put out on plates in the middle of the table.

Lydia noticed the pattern on all the crockery. It was of cartoon doctors and nurses looking after little children lying on beds who looked very pleased to receive the medical attention.

"Here you are my dear, tea." The Doctor put the mug in front of her.

She looked at the concoction in the mug and her mind went back many years to her childhood visits here. Of being told to drink the tea and be a good girl.

"What is this?" she asked, "it does not look like tea."

"It is our special tea. You remember that all you children used to drink this tea and have your cakes and sweeties when you visited?" said the skinny old lady.

Lydia did remember that. The tea and the cakes and the games inside and outside. How long ago was that?

"Do children still come here?"

The grins faded a little.

"Not so often as they used to do, my dear. That is a bit sad for us. We need – we love to have young children around. We all feel so much better when children are about."

"We had thought about going to the Finders Hospital and taking some of the children who don't find homes. They would be happy here," said the fat old sister.

Was it Lydia's imagination, or had the Doctor quelled his sister's speech with a glance and a shake of the head.

"Although I don't suppose that we would be able to do that," said Skinny, "even with Catapult's influence there."

Doctor Catapult got up from his chair and cleared away the tea and biscuits before Lydia had time to drink anything.

"Do you want me to go now Doctor?" she asked. "Only I would like to take a look around the old house. I have thought of it often during my marriage and time away from here."

Doctor Catapult looked unconvinced.

"Do you still have the toys and the games you used to have?" Lydia wasn't sure why she was following this line of enquiry with the Doctor, but she had started so she had to carry on with it.

"Not really, not on display anymore. As we said, there are not so many children coming around as they used to."

"How many exactly?"

"None really." The Doctor's face remained impassive.

"Oh," she answered.

Everyone stayed in the kitchen for almost a minute without speaking at all. Lydia thought she had better push a bit harder.

"Can I have a look round then?"

She thought that his face flashed with anger, but it was possibly her imagination because he said, "Of course my dear, please follow me."

So she did.

CHAPTER SIX *THE TWINS' STORY*

The girls sat down to breakfast as soon as Lydia left for her head-clearing walk.

"I bet she'll be trying to get it all sorted out on her own," said Janey.

"She always does that. Sometimes you wonder if she just wants to be the centre of attention," Alice replied.

"You can certainly tell she is back. All this mayhem and drama," agreed Janey.

"So you are blaming the murders on her, are you?" asked Gran. She was stirring something or other on the stove.

"No, not blaming her at all. It's just that when Lydia is around there is always something going on. I mean really major going on," Alice emphasised.

The girls continued eating, lost in thought. To an outsider, the dynamic in the kitchen was of two children and their granny, not two grown women. Gran had that effect. She made the cottage so comfy that a person naturally resorted to childhood.

The twins finished feeding and taking care of the ponies for the morning. They enjoyed their job and had high hopes for the future of their venture. If enthusiasm was any

94

measure of future success, then they had that in spades. They owned ten ponies so far and had plans for expansion. They spent much of their time training the ponies and encouraging local people to see the benefits of owning one. Just recently there had been a great deal of interest, but as the girls insisted that the ponies only went to approved homes, the sales were not going as quickly as they might.

They had a wonderful idea about the breeding of the ponies. The ponies came in many colours and the twins had chosen a different colour each time they bought.

"If we cross the red pony with the yellow pony, we should get an orange one," said Janey.

"And if we cross the blue pony with the red one, we shall get a purple pony," said Alice. What great plans they had for the future.

"I would rather the ponies were taken care of than just sold for the sake of it," said one.

"I totally agree," said the other, and so it was. They both knew that they were safe living at Gran's and unless they decided to marry, this was how life would be.

Life had not always been this happy for them. Up to that night at the old mill life had been pretty ideal, but after that things changed. Certain episodes in the past of the girls they intended never to repeat. If they kept very, very quiet, then everyone would be alright.

The games they played in the field stopped and from then on, playing was something which was only done in the gardens at home and in the gardens of friends and family. Doctor Catapult and his sisters were kind as always and allowed the children of the whole town to come and play all day and every day. They even bought more toys and had dens and hides built in the gardens where the children could play on their own, or together, or sometimes with the Doctor if he wasn't working.

The keepers understood nothing and only worried when their life was disrupted. The children often wondered exactly why their keepers had fetched so many children from the Finders Hospital, when they quite obviously cared little for them. It was true that when they looked at the way other keepers cared for their own children, few were brilliant, but many at least knew where their children were and noticed when something was wrong. The Prix keepers noticed nothing expect what was happening to them. They liked their own life and their inn visiting. Mother often felt badly done to and would tell anyone who was interested what a hard and busy life she led.

"If only your father earned more money, I would be able to have a big house in the country and take in all the children from Finders that no one else wanted," Mother would tell people.

"If your mother earned some money herself then she could do that, but she just expects me to pay for everything!" Father answered.

Everyone thought that they were such kind and thoughtful people, but Mother Prix acted like a child herself. She was simple in her mind and only considered what affected her and no one else.

Father Prix, the only son of Gran and Grandfather Prix was always ready for a quiet life. When his keepers fetched him from the hospital, he was very pleased to have been chosen he told the girls in a reflective mood one day. He could not remember actually being chosen by them of course, but his life at the cottage by the woods had been idyllic and when he got married to their mother he had looked forward to having children of his own. Being an only foundling meant that sometimes he was lonely at home, but his keepers had never wanted any more children or weren't allowed them or something. He couldn't remember.

"But then I can't really remember how I ended up married to your mother!" he said to the girls and they were never sure if he was joking or not.

He certainly followed his wife in all of her decisions and opinions and his children often felt that if only he were to make a stand every so often, then their childhoods would have been warmer.

There were the wonderful times when Auntie Cal would come waddling up the road to visit her sister.

"Now come on you children, out of your mother's way, none of you give her a minutes peace!" she would say and despite protestations which became louder and more vociferous the older the children got, they nevertheless found themselves either packed off to play at the Doctor's or down to Uncle Cal. The children all had different answers.

"Please mother, please! Don't make me go there, please don't, I don't like the path!" cried Marjoram.

"Mother, I don't want to go, please don't make me!" cried. Alice.

"Father, father, say we don't have to go. Please!" screamed Janey.

"I am not going," said Sadie with determination.

"Make me," said Lydia.

"No," said Michaelmas.

They were instructed to visit Uncle Cal alone as he did not like too many visitors at once. He liked to see the children individually. All protestations were in vain and the children must walk down the wobbly path whenever Auntie Cal decided. It was surprising that either aunt or uncle were still alive, when one considers the depth of hate aimed in their direction by the Prix children. So, down the wobbly path they went on their visits until they were old enough to keep out of the house when Auntie came to call.

Eventually Lydia left with that dreadful Mr Pollack and Sadie left to marry her Charlie and Marjoram ran off with Mr Chariot, although not too far. The twins were left with their brother. Michaelmas then got his job in the forest and the twins moved in with Gran and life went on.

Gran was helpful to the girls and living there meant that they could stay together and follow their dreams. They had a plan which was being followed to the letter, but the plan had gone awry now Michaelmas was dead. How had that happened?

They finished their breakfast and took their dishes to the sink. The door opened and in came their sister Marjoram.

"Hello all!" she said.

"Hello!" they answered.

"Aren't you supposed to be going to the Finders Hospital today to pick up Dotty?" asked Gran.

In the dramas of the past couple of days, everyone else had forgotten about that happy event.

"Well yes." Marjoram's face dropped and she continued, "We thought that we ought to wait until next week, when things have settled down a bit. I wouldn't want my daughter to come into our family in the middle of all this drama. What do you think?"

"I think that is an excellent idea. It will be better for her to wait until we can all pay attention to her. She mustn't feel as though she is not important," said Alice. Everyone nodded, perhaps remembering their own admission into the Prix family.

There was silence for a moment, until Gran piped up, "Any more news about Sadie? Mr Chariot told us about his visit."

"No, there is no more and I am very worried. Bobby said that he saw her going to town yesterday morning and she looked really happy, excited even."

"That is a bit odd, when Michaelmas is dead," said Janey.

"I know, but perhaps she was going to meet someone first."

"You mean that farmer bloke don't you?" asked Alice.

"Probably. I know she has been seeing him and her husband doesn't know about it. Mr Chariot has seen her more than once and so have I." She dropped her head and fiddled about with her mug.

"I think that we should go into Town and visit the Inspector and see what is going on," said Gran. "I want to know where Michaelmas is being kept."

"I can't come with you, I have to get lunch for Mr Chariot and Bobby," announced Marjoram.

"Of course, you get on with your own life Marjoram, let the rest of us sort out the problems."

"Janey!" snapped Alice.

"Well, I'll come if I am really needed," Marjoram answered. "I just thought that four of us would be too many. I will support you in anything you decide."

"OK," said Janey. "Sorry."

"That's alright."

Within half an hour, a red pony had been attached to a cart and the three set off from the house, crossed Wide Lane and trotted up Bell Lane towards Town Street. As they crossed the road, they noticed Lydia in the distance standing outside the old mill.

"She didn't get very far," said Gran. "I expect she has been talking to everyone."

"I hope she doesn't get herself into trouble," remarked Alice.

"She won't, at least if she does she will get herself out of it again," Janey said.

It was true, whatever trouble Lydia got into, she dealt with it herself. But this murder thing was different. It was difficult to imagine what any of them could do to turn the situation around.

Passing cottages, they noticed people in gardens and fields working and talking. Nearly everyone waved to them because the Prix family were known to most. Everyone was also fascinated to see the brightly coloured pony trotting amiably up the street with no hint of tiredness or naughtiness.

Each cottage had a plot of land which was laid to rhubarb and cabbage. Rhubarb didn't do as well now as it used to do back in the days of the mill. When the great fires had been lit in order to power the looms and keep the great furnaces going, there were huge plumes of smoke puffing out of the great chimney. The smoke and soot fell on the land around and onto the fields as well as the washing hanging on the line. While the women complained and washed the laundry again, they also had to admit that the soot made the ground fertile for the rhubarb. These days of

100

clean air and atmosphere meant a drop in the rhubarb production. The villagers were trying to think of something else they could grow which enjoyed fresh air.

As the cottages became more numerous and built closer together, they knew they were nearing the top of Bell Lane. The junction at the top was a precarious one, as the cart had to be held with a brake, while they checked that the street was clear. Bell Lane did not level out evenly at the top, so that process was quite difficult. But the pretty red pony stood impassively, awaiting his instructions.

When the traffic cleared, they trotted off to the left in the direction of the office run by Inspector Glees. The office was opposite the park gates and next to the Lawyer's. Above it was written:

Police Office

The pony stopped outside and the family climbed out. Before Gran had landed on the floor, the pony was surrounded by children.

"I love this Mrs. What is it?"

"A pony."

"Is it for sale?"

"No, clear off."

"Can we look after him for you Mrs?"

"No, get lost. He bites and kicks and tells tales."

"What did you say that for Janey? Now no one will buy the ponies if they think they are vicious."

"They might buy more if they think they are good at guarding too."

"That's true."

They all trooped into the office and closed the door behind them. It was quite a squeeze. There was a counter in front of them and behind it sat a young boy of about sixteen years of age. In order to close the main door they scrunched up to one side of the waiting area, shut it and then spread out again. There was a tiny window looking out on the street, but it let in only a little light.

"Hello, we want to see the Inspector," said Gran.

"He ain't here," was the answer. The spotty faced boy showed little interest in the group. He had a book to read. Alice leaned over to look at it, wondering what Ginger Batty could possibly be reading. It turned out to be a picture book about ball games. No wonder he didn't have any girlfriends.

"Where is he then?"

"Out."

Gran tried again. "I want to know where my grandson is being kept."

"Why, has he been arrested?"

This was too much for Alice. "If you don't stop being so damned cheeky and insolent, I will come round that counter and smash your face into it."

He coloured up and said, "Oh, you are that dead man's family aren't you?"

"And I will help her." Janey's face was set to stern and she meant what she said.

Ginger knew they did and he replied, "He is being kept at the Doctor's house until the burning is sorted out."

The group fell silent for a moment at this news. This information made it all so real.

"What is happening with the investigation now?" Gran persisted with the boy.

"Don't know anything about it, I don't think he's doing anything. He is spending a lot of time sorting other things out," said the boy.

"Is that right? What sort of things?"

Ginger looked confused as if unsure whether to impart any further information. He was frightened of older women and worried about how much information they could get out of him.

"Well nothing much I don't think. There is some sort of do being arranged. I think the Council people are arranging it."

"What do are you talking about?" asked Alice.

"Oh I don't know, I can't remember." He was looking shifty now.

"Try." Alice started to look for the gate to the counter.

"The ones that are going are the Lawyer, the Doctor, all of the Council. The Snooty family, the manager of the Finders Hospital and some of their second in commands," he said quickly.

"Is there a list?" asked Janey.

"Somewhere about, in his office I think."

"Get it for us."

"I can't, not now, it's locked," he whined.

Janey began to open the counter gate.

"Look, I'll make a copy and bring it to you later. Don't say anything though, he'll kill me."

"And I'll kill you if you don't," Gran informed him.

They left the office after shuffling to one side and opening the door and then making their way out. The red pony was standing as good as gold, despite the attempts of several children to spook him.

"He's not half as giddy as a goat Mrs!" one boy announced.

"I'm going to get my dad to buy one of these. What other colours you got?" asked another.

"If anyone is interested, then they have to call at Gran Prix's house and we can discuss terms. They are very expensive," said Alice.

"And we will check out every home. Not just anyone will be able to have them," said Janey.

"I'm going to ask my father," said one.

"I'm going to ask my mother," said another.

As the Prix family climbed aboard the cart and walked off, they waved to the children who, to be fair, had only been curious and not done one bit of harm to the pony or the cart.

"Shall we do some shopping and have lunch in the park and then go down to the Doctor's?" asked Gran.

"I would rather have lunch at the inn, I don't like sitting in the park very much," Janey informed her.

"I thought you liked the park. You two used to play on the swings and the roundabouts for hours when you came here with your Uncle Cal! What about popping in to see him on the way back home? It's ages since we visited." Gran was enthusiastic.

The girls looked at each other and Janey nodded to her sister.

"We hated every single minute we spent with that creepy old man. Why has no one ever asked why none of us would spend time with him when we got old enough to say no?" Alice said.

Gran said nothing.

"He is a disgusting old man and we were made to play with him and I don't ever want to have anything to do with him again. We could tell you tales Gran about him, but you probably wouldn't believe us. Auntie Cal never believed us when we told her." Janey was almost in tears.

"You told her about it did you? She did nothing then? There is nothing to be done about any of that stuff. It's a man's world and it is pointless complaining about it. Some of us have tried, but so far it hasn't done any good."

The girls silently agreed that Gran was well trained in trying to make the best of whatever life threw her way. School did a good job with everyone. Lydia was right, she had always said that no one ever caused trouble and questioned the teachings. And that they really should.

Lydia had done that and ended up at the Doctor's for a week. She had been quieter after that visit, so the twins often wondered what kind of treatment he had given her. It must have been good, the Doctor was always kind and helpful. In fact it was the Doctor who had helped her find a husband in Mr Pollack, even if Mr Pollack was a berk.

"So you think it is alright for him to behave like that towards us?" Janey was shocked.

"No I don't, but it's always best to let bygones be bygones. Keeping anger in your heart only makes a person ill."

Wow, the girls did not know whether they could ever feel the same way about Gran after that. Discussing it that night, they came to the conclusion that Gran was just a product of her generation and hadn't really understood what they were trying to tell her. She probably thought that they meant he told them off or something. Anyway, they decided at that moment that it was no use telling Gran about anything that had happened.

The girls, also known as the twins, were in fact 28 years old, but never treated as such. They had come to the conclusion very early on in their life, as have many with similar disgusting old uncles, that even when you tell an

105

adult, you are rarely believed. These children, when they grew up, were not believed as adults either.

In, truth it really is far easier to say nothing. Michaelmas had said that revenge comes afterwards, in Beyond. Lydia said that one day, no matter how long you waited, there would be a chance of revenge. The girls just tended to ignore the subject.

Shopping done, the three went into the Rat and Handbag for lunch. The mood was definitely more subdued now, but they carried on regardless. What else was to be done? They sat down at a table by the window and the waiter came over.

"Hello Mrs Prix, your granddaughter was staying here the other night, she looked proper poorly when she arrived. I only realised it was her after someone told me."

"Was she? Well, she is alright now," answered Gran.

"As alright as a person can be, when their brother and sister are dead." Alice was feeling peeved.

"Yes, I suppose so," said the waiter. "Not the sort of thing that happens every day!" He was trying to be jolly.

Lunch was finished quickly and nothing very interesting happened. The three hardly spoke, other than to agree that they should call at the Doctor's and visit Michaelmas before the burning. As they were leaving, two very similar looking young men stopped and removed their hats as they came face to face with the girls. They were the sons of the Lawyer and both had a soft spot for the Prix twins.

"Hello, we are very, very sorry about your sad loss," said Jot Scriber.

"If there is anything we can do to help, please ask," said Mark Scriber.

"We will help you catch the person who did this if you want us to," they said together.

"Thank you very much," answered the young women. They were more touched with this offer than they might have expected. The young men raised their hats and let the women pass by.

The pony was waiting patiently, even though the children who had fussed him while tied up outside the Police Office were surrounding him again. They had given him water and some of the hay which was tied to the side of the cart. Pony seemed very happy with himself and his fans.

Soon, the family were on their way along Town Street back to the Mill Lane junction. In order to reach the inn from Bell Lane, they had already trotted past the end of the lane. The geography of the town might seem complicated until mastered, but it is quite easy really. The lanes and streets had been the same for many years, going far back in time and written in all the old records.

They turned into Mill Lane, past the bank and the Council offices and made their way downhill. Twenty minutes later they arrived at the entrance to the old mill on the left, with the sign informing all that properties were for sale. Then they passed the cottages which housed the keepers and there on the right, the turning to the Doctor's house. They turned in and listened to the scrunching noise the wheels made on the drive. It was quite relaxing.

"We shouldn't stop too long. Pony has had a busy day today, he will want a rest," Janey said.

"We won't feel like stopping anywhere else after seeing Michaelmas, I shouldn't imagine." Alice was already dreading the visit.

"We shall have to call in on your aunt and uncle another day. It's a pity really because I should have liked them to see us with the pony."

Great. Gran was going loony.

As they climbed down, Doctor Catapult came out of the front door and welcomed them.

"How wonderful to see you Mrs Prix! I wasn't expecting you today," he said.

"We came to pay our last respects to Michaelmas. We were told he was here," Gran answered.

"Well I am afraid you have been misinformed, Mrs Prix. Your grandson is not here. I don't know where the Inspector took him, but it wasn't here."

The women looked confused and Janey looked as though she was going to cry.

"Now then my dears, don't get yourselves into such a state, come on into the house and my sisters will get you a drink. You have had so many things happen to you just recently. You must be emotionally exhausted!"

His sisters appeared and the three Catapults offered them tea and cakes, which were refused. The Prixs were still full from lunchtime.

"We don't want to stop too long," said Gran, "we need to get back home. I am very tired."

"That is such a shame," said the Doctor. "We haven't had any visitors here for a few days now, we don't get the visitors we used to. We enjoy company."

"Well, we only came to see Michaelmas and if he isn't here, we shouldn't waste anymore of your time." Janey was finding the whole day too much and she was overcome with an urge to leave.

"I am sorry that we could not help you in your quest. Your best plan is to see the Inspector and find out where his body is being kept. You don't want to miss seeing him before the burning, do you?" Doctor Catapult was kindness itself.

"No, we don't," said Alice.

"Yes, they will just get rid of the body without a word to the family, if that's what is decided," Skinny sister informed the women helpfully.

"Thanks for that," said Gran.

The women climbed back into the cart and made their way home. They were all very tired and Gran felt as old as she actually was – a feeling she had never had before.

CHAPTER SEVEN *THE SURGERY*

As Lydia followed the Doctor out of the kitchen and into the hallway the two were immediately plunged into darkness.

"Oh, sorry, there don't appear to be any lights on in here. The flame must have gone out while we were in the kitchen. Just stand still and I shall fetch another lamp to light this one."

The Doctor walked away and left her completely alone.

"Wait a tick, my eyes will get used to the dark very soon," Lydia said to herself, well it might have been out loud, but who cares.

She waited a tick and her eyes did not get used to the dark. The dark remained what it was, dark and impervious.

"Doctor!" she called out. There was no answer.

"Doctor Catapult, are you there?"

She thought of her childhood and the time she spent here under medical supervision. Why was that? Had she spent much of her time in the dark then? She couldn't remember anything about that.

"Miss Catapult, are you there?"

How long had she been standing there? It already felt like half an hour, but couldn't possibly have been. Surely the Doctor should have returned by now?

The dark wasn't getting any lighter, so to speak, so Lydia began to walk forwards holding both her arms straight out. The aim of this action was to touch something and discover exactly where she was. She moved carefully forwards, although forwards is relative when you have no idea where you are going.

Standing still in the dark had felt a bit unnerving, but moving in the dark was positively creepy. It was as if she was beckoning trouble to come to her. Her mind immediately ran riot, imagining all sorts of heebie-jeebies moving silently past her and trying to trip her up. The thoughts made her stop and bring her arms smartly back down to her sides.

Think, think. What was the layout of the hall? She had been here many times before and if she settled her mind she could picture it. Taking a deep breath, Lydia thought. If she could find the first doorway on the left, then she would know that she had found the dining room, for this room faced out the same way as the front door. Then directly opposite this door was the sitting room and the next room along would be the morning room. On the same side as the dining room were the steep stairs up and the door down to the cellar. Next on the left was the entrance lobby and front door. Between the morning room and the front door was the entrance to the surgery. Lydia pictured the detail carefully in her mind and felt safe enough to move around again until she felt a knob. This must be the dining room door. She opened the door and walked forwards.

111

This assumption had done Lydia no good whatsoever. As she lifted her head from the floor, she realised that she had fallen heavily down a steep set of steps and was now lying on a cold hard floor which smelt of damp and earth. It felt alarmingly familiar.

She gingerly felt around her body and decided that there were no bones broken, but a good portion of her frame was bruised. She sat up and looked around. At least there was plenty of light from the lanterns which hung around the walls.

Lydia's bottom was getting cold and the lovely dress she was wearing gave little protection against the damp. She wished that she had worn a jacket. She stood up and swayed a little and felt sick. She pulled herself onto a chair which sat forlornly next to an old table. Her bag was still over her shoulder and she moved it over her head onto the other shoulder in order to keep it secure.

She decided to sit for a little while until she felt more normal. The cellar was quite large, but little seemed to be stored there. There was the chair in which she sat and a table on which she leaned. Upon the table was notepaper and a pen, but nothing was written. In the corner was a cupboard, but the doors were closed so she had no idea what was in there. At the top of one of the walls was a tiny window covered by a grille which probably looked out onto the garden, if only she could get up there to see out. There was another door in the corner of the room, which Lydia guessed led to other cellars.

She felt a little better and decided to get out of there as soon as possible. She was a bit surprised that no one had come to see what had happened to her. She got up from the chair and made her way towards the cellar steps. Taking hold of the rail she hauled herself up. The stairs were very steep and she felt quite sore and stiff, so progress was slow. Arriving at the top she was faced with a solid door which appeared to be fastened firmly shut. She twisted and turned the handle, but nothing moved. No need to start panicking.

She knocked firmly on the door and said, "Doctor Catapult! Hello!"

Surely he must have come back with a lamp and wondered where she was by now? She tried this approach for a minute or two with no result. Perhaps there was another door to the house from another part of the cellar.

She limped down the steps again and headed towards the door in the corner of the room. Upon opening it, she was surprised to see that this room was also lit with lamps. There was more furniture here, a bed and a couple of chairs and a sofa. Down one side, there were some kitchen units with bread and cake on the counter. How odd.

But upon closer inspection there was no alternative access to upstairs, so she left this room and went through another door and into the next.

This room was decked out like a library and even had an open fire. There were floor to ceiling shelves and hundreds and hundreds of books. In the centre of the room was a long wooden table surrounded by chairs. At each end were two huge chairs in the style of thrones. A line of large brass candlesticks, lined the middle of the table, with a centrepiece of an ornate brass cross. There were no windows apart from a covered tiny grille at the top of the room.

Lydia was becoming increasingly alarmed that someone was leaving each room as she entered. That meant that she was following someone – or were they following her?

She went into a further room but this was not so welcoming and light. It was cold, dark and small. There seemed no point to it. Through the reflected light, she noted that there was only the one door and the stone walls held no lamps. Some old chains and iron rings hung from the walls and slumped on the floor was a very small wooden chair. Lydia had to return into the library room and fetch a lamp before she could see what else was going on there.

The lamp revealed nothing further of interest other than a pile of dust and gravel against one wall, and so she went back through the rooms and returned to the original one. When she arrived there, she heard a scrunching noise on the gravel drive above, followed by voices.

She couldn't make out what was being said, but she was sure that she could hear Gran and her sisters talking to the Doctor.

"Help! Help!" she shouted. But apparently no one could hear her.

She went back up the steps and banged on the door. Nothing. She sat there on the top step and wondered what to do next. Then all of a sudden there was a clicking noise and a creak and the door opened.

"Hello Lydia, how did you manage to get here?" The Doctor smiled and his voice was kind and reassuring. "I only went for a lamp and when I got back a minute later, you had vanished! I thought that you must have gone out of the front door and walked home!"

"No, Doctor, I fell down the stairs and no one heard me shouting!" Lydia felt about ten years old telling her father something had happened and suddenly, bizarrely she started to weep.

"Oh, silly, silly girl. We couldn't hear you! Don't upset yourself, come on up here. Let's get you into the surgery and have a good look at you."

Even though the Doctor was being very solicitous, Lydia felt her body grow tense. She was not sure that she wanted this man to check her over. Why was that?

He led her through the hall and entrance lobby. Instead of going out of the front door, they turned right through the door marked:

The Surgery

There was a small waiting room with chairs lined up as though awaiting a theatrical entrance from the direction of the surgery doors. Doctor Catapult led her through the waiting room and into his room and told her to lie down on the blue leather couch which stood in the exact centre of the room.

"I think I am alright now Doctor, only a few bumps and bruises."

"Nonsense, lie down there and I will check. We don't want anything else happening to you later in the day, do we? Never forgive myself, never!"

"I would really rather not." Lydia was firm in her refusal.

"Don't be silly now, just slip off your dress and under things before you lie down. Make the examination easier."

"No, really, thank you." Politeness was still paramount in her refusals.

"I think you are being a bit childish now Lydia, reminds me of when you were a girl. Nothing much changes does it? Come on up you get." He patted the couch.

Always so jolly.

"Doctor, I do not want you to examine me and I certainly will not be taking off my clothes and jumping up on the couch as you so kindly request."

"Now then Lydia. You don't want me to let the Council know that your old mental troubles are coming back do you? There is already enough evidence against you, with you pretending to see a murder and then a monster."

"What do you mean?" This was getting out of control.

"Your uncle told me all about it. You thought you saw things in the woods and caused a lot of trouble for everyone. The Inspector isn't very pleased about it I can tell you. It will help you if I can put their minds at rest with a proper examination. Now, take off your things and pop on the couch."

Lydia felt sick and she wasn't sure whether it was from fear or anticipation. Were they the same thing? Before she could decide on the two courses of action now open to her, leaving or doing as she was told, the surgery door burst open.

"Your sisters told me you were in here, Doctor. I've come for the body. We have got to get it burned straight away, no waiting."

"Whose body?" asked Lydia, frightened of the answer.

"Now, out you go, Emtee, can't you see I am busy?"

The Doctor shooed the man out and Lydia watched the pair go through to the waiting room. The dreadful man was Emtee Oreful, who organised the disposal of all the dead people and animals before they became smelly. He was not liked nor appreciated by the mass of the population, most of whom found him creepy and objectionable.

116

"I'm not always sure that people are dead before he burns them. I heard screams come from his place at night." An informed neighbour told his friends at the inn one evening.

"That's why no one tells him about deaths in the house, not until they are sure they are dead. Gives them chance to get the cart."

Lydia went over to the door and opened it a crack. She saw the two men in heated discussion in the waiting room. She closed it swiftly and went over to the other door, which led outside. She crossed over the small alleyway and opened another door to the little hospital, where the Doctor did some of his operations and where those recovering stayed for a while.

The door was open. Lydia went in and moved quickly along the corridor, opening each door as she did so and looking into the rooms. Nothing, nothing, no one, no one. The fifth door opened as easily as the others and Lydia suppressed a squeal with her hand.

There was her brother's body. He laid flat, cold and stiff on the table. She went over to him and touched his face. He was smiling even in death and the energy around his body felt warm and comforting. She was not going to cry.

"Oh Michaelmas, I will find out who did this to you and I will make them pay, if it's the last thing I do."

"Lydia, move it! Someone's coming!" The voice seemed to come from the body and she was certain the voice was Michaelmas's. She moved quickly into a small storage cupboard at the rear of the room. She heard footsteps coming down the corridor. Click, click. The door opened and the same footsteps sounded, click, click. Then slap, slap. There were two people. There followed the sounds of walking around the room and then the door closed as they left.

Ok now, Ok now. Lydia was proud of herself, she was getting better at this. She came out of the cupboard and looked at Michaelmas lying on the slab. Was it him who had warned her? She liked to think so; he would like to watch out for his sisters when he could.

She listened at the corridor door and heard nothing. Walking back to her brother, she kissed him and held his hand for a moment.

"Take care Michaelmas," she said.

"Don't make such a fuss Lydia, I'm alright. I can do what I like now. Go next door, one further down, check that room out."

Lydia responded to this command as though it were the most normal thing in the world. Upon entering the next room, she saw Sadie lying on another slab. She looked exactly like Michaelmas, but when Lydia touched her, Sadie was still warm.

"Wake up Sadie! Wake up!"

No response.

"Look at that gorgeous man!"

Stupid thing to say, she knew, but Sadie was always interested in men. Lydia was rewarded by a stirring from her sister. Lydia roughly shook Sadie and pulled her legs to the floor, leaving her decidedly sickly looking younger sister dangling off the edge of the slab like an old rag doll.

"You look like an old rag doll," Lydia told her.

"Cheek!" was the slurred response.

"Get moving out of here you two!" said Michaelmas's disembodied voice.

They went out into the corridor and Lydia dragged her reluctant sister back up towards the main door.

"Ssshhh what was that?" Lydia thought she heard some sort of whimpering from the other end of the corridor. She hadn't checked a couple of the doors down there. What if someone was in danger?

"Don't you ssshhh me, Lydia. Coming back after all these years and bossing me about!"

For a moment, Lydia was tempted to leave Sadie there in the corridor, but duty got the better of her and she pulled her outside. They went up the alleyway and into the shrubbery beyond. They could not leave by the front drive. They must go through the gardens and over the wall at the back. The women knew this garden well from their childhood.

If they went over the wall and into the garden beyond, Old Mrs Snailwort wouldn't even notice them. They made their way towards her house. The back door was locked, so the women had to climb on top of a large plant pot and climb in through the window.

"Don't let the neighbours see us." said Sadie.

"Look, who cares, I just want to get away from the Doctor's. A neighbour calling me a burglar will be the least of my worries." They both giggled.

They arrived in the kitchen via the sink and tried as hard as they could not to knock anything off the counter. This was the only way through to the front of the old woman's house and onto the road. There was no side gate.

This road would lead them back to Mill Lane, a little further down from the Doctor's house and away from the view of their aunt's house.

They had done this many times before.

"Ssshhh!" Sadie glared at her sister.

"I'm not saying anything! Stop ssshing me!"

They scuttled through the kitchen and into the hall. They saw Mrs Snailwort snoozing in her chair. The women crept quietly to the front door and tried to open it.

"Noooo! It's locked!" Sadie whispered.

"Smash it down! I'm not staying in here!"

"Hello! Is there any one there?"

Great, now the old bat was awake.

"No! There is no one here," answered Sadie.

Lydia stopped and raised her hands and her eyes to the skies.

"What are you doing?" she asked.

Sadie pulled a face and started to giggle. Lydia felt like slapping her, but instead began to giggle too.

They tried the door again and almost fell onto the street as it gave way under their combined pressure. They scuttled towards Mill Lane and looked right and left. There was no one there and so they walked down Mill Lane towards Wide Lane brushing themselves down and trying to look as normal as possible.

"You are covered in dust and mould and dirt," Sadie informed her sister.

"And you are covered in death," she answered.

The women created a funny picture, holding hands as they walked down the steep hill to Wide Lane. They turned left and followed the stone wall which led them towards home.

"I am really hungry," said Sadie.

"I forgot! I haven't eaten either. But I have sweets!"

The two scrambled up the stone wall and into the field behind. While they made themselves comfortable on the grass, they noted that they were able to see the old mill and all the work going on there. They sat with their backs against the moss and lichen covered wall and faced the sun, which was warm and bright and comforting.

"It's nice just sitting here," said Sadie.

"Yes, I missed it a lot when I was away," replied Lydia.

They took out the sweets and toffees and juice drinks, which Lydia had purchased that morning. This morning seemed a long time ago.

"What happened to you Sadie?"

"I am not really sure. I was walking to the shops and thinking about my shopping."

"And meeting Farmer Hornbeam I gather!"

"Who told you that? He's only a passing fancy. My husband is so boring. I know he is reliable, but really! I could set my clock by him!"

The women giggled.

"I decided to go through the woods because I was thinking that there was something wrong about Michaelmas. You know the way he was supposed to have been killed and no one caring about it. Everyone is just sort of ignoring it. So I thought I will go and see for myself. Perhaps I could find a clue or something."

"Yes, that Inspector is no good at all."

"Well I got to the clearing and I have to tell you I thought I was being followed, but I couldn't see who or what was following me. I kept looking round and calling out and then something grabbed me from behind! I thought I could hear women's voices coming and I wanted to shout for help, but a hand went over my face." She stopped talking and looked scared.

"Go on, tell me what else happened."

"The next thing I can remember, was you shouting at me and pulling me off that bed thing at the Doctor's and dragging me outside. That's all I remember. How did you find me?"

"It's a long story, finish telling me yours first."

"That wasn't a bed was it? It was one of those death slabs. They thought I was dead didn't they?"

"Either that or they knew you were still alive and were going to …"

"Going to what?"

"No idea! This whole thing is getting barmier by the minute."

The women carried on eating and drinking. The high rhubarb and sugar content made them feel energised and strong.

"It's Friday isn't it?" asked Lydia.

"Don't ask me, I've been dead on a slab."

"True. I only got back on Tuesday feeling sorry for myself, getting divorced and feeling badly done to my whole life. I thought, I will surprise my family and finally come back to live a normal life and buy a cottage and start a business or something. I wanted to put the demons from my childhood behind me. Look at me now! All this lot to contend with. Mr Pollack and his fish and his girlfriends were a piece of rhubarb cake."

"You're getting divorced? Tell me how to go about it. I'm going to get divorced too!"

"Not just now, I have a lot to think about."

They looked out over to the mill.

"There's loads of work going on there," said Lydia.

"I know. I hear the places are beautiful and modern. I would love to see inside one."

"Come with me tomorrow then, I am going to look round. I'm thinking of buying one myself."

Sadie looked at her. "You made enough money from your marriage to afford one of those?"

"Not from my marriage," she answered. "No, not from my marriage, from something else entirely." She leaned forward and hugged her knees. That story was going to be kept secret for a little while longer yet.

Sadie looked at her sister with an expression that could have been jealousy or admiration. Sadie had not yet decided which she felt.

The women got up and dusted the grass from their bottoms. Sadie's bottom being twice the size of Lydia's, it took her a little longer Lydia noted with satisfaction.

"I might come with you tomorrow, but I shall probably be too tired and have to catch up with work at home," said Sadie.

"Don't worry, that's alright." Lydia picked up her bag and the few sweets they had not yet eaten.

"I'll take those off your hands if you like," Sadie offered.

What a cheek, Lydia thought but did not say it out loud. She handed the sweets over to her sister. So, that's how your bottom got that size, she said to herself.

They climbed back over the wall and passed in front of the mill entrance. The salesman waved to Lydia, oblivious to the adventures she had experienced in the past few hours.

"She looks as though she has been tumbling with her boyfriend in the woods," he said to his assistant.

"They both look as though they have," she answered.

123

"It was always the other entrance to the mill we went in when we were kids wasn't it?" said Sadie. "The one by the air raid shelters?"

"I only ever went in once and that was from the other end. I did not know you had ever been inside the mill, you never said." Lydia was stunned by this new revelation. There was so much of childhood that the children did not know about each other.

This was another example of how the Prix family were different to others. Other families tended to know what went on with each other. The Prix family didn't. There must have been something going on that kept them all silent from one another. They were isolated by their silence. Once you have been scared as a child and told not to tell anyone anything, the instructions become mixed up and soon you learn to say very little about anything to anyone. Isolation becomes the norm.

"I think I must have been told not to say anything."

"Who told you?"

"Can't remember," Sadie answered. "If I remember I shall tell you."

Passing in front of the tall building where the windows and walls leaned over the street, Lydia had a flashback. She could remember being pushed in a pram and looking up at the mill. It wasn't her mother or Gran pushing her, it was Auntie Cal and she kept leaning into the pram and scaring Lydia half to death, with her fat, ugly face. She smelt too, Uncle Cal smelt, but of what Lydia could not quite recall.

She knew that she was being pushed from Gran's in the direction of home and as she looked up beyond her aunt she saw something. But what?

"Are you alright Lydia, you've gone a very funny colour." Her sister's face was one of concern.

Lydia laughed, "No I was just feeling a bit off, probably from the sweets."

They walked on linking arms for comfort, until they reached Gran's house. The cottage looked the same. Why that was a surprise didn't quite register. Lydia had only left the cottage a few hours ago, but there it was all safe and pretty with smoke coming out of the chimney and roses wafting our their lovely scent in the breeze, as if nothing had happened between then and now.

"Come on in Sadie," instructed Lydia. "Everyone will want to see you."

Sadie followed Lydia into the kitchen and was rewarded with squeals and hugs and demands to know exactly what had been going on.

Gran had gone to bed since returning from town and she had to be persuaded to get up. The twins were there and Marjoram and Mr Chariot and Bobby. After hot drinks all round and a large plate of cakes in the middle of the table, both stories were repeated to the gathered family and no one interrupted until everything had been told. The twins and Gran told of their experiences too.

"It would have been Michaelmas that helped you. I've always known that you can come back from the dead and help the living. That's what I'm going to do anyway," Janey informed the group.

"How do you know you will be allowed?" asked Mr Chariot.

"Because it's not a case of being allowed," she said. "It's whether you want to or not."

"Look, we have to decide whether we tell the Inspector, or whether we are all in this investigation together and try and see what we can find out ourselves," said Bobby Chariot, only a child, but a clever one.

"I don't feel we can trust anyone at the moment. Present company excepted of course. We are finding out a lot as it is, but we are also getting into a lot of trouble. We need to have some plan about backing each other up," Alice surmised.

"Well, you're going to have to decide pretty quick whether to tell Glees anything. He's on his way up the path and he's got David with him." Marjoram told them.

"Follow my lead," said Lydia. "I'll work it out as we go along. Trust me."

The Inspector came through the kitchen door closely followed by David. He did not knock or announce himself. He looked cross.

CHAPTER EIGHT *SELECTIVE MEMORY*

"Hello Inspector Glees," said Marjoram. "Cup of tea?"

"Not while I am on official business Mrs Prix. No drinking on duty."

"It's tea," said Lydia.

"Nevertheless, not just yet."

"What are you doing here today David?" asked Lydia. "You seem to be spending a lot of time with the Inspector just lately."

David smiled briefly and then looked at the floor before folding his arms across his chest.

"Enough of that. I have a list of complaints against your family." Glees took out a sheet of paper from his pocket and unfolded it carefully. He began to read.

1. Pestering and threatening Ginger Batty at the Police Office while he was only doing his duty.
2. Spreading gossip about me not being able to do my job.
3. Arriving at the Doctor's unannounced and asking for a body.

4. Trespassing in the Doctor's house and hospital.
5. Upsetting Mrs Snailwort and using her house as a thoroughfare.

"That's only scratching the surface, I haven't had chance to get round to everyone." He folded the paper and put it back into his pocket.

"You've been moving fast Inspector. Have you managed to find out any more about my brother's death?" asked Lydia.

"I haven't had time for that just yet. I am too busy sorting out other things." His eyes moved round the room in what he considered to be an authoritative manner. They rested on Sadie.

"I thought you were dead!" he said, surprise registering on his face.

David looked at Sadie and said, "So you are not dead on a rock in the woods then Sadie?"

"No I am not cheeky. If you know who is involved in all these things, you should do something about it. I want him investigating for a start," insisted Sadie pointing at Glees.

"Inspector, Sadie was drugged and it was only pure chance that I discovered her," Lydia said. "We would all like to know where the body of my brother is being kept. Gran wants to pay her respects before he is burnt."

"The body will be on its way to Mr Oreful by now I should think. You should have gone earlier and seen him."

"Where?"

Don't get cross. Lydia said to herself.

"At the Doctor's surgery, where my assistant told you he was."

Gran stalked across the kitchen and stood in front of the Inspector. Even though she only came up to his waist, she was not intimidated by him.

She said, "We called at the Doctor's this afternoon and he was most insistent that Michaelmas was not there!"

"Perhaps you were mistaken," David answered for the Inspector.

"Are you calling Gran a liar?" Lydia glared at her former friend.

"No, I just wanted to make sure that everything is done properly," he answered sheepishly.

"Well shut your mouth then!" Mr Chariot had never been impressed with David and his superior ways.

"No need for that," interjected the Inspector. "You lot are in enough trouble already, without insulting my official deputy."

The Prixs looked shocked.

"Deputy is it? We all know whose side you are on David Turncoat!" Mr Chariot said.

"I am on the side of justice and right," he answered quietly.

Lydia stared at him, but said nothing else.

Gran said, "So can we go to the Doctor's now and see Michaelmas? Are you going to come with us?"

"I don't do things like that, I am far too busy," answered the Inspector.

"I'll come with you Mrs Prix, if you would like me to." The offer coming from David so soon after the insults was not expected.

"I should appreciate that, David. Girls, can you get the trap ready now, we have only a little time before it gets dark. I want to see Michaelmas before tonight."

It was soon done and by six Janey was driving David, the Inspector and Gran to the Doctor's surgery.

The Inspector said that he would come with them as he had some business with the Doctor. Lydia was glad that they were all going with Gran. She would not come to any harm if everyone was there. The Doctor would not cause trouble if the Inspector was there and the Inspector would not cause trouble if David were there. She hoped anyway.

Lydia and Alice sat at the kitchen table again. The Chariots had gone home, taking Sadie with them. Mr Chariot promised to take her directly to her house and see that she was alright. Alice and Lydia thought that they should write down a list of things that had happened and see what they could make of it.

"The Inspector and the Doctor are prime suspects," said Alice.

"Uncle Cal is suspicious too and I am not that sure about David," added Lydia.

"There is also the possibility of someone else, someone whose identity we don't know yet." Alice wrote notes as they spoke.

"I know, because when I was in the clearing, someone was about then. But it felt like a something rather than a someone. It reminded me of the thing that got me in the old mill."

"So, describe it to me. If we write the stuff down and look at it coldly we might get more of an idea."

"Right. It was tall and thin and spiky," began Lydia.

"Wow, no wonder we haven't noticed that walking down the street," joked Alice.

"Don't be sarcastic! Write all this down!" Lydia wasn't really cross, it was just that as she was saying the words out loud, the whole experience wasn't sounding quite so scary and yet all of those experiences had been very scary.

"Chill out!"

"Ok. Leathery skin and long fingernails. Smelly breath and very creepy. He shuddered." Lydia said the last part more quietly than the rest. She didn't like the shuddering part and didn't want to talk anymore about that bit.

"I don't like shuddering either," said Alice. "It's not right."

Alice doodled on the page.

Lydia said, "It seems very strong, but doesn't really use its strength, it sort of forces you to do things you don't want."

"Yes, I know," answered Alice.

"How do you know?"

"I don't know how I know."

"Oh."

"What else?"

"I am not sure, I know I am never supposed to tell anyone, but now I can't remember why I have been so determined to keep quiet."

"Perhaps it threatened you?"

"Yes, I think so, but I seem to have forgotten how."

This was strange. For the past twenty years, Lydia knew that dreadful things had happened to her and she could always sort of remember what. She knew that she must never say anything to anyone, or her family would be in serious trouble, perhaps killed. But just at this moment, she could not remember what or why. What was happening to her?

She thought for a little longer, watching her sister draw all over the list they were making. She appeared to be drawing a bonfire with a person on top of it.

"Who is that?" Lydia asked.

"No idea. Someone I used to know I think." Alice seemed unsure.

There was a noise from the front door. It was a sort of scuffling followed by a scratching noise. The women went into the hallway and watched the doorknob twist and turn. Luckily the door was locked, but whoever it was still tried to turn the knob. The women moved nearer to each other and stared mesmerised at the door. They were tense and scared. The door bell sounded.

"Who is it do you think?" Alice asked Lydia.

"Murderers don't usually ring the bell do they?"

"No. Hello who is there?"

"It's Ginger, I've got your list for you!" shouted the boy.

The women both went to open the door, feeling slightly foolish.

"Hello Ginger," said Alice. "Thanks for bringing the list for us."

"Yea, well don't say anything to the Inspector about it. He went mad just because I told you where your brother's body was. Apparently I am not supposed to tell anybody anything."

"Yes, he came round to tell us all off."

"Just keep that list to yourself. See you around."

The boy scampered off down the drive and into the street. He was gone in a flash.

"See if this list shows us anything useful," said Lydia.

She read it, but apart from the usual suspects, doctor, police, mill and the Council lot, there was no one on the list that they wouldn't have expected. Except …

"There are two names on here I didn't expect." Alice looked confused.

"Who?"

"Cal and David Turncoat."

The conversation was interrupted with the sound of the pony and trap arriving back. Alice put the list in her pocket and the two women went out through the back door into the yard. Gran was being helped down from the cart by Janey and Alice noticed that the old lady had aged twenty years this past week.

"Are you alright Gran?" asked Lydia. "You look tired."

"I am tired, you are right Alice. I shall have some tea and go to bed I think. It has been a long and very sad day."

"What happened at the Doctor's Gran?" asked Alice.

Janey shook her head firmly and beckoned her sister to be quiet.

"Take Gran inside Alice and make sure that she is alright." Janey handed over the old lady and turned back to the pony and began removing its harness. Lydia helped and when she was sure that the others had returned safely to the kitchen, she asked about the visit.

"It was dreadful, so sad and emotional, for both of us really."

"Tell me. What did he say about pretending the body was not there when you called earlier?"

"He just said that he hadn't realised that Oreful had brought Michaelmas to the hospital. He said that he was

133

very upset when he found out that he had sent us away like that!"

Lydia felt confused.

"So what did he say about pretending that he had no visitors recently?"

"Just that he thought that you had already gone home. He didn't mention the cellar or anything like that so I said nothing. I am sure that the cellar is connected to all of this somehow."

"I agree about that," Lydia answered. "I am wondering how we can get more involved."

"We need to go and investigate properly. We need to get into all of these places and really see what is going on," Alice said thoughtfully. They finished sorting out the pony and hung up the tack.

"Come on in and have some tea!" shouted Janey from the back door.

Soon the three sat around the kitchen table with hot drinks and cakes. Gran had gone to bed after having very little to say to her granddaughters before she went.

The birds in the ivy upon the wall seemed restless and flit from one branch to another. The birds had been unsettled since Michaelmas had been found dead. Owl was not much happier and he remained puffed up and eyes closed, even when encouraged out of himself with food. He ate a little and hunched back on his log. This unusual occurrence was not helping the atmosphere of the cottage.

Only a week ago it was warm and comforting, but steadily the place seemed to be losing life. The birds felt it, Gran was feeling it and now the girls were feeling it too.

"How are we going to get into the cellars at the Doctor's without raising the alarm?" asked Janey.

"I have no idea how. Unless we can get David's help?" agreed Janey.

"Don't trust him. He's changed for the worse. I am sure that he is caught up in all of this somehow and I don't want him to know anything more than he finds out himself." Lydia was adamant about this. The sisters had the sense not to argue, not least because they agreed with her. David Turncoat was not a friend.

"Even if we waited until the Doctor was out of his house, we still have to account for his sisters," said Lydia, taking another biscuit from the plate. She was going to have to watch this habit or she would have a backside the size of Sadie. She giggled with this thought and almost choked on the biscuit.

"What's got into you?" asked Janey.

"Nothing, I think I am just over tired," answered Lydia.

"So, how are we going to move ahead with all of this? If we are going to find anything out, we must start exploring. I mean I am struggling to see how all this connects with each other," Alice noted thoughtfully.

"Let's go back to the list of clues," said Janey.

"That reminds me! I have the list for this party thing that's going on." Alice took the list from her pocket and smoothed it against the tablecloth.

"I wonder what is so special about this party?" pondered the girls. "I mean there have been parties before, but never this secrecy. No, it's very odd."

"We'll work it out, let's sleep on it." Lydia hoped that soon everything would start falling into place. Trouble was, until then they would have to deal with whatever came along.

The rest of the evening was spent discussing the state of Gran and how worried they were about her. She was not the woman she used to be. She usually had the energy of a much younger woman and didn't let any of life's troubles affect her. The Prix children were used to Gran being around, encouraging them all to be positive.

"You get exactly what you think," she would say.

Even though Lydia had been away for such a long time, the Gran she saw when she returned was the same as the Gran she remembered. But now, only a few days later, she had withered and shrunk to half her size.

"I would take her to the doctor if only we had a proper one," they laughed. But it wasn't that funny.

They went to bed. Judging by the pace of the past few days, tomorrow was likely to be busy and they needed their rest. Lydia, on entering her bedroom and shutting the door, realised how bone tired she was. Her whole body ached and throbbed and as she undressed she noticed just how many bruises and cuts she had incurred from her fall down the cellar that morning.

It was too late to bathe because it took over an hour to heat up the boiler. She intended to have a bath in the morning and made do with cleaning herself from top to bottom with a flannel and a bowl of water. She rubbed some ointment into her wounds, knowing that Gran's remedy would help considerably by the following morning.

She dressed in her night things and climbed wearily into bed. What a funny day. What a peculiar week.

Mill Town tradition dictated that Michaelmas would be burnt and his name written in the Book of Passing which was kept at the Council offices. Name and cause of death alongside the date were also recorded there. The book, huge white and ancient, had been recording the events since Mill Town began. It was said that the book would never run out of paper and the job of writing in it passed down through a line of recorders. This family was related closely to the Scribers.

There was also a record of marriages kept there, except this book was red. The recording was done by the Passing recorders too. Of course the recording of foundlings was done at the hospital. Lydia wondered briefly how long it would be before Michaelmas arrived there again. She had an idea that perhaps she could go there one day and recognise him. Then she would bring him home and be the best keeper possible to him. She had heard that a keeper did not always have to be married.

Now, she must have a proper think about what was actually going on. She made herself comfortable against the pillows and tried to establish the facts.

There is no question about that thing in the clearing being the same as the thing in the old mill. Of course, something had followed her through town that first night. And, why could she not remember anything about it? The memory was just there on the edge, waiting to be recognised, but Lydia could only remember when it was happening again and then she forgot. But it was never forgotten completely. The shadow of the memory was always there circling her thoughts and life. It kept her on edge, fearful and encouraged her to make decisions she did not like. She could be a happy smiling person and then suddenly the memory would come in and ruin the moment. But she could not picture nor verbalise why that would be so, nor what it would take to stop. That was because she had not recalled it fully. Coming back to Mill Town was certainly rattling a lot of cages, elsewhere and in her mind. Fear, instead of circling her and warning her, had been right in her face just recently, she was almost getting used to it. That was mad.

And what about the Doctor? What was going on there? Had all her visits there as a child really been innocent? It certainly seemed a little strange, with the benefit of hindsight. No other family encouraged children to constantly come round and play, all day and every day. Then that weird thing about today and the cellars wasn't normal. Why would the cellars be laid out like that? Perhaps the Doctor liked to have some time to himself away from everyone, hence the books and the fire.

But why would there be such a huge table set out for large gatherings? It looked like a meeting place of some sort. But did large groups of people arrive at the house and then march down those tricky cellar steps for a meeting? Why wouldn't they meet in the dining room or the sitting room? Unless of course what they were meeting for was secret. But what sort of secret? None of it made sense. It was a bit creepy really. And if David's name was on that list alongside all the other men, then he must be involved in some way too.

She heard a noise outside and got up to have a look. She peeped out through the gap in the curtains, but could see nothing or no one. It was probably her imagination and she climbed back into bed, noticing that it was quite cold. She snuggled up under the flowery quilt.

"Are you alright?" Alice shouted from the next room.

"Fine. I just thought I heard something outside, but I couldn't see anything!" she shouted back.

"Well if you hear anything else, give us a shout and we'll go out and look. I don't want anything upsetting the ponies!" Janey bellowed.

"I will!" She snuggled down amidst the lovely peace and quiet of her bed and went back to thinking.

She tried very hard to dwell on the events of today. It wasn't working very well and she let her thoughts drift to the mill visit tomorrow. It was a very comfortable feeling knowing that she was wealthy enough to buy any of those apartments. How lucky that she had agreed to help out the coastguard with his little bit of importing from across the sea. She had been rewarded well for that.

The coastguard did offer her a permanent partnership, but Lydia had waited until she had money enough for what she wanted and could leave. Mr Pollack knew nothing about the smuggling and if he did, he wasn't bothered. The nearest he had actually come to stealing her gold, was asking her if he could borrow some. The divorce would come through soon enough. She looked forward to that.

Lydia had dreams of buying a cottage by the woods, as near to the rest of her family as possible. But the thought of owning one of those swish apartments at the old mill was very tempting. Perhaps she could buy both? She certainly had plenty of gold. She had no real intention of telling the others yet, better to see how things went.

Lydia had no desire to marry again. Marriage was too restrictive. It was odd, because as a child and a young woman, she and other people had taken it for granted that she would marry David Turncoat. But, he had gone cool towards her and her returning overwhelming feeling that she was bringing trouble down on her family, moving away had been a logical step. Trouble certainly seemed to follow her around and bad trouble at that. Lydia felt like a bad luck charm and wanted to keep her family safe. She thought that she was the only person that the shuddering thing bothered with, but now she was not so sure.

She heard a noise again. She got up and put on her coat and shoes and went out of the bedroom to the girls' room. She woke them up with some difficulty and told them about the noises. They jumped out of their beds, put on dressing gowns and followed Lydia down the stairs. There was all sorts of fluttering and flapping from the birds in the kitchen.

"Someone is about out there definitely. The birds wouldn't wake up if it was nothing."

They did not light any lamps, but crept across the hall and into the kitchen. Feathers and bits of hop and ivy floated to the floor where the little birds and bats had been scurrying from one side of the wall to the other. As soon as the women entered the kitchen, the movement stopped. Their work done in raising the household, the little flutterers felt safe to go back to sleep.

The women looked out of the kitchen window onto the yard and garden at the back. The moon lit up the garden beautifully.

"Look over there on the path to the woods!" whispered Janey.

"I can't see anything!" Alice peered through narrowed eyes, hoping that would make a difference.

Then suddenly they all saw together. Michaelmas was standing there in the moonlight waving to them. He was smiling and looking very happy. They saw Treen walk from the woods towards his grandson, wave to the women and then the two men walked away and vanished into the moonlit woods.

The women held each other tightly.

CHAPTER NINE *BACK TO THE MILL*

Breakfast the following morning at Wood Lane Cottage, was a quiet affair

The women sat around the table and watched the birds tweeting and bustling about in the branches. Every so often one of the birds would come to the table, sitting on the back of a chair or perching on the toast rack. They waited patiently for a crumb or piece of bread to land on the table and then took it back to the branches tweeting and singing and telling their little friends what they had managed to find. The sound was pleasant, relaxing and comforting.

Gran was still in her room. She got up for a short time and decided that she needed to spend the day in bed. The women had never seen her do that before. They decided not to tell her about last night, feeling that there would be no point in upsetting her further.

"Tell her when she is feeling better, in a day or two," said Alice.

The women ate in silence, unsure how they were supposed to carry on in this new world in which they now lived. Michaelmas was dead and gone for ever. Gran was going the same way and there was all sorts of weird things

142

occurring. There was no one to trust or talk to outside of their own family.

"You wonder whether it was better when we just held on to all our secrets and told no one. Because now it is as though we have unleashed something," commented Janey.

"I don't see how that could be. What have any of us actually done to make any difference?" Alice passed a piece of bread to a particularly brightly coloured little bird that was doing his best to make himself agreeable to her.

"I came back," said Lydia. "I knew that I had to leave to save everyone and I came back. That's what happened." She looked sad.

"I don't see how that could make a difference. I mean why would that be so?" Alice was not sure what her sister was talking about.

"I just know that I was not supposed to tell and I was not supposed to come back."

"Who have you told?" asked Janey.

"No one. Unless you count my journal, but I burnt that."

They became thoughtful again.

"I am going to the old mill after breakfast, to have a look at the new apartments," Lydia informed them.

"How much money have you actually got?" Janey wondered briefly if she could persuade her older sister to invest in their pony scheme.

"Quite a lot, but don't worry I will help you two out. I just have to be a bit careful until the divorce comes through. I can't be seen spending too much money. It won't matter afterwards."

The twins decided to say no more. Lydia wouldn't have said that unless she intended to help them. Alice

143

visualised the sign they intended to put up outside the cottage:

Prix Pretty Ponies

How nice it would be to be well known and respected in the town. Better than that, to have the ability to earn their own money and carry influence that way. They could get their own back for the shabby way their Grandfather had been treated.

Breakfast finished, everything was cleared away while the women planned the rest of their day.

"I shall leave shortly. Do either of you want to come with me?" asked Lydia.

"I am too busy here Lydia. With Gran in bed, someone has to do the work she usually does. All, the cleaning and cooking and washing and all that." Alice was not being negative, merely truthful.

"I will give you a lift there if you like, I have to take some potatoes and things over to the fish shop then go on to show the pony to someone who is interested in buying. That's good news isn't it?" Janey said helpfully.

"That's really good news. Thanks for the lift. I will have a good look around when I am in the mill, I might find some clues if nothing else!" Lydia was more interested in her visit than she had expected. Was she going to be facing more demons from the past?

Trotting in the cart down Wide Lane was a refreshing experience. The sun was out and already becoming warm, but a slight breeze ensured that it would not get too hot today.

144

"I don't want the pony sweating when I get to the buyer. It would not create a good impression."

"Who exactly wants to see the pony today?"

"Mr Turncoat actually." Janey looked sheepish.

"You mean David?" Lydia turned to her sister, who had coloured a little.

"No, his father. Apparently he wants a pony to pull a cart of their own. He specifically asked for blue." Janey skilfully slowed the pony up as they approached the shop and the mill, conveniently situated opposite each other. "I am not saying I will let him buy. I will see how well he is going to look after him. Plus I don't want to sell my only blue pony, when I can cross him. It is so difficult selling when I can't yet afford to replace. I have to buy more than one when I buy you see."

Lydia leaned over and kissed her sister on the cheek. "Don't worry yourself, everything will work out soon."

The women both jumped down, Lydia walked towards the mill sales office and Janey towards the shop. They agreed to meet here again at lunchtime.

Lydia turned and watched her sister as she went into the fish and chip shop. The large street side window framed the viewing. As Janey entered the shop, Lydia noticed how the two male assistants smiled and cheered up considerably. Janey chatted effortlessly with them and soon they came out and carried the potatoes from the back of the cart and back into the shop. Janey was laughing and joking and Lydia realised that she hadn't seen her sister in male company at all. When she left for Seaside, the twins were not much above twenty and still lived with their keepers, and since she had been back, there had been far too much drama. She remembered that the Scriber boys also liked the girls. Those two had a better family pedigree.

Lydia wanted to help them find more friends. She would try and set them up in business as soon as she was able and they could meet a better sort of husband. The fish boys were no doubt lovely and kind, but life with them would be hard work at a business her sister did not enjoy.

She laughed at herself. There was no evidence that her sisters were interested in the fish boys or anyone else for that matter, but honestly she knew that they must do better than Sadie and Marjoram had done.

Lydia turned back to the mill and walked through the big metal gates towards the sales office. The office, set back in the entrance yard, had originally been the delivery booking-in office. It was here that anyone delivering or collecting would call prior to being allowed into the main yard.

The entrance at the other end of the mill was where the workers and managers arrived and any visitors called. It was the other entrance that Lydia and the other children went through all those years ago.

She went into the sales office and listened to the bell which hung above the door tinkle and call a receptionist from within another room.

"Can I help you?" asked the girl. She was the same girl who had booked in Lydia's appointment. She didn't usually work on a Saturday and Sunday as another girl covered for her. Today that girl had decided to be ill and couldn't come to work, so Cranberry was feeling slightly flustered and overworked. A casual observer might have pointed out that she had a well-paid job and appeared to do very little at all. But Cranberry would not have listened to a casual observer any more than she listened to her manager when he gave her anything extra to do.

"I have an appointment to view some of the apartments this morning," answered Lydia calmly.

"Who did you make the appointment with?" asked the girl rather curtly, while flicking her diary from one page to another.

"You wrote it in your diary yesterday morning when I was talking to your manager," replied Lydia coolly, and then added, "I can't imagine that so many people are viewing the properties that you have forgotten me so soon."

Cranberry stopped flicking and stared at Lydia as though she were a foreign specimen. She looked up and down her visitor, noticing her well cut dress and nice shoes. As someone who was greatly interested in fashion, she knew full well that the clothes had not been bought from anywhere on Town Street.

She didn't like the woman's attitude and superior air and said, "Didn't we see you going past here yesterday afternoon with Sadie Prince all messed up and dirty? You were both lying against the wall in the field next door weren't you?" she nodded her head in the direction of the said field. "Had you been drinking Madam?"

"Goodness, you are a bitch aren't you?" Lydia had been a sister too long to be upset by comments from a silly girl like that. "Get the manager immediately before I ensure that you get the sack." Then Lydia leaned forward a little and said, "Trust me, I am a person of my word."

Cranberry went red and said, "He will be back in a minute. He said that you were to wait."

147

Lydia looked around the office and noting a row of chairs, sat upon one and made herself comfortable, all the while smiling prettily at the receptionist.

However, within five minutes the smile was wiped smartly from her face. She turned to the entrance door as the bell tinkled again and saw a couple walk into the office, arms interlinked, and the woman looking triumphant.

"Can I help you?" Cranberry asked the couple.

"We have an appointment to view some apartments this morning," said the woman.

Lydia almost fainted and was thankful that she was sitting down.

"Hello little Liddy! Fancy seeing you here!"

What on earth were the worst couple in Mill Town doing here? Auntie Cal turned round on hearing her husband talking in a way that always put her senses on red alert.

"Well if it isn't you? I heard you were back, getting divorced and causing trouble. Your husband doesn't want you anymore I hear? That didn't last long."

Lydia didn't know that it would be possible to hate these people any more than she already did, but apparently she could.

"How long we been married now Cal? Must be nearly thirty years, isn't that right Lydia?"

"Something like that," mumbled Lydia, conscious that Cranberry was listening to this conversation with growing interest. Lydia didn't sound so sure of herself now.

Lydia had noticed the shift in the dynamics since they had entered the building and was trying in vain to discover why she felt like she did. The pair were grinning at her and

148

she felt the old familiar shiver when she saw her Uncle wink at her. Horrible creepy old man.

Auntie Cal was dressed in a voluminous dress which was tied unnecessarily with a large belt around her middle. Her pale fat legs were only partly covered by the dress, and her feet were stuffed professionally into painted wooden clogs. Her hair, still dark but unkempt, was partly tamed with a checked headscarf. Her face had fallen into the lines and shape of the person she had always been: a mean spirited, self-involved cruel woman.

Uncle Cal, tall thin and creepy, wore large dark glasses which hid his small darting eyes. His face had razor sharp features and he wore now as always, a pair of pale blue trousers and a striped shirt. His head was partly covered by a greasy cap which Lydia remembered with great distaste, he had worn every time she saw him. He seemed to change shape and size according to the situation he was in. He said very little in public, but all the children knew that once alone with them he would talk in a way that unnerved them.

She hoped that they would not be viewing at the same time as her, but did not hold out much hope. Luck rarely ran her way. In fact the only time she had a peaceful time and had made some money was while she lived at Seaside with her uncaring and unfaithful husband. She was almost missing him and her life back there.

The sales man came back into the reception, all smiles and handshakes. He seemed pleased to have so many potential purchasers in his grasp.

"Welcome, welcome. I am glad you all managed to get here on time. Sorry I am a bit late. You are all related aren't you? That's a coincidence. I am sure that you will have no

149

objection if we all go round at the same time. What do you say?" He smiled at everyone.

"Well we are game for that aren't we Cal?" said Mrs Cal brightly. "It will be good company for us all to view together. We can compare notes and intentions. Who knows? We might decide to live next door to each other and then when the sisters visit Lydia they can visit us! What do you think Cal?"

"I should like very much to have all my nieces live by me again and visit whenever I wish. I have missed the girls coming round to see me in their little dresses and pretty ribbons. It has been a long time since I have touched pretty ribbons," he answered. He put out his hand as if he intended to touch her. Lydia moved back.

"Oh, isn't that lovely Lydia," said Mrs Cal sweetly as she gazed fondly at her husband.

Lydia put her hand to her mouth in order to suppress retching.

"That's settled then," the salesman was happy not to have to do the rounds of the site twice that morning. "If you will all follow me, I should be very much obliged."

Lydia rose from her chair wondering why she was following these instructions despite it being the last thing she wanted to do. Really she should leave right now and go back to Gran's or anywhere else as soon as they left the door to the sales office.

Now, they were all standing in the entrance yard as the salesman decided which way to take them into the maze which was the old mill. It was at this moment when Lydia had the best chance of leaving the party. Here in the yard she would not even have to make an excuse! She could wait until the others turned towards the doors and then she could

150

just walk away from them and go right into the street and never have to put herself in the position of being trapped by the Cals.

Trapped! That is what she would be if she went with them. Yet here she was, following them and walking up the steps and towards the main doors.

"As we go in we lock the doors behind us, thereby ensuring high levels of security at all times. I am sure that you would all like this to be so when any of you move in."

In they all walked, the man ushering them through into the entrance hallway and the door was soon firmly locked behind him. Mr Beesty, for that was the man's name, put the large key around his wrist by means of a chain which he had expressly for that purpose. He smiled at Lydia as he did so and Lydia was suddenly transported back in memory. Not this time to the distant past but the recent past. Keys mean something.

She followed the group through the second door. Mrs Cal was twittering away happily to her husband. He, in return, ignored her and walked in step with Beesty, all the while keeping an unlit pipe in the corner of his mouth. His cap defied gravity by staying on his head as he walked.

Lydia was at a loss to know why she followed them all on this mission. She was quite aware that now she had no means of easy escape without asking the salesman for the key and telling him she wanted to leave. Might as well go ahead and see where the visit took her. She watched the keys swinging on his arm, mesmerised by the tick tock motion of them.

Of course! She had forgotten about the key which she picked up at the clearing that day. Where had she put it now? She tried to think straight and remembered that it was in her handbag which she was holding tightly for security at this very moment.

She remembered seeing another key in the Lawyer's office, when the old lady helped after she dropped her bag on the floor. She had put that key in her bag.

But wait. The key had not been in her bag when she dropped it, so how had the old lady found a key and returned it to Lydia?

That would only be possible if the old lady had left them there in the first place. So did that mean that she was carrying around two strange keys in her bag at this very moment? There is no way she could look now, but vowed to do so at the earliest opportunity.

"Here, were the offices where accounts and letters were sorted out. Now, it will be used by the wardens and security men for the whole community. We will have shops and our own medical person ensuring that anyone who lives here need not leave if they do not want."

"Doctor Catapult won't like that will he? Does he know about it?" asked Aunt Cal.

"There will be maids and cleaners and servants of all kinds," continued Beesty undeterred. "If a resident does not want to do any work in their own house, then they needn't do so."

"Where you going to get all these maids and servants and whatnot from then?" asked Mrs Cal.

"All labour will be sourced from the village and town, ensuring that local people can gain benefit from the venture too."

"Oh, that's alright then. Perhaps I should apply for one of those jobs. You could get a job here couldn't you Cal? You could be a butler or something couldn't you?"

"I would have thought that if you are in a position to buy a property here, you would not want to work here too?" Beesty was becoming a little worried that his potential customers may just be coming out for a Saturday trip out of the house.

"There is no law against us doing that is there?" Cal had the belligerent look of a man not used to being crossed.

"No, no, not at all." The salesman answered quickly, not wanting to upset his clients. "You may do as you please if you live here."

They arrived at the end of the office block.

"If you look across the yard, you will see a large mill building, and in there will be shops of all types. Dressmakers, grocers, butchers and all sorts."

"What will happen about the tradesmen in town?" enquired Lydia.

"What do you mean?" Beesty asked her in return.

"Well, it has always been that each family hands down the business to the next generation and they carry it on. The only people qualified to do any of the jobs will be those who have grown up with it. I can't see any of them leaving their family business to come here?" Lydia said thoughtfully.

"Well, let us just say that we are in discussions with everyone. Who is to say that having a change of face might not be a good thing?" Beesty asked reasonably.

"Well. Lydia was always a posh know-it-all cow wasn't she Cal?" Cal nodded in answer. "Trust her to disapprove of a man trying to get on in the world!"

The couple looked smug. Lydia was too shocked to answer. She should have been used to the unfair rudeness of her Aunt and Uncle by now, but she quite obviously was not.

The salesman chose to ignore the tense atmosphere which existed between the three clients and proceeded merrily with his well-worn sales pitch.

"Every need will be catered for here. Lamps will be constantly lit in the corridors and yards and alleys and if required, the lamps in each apartment will be lit by a warden so that no one needs return in the dark."

"That sounds very useful doesn't it Cal?" Lydia hoped that her Aunt would not have to make a comment about everything they were told.

"How are you going to get water up here for all these people?" It was a fair question, even if it came from such a horrid man. Water for every cottage came from wells and made use of the springs that occurred naturally on the hillsides. These in turn led down to the river at the bottom of the valley. But for so many people requiring water on a regular basis, the old fashioned well used in the old mill would not suffice.

When the buildings had been used in industry, the workers made do with archaic plumbing and the lovely and sadly missed tea ladies waited until the tap from the spring had filled their tea urns. The ladies took turns in filling it as the job was so incredibly slow and boring. There is no way that people paying the large sums of money asked for the properties would stand for half an hour while their containers filled with water.

"Well there will be one of the wonderfully modern contraptions we have invented and are installing at the moment. It is a secret invention, but it uses the force of the water from the river where it tumbles over the weir and

154

allows it to fall into a drain which pushes the water up here by a series of pipes and valves, it is very complicated and very clever." The salesman obviously was not too sure about the details of the contraption.

"Is it anything to do with the big bridge and tunnel thing you have planned for the field next door?" Cal had brought up a conversation piece with such authority that everyone looked at him.

"Where did you hear about that Mr Cal?" asked Beesty.

"I get around to places you might not expect," Cal said more reluctantly. "I just heard about plans to dig a great big tunnel in the field to let the water drain away into a leat and allow it to go back to the river."

Lydia was not interested in mechanical things and so asked instead, "Do you think that we might go and see some of the apartments soon? I have to leave by lunchtime."

"Yes of course Mrs Pollack. Let's get a move on."

They trooped through the door which took them back into a yard. They found themselves standing next to the huge chimney, which looked much spruced up now that it had been cleaned and the brickwork pointed. It no longer looked so grey. That was another thing that Lydia noticed. The old mill did not seem as grey as it used to be. It must have been cleaned all the way through.

Passing beyond the chimney led them to the first large mill building. They mounted a staircase made from stone and iron and arrived at another huge oak door. Mr Beesty used the same key to open the door, allow them all entry and then lock the door behind them again. Lydia found that quite interesting, now that keys were her brand new fascination.

They were standing in a corridor, which would be black as bag if it weren't for the lamps lit and hanging in brackets.

"Let's just hope those lamps don't blow out!" observed Mrs Cal unnecessarily.

"They couldn't all blow out at once Mrs Cal and there is always a way to light them again," answered Beesty reassuringly.

Here, they saw door after door, but Beesty said that there was little point in looking in any of the rooms as they were so far from being completed and would give little clue of their finished status.

It was probably nearer the truth that Beesty only wanted to sell the apartments in the far building because they were almost finished. The sooner the properties were filled, the easier it would be to sell the others. The Snooty mill family also needed money coming in soon so that they could carry on with the work.

Along the corridor they trudged, passing twenty doors at least. It was like being on a donkey treadmill seeing the same hypnotic sight over and over again. Every five doors they passed a set of stairs.

"Where do the stairs lead?" asked Lydia.

"Each apartment goes up two floors from this corridor. But there are two other corridors up there which lead to a door into each apartment again," Beesty informed them.

"So there are three doors on different levels to each apartment?" said Lydia.

"That's right. The same plan applies to all four blocks of apartments. There are two blocks on this side of the centre courtyard and two smaller ones on the other side. It has been very well thought out," Beesty said proudly, as though he had planned and built the places himself.

They left this block via another door and alley, locking and unlocking the doors on the way through. Going to one of those City prisons must be like this. Lydia had been suppressing a rising panic in her body as each lock was turned. There was something about entering this far block which made her heart bang against the wall of her chest. She felt a little breathless and staggered slightly.

"What's the matter Liddy, feeling a bit queer are you?" Cal put a hand on her arm and she jerked away from him instinctively.

"No, no I am fine. I am still not quite recovered from Michaelmas's death," she answered, only partly truthfully.

The group walked to the other end of the corridor. Lydia leaned against the wall as she looked at the huge doors in front of her.

"Did those doors used to lead to the outer reception office?" she asked the salesman.

"Why yes, Mrs Pollack. They are the original outdoors."

"So, where we are standing now used to be the building which housed all the old looms?"

"Yes, how did you know?" asked Beesty.

"I have been here before. Many years ago," she answered.

"I've been here lots of times as well. I don't think we have been here at the same time have we Liddy?"

Lydia could not answer.

CHAPTER TEN *REMEMBERING*

Facing the doors and thinking about another time, she became conscious of her uncle standing behind her. He was breathing heavily and as he put his hand on her shoulder, she turned round and slapped his face hard.

"Don't you ever touch me again, Cal. If you do, I shall kill you."

He backed away, grinning at his niece. He was not perturbed by the slap, merely amused by her reaction. Mrs Cal on the other hand objected seriously to the assault upon her husband. She lunged forward and made to grab Lydia's hair. Mr Beesty, amazed at the sudden turn of events leant forward and took hold of Mrs Cal's arm.

"Ladies, ladies please! What is happening? Let us keep our cool!" Beesty was used to the arguments of the girls in the office, but had never been witness to such violence amongst clients. He suspected that there must be some serious dispute of which he knew no details. Was this likely to affect his sales? On quick reflection he deduced that it very likely would. He must calm this down as soon as possible.

"I am not having that cow hitting my husband with no provocation!"

158

Lydia, although initially surprised that her aunt knew such a long word said coldly, "Cal knows perfectly well what I mean."

"Do I little Liddy? Do I? I don't imagine you know anything that you can prove, or say out loud." The last comment was accompanied with a sneer.

Lydia felt cold and shaky, but was starting to feel a power within her that she hadn't felt before.

Beesty, not quite sure how he had got into this situation, said, "Perhaps Mrs Pollack and I can view this apartment and Mr and Mrs Cal could view the apartment opposite? That way we can cover more ground. I haven't forgotten that Mrs Pollack has another appointment at lunchtime." That should sort everything out, he thought.

"Appointment at lunchtime! You are such a posh stuck up cow Lydia. Your mother would be embarrassed if she could hear you now." Mrs Cal had a practised way of upsetting people, particularly her family. She had been doing it for so long, that it came naturally to her. If ever she had been picked up on her manners, she had come down so hard on the critic that they had not criticised again.

"That is an excellent idea," replied Lydia. "Lead the way Mr Beesty."

"Yes, yes, just go through door number 2 Mr and Mrs Cal and shout if you need anything from me." He was very agitated now that his customers had split up. Beesty liked to keep any potential sales close to him. He was paid very little as a basic wage and must rely solely on commission for apartment sales to pay his bills.

Lydia and Beesty entered Apartment 1. The door opened onto an entrance hall, which was quite narrow. A set of stairs began on the left hand side of the corridor and went up to the next floors. To the right was a door which led to a room with no outside windows. It was fairly square and painted in a cream colour.

Lydia walked around it quickly and came straight out. The room made her flesh crawl. The second door off the corridor opened out onto a particularly bright and large kitchen.

They walked over to the big window and Lydia noted that from this window she could see directly onto the field and into the back gardens of her Aunt's and neighbours, including her own keeper's home. If she lived here, she would always know where her mother and father were. She would also be able to see into anyone else's cottage on that same small row. Of course, Cal would always be able to see into her kitchen and probably her bedroom.

"The kitchen is well equipped with an oven and fire combined, the chimney going up the side of the building where it joins three other chimneys and then goes up onto the roof. There are many chimneys along the roof of each apartment block. It has been very well planned."

"I am sure it has. It just seems so separated from the world."

"I think you will find that is the point. People these days like to have their privacy without danger of someone coming to their house and interfering in their lives."

"I thought everyone liked some interference? I mean here there is only the door to the corridor. Unless you meet someone actually coming out of their apartment at the same time as yourself, you may not even see your neighbours." Lydia was thinking of the lonely years she had spent at Seaside, where everyone kept themselves to themselves. Apart from the friendly coastguard she had got to know no few other people there. No one would miss her, now that she was never to return. How sad.

They left the kitchen and went back to the stairs. These stairs were well made but lacked the character of any stairs at the cottages in and around Mill Town. These were straight and square and Lydia expected that every other apartment was built in this same way. On this floor was a sitting room and bathroom. The bathroom looked out over the field and the sitting room had no windows, as its outlook would have been the corridor.

Lydia thought that not only would there never be any friendly sunlight, while sitting and reading or working, but the bathroom would be overlooked by anyone who chose to stand in the field.

"The water will be pumped through pipes from the pool collected by the contraption I described to you earlier and held in an individual tank in each apartment," Beesty informed her.

They went up to the second floor, and Lydia envisaged that they were now walking amongst the old rafters on the mill. Here were two bedrooms, white and square as all the other rooms here. Lydia decided that there could never be a chance of her living here.

"What do you think now that you have had a look around Mrs Pollack? Do we have a sale?"

She was just about to tell him exactly what she thought when they were both startled by a loud rapping on the upstairs door.

"Well that did give me a turn!" said Beesty as he went to the door, pulled the latch across and opened it. There stood Mrs Cal, her face bright and red and shiny.

"You must come and show us around this apartment Mr Beesty! We have walked around on our own for long enough."

"Well if Mrs Pollack is alright on her own?" he asked tentatively.

"Yes of course, but I do have to leave soon, can I get out another way?" She was conscious of the time passing and did not want to stay here a moment longer than she needed to.

"You could leave by the main door, but I thought it would be better if we all returned to the sales office together and had another discussion about the facilities." He was out in the corridor with Mrs Cal and gone before Lydia could say anymore.

Now she was on her own in this truly awful apartment. Or was she? As soon as Beesty left she had that old familiar back of the neck creepy feeling come over her. She went into the front bedroom and looked out over the field.

Leaning against the windowsill she could see the entire row of cottages and there she saw her mother coming out into the back garden and hang some washing on the line.

What a pity they didn't all get along. Lydia would love to visit her keepers now that she was back and talk about her life at Seaside and why she left and the money she had safely stored. But they would not be interested. As soon as each child left home, the keepers rarely thought of them. It was hard to believe that her father could be the son of such lovely grandparents to the Prix children.

She watched her mother busy at her house work and saw a figure come around the side of the cottage and walk towards her. He seemed to be arguing with her and then mother was wagging her finger at him. She only ever did

162

that if she felt very strongly about something. What could it be?

Lydia leaned further forward to get a better look and as she tried to find a catch with which to open the window, she realised that there was none. Who had designed these ridiculous places? She hoped that mother was not in any sort of danger.

Then the wagging stopped and the man walked to the end of the garden and looked over the field. Then he looked up at the mill and Lydia was sure that he could see her. But he soon turned away again and Lydia realised with a start that it was David Turncoat.

Well that's odd, why would he be visiting mother? Not only visiting her, but arguing with her? She watched them go back around the side of the cottage and out of her view.

Suddenly she was sure that someone was in the room watching her now. She had heard no one enter and no footsteps, but she was sure that there was someone breathing behind her. Her back felt cold and there were beads of sweat on her forehead. She didn't want to turn round, but knew she had to.

She decided to do it quickly and as she did so, saw something dart out of the room. She only saw it out of the corner of her eye, but it was enough to scare her. She pulled herself together and went out of the room, but there was nothing there. She ran down the stairs and looked into the sitting room and bathroom, there was nothing.

Then she could hear scurrying downstairs in the kitchen area, so she ran down the next set of stairs. Why on earth she was running, she had no idea. It was as though some force outside of her control was directing her legs and body. She chose to follow the instructions of the force.

Here she was, standing in the kitchen, sweat dripping from her forehead and her breathing quick and noisy. Her senses were on red alert as she listened for sounds of movement anywhere in the apartment. She closed her eyes in order that she could hear better. It didn't work so she opened her eyes again.

"Aaaah!" Lydia took a step backwards because standing directly in front of her was, Uncle Cal.

"Hello Liddy. Why did you have your eyes closed?"

"I, I ... What are you doing in here? I didn't hear you come in!"

"I have been here for about five minutes Liddy and I've watched you doing a lot of running about."

"You have been watching me, how odd. Where are your wife and Beesty?" Lydia was trying to keep calm while deciding the best way to get out of this kitchen and go home.

"They are busy looking at the other apartments, I said that I would come and keep you company. Don't want you to be all on your own. In these places, it is impossible to hear someone shout."

"I see. Well I think I shall go now, I have seen all I want to see."

"Are you sure you don't want to look around again? I can help you if you like."

"No. Thank you. I wish to leave. Please let me pass."

Cal moved to one side, grinning all the time. He stayed too close to her and made Lydia feel very uncomfortable. Lydia brushed past him and he smiled again.

"You are a proper big girl now Liddy. I remember when you were just a child. Doesn't seem that long ago."

164

"Really?" she answered and went to the door, conscious that her uncle was following her too closely. She slammed the door shut behind her, leaving Cal in the apartment.

She stood in the quiet corridor, taking stock and hoping that the rest of her life would not have so many dramas going on. No one could stand this much pressure and survive.

What time was it now? It must be nearly lunchtime. Standing alone in the corridor, she was aware how vulnerable she was. She looked at the doors which guarded the end of the corridor. They were exactly the same as she remembered, nothing had been altered. Perhaps it would be a good idea to go and have a look. If the doors were open, she could leave the building by that way. Lydia would dearly love to get out and go home.

Home? Where exactly? She could call at her old childhood home and see her keepers. Maybe she could find out what all that was about with David. Was that home? No, she felt more at home at Gran's at Wood Lane Cottage. She was determined to get her own place soon, preferably near to Gran and her sisters. Sadie and Marjoram were not far away from there. Yes, that was the place to live, not these apartments, not here.

She wondered briefly why she even decided to view. Was it vanity, trying to show all of Mill Town that she could afford to live here if she chose? Probably. But if the Cals were thinking of living there, the place was not so elite after all.

This idea that enclosed corridors and rooms, lit only by lamps and locked at either end made a person feel safe was a ridiculous notion. Lydia did not like being here at all. She would leave right now.

Walking towards the big old doors, she remembered that Cal had not left the apartment by the same door as her. She looked behind her just to make sure. Good, no one there and no noises anywhere. Cal must have gone up a floor or two and left that way. He must be upset about the door slamming. Lydia couldn't care less.

The big doors with the small glass panes stood proudly in front of her and Lydia leant forward to hold the handle and as she did she looked at her reflection in the glass. Time seemed to slow down as she saw her face, distorted but recognisable. She looked pale and strained and beyond her reflection she saw the corridor behind her.

The lamps cast shadows and trails of smoke floated upwards. She imagined that someone was walking up the corridor. Why had she brought that thought to her mind right now?

There was the icy tingle of anticipation and fear running up her spine. She squinted into the glass, checking for something following her, but could see nothing. She could give no sensible reason for the search. She knew that she was wasting time holding on to the handle and waiting for trouble, when she could be out of the door and on her way home. Perhaps there was something about the door which prevented a person from going out.

There was definitely nothing there, so why this feeling? Lydia had always hated the thought that something could be behind her. She pulled the handle and felt the weight of the door resisting the pull.

The door opened and Lydia was aware of a very cold draught coming from beyond the door. There was utter darkness out there. This was a choice and a half. To choose to go out into the dark, free from this new prison or stay with the Cals and navigate the many locked doors between her and freedom. She decided to go out into the place she remembered as the reception hall, and took one of the lamps from the corridor wall with her. There was no point in going out there unarmed.

As she walked through, she felt the big door close behind her. It didn't slam like she remembered, but closed slowly and carefully. The lamp, held out in front cast a large, round pool of light but gave few clues as to what was going on in the hallway. This meant that she had to move left and then right in order to see anything at all. The lamp did not show up anything at any distance.

She noticed that the floor was relatively clear and so went towards the old reception office. There was nothing of interest there. Her shoes made a clipping sound on the tiles and each step reverberated up her legs making her aware of every movement. The main doors must be directly in front of her now.

She remembered to be very careful, not wanting to fall down any cellars here. The lamp showed the doors and the glass on the top half reflected the lamp right back at her. Her face looked very spooky and made her smile. The smile could also be due to the fact that she was almost outside.

She pushed the door and nothing happened. It shook and rattled against the strain, but did not open. Perhaps a key was needed from Beesty in order to open the door.

She clipped her way slowly back across the hall so that she could go back through the doors leading back to the corridor. She pushed the handle and there was nothing but a rattle. It was locked now and refused to budge. It must work on some sort of one way lock. She peered through the frosty glass into the corridor. It looked quite dimly lit from this side and she could see no one there.

So, how to get their attention? What if they did not come out into the corridor again and left by the upper floor?

Don't think like that.

She turned towards the main door again. Should she go back there? Then she thought, how was it that she could not see outside through the glass on the top of the outside door? It was the middle of a sunny day and sunlight should have been streaming in. The only way she would not be able to see anything is if it were night time.

But that could not be possible, she hadn't been stuck here for ten hours. Not unless she had gone into a time warp. She must attract the attention of the others.

She turned back to the corridor doors and pressed her face against the glass again.

"No!"

There was a face at the other side of the door. She stood back and almost fell and dropped the lamp. She regained her composure and noticed a shape running down the corridor. Was it Cal again? The shadows cast by the lamps down there, obstructed any clear view. It could have been any of the three people Lydia knew were still in there. She hammered on the door and shouted.

"Hello! Hello! Can someone let me out please?"

No one came. Now she was in a pickle.

Being trapped behind a locked door for the second time in two days was making her look stupid. She was wondering whether to vow right here and now to get the next cart to Seaside as soon as she was released from here. Life there may have been boring and predictable, but at least

168

she knew where she was at Seaside. There had been nothing but trouble from the moment she arrived back from the Lawyer's office and…

Hang on.

She held the lamp in the crook of her arm and pulled her bag from her shoulder. Rummaging around in the bag, she searched from one side to another, looking for something. After a minute she was successful. Triumphantly she pulled out two keys. Don't even think about dropping them Lydia.

She tried both keys in the lock on the corridor door. Neither was any good. She clipped back across the tiles to the main door and tried them in the main door, one almost worked, but nothing. So much for that idea.

Perhaps there were keys in the reception office. She clipped over there, trying to remain upbeat and positive. How long would this lamp last? Stop thinking like that you stupid panicking cow. It will last as long as you need it Lydia. The lamp light helped her to see around the shelves and hooks and pegs in the office but she found no key there.

She opened drawers and cupboards doors and found no key. She also noticed that she could see no daylight from the window high upon the wall. Probably a valid reason for that. Can't think what it is.

She walked towards the last large cupboard in the small room and went to open the door to look for a key in there. She could not look in there as the door was locked.

She stopped and thought, her finger tapping quickly and tensely against the desk upon which she was leaning. Stress, stress.

Try the keys in the door, said the voice in her head which had been alternatively encouraging and frightening

169

her. She took the two keys, tried the first key which did not work and then tried the second.

Click! The door opened. Lydia took the key back out and looked at it lying in the palm of her hand reflected in the lamp light. It was the key from the clearing in the wood. She knew that for a fact, for it was shinier than the other key. She did not wait to see if it were a sign, either good or bad, that she had found the key and been able to use it. She just walked through the door.

Constantly checking in front of her that there was no sudden drop and no set of stairs, she moved forwards. The place was dark and cold. It smelled a little damp and earthy.

Almost immediately, she noticed that there was another door in front, so she opened that too. This was quite a revelation, as upon opening it, light came right back at her. Thank goodness for that.

It was also much warmer than the reception hall. The lack of light and lamps had made the place quite cold and the dress and jacket she wore had been little protection against it. There were lamps in this place and Lydia was sure that she could find a way out now.

The walls and roof were made of large stone blocks and upon closer inspection, so was the floor. Lamps hung in brackets every few feet along the walls, but there was nothing else lying about. This could only be a way to somewhere else. So, there was nothing for it, Lydia must walk down the tunnel, for that was what it felt like and see where it led.

She tried to work out in which direction she was walking, and decided that it could only be east, for the outside door of the mill faced south and she had turned left as she left the office. But, that was assuming that she was

170

travelling in a straight line. If it was east, then she was heading towards the back of the cottages.

As she had never seen a tunnel in Mill Town, it also meant that she was travelling underground and that was scary. She must walk with determination and see what was at the other end. Something caught her eye, glinting in the light. She bent down to pick it up. It was a necklace and it seemed familiar. She put it in her bag. Good job she had this bag, stuff was being put in and taken out of it all the time.

After walking a little further she saw another door on her right. This door was not locked so she naturally went through. Although lit by lamps again, it was darker than the tunnel. Walking along here she was faced with a set of steps, which she climbed and reached the door at the top. This door was locked, so she took out her keys again and used the second one to open it.

As the door creaked open she became gradually aware that she was peering into someone's sitting room. She shut the door and then opened it again. Yes, it was someone's sitting room, worse – it was the Cals' sitting room! What to do?

She knew that the Cals must still be at the old mill, safely out of the way, so they were unlikely to catch her here. Why on earth was there a tunnel leading to the Cals' cottage? Equally where did the other tunnel lead?

She wasn't sure that she should stay here and leave by the door, but on reflection did not want to be seen leaving this cottage, so she turned round, locked the door behind her and returned to the tunnel.

Turning right she carried on walking until she was faced with yet another door. Using the same key, she opened that door and walked through. Lydia you are a brave

171

girl, she congratulated herself. But, if she was going to sort out this peculiar goings on in this Town, then she must trust her instincts and just go. Faced with yet another door, she tried it and upon finding it unlocked, carefully pushed it open. She was in a small room made of stone and smelling as damp and earthy as the tunnel. She recognized this room. It was the end cellar at Doctor Catapult's house.

CHAPTER ELEVEN *THE TUNNEL*

This was awkward. There was no one in this room and she could hear no noises coming from the next room, so now she was left with some more difficult choices.

"If I was talking to someone else," she said under her breath, thinking that the only people she could discuss this with would be her little sisters, "how would we decide what to do?"

She thought for a moment. She could go ahead and make her way through the complex of cellar rooms until she reached the steps she had already fallen down. Even if by some miracle one of her keys fit the door to the house, there would only be trouble if she were caught. Or, go back down the tunnel and leave via the Cals' or back to the mill, which should it be?

Going back down the tunnel was the favourite option. She knew that this tunnel was crucial in the investigation, but it wasn't a good idea to be down here on her own, with no one knowing her whereabouts. She must get out and return with a plan and back up. She trudged back through the tunnel, retracing her steps. As she did so, she mused that as a child she had played games in the field overhead, unaware that this tunnel existed beneath her feet. Her mind wandered to the old shelters which had stood at the back entrance to the mill. They had played there also, but now most of these had been demolished. Apparently there were now only one or two standing.

She thought of their childhood games there, scampering around the buildings and playing hide and seek. Once she had hidden behind an old door so well, that the others had never found her and she had to eventually come out and go home long after they had given up and left.

One of her instinctive thoughts came to her, slowly wending its way through her mind. What if there was an entrance to the tunnel through the shelters? They had been built many years before to protect the workers, but had not been used in anyone's memory. The people were told that they had been built to save them from bombings, but no one had ever heard of any bombings and were not sure why they needed protecting from them. So the shelters remained unused and unaffected by the circle of life.

If there was a way out there, then she had missed a doorway on her travels. She walked more slowly and tried to pay a good deal of attention to the walls, looking for a change in the pattern of the stones or signs of a door having been opened. Soon, however, she was back at the door to the mill having found nothing. She felt weepy, both from strain and the lack of fresh air and so she sat down on the floor. Her dress, she tucked underneath her. Luckily she had worn a long dress today and so she wasn't going to get cold as she sat on the stone.

Necklace! She took it from her bag and looked at it closely. She touched it and moved it around the palm of her hand. The gold chain was light and well-crafted and a diamond hung from it. Someone must be missing it. Perhaps they wouldn't mind if she tried it on.

She pulled her hair back from her face and fastened the chain around her neck. The chain was not long enough to bring over her head. What a pity there was no mirror in which to look at her reflection as she was sure that it complemented her outfit wonderfully.

Sitting on a cold floor, locked possibly for ever in a tunnel, she was concerned with her looks. Some things never changed.

This was more than could be said for the tunnel she was in. All of a sudden she seemed to be in a different place. True, the tunnel was still made of stone and lit by lamps. But these lamps were not the same. They were more ornate and larger, light being cast over a far wider area. There was also ivy and ferns growing from the walls and golden rope fixed the length of either side. She got up, brushing herself off and made her way back towards the cellar again.

She felt warmer than before and supposed that there was more heat being thrown upon her from the larger lamps. She was also very conscious that the walls looked different now, for she could see more closed doors every few feet along its length. Perhaps she should try each door and see what happened.

Door number one would not open, nor door two. The doors were on her left as she headed back towards the Doctor's so these were leading downhill towards Wide Lane. Any doors on her right were leading up to the bombing shelters. But so far two doors on her right would not open either. She decided not to use her keys yet, feeling that fate would take her to the right place.

Hopefully, now she would not bother wasting her considerable energy on fear, but transfer it to positive action and see where that took her.

The third door on the left opened as she pushed it. This was clearly the one to enter. She knocked.

A voice from behind the door said, "Hello Pixie, we are pleased to invite you in."

"Thanks, but sorry, no, I am not Pixie, I am Lydia Prix."

"I know who you are, you are welcome, come on in."

The door was opened fully and Lydia walked into the room. But it wasn't a room, it was a street. There was sky, albeit a night sky. There were shops on either side of the street, and there were lots of people milling around. The lady who had let Lydia in was taller than her and very slender, almost ethereal. She smiled, a beautiful smile which left Lydia feeling safe and warm and comforted.

Some of the people waved to her and smiled in a way that made her think that she must be known to them.

"Come with me and we will take a little walk. Do you remember being here before? I see you have found all your keys." She pointed to the necklace.

"Well yes, I suppose. Excuse me what is happening?"

"Come on in and take my hand. I will take you to meet someone who will explain things to you."

Lydia was very confused and so decided just to follow the lovely lady and see how things worked out. They walked down the street. Lydia noticed men, women and children dressed in winter clothes. They wore long coats trimmed with fur. The ladies were clothed in long dresses and beautiful hats, hands pushed firmly into fur muffs. They seemed to almost glide past and everyone smiled and waved. Lydia was not sure if they were waving to the lady or to her.

The street between the opposing shops was narrow and as Lydia looked upwards she noticed that the tops of the buildings were nearer to each than at the bottom. The buildings were made from stone and wood and brick and were architecturally higgledy-piggledy.

Inside the small paned shop fronts, were colours and light and glittering displays of food and clothes and things. Lydia had never seen such choice and wondered how on earth the residents of this town afforded it all. She was deliberately trying not to remember that this place existed under the field by the mill. She was starting to believe that she was dreaming and had not yet set off from her Grandmother's house this morning.

They turned off the street into a row of spectacular houses, which stood near to the road and were constructed in such a way that the observer could not see how they carried the top floors without collapsing into the bottom ones. People came out of their houses, down wide steps and skipped onto the snow covered road. There was snow on the pavements, the rooftops, the tall lamps and along the tops of railings. Lydia was reminded of winters in Mill Town. She had missed these winters while at Seaside, for it never snowed there.

Everyone was happy and children skipped alongside their keepers and sometimes jumped aboard carts pulled by very large and pretty ponies. The girls would like these, although they were twice the size of the ponies back at

Wood Cottage. Lydia could not see everything at once and turned round and round and tried to take it all in.

"We need to travel further and faster."

The lady held Lydia's hand tighter and as she did so, they went straight up. They floated over the scene, slowly travelling over the houses and shops and fields.

"What is that colourful place down there?" Lydia loved this dream.

"That, Pixie is a circus. There are acrobats and animals doing tricks and jugglers and ice cream. We can stop there if you like," the lady told her.

"I would like to see the person we are visiting first. I can't afford to waste any time. I still have to wake up and find out who killed my brother and drugged my sister. I would like to find out who attacked me. I'm slowly finding out more information every day, but I want to get on with it."

They flew over the old mill and she could see the salesman walking across one of the courtyards.

"I don't understand how this is all happening," she asked the lovely lady. "None of it makes any sense to me."

"It will do eventually," she answered kindly.

They were flying over Mill Town, except not the Mill Town she would have described to another. Some of the cottages were missing with only gardens where they had stood in the Town of her experience. The Cals' cottage was not there, nor the Doctor's.

The Turncoat farm was there and she could see David sitting on a wall outside his cottage. He looked up as they flew over, but neither Lydia nor he acknowledged each other.

The cottage in which she had lived with her keepers did not seem to be fully there. That was another odd thing, some places missing and some almost see through. She turned to ask the lady what it all meant. But she, as if in anticipation, put her finger to her lips and smiled again. They flew over Town Street with arms out, heads forward and legs back. It seems that in order to fly well, one must do it parallel to the ground.

Lydia did not feel cold, only a slight whooshing noise as they glided here and there covering all the places she knew. Still, it was not possible to see the tunnel or anything which would give away its presence. The mill was there. But the more Lydia looked at it, it appeared to match the descriptions she had heard of it from Treen.

The lights inside made the windows shine with all colours and as they swooped down to a lower level on Lydia's instigation, they were able to view inside.

And, there they were. The workers were busying themselves at the tall looms throwing up gold threads which floated everywhere and glinted in the light of the hundreds of lamps hanging from the walls. There were red faced ladies and moustachioed men scurrying here and there, all happy and jolly and working to a common goal.

There were great piles of beautiful cloth being carried out of the front gates and loaded onto carts which then drove out onto Wide Lane.

The tea ladies were back, pushing trolleys at great speed, almost losing their stock of cake, biscuits and sandwiches in their haste. It was a truly wonderful sight and she wished that Treen could be here to see it.

"It is just as he described it to me when I was a girl," said Lydia to the lady.

179

"I am sure it is. Come we must go now." They flew higher, following the contours of the huge chimney from which golden plumes of smoke rose.

Lydia turned onto her back and floated as easily as she had done on her front. She spun round and moved faster and then slower. She stood upright and turned around like the little dancing girl who had graced the music box which Treen had given her.

"Are you enjoying yourself? You've certainly got the hang of it now." Lydia was aware that she was no longer holding onto the lady and was flying by herself.

"I am. I have to say that this is the best and most vivid dream I have ever had!" Lydia had never felt so much joy in her life and would not have cared a jot if she never woke up again. Why, she could go and visit whoever she wanted to and shop in the wonderful shops. The scenery was beautiful; the people friendly and there did not appear to be anyone or anything trying to chase her. Perhaps it would be a good idea never to wake up again.

"Come on, follow me, we have somewhere to go."

Lydia followed as they flew up Wide Lane, turned into Wood Lane, and looked down at Wood Cottage. She could see the ponies happily grazing in the paddocks and her sisters busying themselves with the cart. It was being reversed into a barn where it was kept when not in use. Lydia flew down a little and shouted to the girls, who did not appear to see her. She stood on the ground next to Janey and tried to talk to her, but it was a pointless exercise, as she obviously had no awareness of her presence. She walked over to Alice and pulled her hair. Alice turned round sharply and looked past Lydia. She heard her tell her sister that she thought that something had just touched her and

180

Janey told her that she must be imagining it. Lydia went over to the ponies, which could see her and they put out their noses looking for food. The girls noticed this and said that the ponies were acting strangely.

Lydia laughed, perhaps she was a ghost! Perhaps she was dead!

"Am I dead?" she asked the lady.

"You are extraordinary!" was the answer.

Lydia went into the house, forgetting that she could fly and walked through the kitchen, out into the hall and up the stairs. Standing outside Gran's door she felt quite self-conscious and so knocked on the closed door.

She was surprised to hear Gran say, "Come in!"

She went in and noticed how pale the old lady looked.

"How are you feeling Gran?" she asked.

"I am feeling quite poorly and tired. What is happening Lydia? Everything is getting very peculiar. Why are you dressed like that?"

Lydia looked down at herself and noticed that she was wearing a long silvery dress made from some sort of fine weaved metallic cloth. Her long hair was flowing free and the effect of the dress and her hair was as though she were underwater.

"Can you see me properly Gran?"

"Yes dear."

Lydia instinctively put her hand on the brow of Gran and felt energy leave her and transfer to the old lady. She knew that this gesture would help Gran. She kissed her on the forehead and walked out of the room. She went to the window on the landing and passed on to the balcony. In an impulsive move she launched herself from it, arms outstretched, just to see what would happen. There was a

181

tingling feeling in her middle and she swooped down towards the ground and then up and up like a bird.

The lady followed her and the two of them flew out over the woods. If this was a dream, it was funny that she could remember flying over here when she had been found in the clearing the other day. In fact the two women were soon over the clearing and could see the large stone upon which the bodies had been found. The lady turned and smiled at Lydia and beckoned her to follow.

This she did and they travelled further over the trees towards the cottage of her sister Marjoram and then further towards the Moors and saw the cottage of Sadie. It was daylight now and Lydia wondered briefly whether they had been travelling through a day and a night or whether she had changed her thoughts and so changed her surroundings.

They flew back towards the clearing and went down to the ground. Lydia felt safe and would not have worried even if she were there on her own, for now she could fly away from trouble any time she wanted.

She realised that it was night time again, but there was a warm silver glow in the clearing. The stone was luminous as if it had been painted in a substance which reflected the light. They walked towards it and the lady put her hand flat upon its surface. There was a glow which came from her hand which grew until the light shone out in all directions and lit up the whole clearing.

The stone began to move sideways and revealed a set of stone steps leading down into a tunnel. The lady walked in and motioned Lydia to follow and this she did. The stone closed again over their heads as they descended. This tunnel was very similar to the one Lydia had been in earlier in the day. Was it the same day? Was it a dream?

182

They travelled down it for short while and came to a very large and ornate oak door which opened as soon as the lady stood in front of it. They went through and instead of a street were now standing by a huge river which was straddled by a bridge made from white metal intertwined with trees and flowers. Over this bridge trotted a cart pulled by large ponies upon which sat two people. One was a liveried driver and alongside a bewildered looking man. The carts came over every few minutes carrying men, women and children. As they arrived over the bridge they passed into a beautiful park and towards a huge castle like building.

The lady took Lydia to the castle, saying nothing. There she watched the carts pull up in front of the building and saw the passengers dismount slowly and sometimes a little unsteadily. They were met by nurses, who took their arms and walked their charges carefully up the steps.

"May we follow them in there?" Lydia was curious to see what happened inside the beautiful castle with its tall towers sporting huge narrow flags from many flagpoles. The castle was mainly white and gold and was so inviting that she felt the need to be inside right now.

"No Pixie. If you go in there you cannot come back, not as Lydia anyway. We have a very important job for you to do."

Lydia was going to say something, but stopped herself and instead followed the lady as she made her way around the back of the castle traversing the herringbone brick path which moved carefully through the roses and the climbing plants and flowers. A beautiful scent pervaded the air here, almost hypnotising the young woman.

They arrived at a huge courtyard and saw more nurses. This time holding babies wrapped in soft blankets and placing them carefully in small baskets which were strapped on the back of more carts. These left one by one down another driveway towards another bridge.

The carts went steadily over the bridge and were watched by the nurses until they were out of sight. The nurses turned and went back into the castle.

The lady turned to Lydia and said, "Understand yet?"

"I may be starting to understand," answered Lydia, although if she understood, then the whole thing was crazy. She did not really want to say anything out loud, in case she was getting the whole thing quite wrong. It wasn't as though anything that she was seeing was contrary to things she had been told about during her thirty odd years of living. It was because there was a possibility that this experience was not a dream, but was real.

She turned again to the lady who smiled at her. Lydia was pretty sure that the lady could read her mind. She thought, 'When are we going to see the person who is going to explain everything to me?'

"You have already met her, Pixie. It's you,"

So, she could read minds, but did not make sense. She was saying that she had met herself, and that made even less sense.

The lady began to walk towards the bridge, so Lydia ran after her and as soon as she caught up and began to walk in step she asked, "What is your name?"

"I will tell you that another time because you don't need to know it yet."

"Am I dreaming?"

"No you are not dreaming Pixie. But, you must know that once you are out of here, there is still work to do. You will realise that there are some who have no chance of ever making it back to this place.

There are other places which you cannot visit as the horror of them would affect you too much. The people who are destined to go there want to find a way to get here. They cannot do that as they make the mistake of assuming that it is just a matter of finding the right door, or finding the person who holds the right key.

They will not accept that the truth is simpler to follow and more difficult to understand than that. Until the day they accept responsibility for their own journey, they must return to the other places. There will be few chances for them to leave there again."

"Are you saying that those who are evil will not come here?"

"Yes, but they are to be watched and guarded against. They will do anything in their power to find the entrance to this place. That must never happen, for if anyone lets any of them into this place for even a moment, the darkness will spread rapidly. You must be vigilant and help us to trap these people forever."

"Me! Why should I help against these invaders if they are as dangerous as you say?"

"Because they killed your brother."

Lydia digested this information for a little while. She sat on the banks of the river and watched the swans swim elegantly past, under the bridge and away around a corner.

"Why is this all happening now? Why is it suddenly so important?"

"It has been getting worse for years. They started as two people discussing possibilities and are now many. They believe that they can use evil and find this place. They

185

believe that if they do, they will have strength which can never be overcome and they will be master of everything."

"I still don't think I understand." Lydia was becoming very confused.

"Hello Lydia, I can't stop long."

It was Michaelmas. The shock of seeing him and listening to him speak caused Lydia to start crying. She outstretched her arms and reached out to her brother. He stepped back sharply.

"I am sorry. If we touch you have to stay here. Listen to what she says. The Shudder man wants to find his way in here, he has used children and he is still trying to use you. Treen has always been an enemy of his and he will use his descendants whenever he can. The Prixs are different to the others and he knows that."

"Is that why he always wants to make our lives a misery? He knows that we can come here and he can't? But other people can too surely?"

"But they are not key holders like we are. One of his followers killed me to get here, but I would not let him come. Then he tried with Sadie, but I managed to delay that – with your help of course!" Michaelmas laughed. "We have to stop them now Lydia. They are increasing in number. Seek them out and we will help you trap them. For that is what we must do and then the circle of learning can continue."

"But why me! I am nothing special!" Lydia didn't like all this responsibility.

"You must be, you survived the shuddering all those years ago and found your way back here that night. You have already crossed over here twice in this life. You seem to find it easy to do, so you must be special. Everyone and

186

everything gets exactly what they think. Exactly. Whatever you think is what you get. It's simple but difficult." Michaelmas looked serious when he said this.

"I assure you I am not special, but I will help you if it means that my family are not being killed anymore."

Michaelmas smiled at his sister and vanished. The lady held out her hand and took Lydia up and over the river and then over the woods. Lydia flew with her, but she wanted to wake up now. They landed gently on the ground in a clearing.

An oak door stood on its own with no supporting wall and the lady took Lydia through it. They walked along a tunnel for a little while. There was a set of steps in front of them which went up through a large stone cliff. The cliff, covered in ferns and moss and glistening with water which ran down in rivulets, was another familiar place to Lydia, but again she did not know why.

The lady embraced her and gestured for her to climb the steps, which she did. Lamps lit the stairwell and as Lydia climbed up twenty, thirty steps, she saw a stone door in front of her. She touched it very gently and watched it open smoothly. There in cold clarity was the clearing in the woods at the back of Wood Cottage.

She was walking out of the stone upon which she had seen her sister lie and where she had been attacked by Shudder. It was here that her brother had bravely met his death. She sat upon the stone looking about her, hoping that someone she knew would come and find her.

She lay back and fainted into a deep sleep.

CHAPTER TWELVE *TURNCOAT FARM*

As Janey entered the fish shop, she was greeted enthusiastically by the two young men who worked there.

Scraps and Fry liked Janey and her sister – a lot. But they were getting nowhere with their offers of free fish and extra helpings of chips. The girls told the boys that they did not want to get fat and had other fish to fry and similar stupid jokes. The unsophisticated boys did not know how to answer these quips. They had spent little time in education and socialising, for the family business had been theirs for the taking and there had been no need to chase any other dreams.

Although the girls valued the kindness and friendliness of the boys, they had no romantic intentions towards them. It was useful for the business to flirt, but the girls were careful that it went no further and never gave these boys, or any other, a promise that more attention would be forthcoming.

"Hello Janey! How are you today?"

"I am well, thank you Scraps. How are you two?"

"We are well." The pleased grin on Scrap's face was genuine.

"How are your parents? I have not seen them about lately and Gran has been asking after them." She hadn't, but Janey thought it was wise to mention it in passing.

"They are not too bad, feeling their age I think. They have been talking about perhaps joining the Old Peoples' Club and getting some more energy."

This Old Peoples' Club was always talked about in the town, but it was only a few old people who seemed to know how useful this club was. Younger members of the community heard the tales of the club, but had no interest in finding out more about it.

"I expect they just do things like stretching and knitting and making tea and cake," many said.

"I have heard that they are a secret society and get up to all sorts of adventures," others said.

Most believed the former and then thought no more about the subject. All are taught that old people are pointless and the inhabitants of Mill Town were no different to any other town. Except that there were a lot of very active old people in Mill Town.

The two boys came out of the shop and helped Janey unload the potatoes. It was an opportunity for more banter and the chance to touch her as they helped her with the sacks. Janey laughed and joked, but was soon waving them goodbye and promising another visit next week.

As Janey walked around the front of the cart to take the reins again, she noticed her sister walking towards the sales office at the mill. She wondered briefly why it had taken Lydia so long to get there, but the thoughts did not trouble her too much She had much to do before lunchtime.

Climbing aboard the cart, she clicked and the pony set off again. The sun was getting quite warm now and the day

189

spread itself out in front of her, full of possibilities. If she could get a foothold in the market by selling some ponies, her ambitions would move on another big step.

The Turncoats were well known and respected in the town and if they agreed to buy a pony to pull their cart, others would take notice. In her dreams she saw a day when everyone would own at least one pony.

She travelled to the junction of Mill Lane, turned right and made her way up the hill. Over on her right she saw the mill and wondered idly how Lydia would get on viewing the apartments there. Janey knew that the places were very expensive and marvelled at the idea that Lydia was able to afford one of them.

"I wonder how she managed to get all that money together?" she asked Pony.

Pony did not answer.

Then she saw the Cals walking down Mill Lane towards the junction.

"Coooeeee!" shouted Aunt Cal.

Janey said nothing, merely nodded and was rewarded with hearing her aunt say, "Stuck up lot of cows they are. Always consider that they are better than us."

Cal turned around towards his niece and sneered. Then he winked at Janey and she shivered. A look from that man always made her feel ice cold. The cold was not so much a result of fear as from total withdrawal from life.

She had thought from time to time that those icy feelings were how a person eventually decided to take the last cart ride. Once in that cold withdrawal it was very easy just to stop everything when the awareness of your body has completely gone.

The pony whinnied and shied at something and that brought Janey's mind back to the moment. She glanced at the Doctor's house on her left and noticed the Doctor standing on the lawn looking out at the road. He did not appear to see Janey and he certainly did not acknowledge her.

There on the right was the house in which she had been brought up. She could not see her keepers, but that was not unusual. Even if they had both been standing in the front garden with nothing to do but look out on the road, they would still have only given a slight wave of the hand and carried on staring. Janey knew this to be true, because they had done it before when she had driven past. It became much easier after a while not to bother with your keepers if they are not bothered with you.

Soon the left turning to Traitors Lane appeared and Janey took it. The lane was narrow and there was scarcely enough room to allow the cart and pony through. If she met anyone, they would have to pull into a gateway. The hedges were too high to see over and the banks of earth from which they grew, stood almost three feet high.

It was said that this lane was used by people who used to conduct atrocities many hundreds of years ago in the village which existed prior to Mill Town. They apparently would leave the area by this lane and other similar lanes when caught meeting in the middle of the night. This coven was secret and their identities were not known. Some said they reincarnated directly upon death and never went to Beyond. They may have gone elsewhere, but no one knew where.

There was also a group of good people who spent most of their time counteracting the work done by this coven and they were a secret group too.

Traitors Lane was used by the ancestors of the Turncoat family who were said to be good people turned bad. Upon discovery of the treachery one Turncoat ancestor had been pursued down this lane and locked away somewhere.

That was the story anyway, but it had apparently occurred so many years ago that the legend had disappeared into popular culture and was not believed by most. Much of the tale may have been altered with the telling, but who could say? The Turncoat family, a well-known and long respected family, had always disputed this story. They preferred to encourage tales of their charity and respectability.

Traitors Lane had remained the same because no one wanted to widen it and allow the threat of evil spirits to return. It is well known fact that spirits do not approve of their domain being changed without permission.

It was only a few minutes before they arrived at the entrance to the farm. A sign made from a large stone had been chisel engraved with the words:

Turncoat Farm

The house was larger than the cottages in which she had been born or lived with Gran. It was more on a par with the Doctor's house.

The Turncoat family had a lot of money and often flashed it around buying clothes and jewellery. They had the best furniture, the newest cart and there was never any maintenance needed at the property which wasn't completed immediately.

192

Janey didn't care too much about that, so long as they bought a pony from her.

David was in the yard and he came across to greet her. He patted the blue pony and the blue pony nuzzled him back. Janey was interested to see how easily David was making friends with it and how comfortable the pony was with him.

"Father is waiting to see you. I will give him a call. He is looking forward to looking at the pony."

David shouted the keepers and soon his parents and two sisters were fussing around the pony and chattering away.

"Father, you really must buy the pony. He is so beautiful and sweet!" said one girl.

"Father he loves me the best! See he is eating from my hand!"

This is going well, thought Janey. She knew that Mr Turncoat could not resist his daughters' demands. Any shopkeeper on Town Street loved it when these two girls arrived with either keeper. A sale would always follow.

"I know, father," said Mrs Turncoat, "We shall buy two ponies of different colours."

"What other colours do you have Janey?" asked David.

Janey felt a bit funny now, as though she were being asked about the colour of her children.

"All sorts of colours. Pink and blue and white and yellow. Next year I shall have orange and purple and green …" she began.

"Wonderful!" said Mr Turncoat. "We can change colour each year. You can match the ponies to your outfits," he said to the women.

"No, no, no!" interrupted Janey. "These ponies live for many years and must be looked after until they reach the end of their time. They cannot be put to one side when you want a new colour!" She could not hide her horror at the lack of caring about her lovely ponies.

"Don't worry yourself Janey. Any animals we have at this farm are cared for to the highest standard and any ponies we had will be looked after just as well." David looked across at his sisters with much emphasis. "Any new animal will be added to the family. They will end their days happily here."

Janey had always trusted David, but she was uncomfortably aware that Lydia now considered him to be a suspicious character.

"I am convinced David is something to do with all these troubles," Lydia had said sagely. But then Lydia was always so sure of her own opinions and would never consider that she could be wrong about anything.

Emboldened by the thought that she was now a grown woman and not a child, Janey said, "If any pony was ever to be sold at a later date, then that must be done through me and Alice only. We would ensure that a good home is found. That will be written into the sales contract." Janey had just made that up, but thought it an excellent idea nonetheless. After all, they could make money out of the next sale in addition to finding a good home.

"Very well done," David said to her. He had always treated the Prix girls as though they were sisters and Janey thought, not for the first time that it was a shame he had turned a bit funny since he got older.

"Thank you," she answered.

Tying up the pony to a post, leaving him enough rope to eat grass, Janey followed the Turncoat family into their house. The place was just as she had remembered it from her last visit with her Gran.

The house was beautifully decorated and furnished. It was a pleasure to sit around the table in the kitchen and take in the view. After a hot drink and some cakes, a deal was struck which was satisfactory to both parties. The Turncoats would take delivery of a blue pony and a pink pony in one week's time. This would give the Turncoats time to set up living quarters for the animals and adapt a cart. It had also been discussed whether there may be a possibility for only leading the pony around and not putting it to work.

This idea created more thoughts in Janey's mind. Alice had said a few days ago that she felt like jumping on the back of one of the ponies and seeing if it could carry her around. If this were possible, then there would be no need for a cart. They could train the ponies to be ridden. She smiled and vowed to discuss this with her sisters when she got home.

Out in the yard, she untied the pony and jumped aboard the cart.

"Don't leave just yet Janey. I want to show you something before you go." That sounded so interesting that she jumped off the cart again and followed him out of the yard and around the back of the farm.

He pulled open a large blue barn door which resisted him every inch of the way.

"Father doesn't use this building much," he explained.

It was very dark inside and although David walked in confidently, Janey found it difficult to adjust the light.

Once she did, however, she was amazed at what she saw. A room of unbelievable beauty presented itself to the young girl. David lit some lanterns so she could see more clearly. The walls were covered in exquisite paintings that she could not stop looking at. There were chairs of fine workmanship and ornaments of gold and silver.

"This place is fantastic David, what is it?"

"This is my place Janey. I wanted you to see it so you could tell Lydia. I would like to show her this one day. It is very special and sort of, well, magical." He sounded wistful.

"How did you get all these things together? I have never ever seen such wonderful things anywhere." Janey was truly amazed at what she was seeing. "They look as though they are from another world!"

Janey stroked some of the ornaments and touched and caressed others. She picked up a necklace which particularly took her eye and moved it around in her hands. She moved it towards her neck.

"Don't put it around your neck Janey, you can't do that."

"Why ever not?" She was a little embarrassed at his sudden outburst. She hadn't expected that reaction.

"It's just that, well, don't do it." He took it from her and put it back in a little box.

Janey walked around the edge of the room bringing her hand up and moving it along the wall as she walked.

"There is a door here," she said. "Where does it lead?"

"Somewhere you will only ever want to go once," he answered solemnly.

Janey looked at him and said, "You are funny!"

She stayed, looking at everything for a bit longer before she announced, "I must get back to the mill as I have

196

arranged to pick up Lydia at lunchtime." David accompanied her to the yard.

He flushed a little around the cheeks and said, "How is Lydia really? She seems very tense since she got back?"

"You know she is getting divorced?"

"Yes," he answered brightly. "Is she alright?"

"She wants to find out what happened to Michaelmas and Sadie and she won't stop until she finds out. She said that she has had enough of being scared."

"I understand that." He fiddled with the pony's mane. "She has had a lot to be frightened about."

Janey looked at him. He had gone a bit odd. She clicked the pony on and went through the gate, waving to her friend. He sadly, Janey thought, waved back. She watched him sit down on a wall and stare into space.

As she arrived back on Mill Lane, she noticed a few people heading back towards their houses. It must be nearly lunchtime. She trotted on, not wanting to miss meeting Lydia. It would be dreadful if she were standing at the gate on her own, looking right and left wondering where her lift was.

Lydia had told her of a time when father was supposed to pick her up from school early. Lydia had waited for two hours before giving up on her father and going back into the school. She had been the butt of jokes for several days after that. No one else's keepers ever forgot to collect them.

As she arrived at the gates of the mill, she saw the Cals coming out. They were very jolly and making a huge fuss of the salesman. They all shook hands and Janey wondered idly if they had been viewing an apartment.

There was no sign of Lydia, but Janey waited patiently. She looked over at the fish shop and waved and smiled to

197

the young men who were watching her from the window. They waved back enthusiastically.

She waited a bit longer, but still there was no sign of Lydia. So, she jumped from the cart and went into the sales office. She saw a surly looking girl and asked her if she knew where Lydia was.

"She didn't come back with Mr Beesty. He says that she must have left when none of the others were looking. He said she was acting a bit weird on the viewings and that she probably just went home."

Janey's heart beat a little quicker and she left quickly and climbed back on the cart. It was a good job she had a cart and pony, they had come in very useful today. She trotted on, looking about the road for any sight of Lydia, but saw nothing.

She passed the cottages and the sweet shop and the inn and was soon turning into Wood Lane. By the time she arrived home, Janey was barely controlling panic. Where was Lydia and had something happened to her?

Arrival home soon informed her that Lydia was not yet back and the twins discussed what could possibly have happened.

"Perhaps she has gone into the town or called at the keepers'," Alice said. Although worried, she did not want to create more tension.

"Yea, I never thought of going there. Shall I go and find out?"

"No, she will make her way home. She probably just lost track of the time and forgot about meeting you."

"Yes, probably," Janey agreed. Neither believed that conclusion was likely.

They cleaned the blue pony, fed him and returned him to the field with his friends. They also cleaned the cart and put it into the barn. Suddenly conscious of a tickling sensation, Janey rubbed her ear. Alice shouted at Janey and told her not to grab her hair. The girls bickered for a short time, before laughing at each other.

The ponies came to the fence and stood in a line watching their mistresses.

Finishing their jobs quickly, they went back into the house.

"How's Gran been today?" asked Janey.

"Really bad. I have been thinking that she might be going to die. She has been weak, but more than that she seems to have given up."

"Perhaps we should take her up some food and a drink. If we get her to eat, she might be a bit brighter…"

"Good thinking."

The sisters busied themselves in the kitchen making lunch. Every so often one of the birds came for food and hopped back on the branches. They put a tray together for Gran, with a linen cloth and the best crockery. Alice put a flower in a vase and completed the effect.

"Beautiful!" said Janey.

"Beautiful!" agreed Alice.

As they were admiring their handiwork, a noise behind them caused them to turn round quickly. They were amazed to see Gran standing there, all washed and cleaned and looking like her old self.

"What are you two standing around here for?" she asked.

The girls were speechless, if only for a short time.

"I thought you were really sick Gran. I am so glad to see you are feeling better, just a bit surprised."

"Well I was ill until that spirit woman came into my room and cured me."

They looked at each other, wondering if their Gran was going a bit dotty.

"Funny, she looked just like Lydia, only a dead Lydia." She went on about her business.

The last comment really spooked the girls. It was so loaded with possibilities. So much had gone on just recently that anything was possible if not probable and neither felt like going any further with the thoughts just now.

They spent the rest of the afternoon doing the many jobs which were required around the place. They were used to putting troubles to the back of their minds without addressing them. Many things had happened in their childhood and they learned that the back of the mind is a brilliant place to shove worrying thoughts. It is perfectly possible to go through a day, in fact an entire lifetime without looking at a thought about the bad times. It wasn't a very healthy procedure according to Lydia. But Lydia said a lot of self-righteous things.

They worked through to supper time and as there was still no sign of their self-righteous sister, they decided that they must go and look for her.

"But where?" asked Janey.

Alice did not have time to answer because just at that time Marjoram and Mr Chariot came scurrying across the yard and in through the back door.

"We have heard that something is happening in the clearing!" said Mr Chariot

"Lights and noises and stuff like that! We thought that we all ought to go and find out what is going on."

So the family trooped out of the house, three sisters and one brother out through the garden, past the water areas and into the woods. Dusk was falling and the woods seemed cold and strange tonight.

"Can you hear that?" said Marjoram.

"I can hear all sorts of things and none of them are good." answered her husband. "It all sounds very creepy." Mr Chariot was not the bravest man in town.

The twins walked ahead of the other two, knowing that they could not rely on their sister's husband to save them in an emergency.

Before long they were out of sight of the others. They strode ahead wanting to reach the clearing as soon as possible.

They arrived in the clearing and saw the large stone slab in the middle which stood like a dark monument to recent events. People often found themselves at this spot and it was hard to tell whether the clearing had been created because of the many tramping feet or if it had been there all the time.

And on top of it a body. Why be surprised? Just lately there was always a body on top of the stone.

"No, no, no!" Janey ran towards the stone.

"It's Lydia isn't it? She's not dead is she?" Alice daren't go with her sister; she couldn't bear to find a body.

Janey reached Lydia, who was making a low moaning sound and looked very pale.

"Lydia, wake up! What is the matter with you? How did you get here?"

Lydia did not answer, but did moan more loudly. This was a satisfactory response at least. Joined by Marjoram and Mr Chariot, they soon had Lydia sitting up and breathing normally. Alice gave her the coat she was wearing as Lydia seemed cold. But she refused to tell them where she had been or how she had ended up on the stone.

"Help me back home, I shall be fine after a sleep," was all she would say. They helped her walk and the girls noticed that although she looked dreadful, Lydia did not seem upset or worried. In fact she seemed very calm.

"Don't forget my bag!" she shouted to Alice, who immediately scampered back to the clearing to fetch it. The clearing and the wood was dark, it was getting late.

It was also quite scary now that she was on her own. Looking around the stone, she soon found the dropped bag and bent down to retrieve it. As she did so, she was conscious of someone standing behind her. She froze in the position she was in and stopped thinking. A hand on her shoulder was enough to stop her moving and she was vaguely aware of the shuddering.

The rest of the family were back at the cottage in the warm kitchen and drinking rhubarb tea. Gran had insisted that Lydia's contained extra sugar to help her with the shock. Everyone ate biscuits. The fire lit and crackling, cast an orange glow over the room. The birds were roosting comfortably in the branches and the only noise was the soft slurping of drinks.

Alice walked in, looking bemused.

"Where have you been? We thought you had got lost!" said Janey to her twin.

"No, I just lost track of time. Here is your bag Lydia."

"Thanks. Are you alright?" asked Lydia.

"I think so. I can't quite remember what happened this evening, must be overtired. A lot has happened today. Yes that is it. I must be tired."

"Get off to bed Alice. I will bring you a drink and something to eat. You will feel better after that and a rest." Gran was back to her old self looking after her grandchildren.

Lydia sat up straight and looked around at the family. Something had happened to Alice, she knew. She was vaguely aware that she was able to guess what people were thinking, no not guess, she knew. She was different since her visit to Beyond, she could not tell the others about the trip, but from now on everything would be different. She would think and think during the night and come up with a plan for tomorrow.

She became aware of the rest of them discussing the Finders Hospital.

"So we are going there in the morning to fetch the new baby," said Marjoram.

"May I come?" asked Lydia.

"Of course, be at the house by nine, we are leaving at half past."

So it was arranged. Lydia knew she had to go there to the hospital. There would be information there.

"I have just remembered!" Janey said suddenly.

"What?" asked Marjoram.

"David showed me a room which was filled with all sorts of things that did not seem as though they fitted in with this Town."

"The Turncoats' place is filled with stuff that no one else has ever seen," said Marjoram. "I expect he was just showing off."

Janey wasn't so sure, but as soon as she had said out loud the things she had seen there, she thought that silence was probably a better policy.

CHAPTER THIRTEEN *FINDERS*

Marjoram had been to the Finders Hospital four times in her life, including the time when she came there from Beyond and awaited collection by her keepers. Then there was the time she had to arrange about Bobby and the next time to fetch him. The fourth time was to arrange about Dotty and so today would be the fifth. It had taken her eight years to decide about another foundling, but after discussions with Mr Chariot they had decided upon a girl. One had arrived last week which had been allocated to her, but due to the murder, the baby was looked after by the nurses for the first few days.

"I am so excited," she said to Lydia. Her excitement was obvious. She fluttered from one room to another picking up this and that for no apparent reason and then putting it back.

"Well settle down a bit or you will be worn out before you get there. You won't be getting any sleep for about three years after today!" Lydia was not a huge fan of babies.

"I shall, I will just nip upstairs and fetch my coat." This she did.

Lydia stood in front of the kitchen window looking out onto the back garden. She watched Bobby playing with his father. Those two got on very well and Lydia thought, rightly, that Marjoram wanted a daughter in order to be her baby only. She didn't blame her at all.

The Chariots lived on the edge of the woods, bordering Wood Lane, but further up than Wood Cottage where Gran lived. They were the other side of the clearing. With Michaelmas having lived in a cottage in the wood and Sadie just outside near the moor, Lydia wondered how they had all ended up here, literally in this neck of the woods.

After yesterday, there was no way she was going to live in the old mill and was idly considering where she could live near the woods, when Marjoram tapped her on the shoulder and made her jump.

"Gosh, I did not expect you to jump like that, you frightened me!"

"Sorry, I had a bit of a day yesterday. I think I am still recovering from it."

"What actually happened to you?"

"I am still trying to work it out in my own mind. There was a lot to take in. Come on! We had better get going if we are to be on time."

The family set out. There was Marjoram, her husband and Lydia. Bobby had gone to his friend's cottage. They jumped on to the cart with two goats.

"You will have to get a pony for this cart," said Lydia.

"Yes, perhaps," answered Mr Chariot. He was not so convinced.

The cart pulled them steadily along Wood Lane towards the Moor and Finders Hospital. The journey wasn't too long and took them past cottages and more woods towards the river. They turned off the road and went through a set of stone pillars supporting large iron gates. These had been made by the same men who made the mill

206

gates and the park gates. The iron was forged into the words:

Finders Hospital

They travelled up the long dark drive, bordered by trees and bushes which had overgrown and intruded onto the path. Suddenly there was light, so bright after the tunnel of trees that each blinked until their eyes became accustomed.

They arrived at the large red brick building which backed onto the fast flowing river.

The rows of windows three storeys high and the huge turrets which towered towards the sky made this place seem menacing, even though all who entered did so willingly.

Mr Chariot stopped the goats and the two women alighted by the stone steps leading to the front door, while Mr Chariot took the cart around the back of the hospital. They walked up the steps, semi-circular in design, and went through the oak doors which were already open. Inside it seemed dark, but only until their eyes became accustomed again after the brightness outside.

"I can't understand why it always seems so dreadfully bright outside this place," said Marjoram.

"I just feel very nervous here. I haven't been here since I left as a baby and the weird thing is that I can remember it!"

"Well I can't remember that, you are probably just making it up!" Marjoram did not believe in anything she could not see, hear or touch.

"Perhaps I am," Lydia agreed.

Met at the reception desk by a busy looking nurse, they followed obediently into a corridor. Nurse Hickson, for that was her name, was a tall angular woman with a look of the very haughty. She stood poker straight and kept her lips in a perfect line, Lydia surmised that it was unlikely that she had ever smiled.

However, the nurse was perfectly polite and had the reputation of being a kind nurse. She took them down one tiled corridor and then another. The cream and dark green tiled walls and the cream floors in the corridors set off beautifully the large oak doors which swung to and fro as the nurse pushed them aside and the group swept through.

The rhythmic noise of clicking shoes was very calming and for a while at least there was no need of speech. There were no windows in these corridors and that meant the lamps gave off ghostly shadows against the shiny mirror tiles.

The smell of very clean indeed met them at every turn. The doors along the corridor, all firmly closed, gave no indication of what lay within. Lydia did not find the place unnerving as much as bland. A person could walk along these corridors on their own and find themselves in a maze, with no clue of how to return to the outside world. There were no signs on the walls and no one to ask.

"Has anyone ever become lost in here?" she asked Nurse Hickson.

"No," she answered without breaking stride. Stilled by the lack of friendliness, the three continued to follow her along the corridors and upstairs and then downstairs until finally they walked through some more doors and were in a room in which there stood cot after cot, lining the walls as far as the eye could see. Both sides were full, but there was no crying and no smell or sight that gave an indication of who was in each little bed. The cots were set high up off the floor, almost higher than eye level.

Marjoram walked straight over to the first crib and started to peer over the edge. Nurse Hickson shot over to her and placed a firm hand upon her shoulder.

"Now then Mrs Chariot, we are only interested in your foundling I think." Marjoram turned a deep shade of red, which it has to be said was a very unflattering colour alongside her shade of hair, and slunk back to her husband's side.

Lydia looked at her feet, because for some strange reason she found the scene amusing. It was probably because she found the process of picking up a foundling embarrassing and sad. There was no chance of her being able to do so now she was getting divorced and she had no desire to marry again.

"Do single people ever pick up foundlings? I mean is it allowed?" She had said that out loud now and it was too late to bring the words back.

Nurse Hickson turned to her, looking at her with new eyes and replied, "That would be against everything we hold dear. Only two keepers, a man and a woman are capable of looking after a child."

"Well that's not technically true is it? I think a single person could do as good a job," answered Lydia.

"Ssshhh! You will wake the babies." That appeared to be the end of that discussion.

The Nurse walked on her tiptoes with her finger against her mouth. They followed her lead and tried desperately to make no noise, but failed miserably because Mr Chariot's shoes creaked dreadfully and Marjoram's skirts rustled.

'Perhaps I should take out a biscuit and start crunching that!' thought Lydia and giggled. She soon stopped that when Nurse Hickson looked at her using the same face Lydia's old teacher had used to quell classroom noise.

They creaked and rustled to the far end of the ward and at last reached the last crib on the left. Nurse Hickson pulled a pink cord which gently lowered the crib to the floor. There inside was a sweet little girl, all tiny and soft, wrapped in a pink blanket with her thumb in her mouth.

Marjoram looked enquiringly at the Nurse who nodded sharply and soon the new keeper had her daughter enveloped in her arms with love. All faces, including the stern Nurse softened and smiled.

"Little Dotty," said the new mother, "welcome to our family."

Lydia felt tears in her eyes and tensed herself quickly. This was no place for jealousy, for she was suspicious that that was what she was feeling.

"Come along to my office, we have plenty of forms to fill in." Nurse Hickson was back to her old self. Marjoram followed in a cloud of happiness and Mr Chariot followed her, pleased about the new addition, but unsure as always of how he should react. Lydia followed him, feeling a little left out.

The office was the first door they came to and as they trooped in, Nurse Hickson began to shut the door in Lydia's face, informing her that this was keeper business and she could not be part of it and must wait outside.

Lydia stood for a moment, looking at the closed door and turned around, unsure of what she ought to do. There was nowhere to sit and so far she had seen no one else other than Nurse Hickson. Surely she was not the only person here?

210

She walked along the corridor for a minute and came to another corridor. Thinking that she saw another nurse along there, she shouted, "Hello! I say, hello!" There was no answer, so Lydia decided to turn back. Now her problems really started. She could not find the door back to the others. It wasn't as though the door had vanished. It was that she couldn't decide which one was the door through which she had come. There were several doors and they all looked the same.

Lydia could not decide which one to open or how far she had walked while shouting to the imaginary nurse. The lamps flickered and dimmed as if a draught had passed along the corridor. Great, it must be at least a day since she had been stuck in a creepy place on her own with no way of getting out.

Hearing footsteps coming along the corridor, she was reminded that she had no idea of how to get back to where she was supposed to be.

The footsteps continued, but no one arrived along the dimly lit corridor. This was tiled in the same style as the other corridors along which she had already travelled.

Here, however, the lamps appeared to be running out of oil and flickered alarmingly. Rather than look for the ward door, Lydia decided to go onwards and see what came to her. She clipped along, making the same noises with her feet as before, only this time the noises were not quite so comforting.

Her hands went into her pocket and fell upon the necklace which she had decided to bring with her today. She resolved to take it with her every day. Putting it around her neck, she experienced the familiar wobbly sensation, and soon was aware of a shift in perception.

Rounding a corner along the corridor she arrived at a set of steps. She no longer remembered whether she was up a floor or down a floor, but as these stairs only went up she took this as a sign she was going up.

Reaching the top of the stairs, she saw that she was at the entrance to another ward. This was set out very similar to the other ward, only the cribs were on the floor, rather than in the air. There was no one about and there was no sound. She crept over to the first crib, glad that her shoes did not creak nor her skirts rustle. She did not feel like laughing either.

She looked over the top and saw a baby lying there. Only this baby was not pink or wrapped in a sweet blanket, it lay on its back. On his back, eyes wide open and staring at Lydia. She held her breath involuntarily and put her hand to her mouth. Then she looked around the ward to ensure that there was no one else there, for she felt as though she were being watched. Turning back, Lydia bent over the crib again. Horrifically, the baby was sitting up and looking directly at her. He opened his mouth and said, "Hello Lydia."

She nearly fainted.

After swiftly deciding that there had been rather too much fainting of late, she stayed upright instead.

"Gave you a shock did I Lydia?" The baby was no bigger than Dotty, but talked to her as though he was an adult and it was very unnerving. As he sat up, Lydia noticed that he was dressed in a miniature version of a grown man's clothes.

"Well yes you did rather. What or rather who are you? Please?"

"We are from the other place and are waiting to be collected. We are the ones who Beyond won't let in."

"You mean the ones who have been bad in their life?"

The baby smiled, showing that he had no teeth. He wouldn't have had teeth at that age, though would he?

"The ones who the warped minds in Beyond consider to have been bad. We are inclined to disagree though."

Lydia heard something scurrying behind her. This time she turned around slowly and was rewarded with the sight of a ward full of baby people sitting up in their cots and looking at her. The babies made no noise, they just smiled at her. This was the most frightening sight Lydia had ever seen in her life. She had seen a few odd sights recently, so the comparison was valid.

Her hand went to the necklace at her throat, noticing that the talking creepy baby was looking at it constantly.

"May I try that on please?" His hand was outstretched.

"No, you can't."

The baby's face puckered and he began to whimper, shaking his lower lip while tears sprang to his eyes.

"Please, let me have it. Just for a little while. We receive no attention here and have nothing to play with. We are so lonely. Please!" This plaintive cry had a small chance of working when tried by a normal young child.

"No, I am afraid you can't. It is very precious to me."

All the babies whimpered and their lower lips shook. Lydia looked from one to another and within a few moments, the whole ward was crying and shaking. The noise was terrible and frightening and Lydia considered giving in to his request just to make the noise stop. But that would be a stupid thing to do. She could not risk Shudder getting access to any of the keys or the necklace.

The first baby suddenly stopped crying and said quite calmly, "You just thought about Shudder didn't you?"

"I don't know what you are talking about," she answered, although she was more taken aback than she would admit.

"Yes, you did. Would you like me to call him? You could give him the necklace."

"Don't be ridiculous baby, I shan't allow you to call him."

"You can't stop me. We are going to find a way into Beyond very soon. We are almost there and no one will get in our way." The baby seemed to be growing as he was talking to her. He looked taller and spikier somehow.

"I can stop you and I will. You other babies, do you have anything to say for yourselves?"

There was no answer, they had stopped crying, but were saying nothing at all. They didn't look real. Lydia had seen a man perform a play with wooden puppet dolls at Seaside once and these babies reminded her of them. Back then she had kept expecting the dolls to jump from the stage and walk towards her. She had been more than a bit tense that day.

"Lie down baby and go to sleep." She pushed him back into his crib and tucked in the blankets so tightly that he could not move. She pinned the spindly arms underneath the covers. The baby might be unusual, but appeared not to have much strength.

He wriggled about, but Lydia made sure that it would be a while before he could get himself free. The other babies became uncomfortable about his discomfort and started to cry again.

214

"If you start crying, I shall do the same to you all. If you want to get into Beyond, you don't need to be weird and horrible like Shudder, you just need to be good and kind! Then you get in for free! It's easy really."

The whimpering stopped and Lydia turned to leave.

"What are you doing in here Mrs Pollack?"

It was Nurse Hickson, arms at her sides and her sternest look upon her face.

"I, I, got lost and ended up here," blustered Lydia. "I didn't mean to upset the babies."

"I have no idea what you are talking about young lady, this is just a corridor."

She was correct. It was just a corridor and nothing else. In her pocket, Lydia felt the necklace, now settled safely in its depths.

Following Nurse Hickson back to the front door she thought hard about what she had just witnessed. She gathered correctly that the Nurse was not someone with whom she could discuss the matter.

Nurse Hickson brought her back quickly to the baby ward where the Chariots were holding Baby Dotty and waiting by the door.

"Come on Lydia! We want to get Dotty home and in her own bed!"

"Sorry, I got lost," she answered quickly and accompanied them outside.

As the Chariots climbed into the cart, Lydia asked if they minded if she walked back rather than rode with them. She told them that she needed the fresh air and thought that they would be better getting the baby home quickly.

They agreed and soon she was on her own, standing on the dark part of the drive with the overhanging trees. As soon as she was sure no one could see her, she put the necklace back around her neck and was rewarded with the sight of an open green space in place of the trees and shrubs.

It was beginning to snow, falling lightly upon her shoulders, and dusting the ground. The driveway which lay out neatly in front of her, meandered through a set of gates with stone pillars holding them upright. It continued through the green lawns and arrived at a beautiful building with a high tower topped with a tall spire. As she strained her head back to look up, the cross upon the top of the spire came into view. The other part of the building was still large but with a normal pitched roof. The windows, tall and paned with brightly coloured paintings in the glass, were lit from behind by lamps. The tall oak doors at the base of the tower looked welcoming and friendly, so Lydia walked in.

Inside were rows of finely carved wooden benches on either side of the room. At the far end was another set of carved wooden benches at right angles to these and in between the two, a lectern. Lydia had no idea what this wonderful building was, but she felt very comfortable walking in and going through to a table at the other end. Upon this table stood a gold cross and various bowls and cups, all shining brightly and covered in jewels.

Lydia had never felt as warm and safe as she did at that moment. She placed her hand gently upon the cross and felt a warm glow coming from it. Turning around she noticed that the whole room seemed to be bathed in light, although only lit by a few lamps. No Shudder man could follow her here, she felt sure.

Lying on one of the benches to her left, she noticed a beautiful fur coat, on which was a letter addressed to Lydia Prix. Upon opening it, she read:

Wear this and keep warm.

So, naturally she did.

The coat was lovely, so Lydia decided to go back outside and see what she could see. Warm as toast, she walked back into the snow which was now coming down thick and fast. There was no one about, so stepping out onto the driveway would not cause any problems. At the moment the entrance gates were still visible, but as the snow was increasing, they would soon be blocked from view.

To her right was a path which led around the back of the lovely building and to her left a path leading to another stone building. Both beckoned to her.

She decided to take the right turning before the snow became too heavy. The path wound its way through bushes which made passage difficult for her and would not have allowed another person to travel alongside. Stones planted here and there were covered in chisel carving. The path spilt into two and on the corner was a mock stone entrance to a house. Lydia could only see part of the feature when she first came upon it and as she walked around to the front, saw that there stood a woman staring into the distance.

"Hello," she said to the woman.

But there was no answer and it wasn't long before she could see the reason. The woman was made from stone. She was a statue, albeit an excellent one. Looking at her face must have been exactly the same as looking into the face of the woman after whom her likeness was created. Lydia reached out to touch the cold face and felt a tremor within.

She knew that the woman was sad or had been the cause of great sadness. The stone lady stood impassively in front of the stone door and under the shelter of a stone porch. The door behind her was slightly ajar and when Lydia tried to look beyond the lady and the door, she could only see another wall. Lydia shivered a little when she thought that the lady moved and pulled the fur coat around her shoulders for comfort. She must pay more careful attention to the statue lady and make sure that she didn't suddenly come alive and chase her down the lawn.

The beautiful stone lady, dressed in the old fashioned style was reminiscent of the old paintings Lydia had seen on the walls of the Town Hall. In one hand she held a handkerchief tightly, as if for security. Her other hand rested against her dress held a solitary flower. The porch roof stood on ornate stone pillars and the door itself, although made from stone, looked exactly like carved oak. Next to the door, underneath the bell push was a sign:

Lady Gladys Ailwood, my darling wife and companion
Taken from me by the Shudder Man
I shall never stop looking
Don't despair
Lord Edward Ailwood

Goodness! That was odd! This discovery made the trip through the lawns all the more relevant. Excited and hopeful, Lydia walked briskly to the next monument, a huge stone angel upon a pillar and read:

Mitzi

Stolen by the Shudder Man
Not forgotten

Then a memorial, again of stone and surrounded by iron railings:

Tamson
We won't stop looking
Don't be afraid
Mummy and Daddy

Lydia travelled along the snow covered paths and saw more monuments, memorials and plaques, all with similar legends. She continued walking around the overgrown park, never seeing a living soul but feeling comfortable with the dead. She rounded a corner and she saw a field with hundreds and thousands of stone ornaments stretching out before her.

She stood and watched the snow coming down so fast that it obscured the sky and the trees and bushes and memorials as if shutting down her knowledge of what she had just seen. The only monuments left in view wore snow hats and coats and stood out against the white background creating a peaceful effect.

Lydia continued with her walk, turning right and then left until she was back at the memorial to Lady Gladys. There she saw that the door behind Gladys was now completely open. Lydia, with the innate curiosity of all women, naturally looked through it and noticed that the stone wall she had seen previously was in fact the entrance to a passageway. She excused herself to the Lady and squeezed past, travelling through the door and into the corridor.

No light was necessary because soon she came upon a door which gave way reluctantly against her strong pushing. On the other side of this door was what appeared to be a large barn.

Inside was dark but the gap under the main doors at the other end of the room, threw in enough light to enable her to make sense of outlines. There were so many things lying about the floor and the walls, that she found it difficult to take it all in.

Suddenly she heard a noise – someone was opening the doors. Lydia stood back into the corridor and shut the door leaving only a small gap. Hearing voices, she kept a firm grip on the handle, getting ready to close it firmly and run if necessary.

"Father doesn't use this building much," she heard a man say. It was David Turncoat and he was accompanied by her sister Janey.

Lydia thought about this, for she had to take into account that not only was she now able to travel from one place to another via another dimension, she was also travelling in time. Perhaps there was no such thing as time.

Lydia watched the scene unfold just as her sister had described it to her. She thought David looked sad, but he must have something to do with all of this and she still could not trust him. How could she know which side he was on? She closed the door and walked back through the doorway, past Lady Gladys and onto the snowy path.

It was hard to tell if it was dusk or daylight, with the sky and ground joined by steady snowfall. Looking up and blinking against the flakes falling into her eyes she smiled. Were things coming together quietly in her mind?

She went back to the large building and walked to the table at the front. She removed her coat and shook it, then placed it carefully where she had found it an hour or two previous. She said thank you, to whoever may be listening and walked back to the main door. Turning round for another look, she felt strongly in her heart that she would return here.

The snow had stopped and Lydia saw that although there was a thick layer covering everywhere, she had a clear path to the main gate. Was this the place where she would find her answer to the Shudder Man? She certainly now knew that she was not alone in her experiences of that devil. Perhaps it would be down to her to stop him.

Once outside the gate, the snow had gone and she soon realised that she was back on the pathway to Finders Hospital.

Her hand went to the necklace, and she wondered whether or not to remove it, but swiftly decided against it. She was getting some sense of the difference between her world and this other world. She would be more protected wearing the necklace, she was sure.

Now she felt that she had an idea of the direction she needed to go in order to solve these mysteries.

It didn't take her long to arrive back at Gran's and tell the family all about the visit because she only told them about the new baby and waiting in a corridor and walking home. Lydia thought that she must now keep certain information safe in her mind until she needed to pass it on. She must wait until she had more answers than questions.

CHAPTER FOURTEEN *DAVID*

It was very important now that Lydia should see David Turncoat and find out what he knew about all of this. They must not argue, just talk. Lydia was determined that they would not argue. She had a quiet lunch with Gran and the girls and answered any baby questions she was asked. The twins were as disinterested in babies as she, but Gran wanted to know every little thing about Dotty.

"Gran, I hardly saw her at all. She was wrapped in a blanket and then they took her in an office and then straight home. I wouldn't recognise her again!"

"What was the point in your going then? You didn't learn anything!" Gran was a bit cross, Lydia could tell.

"Well go over there yourself this afternoon!"

"I shall," she informed them, then said, "Will you give me a lift up there please, Alice?"

"And will you give me a lift to the Turncoat Farm Janey?" asked Lydia.

"Why? What are you going to do up there?"

"I am going to see what David knows about everything."

"Great, can I watch the fireworks?" asked Janey.

They were on their way an hour later, Alice rather upset that she had drawn the short straw of the baby visit. The weather was fine and dry and Lydia thought briefly about the snow storm she had been in only an hour or two previous.

Rounding the corner into Wide Lane, she asked Janey to stop at the sweet shop. She had an idea that Mrs Ladywoman would be able to give her some help.

Janey went in with her sister, partly because she liked sweets and partly because she did not want to miss out on anything exciting which may occur. Mrs Necessity Ladywoman arrived behind the counter from the back of the shop upon hearing the jingle of the doorbell.

"Hello Lydia and young Janey too! How lovely to see you both! Something you want to ask me dear?"

Straight to the point.

"Well first we want to choose some sweets, for Gran and Alice too and then I have something to ask you, but I am not really sure how to phrase it."

"Best just to come right out with it, I should think." She was putting sweets into brown paper bags while listening.

"Something is happening in this town, Mrs Ladywoman, and you said to me that you could help if I was stuck. What can you tell me?"

The lady stopped what she was doing and looked at Lydia for a full five seconds as if deciding what to do next.

"Follow me," she said at last.

The girls went around the back of the counter and both felt quite excited at the prospect. It doesn't matter how old a person becomes, it still feels naughty doing something that would have been forbidden when a child.

They went through the heavy curtains which separated the shop from the house at the back and stood in a room with no obvious outside light. The girls could see no windows, only lamps flickering around the place.

A desk in the corner with books and a pair of glasses inferred that a studious person had recently left. There were some papers on the floor and Janey bent to pick them up, but Mrs Ladywoman was quicker and she put them upside down on the table.

Lydia and Janey looked at each other and then Janey said, "So what do you need to show us?"

"Patience, please. You have heard the tales about the olden days of witches, both good and bad?"

"Yes. What has that got to do with anything?" asked Lydia.

"It has everything to do with what is happening now and everything to do with what has always happened."

"I don't understand!" said Janey.

They were interrupted by the sound of the shop doorbell ringing and Mrs Ladywoman going to answer it. She returned a few seconds later accompanied by Alice.

"I don't see why I should miss all the fun, you two. I always get left doing the boring stuff, so I followed you! You didn't get very far did you?" She sat down on an armchair without being asked.

"What about these witch stories then?" Janey wanted the woman to continue.

Mrs Ladywoman smiled and sat down in the other armchair leaving two straight chairs for the others to take advantage of.

"For thousands of years these witches have been battling for supremacy over the souls of the people here.

The bad witches have been meeting at the same site forever and arranging who to recruit and who to give orders to. They also know which children to groom and overpower.

"They learned early on, that to have a child's mind and his or her memories would ultimately control what that child did, even when an adult. The good witches have been battling against them and mostly winning. They protect the children where they can and save them where possible."

"So who is who?" asked Lydia.

"That is one of the problems we have!" answered Mrs Ladywoman.

"So do we," murmured Alice. "Tell us more."

"There are many of us in Mill Town and most of us are quite old now. In fact some of us are very old, but we know that we must keep going as long as possible and not move to Beyond. There has been no one to take over from us until these last few years. We are hoping that Shudder can be finally captured and killed off. We think that you are the only person who can do it Lydia." She paused for dramatic effect.

"Me! How can I do anything?" she asked.

"Who is Shudder?" asked Janey, she and Alice knowing nothing of the story to date.

"You will soon get to know your abilities, even if not immediately, then as you need them," Mrs Ladywoman announced sagely.

"What are you two talking about?" The twins wanted to grasp this very interesting turn of events.

"You must come to our next meeting Lydia. It takes place Thursday next. Meet me here at 11pm and I shall take you to the place," Mrs Ladywoman continued.

"Can we come?" the girls said in unison.

"No," answered the other two women.

It was decided to take one pony and cart back home so that the three sisters could journey together to Turncoat Farm.

David was not there when they arrived, but his parents made them welcome, offering tea and cake and company.

"David should be here soon," his father informed the group.

"May we walk around the farm Mr Turncoat?" asked Lydia. "I have not done so since I was a child."

"That is an excellent idea," he said as the conversation had been muddling along for over half an hour and he would be glad to get back to his own room. "Would you like me to accompany you on this walk?"

"No, Mr Turncoat, we can manage well on our own. If that is acceptable to you?"

"Yes, of course," he answered with much relief.

The girls left the stuffy kitchen and went out into the yard and the sunshine.

"I want you to show me the barn," said Lydia quickly.

Janey beckoned the other two to follow her and soon they were pulling at the barn door and making their way inside. Again, they were swiftly aware of the contrast of the cold, dark shed and the warm yard, but they went in anyway.

As they walked to the middle of the barn, there was a loud scraping noise and then a bang. As the girls wheeled around, they saw the barn door slammed firmly shut and the only light in the shed was coming from around the doorway.

"No! How on earth did that happen?" screamed Alice.

"I don't know. The door has been too difficult to open and close up till now. Someone else must have done it." Janey was sounding much calmer than she was feeling.

"Hello! Is that you David?" shouted Lydia, but no answer came.

"You don't think that he would be stupid enough to shut us in here in the dark do you?" Janey asked.

"No, I shouldn't think so. David! Are you out there?" Lydia shouted again.

"What was that?" Alice spoke quickly and grabbed hold of her sisters. They stood like statues, straining their ears to listen to the silent darkness. There it was again, a creaking noise, followed by the sound of footsteps walking very slowly.

"Have either of you got a light?" whispered Lydia.

"No," answered Alice.

There was the sound of heavy breathing somewhere nearby. The girls remained locked in their positions, unable to move. Janey could feel steamy breath on her face, but in the dark did not have the strength to move away from it. This had happened before, she was now sure. She was unable to remember when or what, but she knew this had happened to her before.

"Alice, Lydia! Please make him stop! I want him to stop." There was no answer, the girls were immobilised and could not help her. They were not really aware of what was happening to their sister, for they were scarcely in their bodies.

Shudder touched his victim on the face and whispered hoarsely, "Hello my little girly. Have you come here especially to see me?"

"No, I haven't." Janey did not recognize the voice she heard. Where were the others?

The stick-like hand moved slowly over her head and another hand on her shoulder. The hands moved carefully all over her body and made her shake uncontrollably. She knew what was coming next. As the hands moved over her frozen body like an expert, Janey once again submitted herself to Shudder.

It was over an hour later when the barn doors opened and David Turncoat stood in the doorway.

"Lydia! Are you in there?"

"Yes, we are here. Why did you lock us in?" Lydia was very quiet when she said this.

"I didn't," he said and came into the barn quickly. "What has been happening?" He was white faced and shocked as he rapidly looked around the three Prix girls. They in turn were almost catatonic and staggered out of the barn and into the fading light of the farmyard. Alice noticed that the pony and trap were not where they had been left an hour earlier, but beyond that she did not care.

"What has happened to you?" David looked concerned.

Lydia fixed him with a steely stare and said, "You must know what has been going on. Someone locked us in the barn and then allowed him to find us again. You should know better than that David." Lydia could feel her blood boiling. She was sick and tired of having stuff happen to her and her sisters and no one caring about it. Necklace this and meaningful talk that, didn't alter the fact that Shudder and his little friends were able to do what they wanted whenever they wanted.

Yes, she was sick of it.

"I didn't lock you in there! Why blame me! You always blame me!" David stopped and took a deep breath, saying more calmly, "What has happened Lydia? Tell me."

"I can't." Tears were welling in her eyes, she didn't want that. "Look David, I came here to ask you about some things and perhaps tell you some things. It has been very odd since I came back and I know you are involved somewhere along the line. I just can't work out how. I am not sure if I can trust you David. I used to be able to, but now I don't know."

David held her hand tightly and said, "You can trust me Lydia. I promise."

She looked at him again, trying to read the truth in his eyes.

"There are many things I need to talk to someone about. Major things."

"Talk to me."

"Not yet. The secrets are too big, if you are not to be trusted." She dropped her head into her hands feeling the weight of the past week. No, her entire life was exhausting.

"Shudder is back," she said.

"He never went away Lydia, he never went away."

The girls came over to them and Janey said, "Come on Lydia, let's go home. I am so tired."

"Yes," she agreed.

The pony had been put away in a field and was merrily eating grass, unaware of the dramas which had been taking place. Lydia walked towards the barn again and went in. She felt braver now that the yard was full of people and her exit was safe. She could see no evidence of what had recently occurred. There was no sign against the wall, where the Shudder man had made two girls wait as he...

229

Lydia looked behind her and saw that everyone was busy talking and no one had noticed where she was.

She took out the necklace and looked at it in the palm of her hand. Why hadn't she taken it out a couple of hours ago when he was attacking them? Because she forgot about it, because when Shudder was about she could think of nothing.

She must practise focusing, practise centring her thoughts so that she could act properly, no matter what the distractions might be. Looking over her shoulder, she saw that no one was looking and she put the necklace around her neck.

The room remained the same this time, she was still aware of the others on the yard, but she could not see a doorway in the wall. She knew there was a doorway there, for she had stood in it only very recently, but now there was no sign of it. Had the Shudder man done something to it?

"Lydia!" shouted David behind her and she jumped.

"Lydia!" he repeated.

He could not see her. She put out her hand and touched him on the shoulder lightly and he moved to brush her hand away. He could not see her.

Lydia was happy to see him looking worried, it jolly well served him right to be worried. There was something else she could see too. In the shadows of the barn were shapes of, well, things. They scurried about to and fro, but seemed unable to come fully into the barn. Lydia was reminded of the babies at the hospital and shivered involuntarily.

She made her way around the walls of the barn and tried to find the door to the graveyard, but there definitely was none. She assumed that she could only travel here from

230

the other side. Lydia decided there and then that she would not go back with the twins, but would do some more investigation under cover of the necklace. This could not go on any longer and she needed to solve these mysteries once and for all.

She took off the necklace and walked out of the barn. David looked amazed to see her as she shouted to the twins, "Let's get going now and then I want you to drop me off on Mill Lane and I shall walk home."

The girls gave her a quizzical look, but did as they were told and within half an hour, despite several protests, Lydia had been dropped off at the end of Turncoat Lane and was watching her sisters trotting off in the cart. David had been insistent that he come with her and she had quite naturally refused. Now, all alone she walked the short way to the house of Doctor Catapult.

Passing her childhood home unsettled her rather as it always did, but she was never sure whether it was for good or ill. As it was, no one was looking out of the window at her or in the garden, so she did not have to heighten the awareness of her presence.

She smiled and waved at the people she passed, knowing that they were on their way to the inns on Town Street.

Walking the few steps further on from her home, she came face to face with Cal.

"Hello little Liddy," he said in his usual creepy way. He held out his hand towards his niece and momentarily touched her shoulder with his long fingers and allowed these to touch gently against her chest. She withdrew quickly and fixed him with a stare.

"Keep away from me Cal. You are disgusting and I hate you."

He carried on grinning, but took his hand away. "Isn't it about time you called me by my first name, Liddy?"

"No, I don't want to call you anything. I would rather not speak to you at all," she said with feeling.

Smiling again, he answered, "My name is Invention. You call me that from now on. Now you are a big girl, you are not so interesting to me. But I imagine you are still attractive to others." He showed his black teeth and close up, Lydia was aware of how old and evil he really was.

Connecting with him thus, she felt almost hypnotised, but soon broke free and ran towards the Doctor's. She turned into the driveway and upon doing so looked to see if Cal was following her. He wasn't, so she made her way to the front door and rang the bell. She had to ring a few times before it was answered by one of the Misses Catapult.

"Oh, hello Lydia, what brings you back here?"

Lydia had absolutely no idea what had brought her back here, she just knew that she needed to be here to find out the next step.

"I, I lost a ring when I fell down the cellar the other day and I wondered if you would allow me to go back and look for it. It is a very precious thing and I would not like to be parted from it for too long." Lying came easily to her.

"Come in do, but Catapult has not mentioned finding a ring. My sister and I never go down there, the steps are too steep, but Catapult keeps it clean and tidy, so he tells me anyway." She seemed less sure of this fact. "But he has not mentioned anything about a ring to me."

Lydia followed the old lady into the hall and noticed how nervous she seemed.

"Are you alright Miss Catapult?" she asked her.

Miss Catapult turned to the young woman and looked for a moment as though she was going to embark on a confidence, but she soon decided against it.

"Would you like to come through to the kitchen? The Doctor should be back a little later, he went out somewhere, I am not sure where." She was definitely nervous.

"Perhaps you would allow me to go down to the cellar and have a look for my ring?"

The old lady looked again from one side of the hall to the other and then answered in a hushed tone. "I am not really sure if my brother is already down there. I know that sometimes he will go without telling us and we only find out later on."

"Is there something the matter Miss Catapult? You seem worried."

"No, no I am alright my dear. Everything is fine." Miss Catapult straightened her skirts with her black gloved hands and smiled at Lydia.

"You go down the cellar and I will put on the kettle for some tea when you come back up."

Lydia watched the old lady walk across the hall and go through the kitchen door. Now, alone again in the hall she shook involuntarily and went to the cellar door. It opened easily and Lydia carefully made her way down the stairs. The room although dimly lit was bright enough for her to see all around it. Nothing was changed from the other day and the door to the next room was clearly visible. Lydia went to that door, opened it and walked through.

The fire, still lit, cast its shadows around the library shelves. Again it felt as though people were about to enter the room or had just left it for a moment, an unnerving feeling considering all that had happened recently.

Upon the long table, the candles were lit and added extra shadows upon the walls. The notepad and pen sat on the table and Lydia remembered that last time this same pad was in the cellar room. Curious, she walked over to it and turned it round so that she could look squarely at the pad. Nothing was written on the top sheet, but this time she picked it up and flicked through the pages. There was writing on one of the sheets of paper. Lydia read and said the words out loud:

Lydia, if you are reading this you are in great danger. You are still not aware of the truth but soon will be. Shudder does not realise your power yet and neither do you. Think more slowly and carefully in every situation and do not accept what you see as being the truth. You are not in the place or time you think you are,

Lydia

She had no idea what that meant and why write her name twice?

Was that a noise behind her? Wheeling round, she saw there was nothing. The shadows still danced menacingly around the walls. Lydia decided to walk around the room and see what she could make of it. There were ten shelves of books, floor to ceiling and covered the walls, with the exception of the fireplace and door areas. The books were of different sizes, but all appeared to be leather bound and very old. Mainly in brown, but some red, cream and green added interest to the overall effect.

Leaning over to the books, she began to read the titles:

History of Mill Town

This covered a large area, being a 132 Volume set:

Ancient Spells

Witchcraft

Sea Beasts

Terrors of the Old Days

There were many titles in the same vein and one or two Lydia took from the shelves and thumbed through the pages. The pictures were scary and the writing large. Some books felt as though they had a life of their own, whereas others felt like nothing special. She moved along the shelves, becoming lost in the job of examining the books and their contents. The subject matter seemed to be allocated in sections covering history, magic and doctoring of one form or another. When had all these books been collected and by whom? The Doctor was not old enough to have bought these books new.

One book caught her eye and she took it from the shelf immediately she read the title:

The Turncoat Family and their role in Mill Town History

By Dewr Beau Bradwr

Taking the book over to the table, she dragged out a chair and with her back to the fire she began to read.

The story told was of the Turncoat family history going back many generations. Names and dates were written along with the story of their contribution to the community life. Lydia learned that contrary to the stories told now, the Turncoat family had been influential as good people and had ensured the safety of the locals. There had been and apparently still were, a group of inhabitants who were intent

235

on control and took money and power by this means over the rest of the community. This small group controlled how the community worked, lived their lives and whether times were good or bad.

Whenever there seemed to be surplus of money or good feeling amongst the locals, then jobs would be lost and money tightly controlled by the elite. The group of ruling families swopped and changed their business interests depending on where money was to be found. They never lost money.

The Turncoat family amongst others had infiltrated this group on several occasions and often stopped the worst of the excesses. But some had remained with the other side preferring money and riches to poverty and righteous feelings. Turning the pages showed that the Prix family and the Ladywomans amongst others had altered their political allegiance over the centuries. Lydia read quickly with growing interest. She saw names she recognised from books they had at school or from conversations with her grandparents. Pictures of the main parties made Lydia aware that many descendants of these great families still looked the same now.

Every generation would produce some special children capable of overthrowing the secret regime which had become more malevolent as time went by. The only way it would be possible to stop this happening once and for all, Lydia read, was by changing the minds of every single person in the neighbourhood. That was impossible as it is the inherent nature of all to want more. If one group lose their power, another will take it immediately. That is and always has been the truth.

The only freedom for anyone was individual freedom. That must be achieved by changing the way they viewed their own world. See that the mind is a small version of the outside world and that the mind has all the power. It seems that hardly anyone believes it though and so those with the knowledge will always rule. The special children must remove the most malevolent in order that the worst excesses could be avoided.

"Heavy stuff," Lydia said.

The fire was dying in the grate and she automatically threw on some more wood. As it burst back into life she read on.

The writings told her that these special children had an unusual ability to travel from one place to another and as soon as this skill was accepted they would be able to achieve far more.

"Must mean me," she said.

There were pictures of people good and bad, past and present. She saw her own likeness in the Prix section. Pixie Prix looked so much like Lydia. It was as though she were looking in a mirror. Did the image smile at her? There was a picture reminiscent of David but the writing underneath informed her that it was the author Dewr Bradwr.

She closed the covers of the book and wondered whether to take it with her. But how could she get it past the Doctor and his sisters? That thought made her sit up straight. She must have been here a long time. A glance up at the grille in the wall showed her that there was darkness outside. Great, now what was she supposed to do?

Then the simple answer came to her. She could put on the necklace and take the book out without ever being seen. She would inform the sisters should they ever ask her in the future that she had gone straight home earlier in the day. That was what she would do.

The sound of voices interrupted her little plan. Male voices, one of whom she immediately recognized as Doctor Catapult, were making their way to this very room.

Think, think, and think.

She put on the necklace and picked up the book. To this she added the notebook and pen and moved the chair back to its original position. Looking round swiftly to make sure the room was almost as she found it, she made for the door and slipped quickly into the far room.

As she stood on the cold stone floor she heard a group enter the library, laughing and joking. She peeped around the partly open door and looked at the assembled men. She knew most of them.

Bringing her head back, she pondered for a minute or two what her options were now. She could walk past them hoping that they were incapable of seeing her. But that may not work if they had any abilities such as those horrid babies at the hospital. Or wait until they had finished and find her way out then. She could go out through the other door and back down the tunnel.

She must make a decision quickly and stick to it.

CHAPTER FIFTEEN *REVELATIONS*

There was much joviality in the library. Everyone was socialising and passing round drinks.

Lydia meanwhile, was still debating whether or not to walk through the library under the disguise of the necklace while everyone was milling around, or wait and see what this gathering was about. If she stayed, she was very likely to discover some useful information.

At that moment, however, she heard Doctor Catapult shout above the noise and tell the group to sit down and pay attention.

"Come along, everyone settle down. We have a lot to get through tonight. That means you too Invention, stop looking through the books and sit down. You won't find what you are looking for in any of those books."

Laughter followed the remark and Lydia listened to chairs dragging across the floor and feet shuffling and within a few minutes there was silence.

The Doctor spoke. "I had to call this emergency meeting due to the interference of certain people who seem intent on upsetting the equilibrium of the Town."

"We all know who you mean," said a man, who Lydia knew was Peter John Burgess, a tradesman of the town. She had seen him on her first glance around the door.

"Why is that door open?" asked another.

Lydia stopped breathing as she realised the owner of the voice was referring to the door behind which she stood.

"I have no idea," answered the Doctor. "Go and close it, but check out the waiting room before you do."

So this was it, make a decision now Lydia.

Burgess opened the door wide and looked into the small stone room. He could not see her, or the things she was carrying. That was a relief. He walked past her and would have walked into her had she not jumped to one side at the last minute. He went directly over to where the tunnel door was hidden within the stone work, obviously well aware of its existence. Trying the handle and discovering that it had not been recently tampered with, he turned ready to return to the library. Lydia took the opportunity to jump into the room before him and made her way around the table as he closed the door to the stone room.

"Lock it," instructed Doctor Catapult. It was done and Lydia did a little dance, glad that she had made the right decision to enter the room. She leaned against a shelf of witchcraft books and looked around at the gathered group.

Doctor Catapult, Inspector Glees, Invention Cal, Peter John Burgess, Emtee Oreful and several others sat around the table. Lydia was shocked to see David Turncoat there. He was paying little attention to the rest of the group, reading a sheaf of papers on the desk in front of him. Lydia made her way over to him and leant across his shoulder trying to read what was there. Her breathing caught his attention or appeared to, for he said in a whisper, "Be careful, they may see you."

She jumped back, startled, but David made no attempt to lift his head from the pages and Lydia was unsure whether or not she had imagined the voice in her state of nervous tension. She leaned back and noticed that the top paper said only:

To be read by addressee only

A loud noise made her jump again. It was the sound of the small hammer which Doctor Catapult banged on the table as he said, "Please let us begin the meeting without any further delay."

So the meeting began. The fire flickered happily in the grate. The candles and lamps upon the table gave audience to the proceedings. Lydia leant against the shelving and listened intently, discovering that the initial half hour appeared to be taken up by formalities.

'It is obvious that this meeting is run by men,' she thought to herself. Any group of women tend to talk about anything other than the agenda and achieve far more in the process.

Eventually the proceedings turned to something a little more relevant.

"Now then brothers. As I said before we have trouble in our midst," Catapult began.

"You mean that Prix girl. She always has been trouble. When she was a child she tried to accuse me of something. Mrs Cal was having none of it and gave her a good hiding and threw her down the steps. She told her sister and she

241

ended up here in the hospital and I know that she has always been a liar."

The group looked at their fellow member, amazed at the irrelevant tirade.

"Thank you Cal, although I don't think anything you said will help us here."

"I think it will. I know she is a liar and I am telling you that she is."

Lydia had stiffened on hearing her uncle speak, but did nothing about it. She intended to do something about it later.

"Lydia Prix has found the tunnel and been down it. We don't know how she discovered it or what happened when she was in it. But now the situation has been exacerbated."

"I also am sure that she has been travelling elsewhere. Shudder will not be pleased and will now see her as a target. He will want to remove her from this place because of the damage she is capable of." David had joined the debate and Lydia was shocked to see how knowledgeable he was about Shudder. Surely he was enemy to David too? But no, he appeared to be one of his followers.

"Shudder will do as he pleases. He always has done. But the truth is that now we are all going to suffer from his anger. Once the tunnel was breached he went on red alert. He will make everyone pay in one way or another."

"That is why we must stop her. If she and the Prix family start making too many enquiries, the whole project will be upset." David looked gloomy.

"It was only luck that I managed to cover up Michaelmas's death. If the truth of that got out – well I don't like to think of the consequences for us all." Inspector

Glees shook his head. "And that near disaster with his sister. It would have been better if she had died."

"At least I managed to get the body out of the way before there was too much investigation," added Emtee Oreful.

Lydia tried to stifle a cry which insisted on vacating her mouth. It was soon clear that the group were able to hear her if not see her.

"What was that?"

"Did you hear it?"

"Ssshhh, what was that?" comments flew around the table.

David looked startled and Lydia was quite sure that he was staring at her directly.

"It is probably our imagination," he comforted the group. "I would have thought that no one would be stupid enough to come and listen to our meetings. They could get into serious trouble, playing games like that."

Did he know? How could he possibly know she was there?

"It is not better that Sadie should have died," he continued. "We are not happy with any deaths. I think that should be made clear on the records of this meeting."

"I concur with your views David," said Doctor Catapult.

"Well I think you are all getting weak. Shudder can be admired for the power he possesses. No one else has that power." Cal was speaking again. "I am not like him, but some of the things he gets away with. You just have to admire him."

"Shut up Cal. Nobody is interested in your views." David was firm in his response.

243

Cal pursed his lips and leant back in his chair. He clearly was not bothered about David's opinion.

Lydia listened intently to everything which was said and looked closely at all the people sitting around the table. She wanted to remember everyone.

She felt something stroking her shoulder lightly and instinctively shrugged off the hand. It happened again and she looked to her right, in sudden realisation that no one should be able to see her.

"Hello," said the owner of the hand.

The girl standing next to her was about ten years old, very pretty with long dark hair. She wore a pale blue dress, black shoes and a white cardigan. She looked dreamy, quiet.

"Are you dead?" the girl asked.

"No," answered Lydia. "Are you?"

"I think so," she answered, "I haven't seen my parents for a very long time."

"How did you die?" Lydia was accepting of anything that happened to her recently, how could she be anything else?

"I am not really sure," was the answer.

"Oh. Can't you remember?"

"I don't know. I was alive and now apparently I'm dead. I didn't feel any difference when I journeyed from one state to the other. I thought it would hurt or feel spectacular when I died. But it didn't." The girl was very laid back about the situation in which she now found herself.

"Oh I see," Lydia replied.

"What's your name?" asked Lydia.

"Tamson," was the reply.

Lydia was vaguely aware that she had heard the name recently. She also suddenly became conscious again of the others in the room. It seemed odd that she had not noticed them while she was speaking to Tamson. Had they still been there? And now it seemed they could no longer hear her.

"They can't hear us now," said Tamson, as if reading her thoughts. "I've seen to that."

"Oh, how?" asked Lydia.

Tamson lifted a necklace she was wearing and turned a key which was sitting in a locket.

"Have you got your key for your locket?" the girl asked. "They will never be far away from each other."

The discussions in the room appeared to be continuing in the same vein.

"So we are all agreed," announced the Doctor. "We shall close all access to the tunnel. That way Shudder can be happy and content."

David spoke up. "So what gates are we closing? We don't want to miss anywhere."

The Doctor looked to the ceiling thoughtfully and began counting on his fingers.

"There's the Mill office and the one at the back of the cellar."

"The woods."

"Finders Hospital."

"Town Street."

'Everywhere,' thought Lydia.

"My house," said Cal. "And your house," he added, looking across at David.

"Yes my house," he acknowledged.

Lydia looked at David and then at Tamson, who was giggling.

"I know the door at Turncoats. It calls to me."

"Have you been through it?" asked Lydia.

245

"Just once," she answered.

Lydia remembered where she had seen her name.

"Did your parents ever find you?" she whispered.

"No. They don't know where to look," Tamson said sadly. "They have all been in Beyond for a long time and there is no way to get from there to here."

"Oh but there is," Lydia answered. "Are there many of you?" she asked the girl.

"Hundreds," was the answer.

"Where are they all?"

"Stuck in the tunnel."

Their conversation came to a halt as the meeting appeared to be breaking up. Lydia had now to find her way out of the room and cellar without attracting any attention. She must do it quickly.

Beckoning to Tamson, she made her way out of the room and into the first cellar. As she stood on the bottom step, she noticed that Tamson was not following her.

"Come on," Lydia said. "We need to work on a plan!"

"Can't come," replied Tamson." I'm going back to the others."

"How can I find you again?"

"Come to the shelters and light a candle. I will come straight away."

"Right." Lydia could not afford to waste any more time. She scampered up the stairs and pushed the door at the top. This time, thankfully, it opened easily and she stood in the hallway. Lydia noted how bright it was up there and then inexplicably began to look at the pictures on the walls.

There were pictures of the Doctor with his brother and sisters and an older couple who Lydia knew must be their keepers. She had heard tales of old Doctor Catapult and his wife. Doctor had been well known and apparently well-loved in the village and the town. He had at one point been Chief Council man and had great influence.

Lydia looked closer at the picture and noted that the Doctor's wife did not look as proud and confident as her husband. The girls did not look too happy either.

The Doctor's younger brother was never really talked about. All Lydia knew was that he had been angry that his elder brother would become the Doctor for the town and that he must find his own way in the world.

Another picture was of a group of people: some men, some women and all dressed the same. Their uniform appeared to consist of pointed shoes and long brown cloaks. Again she moved closer to the picture to enable her to peer at the occupants of the metal benches.

"Hello Lydia. Did you find what you were looking for?"

She jumped back with a start and saw the Doctor's eldest sister staring at her impassively. She had her hands folded in front of her black dress giving a good view of a ring fashioned in the style of a large brass key.

"Err yes, well no. No I didn't. Sorry Miss Catapult, I was so absorbed in the pictures, I quite forgot where I was," she said more confidently.

"I thought you looked busy. I had wondered where you were as you were gone so long. Did you see my brother down there?" The latter question seemed to be added with a little less confidence, a slight tremor appearing in her voice.

How to answer? The truth was the only way. When in doubt speak the truth.

"Yes, I did. He was having a meeting with a lot of men from the Town."

"He didn't see you then?" she asked.

"No, he didn't."

"No, or you wouldn't be up here would you my dear?"

"No, I suppose not." Perhaps now would be a good time to ask questions.

"Miss Catapult. Is something going on that I should know about?"

The old lady looked uncomfortable and fiddled with the rings on her fingers.

"I don't think so Lydia."

Then, as an afterthought.

"Perhaps you would like to see your old room?"

"My old room?"

"From when you stayed her as a girl. You do remember that don't you?"

"I most certainly do," she answered with emphasis.

Then, perhaps with less certainty, "At least I think I remember most of it."

"Perhaps not everything, Lydia. It may be of help to you to put yourself in the mind-set you were back then. You may feel quite different in that."

They heard the sound of the Doctor's voice and Miss Catapult said, "Quickly, go up the stairs. It is best you don't bump into him."

The two women went upstairs, Lydia swiftly and Miss Catapult slowly and sedately. Her long black dress ruffled at the front, as she lifted it carefully.

They climbed up eight polished hardwood steps until she came face to face with a stone fountain built into the wall. Water poured from the mouth of the face of an imp and into the oblong trough in front. The imp seemed displeased with his task and glared at Lydia as she dipped her hand in the water.

It was funny, she thought, the stone face used to remind her of her Uncle Cal. The thin face, the spiky hair, the creepy leer. Come to think of it, it looks like Cal even now.

"Come on Lydia, up the steps," insisted the old lady as they heard footsteps coming out of the cellar.

The stairs split in front of the fountain. The women turned right. Miss Catapult because she knew exactly where she was going and Lydia because she was following.

"I remember looking out of these windows when I stayed here. Wishing my keepers would come for me. We would stand for what seemed like hours staring and praying. But no one came. We could see our friends and family walk up and down the street and wish they would come. I once saw my mother walk past the end of the drive and she never even looked in. I prayed that they would come and fetch me home but they never did. No one even came into the gardens to play. It was so sad."

"Yes I imagine so. But you were here on the instructions of your teachers and the Council. There was nothing we could do." Miss Catapult lowered her eyes.

"Wasn't there? Are you sure?"

Lydia realised that she could see directly into Cal's house. She remembered that too.

Lydia noticed that there were none of the men she had seen at the meeting crossing the lawn or walking down the drive. She had seen the meeting break up and knew that Doctor Catapult had left the cellar, but it looked as though no one had left by any of the house doors.

They must have left the cellar by the tunnel. But they hadn't entered by the small stone room. So, from where? There must be yet another entrance.

Lydia turned her attention to the landing. On the right of the corridor were the doors to several rooms. Five in fact. Each door made from solid oak with brass handles and hinges. They were built to stay in place.

"Which was my room?"

"This one," answered Miss Catapult as she opened the door.

The room was tiny. Lydia understood that places seem smaller when reviewed as an adult, but this room really was tiny. No window, just a small bed and a cupboard.

"I didn't spend much time in here did I?" she asked.

"Not alone."

No pictures on the wall either, she noted as the door closed. So what was the point of having been here?

They moved along the corridor, Miss Catapult in front of Lydia, walking purposefully.

Was that a whimper or a cry?

Lydia turned around and looked back down the landing, lace curtains at the windows blowing in at various intervals and for a moment, Lydia thought she saw a young boy standing there. The curtain blew in again and he was gone. She gasped and pointed her finger while turning to see if Miss Catapult had seen him too. She was still walking ahead, so Lydia dropped her finger and turned to join her. Lydia shivered a little because of the whole effect of that scene was made worse by the dark outside and the flickering lamps inside.

Then she heard a small voice saying, "Pixie! Help us!"

She would.

As they made their way to the end of the landing, Lydia asked, "Where are we going now?"

The smile that the old lady gave her almost made her stand still. She looked exactly like Cal.

"What happened to your brother, Miss Catapult?"

"Oh I expect he is doing some work somewhere about the place."

"I mean your younger brother."

The lady stopped and narrowed her lips before replying. "He lives a quiet life in the village, intent on being a good and honest citizen."

"In this village? Is he married to my aunt?"

Lydia's heart was banging away inside her chest and she felt the familiar leg wobble and sweat on her forehead. She knew she must ignore these feelings or her mind would move into the place where there was no clear thinking.

Miss Catapult did not reply. She opened the big white door at the end of the landing and half pushed Lydia through it. As her eyes became used to the bright lights within, everything came back to Lydia.

Everything.

CHAPTER SIXTEEN *DAVID'S STORY*

David began putting his papers in order as Doctor Catapult closed the meeting. He filed in order of importance and then in order of date. But still he did not feel satisfied with the result. Ever since he had heard that Lydia had come back to town, David had felt very unsettled.

Perhaps he had become more agitated when he heard that Michaelmas had been killed. That event had brought back so many memories of his rotten childhood and rotten schooldays and the only family who had made those years bearable, the Prix family.

"David, I wish to talk to you once everyone has gone," the Doctor informed him.

"Oh, alright," he answered.

David stopped filing his papers, put them into his leather satchel and returned his attention to Doctor Catapult.

"What is it that you want?"

"Not here David," he said. "Let's go upstairs."

The other men were leaving the room, talking and laughing, through the doorway in the library shelves. This door led into another part of the tunnel and on to the air raid shelter. Or, what was left of the air raid shelters after all the work at the old mill.

These old buildings were being converted into the entrance to the complicated water supply system. The guard there would need to be one of their own men.

"Fine, I'll come now."

The two men walked through the other rooms and came to the cellar steps. This latter room never ceased to make David quake inwardly, for he had bad memories of it. He followed the older man up the rickety steps and heard the familiar voices he always heard in the cellar.

"David, don't forget."

How could he forget?

"I think we should go directly into the hospital today, David. There is something important I wish to show you. Come on man, you are slow."

As they entered the hallway, David was aware of a swishing noise going up the central staircase and was quick enough to see Miss Catapult making her stately progress up there. He also thought he saw someone else ahead of her. Had he?

David was getting so tired these days. Life was one constant struggle and part of him felt that it was of his own making.

Crossing the entrance hallway they made their way through the waiting room, the surgery and then out again into the alley which led to the hospital. This place never failed to unnerve David. He had seen so horrible things happen since he joined this special Council group, but even they did not measure up to the memories of the Doctor's.

"Is there something the matter with you today David? You seem distracted." The Doctor fiddled with the lock, opened it and beckoned his friend in.

"I am not sure if I am coming down with something. I feel a little lightheaded today. I had a temperature this morning and would have stayed at home had this meeting not been called," and as an afterthought, "Perhaps I should go straight home now and have a lie down."

"Nonsense," said the Doctor. "Come with me and I shall give you some pills which will cure you immediately."

With a lifetime horror of taking medicine, David immediately replied, "No, no, I shall be fine. Let's just get this done quickly. What is it you want me to do exactly?"

Doctor Catapult pushed David into the hospital corridor with unnecessary force. David did a sort of shuffle and put out his hands against the far wall in order to keep his balance.

"What was that for?" he asked as he brushed himself down, quite cross and a little flustered.

"Sorry David. I didn't do it on purpose. I was just helping you in." However, he didn't look sorry and David began to feel more anxious as they made their way down the corridor.

The only noise was that coming from their shoes as they walked down to the far door. All doors on the corridor were closed, and David felt an atmosphere of menace behind each one. He had been here a few times in his adult years, but the experience which reared in his mind was the time he was a child of eleven.

He and Lydia had been sent there by their keepers after being advised so to do by the Doctor. Lydia had displayed argumentative behaviour and David was speaking to no one.

"What has happened to your boy to make him this way Mrs Turncoat?" he had asked.

"Well, nothing that we know about Doctor," was the answer. "He has a good home at the farm and as you know we are a good respectable family."

"But I am sure that he must come for a little visit with me at the hospital and he will soon be well again."

"I would rather he stay at home. If he stays away from school for another week, we can soon have him back to his normal cheeky self."

"It is out of your control now. The teachers told the Council and they have decided that he must come here to recover. It's best that you accept the situation and leave him here with me."

"But Doctor, I haven't brought his clothes!"

"You can drop them off at the surgery later on today and I will see that he gets them."

And so it was.

David, remembered sitting next to his keepers in the surgery wondering what was happening. Ever since that night at the mill he had said as little as possible. He was constantly frightened of giving the game away. It was difficult to learn how to ask questions after that.

Sister Catapult passed them in the corridor and stopped to speak briefly in her brother's ear. She walked out of the main door without a backward glance.

They reached the door at the end of the corridor and David turned the handle, following some agitated finger beckoning from Doctor Catapult.

"In you go David. Hurry up," he said.

They entered the room. It was a white shiny clinical room, very much like the other rooms. Some of which he had been in.

"What is it you want to show me Doctor?" he asked again.

"That," said the Doctor as he pointed at the table against the wall. The table had a large object upon it covered in a cream sheet. David walked towards it as if in a trance and stood before it.

"Sheet off, David. You know the drill." Doctor Catapult prodded the younger man in the arm.

David took the sheet off and felt his legs give way when he saw his friend Lydia lying on the trolley, motionless.

"Is she dead?" he asked quietly.

"I am afraid so David. Yes, she's dead."

"What happened?"

"She was found collapsed in Mill Lane by Inspector Glees and he stopped a passing cart man and between them, they managed to get her on board and up to the hospital."

"But when did it happen? If we were all in the meeting, how could you possible know that she was in here?"

"I was just told," grinned the Doctor as he tapped his nose. "We don't need to worry by whom."

"I'm sorry, I don't understand. Why is she here and how did she die? This doesn't make sense." David sat on a chair because he didn't feel as though his legs would support him.

Doctor Catapult's voice took on a different tone as he said, "I warned you not to let your guard down nor speak to anyone about anything. He will always make us pay for betrayal. He makes everyone pay in the end."

"I haven't said anything."

"Go into the little room at the back and lie down and have a rest. I need to deal with the problem we have here."

He handed two tablets and a glass of juice to David, who took them without question and walked towards the couch. He climbed onto it and curled up like a baby. He was vaguely aware of the Doctor rummaging around, but felt too exhausted to pay much attention. He heard the sound of trolley wheels being moved and shuffling of feet and was that the sound of voices?

David fell into the state of mind somewhere just before sleep, where dreams have not quite started and the craziness of life is left behind.

He was back in the mill as a child, standing next to Lydia. They had been such friends before then and grew apart little by little until the stay at this hospital. After that everything changed and they were no longer close.

"You let me down David, you let me down," she had said.

He probably had let her down, he thought many times since. Memories came flooding to him. Playing ball in the field, seeing the light in the mill window and the decision to go in and investigate. Oh, he had been so arrogant and full of himself.

Even at that young age he loved Lydia, loved her family and had intended to be part of it for the rest of his life. That evening had been a chance to prove how strong and brave he was. He had learnt since that the slow game proves more satisfying, if only he could stand it.

He remembered the feeling of those hands and fingers on his back. That finger, a pointy finger, had started at the top of his head and had then moved slowly down to his neck. He had shivered and goose bumps appeared all over his body. He shivered even now at the memory.

257

The finger moved down his back and then across to his shoulder. Rigid with fear, he had looked across at the girl he intended to impress and all he could think of was not wetting his trousers. Tears rose in his eyes and he became painfully aware that Lydia could see him cry. She seemed as strong and resolute as ever.

The finger moved over his shoulder and then the hand suddenly grabbed his arm and shoved him firmly against the door. As David moved towards the door, he caught sight of the man thing that was assaulting them. It was the face to which he was to become accustomed during his adult years.

And he didn't like it.

He remained face up against the door, incapable of experiencing anything other than a paralysis of mind and body. He felt the shuddering and then it was over almost as soon as it had begun. Lydia tapped him on the back and said, "David, are you alright? You look so white and frightened." And adding for good measure, "Have you been crying?"

"No. I haven't," he had replied. He was upset that Lydia seemed to be able to move and he didn't. "What just happened?"

"I am not really sure. I know that it hurt and was wrong and, and he smelled terrible."

"We have to go and tell Inspector Glees and our keepers." David had wanted to take charge of the situation and this was all he could think of doing.

Lydia was forceful. "No, no we can never tell anyone about this."

"Why on earth not?"

"He said he would seek out and kill our families. I believed him. He said he has been watching us for years and what's more, he is going to see me again."

"Where?"

"I don't know. He said he liked my company and felt better for seeing me."

"We should still tell."

"No. He said that if I didn't keep company with him, he would keep company with my sisters. I can't risk that."

But, David could not keep quiet and he had told his father and his reward was a good hiding.

Mr Turncoat had then taken him to the police station on Town Street and Inspector Glees had laughed out loud and told him that it sounded as though he was going a bonkers.

Later that day the Inspector grabbed David while he walked back from school on his own. He held him by the neck and said that if he caught him talking about the mill or anyone he may or may not have seen there, he would personally see to it that David was taken away. David knew that he had that power. So he kept quiet, very quiet from then on.

But, as the weeks passed Lydia would not keep quiet. She never mentioned to anyone other than David what had happened at the mill. But she would no longer do as she was told and caused a lot of trouble in class.

There were interviews with teachers, keepers and Doctor Catapult and the two ended up here. For their own good, apparently.

"David!" the Doctor shouted.

"Ummm?" he could hardly hang on to consciousness.

"I will leave you here. I've done all I can for you."

Doctor Catapult switched off the light as he left the room. He closed the door and David became vaguely aware of shuffling footsteps.

When his keepers left him in the surgery after that interview, David felt desolated and small. After a few minutes he had been led into the hospital by the Doctor's sister. Of the two sisters, he had been too young to know which was which. They used to be kind, he remembered when they played there in the afternoons after school and brought tea and cake. But, when he was brought to the hospital, they were very short with him. They pushed the small boy and jabbed him in the back with a sharp object which he later discovered was a key. A big, brass, jabby key.

Pushed into the hospital room that day, he had been terrified and he never forgot the experience. He was as scared as the night at the mill?

The sisters laid him onto a bed in one of the little rooms in the hospital, bright and white and shiny. Then they put him in a white gown and examined him and gave him some medicine and various ointments. Sometimes this happened when he was in the hospital and sometimes in a room in the Doctor's house. Never did his parents visit and never did he see anyone else.

Except of course for Lydia.

Lydia. At that memory he came back to consciousness a little. He'd forgotten that until just now. That Lydia was at the hospital the same time as David was. He kept forgetting that.

"You let me down David. You let me down." He remembered her saying that now. What had he done to let her down?

260

He sat up in the dark, trying to go over the past few minutes. Lydia dead? Was that possible? The room was empty now except for him. It was dark and cold but in some way that was helping him get together again. He put his feet onto the floor and had a look at them.

He had little feet, as all the inhabitants of Mill Town possessed. They were clad in blue and white shoes, made by the shoemaker on Town Street. He kept details of everyone's sizes and made shoes for each person once a year. He knew when there was an arrival from Finders and when there had been a cart departing and adjusted his stock accordingly. Some say he knew before anyone else did, so that he never held incorrect stock.

"Why am I thinking of that? Must be the shock," he said out loud.

He stood up and walked carefully over to the door. It was locked. That was confusing. He felt his way along the wall until he found a door at the back of the room. This should lead to the next room, but this was locked also.

"Hello Doctor! Can you let me out please?"

No answer. He tried again and eventually began hammering on the door and shouting but there was no response.

"This is ridiculous," he said to no one in particular. He felt the need to stop noticing the hammering heart and the wobbly legs. He went to sit on the bed and was soon lying down as he felt so weak.

Closing his eyes, David allowed his mind to wander back twenty years. After a few examinations followed by sweets and cakes, David was getting used to the routine. He hated the examinations but knew that as soon as the sweets were placed in front of him, it was all over until the next time.

One night, while he sat alone in his dark little room in the Doctor's house, he heard noises in the room next door. There was shouting and scuffling and more shouting followed by silence. He heard a door slam and footsteps moving away.

"Hello! Doctor!" he had cried out. The footsteps stopped and he thought he heard voices, but soon the steps moved again and there was nothing else until morning. As was usual there was a click as the door was unlocked and then opened by a Catapult sister, bearing a tray of food and drink.

"I heard noises last night. Is someone else here?" he dared to ask.

"How clever of you to notice, David. Someone else did arrive last night, but you needn't bother yourself about who it is. All we need to do is concentrate on getting you better. Now there won't be any examinations today. The Doctor has to look after our new patient."

That was the end of his examinations. Doctor Catapult seemed to lose interest in him after Lydia arrived for her hospital stay.

David did not see Lydia for three days and when he did he was shocked at the change in her. Prior to that he had seen her at school, arguing with the teachers about the benefits of the subjects they were teaching the children. She was always questioning.

Lydia looked pale and drawn and her eyes darted from him to the window, then the door and never focussed on anything.

"Are you alright Lydia?" he had asked in a faint voice.

"Do I look it?" was her only answer.

They had met on the landing of the Doctor's house. David had been accompanied down to the hospital for some medicine and on the way back to his room, Lydia was being taken out by a Miss Catapult. Her dress was dishevelled and she looked dirty.

"Come on, bath time," encouraged the old woman and Lydia moved along with her. Looking back Lydia winked at her friend and gave him the thumbs up. It had seemed so strange.

That night, he heard someone knocking at his bedroom door and an urgent voice telling him to come out. He was greatly surprised to see with Lydia when the door opened. She held up a key and said, "I stole it from the sister. Let's get out of here before she finds out what I've done."

David followed her out, but was a little worried that they might get caught. He was tempted to stay where he was, but her sharp tugging at his elbow brought him out into the dark corridor. They looked out of the window onto the driveway and the gate and lane beyond. The lights of Cal's house glimmered and they could see the horrible pair moving around their room.

"What are we going to do Lydia?" he asked.

"Don't know really. I want to just leave, but if I go home my keepers will send me straight back. I could go to Gran's, but she might get into trouble. I thought of just running away."

"Where to?"

"Seaside I think. I heard you can be free there. If the land gets too bad then you can go to sea."

"Oh, I don't know about that," answered David.

263

There were noises behind them which caused them to turn around. As they did, they came to face to face with a small boy and girl who were smaller and younger than them. These other children were poorly dressed, thin and smelt of moss.

"Where are you from?" asked Lydia.

"We are from the Town. The doctor keeps us here."

"Why?" asked David.

They did not answer, but melted into the shadows so quickly that Lydia and David wondered if they had imagined their presence. They looked at each other and then moved towards the end of the landing.

There was the door which led down to the hospital and together they made their way through the unlocked door. The revealed stairway led down to the hospital and the children ran swiftly down.

"I want to see what goes on down here. When I am brought for examinations, I just get pushed into the first room and I know there are other rooms. I've heard screaming coming from some of them." David was glad that he could talk about what had been happening to him during his stay here.

"So have I. But I haven't always been brought to the hospital, sometimes I've been taken to the cellar," Lydia informed him, though with less enthusiasm.

"Have you? Why?"

"Apparently the Doctor is writing about my case and doesn't want to be disturbed."

"Oh."

"Sometimes other people come. He said it is important."

"Oh." David didn't really know what to say.

264

They arrived at the corridor of the hospital and their little shoes clicked on the white tiled floor. The lamps were only half lit and there were shadows dancing upon the walls.

Some of the doors were locked and the children knocked on each one asking if anyone was there. They got an answer from only three.

"Who are you?" asked Lydia.

"Timmy," he said. "I'm from the Moor. I have to be here for examinations."

"Why?" asked Lydia

"Don't know," the boy answered. "Been naughty I think. But so long as I am good and do whatever I'm told, they said that I can go home soon."

"What about your keepers?" David wanted to know.

"They don't know where I am. Because I was naughty, the policeman took me away."

"We will let you out," said Lydia as she pulled the door.

"No, No." The boy insisted. "If I'm naughty again I won't be able to go home."

His cries were so loud that Lydia and David decided to leave him there for the time being. At two other doors, there were answers from children, but none wanted to leave.

"We have to get help," insisted Lydia.

"I know. We have to think of a plan."

"Thinking isn't going to do much. We have to take action." Lydia found a large cane and began to try and batter down the door. The only result of that was being grabbed by the Doctor and two other men from the village who must have entered from the surgery end of the corridor and soon the two were being thrown back into their rooms.

Two days later, David was sent home to Turncoat Farm under strict instructions to never speak of what he had seen or experienced or his family would suffer.

Lydia always believed he had let her down, but the boy had determined to play the long game. He behaved and conformed and joined the right committees and became a respected and trusted member of the Council, determined to break it.

He had seen many things on the journey that he never wanted to share with anyone and part of him wondered if he had forgotten his original intentions. Perhaps he had.

Now Lydia was dead and he was to blame.

CHAPTER SEVENTEEN *LYDIA DIED*

As soon as Lydia went through the door, she knew she was in trouble.

The memories of twenty years ago came back to her in a flash. The two women looked at each other. Lydia's mouth opened in horror and Miss Catapult's face set to stone.

"You horrible woman! How could you? All those children, they trusted you."

"Don't make judgements on subjects you know nothing about." All pretence at conviviality had gone.

"But I do know, you old witch. You are not getting away with anything anymore. You were safer when I had forgotten."

"You don't think I'm safe now? You are the one who is in danger Lydia, not me." Her grin was horrible and showed not one ounce of compassion.

Hillary stopped talking, while making the assessment that just at this moment, she was not in a position to make too much of a fuss.

"Well my girl, if you have remembered everything, then you will know what is going to happen next."

Miss Catapult grabbed the younger girl's arm and pushed her smartly down the stairs. Lydia did not, indeed, could not, resist.

It was as though her feet could not reach the floor. Miss Catapult had super strength and she forced her charge through the doors leading to the corridor in the hospital and towards a familiar door on the left.

Inside, while Lydia blinked in order to get used to the light, Miss Catapult let go of her arm and left her standing in the middle of the room. A lamp was lit and the surroundings revealed. In front of Lydia stood her Uncle Cal and next to him were Inspector Glees and Peter Burgess.

She knew she was in trouble, she had been here before. These people were Shudder trained and Shudder loyal.

Her memory had returned.

It had been day two of her childhood hospital stay that she had been introduced one by one to the members of the Council. She was taken down to the hospital by a sister and taken into this very room. A large tub of water stood in the corner and she was directed to the same and ordered to undress and wash.

"You smell of the poor Lydia, you must wash."

Red faced and full of shame at these words, she slowly and shyly undressed and sat in the water, soon discovering that it was ice cold. The sister stood over her, looking very stern and crossing her hands in front of her body. She held a brass key.

"I don't smell," said Lydia.

"Oh yes you do Lydia. Everyone thinks it, it's just that no one says it," she added. "All your family smell of the poor."

Lydia hid her face by letting her hair fall forwards. She knew she was blushing and didn't want the old woman to see her. She washed quickly using the bar of rhubarb soap which had been handed to her. Smelly indeed. How could she say that! They all bathed twice a week. It wasn't possible to bathe more often, because there were so many of them.

It didn't help that her keepers actively discouraged them wasting soap and water, they needed any extra money for themselves, apparently.

As she finished she asked, "Where are my clothes?"

"They are going in the wash. You can put on that gown from the back of the chair."

The yellow gown looked more like a nightie and as Lydia put it on she thought that it made her look younger than she was and she didn't like that. Mind you she didn't like much of what was going on at the moment. The whole thing was very discombobulating.

The sister roughly brushed Lydia's hair and pushed her out of the door.

"Where are we going?" asked Lydia.

"Nowhere for nosies," was the answer.

Lydia followed the woman out of the hospital and into the surgery via an outside path. The change in temperature shocked the little girl so recently out of water and her regular clothes. She shivered and said, "I'm not frightened."

"I don't care," said the sister.

Nothing more was said, even when the cellar door was opened and Lydia dragged down the steps. There was a table and chair in the corner of the room and Lydia was instructed to sit there and wait until called for.

As Lydia watched the sister walk into a further room and close the door, she took note of her immediate surroundings. There was always a chance that an escape route could be found, although the escape destination was not clear. On the table was a pad and paper and so Lydia began doodling on it. She wrote a message to herself, hoping that it would give her confidence.

Lydia became aware of a presence in the room and as she looked up from her writing she came face to face with a girl about her age.

"Hello Lydia," said the girl.

"Hello," Lydia answered.

"It's going to be horrible for you for a bit Lydia. I wish I could stop it. Lots of us have been there, but you are not going to realise how you can escape yet."

"That's not very helpful."

"I know, but until you have been through some horrible stuff you won't be able to get strong."

"I don't know what you mean."

"I mean, Lydia, that a person's strength is directly related to the magnitude of problems they have faced…"

"Whose idea is that?"

"And the way these problems have been overcome. It's not anyone's idea. It's just how it is."

"Why is it that?" Lydia could be forgiven for being irritated by the statements by this ghostly, wispy, serious looking girl.

"Because we are always what and how we think. If we choose to see that, then the strength and power and freedom which come to us know no limits."

"What if we don't?"

"Then Shudder has us in his power. If we believe we are powerless, then we are. We are always at the beck and call of someone or something else."

"If that's true, why are you down this cellar?" Lydia asked reasonably.

"I'm helping the others," she said.

The door in the corner of the room opened and Doctor Catapult appeared.

"Hello Lydia. All ready for the tests are you?"

"No. Tests? What tests?"

The Doctor took her by the arm and lifted her sharply from the chair. Lydia noticed the young ghostly girl blow her a kiss and mouth silently.

"Rise above it Lydia. Rise above it. Rise so high they can't reach you."

He took her through the door and into a kitchen area. Turning around she saw a bed and some comfortable chairs. The bed was made up in pink and a dolly and a bear were snuggly propped up against the pillow. Sat upon the chairs and looking uncomfortable, were the Inspector and her Uncle Cal.

Someone was sitting on the sofa, but she couldn't make out who that was. He was covered with a large shawl and cape, made from some sort of brown sacking.

Pushed in the back and forced to walk nearer to the group, Lydia realised that the brown caped man emitted chattering sounds as though his teeth were banging together quickly. He seemed to be having a high-pitched conversation with himself. The others were ignoring him.

Lydia resisted the pushing and tried to stand still and turn and run away.

"No point doing that little Liddy. This has to be done and we are all here to witness it. It's important," he said, in no way making her feel more comfortable with the situation.

Lydia was scared and had no idea what was happening. Doctor Catapult stopped pushing her and dragged her onto the bed.

"Get on the bed Lydia and lie down." In a trance, she did as she was told.

The caped figure did not move, but the other men stood around the bed as Lydia manoeuvred into the centre. She took hold of the dolly and then the bear and hugged them to her body.

The three men grabbed hold of her arms and legs and the tall chattering figure stood up and moved to the end of the bed. He removed the cape from his head and revealed his long face and teeth. He appeared to be made from leathery twigs. He still chattered and clicked and muttered and shuddered. The men began chanting and he moved onto the bed.

Lydia went rigid with terror and closed her eyes. Suddenly remembering what the girl had told her only a few minutes before, "Rise above it Lydia!"

Lydia let go of the terror and the room and the situation and rose above it. She rose to the ceiling and with only a quick glance at the bed, she floated right out of the room and through the wall.

Now, in a library, she saw at least twenty children sat around a large table. The girl from the first room was there too.

"You remembered Lydia."

"Yes I did," she said. "It worked. Am I dead?"

272

"We all are," was the answer. "The difference is that you have to go back. We can stay here!"

Going back was not a welcome prospect. The group of children looked as though they regularly sat around the table, meeting and discussing.

"What happens now?" enquired Lydia.

"We enjoy ourselves!" said the girl and she moved silently towards another door. Holding the handle of the far door, she turned and said to Lydia, "Come on Lydia, we've got things to do. Let's go."

Lydia followed her out of the room which echoed with shouts from the others. "Be quick Tamson! Shudder will not stay there forever."

"I know! Don't worry about us."

They went through a little stone room and Tamson opened another door and they were in a tunnel. The tunnel was dimly lit and warm.

Lydia felt at home here. So apparently did lots of children. They played here and there, sitting or crouching on the dusty ground. Some walked along holding hands or chasing each other. Girls and boys, some were shabbily dressed, while others were smart.

"Why are there so many children, Tamson?"

"Most worked at the mill and were taken by the Council. Others just lived in Mill Town or Village and ended up here. This was the only place they could escape to."

"Did the same things happen to the children that happened to me?"

"Yes, sort of."

Lydia watched the children play for a while before she followed Tamson further up the tunnel. Child after child

273

passed them as they walked. All seemed happy and waved and smiled at Lydia and Tamson as they walked towards the far end of the tunnel.

"Let's go a bit further, come on quickly!"

"Don't I have much time left?"

"You are extraordinary Lydia!" she exclaimed. "There is no such thing as time now!"

With this alarming thought they proceeded along the tunnel until they came to a door on their left.

"That leads to an evil house. Cal's."

"Oh," answered Lydia.

They carried on, passing another door to the left.

"That leads to the air raid shelters." As Tamson said this, a group of giggling girls pushed open the door from the other side, saw Lydia and Tamson, curtseyed and ran off again.

They walked on and after a little while arrived at a large wooden door.

"This leads to the mill," Tamson informed her.

"I've been in the mill."

"I know."

"It was horrible, it changed my life."

"You met Shudder for the first time. But it didn't change your life Lydia. You knew years ago that you would be coming here and have a serious job to do. You will work it out eventually."

"You mean I have to go back? I don't want to go back."

"I know, you will leave a few more times yet, but will always go back. Once you have finished what you started, you can do as you please. I promise. Do you want to have a look in the mill?"

"I suppose so." All this talk was confusing her, even though there was a small part of her thought that this was not the first time she had been given the information.

Tamson led the way confidently through the door and they stood in a small office. There was a man sitting in a chair, smoking a pipe. He had his eyes closed and snoozed gently. He seemed very content and was not disturbed by their presence. Lydia was worried because she did not want to be caught by the security guard.

"He can't see us, silly!"

They walked past him into a reception area and Lydia wondered vaguely whether they could move through the man and put out her hand to a lamp on the counter. It smashed. The man jumped up, dropping his pipe in the process and burnt his leg. The girls laughed as they watched him alternate between brushing his legs and looking round to see what had happened.

They went through the huge doors, Lydia recalling the time when she had come here with her friends. It wasn't dark and terrifying today, however.

The noise in there was almost deafening. It was of men and women scurrying here and there amongst the golden cloth and embroidery which waved from the big looms. Everyone looked so happy and jolly and the atmosphere was welcoming. Lydia liked this place.

Tamson's beaming face turned to Lydia and became solemn as she said to her, "If you don't solve the problem, it will be as though this never happened. All the children must be freed. These children have gone missing for years and years and the tunnel is full. The Town can't hold onto these problems any longer. Everyone's future is being dragged down now. You must go back." Lydia became agitated, she didn't want to go back. Not ever.

Hearing noises behind her, she turned to face a mass of children.

"Please Pixie, help us. Without you we can never be free." The begging came as a crescendo and Lydia put her hands to her ears.

"Alright! I'll go back," she screamed.

Seconds later she was on the bed in the cellar, curled up and sobbing.

"I thought you'd killed her," said Cal.

"That medicine never fails," said the Doctor. There was no sign of Shudder, but his smell remained.

"Get up girl!" instructed Doctor Catapult. She did so, but felt so old and so tired. The weight of the world was now about her shoulders. She slithered off the bed, noting how untidy she was and made a slow and painful progress out of the room and up the stairs.

Oh yes, Lydia remembered everything. Now would begin the end of Shudder and his horrid band. She would see to that.

CHAPTER EIGHTEEN *HE KNOWS*

Lydia wasn't shaking anymore. Neither was she nervous, scared, frightened, tense or tearful. Lydia had remembered everything that had happened to her.

Dying is easy and not to be feared. Death is not the worst that can happen. Even terrible torture can be escaped if a person remembers to rise above it.

Good people go to Beyond and do not have to fear anything there. Standing in front of this rabble did not, could not, scare Lydia. For she knew where she was going when she died and they did not. They had chosen to spend an eternity with Shudder and no one in their right mind wanted that.

"Well boys," she asked. "What are you up to?"

This is an odd reaction, thought the men and not one they were expecting at all. Where was the timid and acquiescent girl they had all come to love?

"Why have I been brought here?" Turning to sister Catapult she remarked, "You are a disgrace to women and decent people everywhere. You will pay for what you have done."

The old woman looked momentarily abashed, but soon raised her head and stared at the young woman. She could not understand the sudden change in Lydia's manner.

"Just shut up and do as you are told Lydia. It will be easier for you."

"Do you all think that you can get away with the things you have been doing to all those children? There are so many of them and none have forgotten what you did. Your punishment will be magnified by the amount of things you have done."

"What are you talking about Lydia?" asked Cal. "They are dead, they can't do anything now. Dead is dead."

"You know that isn't true Cal. You have seen enough to know that. Is Shudder dead or alive? Do you know that?" demanded Lydia.

"Shut up!" shouted the Inspector. "Dead is dead. Once you die, that's that."

Lydia laughed out loud and looked directly at each person in turn. The superior, knowing look she gave them unnerved them all. Unlikely to admit the fact to each other, they fidgeted and moved about the room.

"You are all scared aren't you? Quite right, you should be," said Lydia. She wasn't even stopping to think how confident she felt. She certainly felt much taller and straighter now. Perhaps she had been walking slightly stooped prior to this. Up to now she felt as though she had been carrying everyone's problems on her shoulders. She perhaps still felt like that, but now she knew that she could cope and that is a different feeling.

She smiled again, noting that although there were several people standing in front of her, none had made a move towards her. They must be feeling vulnerable. That's interesting, she thought. Stand up to a bully and mean it and the dynamics change.

"Well?" she asked enquiringly. "I wish to leave now."

The others looked from one to the other, before Burgess finally took control.

He grabbed Lydia's arm and pulled her towards the bed which stood in the corner of the room. The others joined him and held Lydia's arms while sister Catapult forced a potion down her throat. Unable to resist the many hands which pulled at her body and her closed mouth, she eventually had to allow the liquid to enter her mouth. Sticky and brown, part of the liquid dripped down her face. Just like Shudder, sticky and brown she thought as she slipped into unconsciousness.

"So much for her fighting talk," said Cal as he let the girl fall to the floor.

"I am not so sure about that," answered the Burgess slowly. "There was something different about her and what with all the other stuff happening, it does make you think."

"Other stuff?" asked Cal.

"You know, her being everywhere all at once since she got back. And why did she come back? She did manage to rescue Sadie and has outsmarted Shudder," Burgess replied.

"Don't ever say that about Shudder!" exclaimed Cal. He hero worshipped Shudder and disliked his fellow committee member.

"He hasn't done a great deal for you though has he?" asked Burgess. "You don't have much and your wife is hardly anyone to brag about."

"Now stop that," said the Inspector. "We don't want to break the code do we? Shudder says we must stay together even though others try and break us down."

"What are you talking about Glees? One woman can't change anything you know. Things will be as they've always been." Cal was adamant, he needed to be.

"You are very blinkered Cal, if you think one person can't change anything. Shudder did."

Bringing Shudder into the argument, Glees felt settled the question.

"Don't boss me about Glees, I know everything there is to know about you and I'm not above making it public," Cal informed him.

"Don't you threaten me you rotten little creep," he answered and hit Cal over the head with his stick. They fell about the room fighting until Burgess raised his voice and told them to behave.

"Shudder will be here soon as you well know, so stop this now. Come on, we've got to sort this girl out now. Things are getting out of hand."

They moved over to the inert figure on the floor and lifted her bodily onto the bed.

"Is she just supposed to be knocked out Miss Catapult?"

"Why do you ask?"

"Cos she seems dead to me."

"Dead?"

"Yes dead." Cal stood back from Lydia, hands on hip and looked from the Miss Catapult to Lydia.

"I know I'm not a doctor," he added, "but I've seen dead and that's dead."

Miss Catapult moved quickly towards Lydia and put her hand over the girl's nose and mouth.

"She's dead!" she said.

This pronouncement cause quite a bit of consternation amongst the others.

"You'd better let Doctor Catapult know," said Glees to the old woman.

"Right," she said. "You lot clear up here and I will tell him. He should be here soon." She swept out of the room and into the corridor. She noticed David Turncoat coming towards her, followed by the Doctor. Pulling her brother to one side, she whispered in his ear and left him to deal with the problem. She carried on along the corridor and left the building by the main door.

Shocked, but unfazed by the news he had just received, Doctor Catapult opened the door to the room and led in David. The girl was lying on a bed, covered with a sheet.

He gave David the news of her death and was amused to see how the young man crumbled under the weight of it. Ensuring that David was safe, partly inert in another bed, he carried on with the job in hand.

Burgess, the Inspector and Cal opened a connecting door and he beckoned them to help him move the bed containing the dead girl from the room.

"She just died!" said Cal, immediately. He didn't want to be associated with yet another death.

"She can't have just died," answered the Doctor in an impatient way.

"Well she did," said Cal.

"After your sister gave her that medicine," the Inspector informed him.

"Oh no. She is stupid. Why didn't you stop her Cal?"

"Don't you start making this my fault Drug. You always try and make things my fault."

281

"If it wasn't for you messing about all those years ago, we wouldn't have the Shudder problem at all."

Burgess and the Inspector listened intently to the exchange. Many rumours abounded amongst the group that the Catapult family had brought Shudder back from the place he had been imprisoned many hundreds of years ago by casting a spell or opening a book or some such thing.

Drug Catapult leapt across the room and put his hands around the throat of his brother Cal. They hated each other, always had done. The two men rolled around the floor, punching, slapping, scratching and squealing. No one heard the door open or saw the entrance of the sticky, brown chattering creature they all counted as their hero.

A high-pitched screech and increase of the chatter brought them all to their senses. If sense was what it could be called. They looked in shock, hair tousled and clothes in disarray.

Shudder pointed at the two fighting men and his eyes burned a brighter shade of red than usual. He moved over to them and slapped the two men hard. They fell to their knees, heads bowed as Shudder screeched and chattered.

"We are sorry Shudder!" shouted the Doctor.

Shudder turned to look at the dead body of Lydia and moved jerkily towards her. He put out his hand and touched her. His long stick forefinger shot out from his fist and reached the top of her head. He moved it down her hair, the back of her neck and back.

Her body rose and fell under the pressure of his touch. He moved further down her body, moving from side to side and his chattering changed to a sighing and moaning as he did so.

"She's dead," Cal informed his master.

Shudder stopped his fondling of Lydia's body and turned slowly to Cal. He stared at the man and chattered in a higher pitched tone than usual.

Cal appeared to understand him and stood up. He moved over to Lydia and pushed the trolley bed away from the group. He moved the bed out of another door and into a back room. This was not as the other hospital rooms, clean and white and shiny. This room was made from stone and was very small. Once Cal had shut the door behind him, he shuffled round the bed and pushed a stone on the far wall. A door of stones opened and revealed a ramp going down.

Because the ramp was dark and uninviting, Cal hesitated for a few seconds, but the sound of chattering and screeching in the other room encouraged him to move on quickly down the stone walkway. It was cold and creepy travelling down here. It reminded Cal of when he was a boy and had been sent down to this same cellar. He hadn't like doing that, the examinations and the punishments. But it had all turned out for the best, Shudder was his friend. Well perhaps not his friend, but they were part of the same team. He was part of something important and now fully understood the need for these examinations. Children were born useless and if some didn't make it through those examinations, it just proved how weak they were.

He could hear voices and scuttling about. He didn't like that. He made further progress down into the cellar rooms, coming out into the library. Manoeuvring past the big table he again heard voices.

"Cal, O Cal!" the voices said.

"Shut up," he answered. "You don't scare me."

The sound of children laughing didn't help his manoeuvring of the bed. Bending down and pushing in one

283

direction the wheels insisted on going the other way. He became aware of eyes staring at him and he looked up quickly, but saw nothing.

It was an uncomfortable thing for Cal to admit, he never would to anyone else, only to himself, but as he got older he was becoming a lot more scared.

He had just small shadows of doubt about some of the things he had done or watched happen. He knew about the kidnappings and the deaths, some going back further than the oldest person's memory and he had not cared. Even now, he did not care about the children themselves. He cared about what may happen to him.

He had heard tales, mentioned by some of the old folk that those who died after leading an unacceptable life had a different passing. It was true, they said that a cart came to fetch them, but the stories of the place the cart took them to and the rebirths in Finders were alarming.

The two lamps in the library went out and left Cal with only the flickering light from the fire in the grate. The fire was nearly out and subsequently very little light was available.

Cal eventually pushed the bed through the doors, into the little waiting room and after more pushing and twiddling, he arrived in the tunnel. Why was it even darker in the tunnel? It was as though this was planned to unnerve him to the limit.

Shudder had instructed Cal to take the body to his own house and hide it there until he received further instructions. As he pushed the bed down the tunnel, he was becoming as worried about the reaction he would get from his wife as much as the voices he could hear and the darkness of the tunnel.

Cal was relieved to reach the door on the left which led to his house. He had never felt so worried in his life, his adult life anyway. Perhaps, yes perhaps he could just remember how scared he had been as a little boy, when his father, his trusted old Doctor father, had first brought him down into the cellar. Cal stopped pushing, because his legs were shaking so badly that he could no longer proceed. He was sweating and crying and could hear children's' voices.

"Cal, Cal. Remember us Cal?" he heard.

In the darkness and the shadows, he thought he saw children running and skipping about. He braced himself against the bed and pushed hard, bashing through the door to his house tunnel and hearing the door slam behind him. He parked the bed up and made his way along the tunnel.

Within a couple of minutes he was through the next door and standing in his sitting room. His lazy, fat wife was sitting in a chair by the fire, smoking a pipe and working her way through a rhubarb mousse. She looked up from her troughing and said, "Well my love, where have you been until now? You said you were going to come straight back." She took another bite, and without waiting for his answer said, "What have you been doing? You look all sweaty and bothered. You haven't been messing and shaming again, have you?"

"No. No I haven't. What do you mean? You are always accusing me of something, you old cow. I have just been doing my Council duty, same as I always do. Nothing else. Stop accusing me and blaming me. If it weren't for me and the others, the Town would go to rack and ruin. Leave me alone."

He stopped and caught his breath, looking in the dirty mirror which hung on the cottage wall and noted his white

285

scared face and the sweat marks on the underarms of his shirt. Should he tell the old trout about the body in the tunnel?

She would go mad he knew. Not about the fact Lydia was dead, she wouldn't care about that. No, she would care about him having to do more work than the other committee members.

"What are you up to for the rest of the day?" he asked her.

"Working around here, I should think. Plenty of housework to be done, this place doesn't clean itself," she spat out.

A casual observer might have noted that not only did the house not clean itself, but there was little evidence that anyone else was cleaning it. The place was and always had been a filthy hovel. The previous owners of the cottage would have been disappointed to see the carefully manicured garden and beautifully kept house in the state it was in now.

The birds and bats had left not long after the Cals arrived and nothing would grow in the garden, not anymore. The rocks and stones which used to make up the walls around the field had fallen into the garden and covered up any chance of green growth. The cottage was filthy, smelly and nasty. Fluff and dust lined the sides of the rooms and the stairs. It was only the pair of them moving through the property that disturbed the dirt and pushed it to the sides. The toilet room was disgusting and needs no further mentioning. The bedrooms stunk and the Prix children had memories of childhood visits and could recall the dirt and smells with a quick close of their eyes.

The kitchen had to be seen to be believed. The stove had wet socks and pants dangling over the metal bar which stretched from one side to the other. The wall next to the stove was discoloured and covered in mush and stains. The bin underneath it was rarely full, because all rubbish was only thrown in its general direction, firstly hitting the wall and then slithering down and eventually falling on the floor.

Every few months Cal got a shovel and dragged the rubbish out of the back door and scraped it down the three stone steps which led to the path. Cal shaved in the kitchen and there was evidence of years of whiskers over the kitchen worktops, sink, table and floor. Neighbours didn't like to eat there, nor did his Shudder chums.

Cal was aware that his wife knew about the tunnel, but it was rare for her to go down. She was afraid of the dark and the spiders and also the beatings which Cal would inflict on her if she made a move to go there. Her knowledge of the tunnel consisted of childhood experiences of the kind which many a Mill Town child had known over the years. For that reason, she very rarely entered it. It was unlikely that she would find Lydia's body.

He looked back over at his wife, who was still shovelling rhubarb into her face. She was in her favourite chair facing the kitchen door. The chair on the other side of the fire which faced the front window belonged to Cal and he sat in it now, picking up and lighting his pipe. As he puffed and drew on the pipe he tried to think about what he should do next.

Shudder had told him to hide the body at his cottage and failure to do so would be met with punishment. Cal didn't like punishment. Childhood punishment had been metered out to him by Shudder and his cronies in the same

287

way they had done it to many other children. Joining the team as an adult had not ensured that he would never be punished again, but at least he got to join in the fun a lot.

The initiation with all those Prix children had meant that he was a trusted member of the inner circle from early on in his Shudder career. Oh Happy Days!

But they were long gone now, the excitement he had felt when first accepted was not so excitedly felt these days. He needed to commit more and more acts in order to try to satisfy this hunger which could not be satisfied.

But no one or nothing could punish him more than Shudder – could they?

CHAPTER NINETEEN *HE AIN'T HEAVY*

As soon as Cal went through his door, Lydia swung her legs over the side of the bed and jumped down. Although it was dark, Lydia had no problem in seeing where she was.

It was true that the medicine given to her by Miss Catapult was meant as a sedative, but she had not swallowed. She held it in her mouth and while the others were messing about, had spat it onto the floor. She decided to rise above it as she had been so recently taught, but this time she concentrated on her breathing and not on the dramas which occurred around her. As soon as she got into this mind-set, she discovered that she was aware of all that was said and done around her, even while feigning death.

She was not becoming aware through tension, but through acceptance and relaxation. She had heard everything that had been said. And now it was time to act.

She made her way back to the tunnel door and walked through it. Turning left, Lydia walked quickly along, reminding herself that only a few days ago she had no conscious knowledge of the place and now it almost felt like home. Lydia was aware that the dead children were mooching about, but she acted as though she were one of them, nodding and smiling where necessary.

289

Here was the door on the left wall which she knew must lead to the air raid shelters.

Tamson had told her to meet her there and she guessed that now was as good a time as any. The door moved easily and soon she was walking along. After a few steps, passing a door on the left, she stopped and stepped back to it.

There was a sign on the door which read:

Pixie Prix was born here

Viewings by appointment only

That's mad, she thought. But what was a girl to do? She must check it out of course.

She pushed open the door and found herself in yet another tunnel. Only this one was different. It was decorated with tiny little lamps instead of the large lamps situated everywhere else.

Oh and by the way, she said to herself. Who lights and maintains all those lamps anyway?

Returning her mind to the job in hand, she noted the pictures and small dollies tied with ribbon. They bore notes such as:

Help my keeper, Pixie, he has backache

Dear Pixie my mummy is poorly, please look after her

My doggy is ill

Make me pretty, Pixie

And so on. These dollies were tied in bunches around the walls, while along the edges of the floor were shiny little presents and gifts.

Lydia picked some up and ran her hands over others. Was Pixie some kind of good luck charm for these people?

As she moved up the tunnel in the direction of her old cottage, her steps quickened even though part of her mind

290

was dreading what she might find on the other side of the door. It transpired, however, that there was no door.

The light increased as she moved along and soon she stood under hanging branches. Intermingled with the trees were flowers of every colour and scent. As she passed through it, Lydia was sure she could hear the most beautiful singing. She had tears in her eyes as she came out into the sunlight of her childhood garden.

Monday morning had arrived while she had been faffing about at the Doctor's.

Her mind came back to earth with a bump, for the garden was just as she remembered it, if a little more neglected. There were the swings they played on as children and an upturned and rotting cart. Painted in blue and black, Lydia recalled the time her Grandfather Prix had brought it round for the family to use. It was a classic old model and Treen had looked after it so well. But it had been sadly ignored by her keepers and fallen into rack and ruin as plants and weeds grew over it and furry animals and birds made it their home.

And there in the corner of the garden, bending down over his fruit and vegetable patch was her father. She had seen him briefly at Gran's when she first arrived, but it had been so long since she had seen him working in his garden in an everyday manner. She felt a huge welling of emotion within her heart.

"Hello," she said in a quiet voice. She had forgotten temporarily the harsh words spoken between the two of them when she had left in the marriage cart with Mr Pollack. Goodness that seemed a long time ago. It was as though she had never been married at all. A busy life stops time dragging, it appears.

291

She hadn't been in a state of mind to talk to her keepers at Gran's.

He stood up from his stooping position and rubbed his back as he did so. Then he pushed the hat back on his head. He was still a handsome man, but looked older and more ill than she remembered. He smiled at his eldest daughter and said, "Welcome home Lydia. You've had a lot of adventures since you came back."

"Yes," she replied, not asking the question she wanted the answer to. Why don't you care that I didn't come to see you first and what about Michaelmas?

"Your mother is inside," he informed her. "Tell her I want some tea when you go in, will you?"

It was as if she had never been away.

"Alright," she said and walked around the side of the cottage and into the kitchen.

There another surprise awaited her, for sitting with her mother at the table was David Turncoat. When he saw her, he got up, staggered about and slumped back in his chair. He was sheet white and shaking.

"Lydia I thought you were …"

"I know," she answered. "But I'm not."

Her mother, who obviously had not been told anything by David, merely smiled at Lydia and said, "Didn't your father say he was ready for his tea?"

"Yes he did. He said he would like you to make him a drink." It was as though her keepers noticed nothing outside of their own little world. It seemed best not to interfere.

"Righto, my dear. Would you like some tea? And cake perhaps? Or I have some rhubarb mousse your Auntie Cal made." She chattered away while making the tea.

292

"No. I don't want any mousse. Cake perhaps. Did you make the cake?"

"Gran Prix made the cake."

"I will have some then." Granny's cake was safe.

David had not taken his eyes off her and when their eyes met, he whispered, "Well, what happened?"

"What do you mean, David? I don't know which side you are on."

Before he could answer, her mother was back at the table.

"Now then, Lydia. Here's your tea and cake." She sat down between them.

"Why were you two arguing in the garden the other day?" Lydia asked them suddenly. She thought she might as well provoke some answers. It felt to her that time was running out.

David thought for a moment and then answered her. "We were arguing about whether to tell you something."

"I said we should keep it quiet," said her mother.

"And I wanted to tell you," said David.

"Tell me what?" Was it possible to become fed up of new information?

"You can trust me Lydia. I'm your brother."

Lydia looked puzzled. "How can you be my brother?"

Her mother spoke up.

"When we went to get you from Finders, there were two of you and we didn't want to split you up."

"We had only wanted one child, but couldn't choose between you." Everyone turned round to the doorway as her father joined in the conversation.

"Were they making you choose? I thought you booked ahead for a baby," said Lydia.

293

"We did, but we were presented with the request to take both of you and we were a bit flummoxed," her mother informed them.

"I wanted a girl," said her father.

"I wanted a boy," said Mother.

"Why did they say you must take both?" asked Lydia.

"They said it was important and we would find out in a few years' time. So, we did as we were instructed and brought you both home," Father said.

"I was here for a few weeks wasn't I?" David had his hand on Mother Prix's arm. Lydia noticed it and felt a little weird about it.

"Yes you were, my David." She patted his hand and smiled at him.

"So what happened?" Lydia was feeling quite the outsider, a situation she was used to in the cottage.

"Your father got talking to his friend Mr Turncoat." She scowled at him.

"Well, they had been waiting and waiting for a child and no boys had come and it's very hard work looking after one baby, never mind two."

"I didn't mind," her mother muttered.

"Well, I said, it's not fair us having been given two and them wanting a boy and me really wanting a girl and so it was decided that David went to Turncoats and you stayed here."

"So, if they wanted a girl it would have been me not David?"

"No, because I wanted a girl." Father Prix seemed surprised these questions were being asked of him.

294

Lydia was turning the sugar bowl round and round. She was recalling the many arguments and sniping conversations about the Turncoat family.

"One day, two weeks after you both arrived, Mr Turncoat came and took David away, only I hadn't called him David, I called him Beau. Mrs Turncoat never gave him the love I would have given him." She looked into his eyes.

"You loved me like I was your son anyway, didn't you?" said David, returning her gaze.

"You had all of us though Mother! Why didn't you love us?"

"Because you are not my first son," was the answer.

"What about Michaelmas? Don't you care about his death?"

"I care about David and always look after him."

Lydia stood up and looked around at the three other people occupying the kitchen. She said nothing more, merely walked out of the kitchen door and into the garden. As she made her way to the boughs, David caught up with her.

He grabbed her arm and said, "It's special between you and me too Lydia. Don't feel left out."

She shook her arm free and stared at him.

"Why were you arguing with her in the garden the other day?"

He seemed surprised at the question, but answered it nonetheless.

"I was worried about you and wanted her to go back to Finders and ask about that first day."

"But she wouldn't go?"

"No, she wouldn't go."

"I thought you saw my dead body."

"I did, it upset me a lot, and I was just wondering how to tell the family."

"You don't seem too bothered now."

"Well you are not dead Lydia."

"I know that, but you weren't that shocked to see me come in the kitchen."

He grinned at her and put out his arms to her. Lydia considered for a moment that he was actually mad, insane.

"David, I really, honestly do not care about you. Go back to your family, I have things to do."

She walked away from him and entered the bough of trees. Turning again she saw that he stood on the lawn, waving at her and still grinning.

Something made her glance up at her old bedroom window. Staring at her out of the window was her young self. Only, she wasn't looking at the older Lydia, she was looking over at the old mill. She looked terrified and pointed at the upper windows to which Lydia turned. The window in the first apartment on the upper floor was glowing. She must investigate that apartment again.

Thoughtfully she re-entered the tunnel, walking through the lights and the tributes.

Her whole life had been a lie. She had left Mill Town to marry and protect the family and so much was being revealed to her day after day. She felt as though she was turning into another person. Nothing seemed real.

Was it like that for everyone who lived? They think they are being one character in a play and if they ever stop to check, they discover that none of the other actors are in the same play. Or perhaps they didn't exist at all.

Everyone is just looking after themselves, and only their world is the real one. That must be how creatures like Shudder get control. No one noticed what he was doing.

It may also explain the willingness of people to take the last cart ride. Once you started realising that things were not as you think they are and all the people and family you have done things for and made sacrifices for, don't even know nor care. Well, you are left with nothing really.

Perhaps that is why the Snootys and suchlike just kept trying to earn more money. At least there was some point in that.

She suddenly remembered her father walking down to his mother's cottage on a Sunday afternoon, just to sit there at the kitchen table. Gran Prix had said how sad he was much of the time. So why did he give away David and not love the rest of us? Perhaps he was depressed or something. What kind of mother gives her son away to another family because they couldn't be bothered to wait?

Mental.

Her musings had brought her to a door which on opening, Lydia realised was the air raid shelter. Tamson stood there, or rather floated there.

"You came!" said Tamson with great enthusiasm.

"Eventually, I had a bit of a stopover on the way."

"I know. Exciting isn't it? All these adventures!"

Lydia followed the girl into the room and then down the steps of brick, which took her even further underground.

Tamson pointed to disturbed ground against one of the walls.

"That's where they are doing that mad water system for the mill."

"Yeah, the salesman told me about it. It brings water up from the stream by valves I think. They need it for the new apartments."

"Yes and that will mean that there is less water for the rest of the village and their animals. Come on Pixie, we need to trot on."

The girls moved swiftly on down the brick steps until they reached the oak panelled hallway. Hundreds of doors lined the corridor to the left and the right. Each had a glass case mounted on the wall to one side. In each case were pictures of young people, dressed in fashions spanning a hundred years.

"All the missing children live here now," said Tamson.

"They can't be missing then."

"Nobody likes a smart Alec, Pixie. They cannot go back to their old lives and they can't go back to Beyond, not yet anyway. Not until the way is clear."

"How's that going to happen?" she asked, recognising that their freedom was probably going to depend on her in some way. Maybe she would have to go through some sort of torture and drama. She wondered if there was a well-paid job that required those qualifications. She would be able to make some good money at that.

They reached the end of the corridor and stood in front of a set of double doors. They were a set of very tall and wide double oak doors.

"We are here," Tamson informed Lydia.

"So, apart from the obvious fact I am standing in front of a big set of doors, what exactly does that mean?"

"Do the doors remind you of anywhere?"

"No." She thought for a moment. "Unless you mean the doors at the mill?"

Tamson smiled.

"Perhaps my master lives on the other side of the doors," she said.

Lydia suddenly went cold. Up to that point she had assumed that Tamson was a good girl, but what if it turns out that she was with the other side? Pushing open the doors with surprising ease in spite of their size, Lydia made her way beyond the door and found herself back in the old mill.

CHAPTER TWENTY *CAL BETRAYED*

As soon as his wife had staggered upstairs, Cal jumped up from his chair and went back through the tunnel door.

Sitting in the room in an agony of tension for the rest of the night, drumming his fingers on the chair arm while his wife had twittered and moaned about everyone in the village, had almost driven him insane. Now it was Monday morning, yet another day and he still had problems to deal with.

As soon as his wife decided that she needed the toilet room, he had the chance to escape. But his relief from anxiety was short lived when he returned to the hospital bed and discovered it empty. The only evidence of occupation was a sheet which was falling off the side and trailing on the floor.

He stared at the bed in total disbelief, alternately putting his hands behind his head and to his sides. In spite of this action, Lydia did not reappear on the bed.

"Shudder is actually going to kill me," he said to himself.

That was true, although the chances were that he would not kill him immediately.

Cal moved the sheets around and shook them in a style which would be recognised by his wife. Hopefully and with no method, he expected the set of keys to turn up, or the body. Neither did.

He walked down his house tunnel and arrived at the door to the main tunnel and opened it. Peeping outside, he looked to the right and the left. In the darkness, he saw the fleeting shadows of children dressed in old, dirty and ragged clothes.

They frightened him now. In all his adventures with Shudder and his contemporaries, he had beaten, bullied and played with these children and seen many die in front of his eyes.

No cart had come to fetch any of the children and this fact reiterated his belief that all those children were inherently bad. Shudder had told Cal that he was also bad and must act in the instructed way if he wanted to avoid an eternity of exclusion.

He shut the door and leant against it. His sweating, shaking body was no longer his friend and companion. He certainly didn't feel like playing with any of the children now.

He walked back into his cottage, through the sitting room and kitchen and out of the back door. Walking into the back garden and looking left he could see Lydia walking into her keepers' garden.

He was not surprised to see her alive, just annoyed. And frightened.

He turned quickly and ran down his drive, across Mill Lane and down the drive to the Doctor's house. As he ran across the lawn, he looked over to the house and seeing no one he made his way to the hospital.

When he ran into the building, he did not go down the corridor. He went into the room which was only used by the brothers in times of crisis. Father Doctor had kept the children locked in here for hours and sometimes days at a time, when the upstairs bedrooms were fully occupied with children from the mill.

He pushed his way through the door and the familiar melancholy which enveloped him as he entered the room, dropped on him yet again.

An observer might ask why no villagers noticed the disappearance of all those children. The only children who worked in the mill had been collected directly from Finders, thanks to an arrangement with one or two of the nurses there. No keepers looked after them or gave them a name.

Others that vanished, the ones who had belonged to decent homes, were lovingly searched for and mourned. Years of prayers and tears to a higher power had resulted in the gravestones and memorials materialising and waiting until the prayers could be properly answered. The sad thing was that very few knew that their prayers were in solid form, noticed and protected. They would have had more faith in themselves had they known. They might also have been more careful of what they wished for, because thoughts are things.

Someone was going to free the children and the lost. She just had to free herself first. Someone was praying for that too. When that worked, the final cart would be full to bursting.

But of course, there are those who have hurt and abused. Cal knew the tales from his encounters and meetings. They had learned more than the ordinary townsfolk, for Shudder insisted that everything was known by his followers, in order for it to be negated.

It was said in the old writings that those who have been hurt, sent up prayers and curses, some very terrible and frightening in their pain. These had created curse memorials which would be honoured one day.

Cal had heard that once the final cart comes for bad people, the destination depended on how many good stone memorials and how many bad he had collected. That was a worrying prospect. But perhaps it would be alright though. Shudder said to them all that he had the final say.

"He does have the final say, he's my master!" said Cal out loud.

There was giggling and sniggering around him. Cal stopped breathing.

He held his breath for a minute or more in the way he had done as a boy when father keeper had dragged him from his bed in the dark of the night and brought him down to the cellar for Shudder and his friends to play with. He closed his eyes tightly and felt the hands and the fingers over him again and again.

He opened his eyes and saw… Things!

They weren't men or children or any animal he could recognise. They laughed and pawed and chattered and moved around the room. They floated, they did not walk or run.

Their faces were elongating and changing colour, then they opened their mouths to reveal teeth of ridiculous sharpness. They had tails, long pink, waggling tails which whipped from side to another and touched Cal. When they touched him, he screamed.

303

"Aaaaaaaaaaaaaaaaaaaaaahhhhhhhhhhhhhhhhhhhhhhhh h!"

"What is happening? Cal, pull yourself together! We need to keep our self-control now!"

It was Drug, holding the arm of his brother tightly. Seeing that this was not bringing his brother to his senses, he changed tactics and slapped his face very hard. Cal slapped him back and the brothers stared at each other.

"You ask me what is happening Drug? Everything is falling apart! They are coming for me. I know they are!"

Cal looked broken.

"Who's coming for you? We are protected, you know that."

"I don't think we are. Perhaps Shudder has stopped his protection. Perhaps he can't give it. Something's going wrong."

Drug slapped his brother again. It cannot be established whether this was for effect or pleasure.

As Cal rubbed his rapidly reddening face he stared at Drug and said, "Don't you ever do that again or I will kill you."

"Oh, just come on," said Drug, who had also been feeling the tiring sensation of doubt.

The two men walked towards the back wall and opened a cupboard there. Shelves of documents and manuscripts were moved about until Cal triumphantly held up a large roll of paper.

"I found it," he informed his brother.

"Let's have a look."

They unfurled it on the table and held it open while they poured over the details. Written in ancient script and painted in beautiful colours, they looked upon it. It was the first time either had seen it open for many years. They had been told by their mother keeper a long time ago that answers would be found there, if ever trouble loomed.

Scanning the words and pictures revealed nothing immediately obvious or helpful. There were details of spells and pictures of men and children.

"Shudder has the power to protect us against anything which may be thrown at us," Drug said.

"I hope he has, because I am sure something is going to happen to one of us. I've just got this feeling." Cal's sulky facial expression did not add to his good looks.

"We've got to get off to this do in half an hour."

"What do?"

"The one at the Dragon Inn. Don't tell me you have forgotten? It's important, everyone will be there."

"O Diddle. I'd forgotten. I will have to get changed."

"And washed."

"Why? What's wrong with me? I'm not going back home to get changed. She's in a funny mood. I will have to do it here. All my old stuff is here."

"I don't care. Just be ready, it reflects on me when you look scruffy."

"Reflects on you! I don't care about you! Mother was always telling me that you think too much of yourself and I agree with her. I was her favourite. She loved me the best." Cal left the room and went into the house to get changed. Drug followed, muttering.

"Mother's favourite were you? I don't think so. Mother loved me the best. Father just used to do things for our own good. He said that way we would be protected forever so long as we passed the tests." He muttered the last bit without much conviction.

305

As Drug Catapult crossed his hallway and was about to mount the steps, he heard knocking at the main door. Perhaps the knocking could be better described as hammering, because not only did the door appear to shake, but so did the air.

"Who could that be?" he asked, in the time honoured way.

"Don't answer the door, it will be trouble!" he heard a voice say. Looking up the stairs from where the sound seemed to originate, he noticed the lips of the fountain man move. Built after the death of his Doctor father, his death mask had been used on the fountain. The brothers had laughed as they made the hole in his lips in order that the water could pour out satisfactorily.

"He would be so cross that we used his best cane," said Cal.

"He shouldn't have used it on us," answered Drug.

"Or Mother," returned Cal.

The hammering continued and was accompanied by the shouts of, "Open this door!"

"We'll smash it in. Then we'll smash you in!"

It was the young Prix girls. Doctor Catapult wasn't scared of them. He strode over to the door and opened it, meeting the fierce little faces with the look which had quelled braver people than they.

"You have our sister in here! Where is she?" screamed Janey.

"I do not have your sister in here. I can assure you of that. What on earth are the pair of you acting like that for? Hammering on my door?"

"Necessity Ladywoman came to the cottage and told us that you had Lydia here and were torturing her."

"And that we had to get here quickly to save her, before you killed her!"

"Don't be so ridiculous you silly children. Go away from here!"

"Not until you let us search the place!"

Drug looked beyond the women and noticed that they had arrived on one of their carts. It stood grandly on his driveway and was fastened behind a pony of the most beautiful colour of gold.

He said, "I like the colour of your pony. Is it for sale?"

"Well, not that one, but we have some others which are. Why, are you interested?"

Janey thumped her sister on the arm and glared at her.

"This is not the place to try and get a sale!" On returning her glare to the Doctor, she said again, "We want to come in and look for our sister!"

"No," he answered and slammed the solid door in their faces.

The Doctor had to run up the stairs if he was to be ready in time. Passing the fountain, he noticed the face looking at him with an expression of disdain.

"I know father. I will get it all sorted, I need to be firmer from now on. Heads will fall."

He continued his journey upstairs and into his rooms.

"Your clothes are all ready," said his youngest sister pointing to his bed.

"Right," he answered. He never said thank you to his sister, or anyone else for that matter.

He dressed quickly and met his brother back in the hallway.

"Have you got it?" he asked Cal.

"Of course," answered his brother, holding up a large leather bag.

"Come on then."

They left the house and walked to the gate. As they stood at its entrance they looked right and left along Mill Street. There was no sign of the young Prix women and so they began their long, steep walk to Town Street and the event which had been recently arranged by their Council.

As they passed the Prix house they saw that the golden pony and cart waiting in the yard there. Standing by the main gate was a tall and handsome, dark skinned man who stared unblinkingly at the cottage. He did not notice the two men walking on the other side of the road and when Drug looked back he noticed that the man had gone into the Prix yard and out of sight.

"Wonder if that's her husband?" asked Cal.

"No, he was blonde. Don't know who this one is," answered Drug.

"Oh."

They carried on their walk, up the hill and to the junction of Mill Street and Town Street. They were to meet at the Dragon Inn which was opposite the Lawyer's and next to the park. As they trudged towards their destination, they met up with others making their way to the meeting and lunch.

There was the Inspector and Emtee Oreful walking together, seemingly deep in discussion. They heard the sound of many feet trotting along in unison and they saw Mr and Mrs Snooty being carried in their sedan chairs by their servants.

Many in the town were curious to know how the couple could remain so calm while being wiggled and

308

jiggled on their travels. But keen to show their superiority by not walking, the Snootys maintained the chair in spite of bad backs and sore bums.

They arrived at the entrance to the inn and entered quickly. Although still only the middle of the day, it was almost dark outside and both men realised that they were mentally revisiting childhood fears. They were very anxious and jumpy.

At the bar there was a tangle of bodies pushing to get served. They all knew that unless they got a drink quickly, they would have to endure the long and boring speeches thirsty. Food and drink was never served together.

Called to the people's function room at the rear of the inn, the members jostled and pushed each other to get the best seat. The best seat was not at the front of the room, but at the back near the food. They wouldn't be allowed to eat the food until after the donations.

No one really wanted to be near Shudder if he got cross at all. Shudder had a habit of getting cross at these meetings. He didn't like dinners where everyone ate and enjoyed themselves.

The gathered associates sat in rows facing the front of the room, trying to ignore the tables laden with the food which surrounded them. The only variety anyone else had in their diet was if they could remember the ancient knowledge which had been passed down through some families. This told them how to make wonderful recipes from common ingredients.

Who paid for this abundance?

Inspector Glees stood at the front of the room and banged his mallet on the table. The muttering and chattering in the room stopped after a few seconds and he began,

"Friends and fellow Council members! So pleased to see you all again and I find it difficult to imagine that another year has passed since we were here before. Again nothing has altered and the running of the Town and the Village remains the same!"

To this he raised his hammer high and the whole room cheered in agreement. They raised their arms high in answer. These people were in control of everyone else.

"Later on today, Shudder will attend our excellent event as usual and will take note of everyone who has attended. He will move amongst you, taking promises and gifts and in return you will continue your good fortune and long, long life. We have many reasons to thank our glorious leader."

Another cheer raised the roof.

"So, get your gifts ready, for they will be picked up by the Shudder helpers." He pointed to the young girls and boys, dressed in bright, little white outfits and standing at various points around the room.

Glees addressed the children saying, "Children, do as we discussed and you shall be rewarded later this evening."

The children looked at each other, unsure about how to react. Some of them had been collected from Finders, unwanted children, who were the wrong colour or look. The rest had been fetched from Mountain and Moor, where people of less caring lived.

Some were returned to Finders to be recalled later on when needed and some just vanished. But no one ever checked the numbers.

The children moved amongst the attendees handing round sweets and collecting gifts and prizes and putting them onto a large table, which rocked under the weight.

Everyone was aware that the larger and more unusual the gift, the more pleased Shudder would be. Over the years, Shudder had gained land, gold, children and souls this way. Each gift carried a label from its contributor to ensure that there was no mistake. It was imperative that the correct reward was given to the correct donor.

The gathering began their meal and ate far more than was good for them. There was singing, and playing with the children who acted as waiters.

After the meal, the children performed a carefully rehearsed act for the enjoyment of everyone and at the end of the show, there was extra loud clapping and chattering.

Shudder entered the room. He climbed and staggered onto the stage accompanied by two of the nurses who also worked at Finders.

To the gathered throng, he chattered and chattered, his voice gradually increasing in volume. He stroked two of the children who stood in front of him and who appeared to be on the verge of tears. One child turned to a nurse and his eyes searched her face. She smiled indulgently at him and told him to turn round and face the front. This he did, although not altogether willingly.

Shudder continued his speech and soon became more agitated. He stood taller than usual. His brown sacking cloak covered most of his body and only his long spiky arms and hands and legs showed. Sometimes his cloak gaped open giving an alarming show to the audience.

His long, brown leathery face could have been made from branches and sticks. His eyes, yellow and bloodshot, embedded deep in the skin showed his great age.

A yellowing document was passed to him by the Inspector and Shudder unfurled it and began to read from it

311

solemnly. Everyone shifted in their seats and one by one turned to look at Cal. He, understanding the charges which were being read out, became paler and tears entered his eyes.

"I am not a traitor!" he screamed.

But it was too late. The men in the audience stood up and they grabbed Cal by his arms, legs and body. He was screaming pathetically.

"No, No, no! Please, mercy! I am not a traitor! Drug, please help me!"

Drug smiled briefly and said. "Yes, do it. Burn the traitor!"

Cal was dragged outside through the back door of the Dragon Inn, towards a large wooden post used for such events. No one had been burned in Mill Town since the witch trials of many years ago.

The logs and kindling sitting about the base of the post and the leather straps dangling partway up showed that a burning was going to happen again tonight. The screams were heard along the Town Street and down towards Mill Village. Many listened for a minute and then ushered their children back into the house and shut their doors.

The screaming stopped eventually and the Council went back into the inn to finish their meal.

CHAPTER TWENTY-ONE *THE TWINS*

"I am sick of Lydia bossing us about."

"Yeah, I know. It's always, drop me off here, and just do as I say, as though she is some sort of secret agent."

"If she told us more of what was going on, then we would be able to help her."

"I know, she's always the same. Before she left she never told us anything, keeping it all herself. Why did she think we wouldn't help?"

"Don't know, probably thinks we were too young and couldn't take it."

"But we were taking it."

"I don't expect she knew that back then."

"No, Cal kept us all in the dark, too afraid to tell each other, let alone the keepers."

"I expect that's how it works. If everyone keeps quiet, then no one gets to realise how common it is. And when it's talked about later on, everyone thinks it's exaggerated. I hate him. I hope he dies a horrible, horrible death. I've always wished that."

"Yeah."

"But she's still bossy!"

They laughed out loud. Just at that time they were passing the fish shop opposite the mill entrance again and the sound of their laughter entered the shop. The boys looked up from their work and cheerfully waved to the girls, who waved back, but did not stop.

They trotted on past the old mill and looking up at it, Janey noticed how dark and uninviting its exterior was. It was nothing like Gran Prix's descriptions of light and bright and jolly, which she referred to sometimes in melancholy.

As they passed the old sweet shop, Mrs Ladywoman ran out in front of the cart, raising her hand and forcing them to stop.

"What's the matter Mrs Ladywoman? Has something happened?"

"Something is going on within the Town, something very dangerous and we have to bring forward our plans. Where is your sister? Lydia I mean."

"We just dropped her off at the Doctor's." The girls looked at each other and pulled faces, in view of their recent conversation.

"Right, that's not good. Why was she going there?" Mrs Ladywoman was looking at the road and rubbing her chin in contemplation.

"Not really sure," said Alice. "But I expect it was important." The family could moan about each other, but no one outside was allowed to know the troubles.

"This is not good, not good at all."

The girls parked up at the side of the road, with Mrs Ladywoman still standing in front of them and the neighbourhood walking past them, turning and pointing and whispering.

314

The old lady seemed to realise that they were all attracting attention. She for one had never been seen to behave in this way.

"Go home girls and tell your Grandmother all that has occurred. Get her to open the shed. Tell her I said she must come back here!"

The twins did as they were told and encouraged the pony to trot on quickly.

When they did arrive home, Alice left Janey to care for the pony and ran into the house calling for Gran.

"Gran, Gran! Where are you?"

There was no answer. Not from Gran, but the birds and bees and bats, squawked and jumped and flapped about in response to this unexpected disturbance to their nap.

Alice scampered all over the house, but Gran was nowhere to be seen. She shouted to her sister from the upstairs balcony.

"I can't find her. She's not in the house!"

"She won't be far away, let me just finish here and we'll check the garden."

Janey led the pony to the field to join his friends. The other ponies stood at the gate, hoping that they would be chosen for the next trip.

Alice joined her sister and handed a flower to her favourite black pony, Jangles, and he responded gratefully, by eating it.

The girls made their way to the garden and although they shouted Gran, she could not be found, so they searched a little further by going past the ponds and into the woods.

"Why don't we open the shed? Do you think we dare do that, ourselves?" They were standing outside the multi-

315

coloured little workshop of Treen's and tried the door handle, which as usual would not budge.

"She'll go mad if we do," said Alice.

"I know," answered Janey. "Let's leave it a bit."

They continued their trek into the wood and didn't look back. Which was a shame, because if they had looked they would have seen their Grandmother hammering on the shed window, trying to get their attention.

Gran Prix watched in dismay as her grandchildren wandered into the woods, giggling. She realised that she was now a victim of her own rules, having instilled in the family ever since Treen died that they must never, ever go into the shed. This was the one rule that the girls had decided to obey.

Gran sat back down on the bench which Treen had sat on over the years, making his beautiful wooden tools for villagers. She looked at the tools hanging on the walls, still in the original positions which had been allocated according to their size and use by her late husband.

She did miss him. More than she ever admitted to the others. Indeed if it weren't for the family, she would have caught a cart and followed him. It is a sad fact that when a person gets old, youngsters might imagine that the happy relative who meets them every time they visit, feels like that all the time. Whereas often, the older person prepares for that one odd visit and tries to ensure that everything is perfect. At all other times, they can be very lonely.

The twins coming to live with her had totally changed her life. Their constant busyness and noise and ideas had given her a reason to get up every morning and keep a home. Not that it was doing her much good at the moment.

Earlier in the afternoon, she had decided to get things ready for their meeting. Her granddaughters had all gone off on their adventures and she knew that she would be safe to retrieve some required documentation.

Fetching the shed keys from their hidey hole in the branches of the kitchen, a Cornish chough having kept charge of them, Gran made her way out into the garden. It was a beautifully sunny day and she felt elated at the possibility that after the meeting, fortunes could change for the town.

Perhaps she was humming and paying scant attention as she opened the three locks on the door and pushed it, enjoying the smell of wood and wax which met her nose. Whatever it was, she was shoved in the back and fell forwards into the shed. As she lay dazed on the floor and tried to get up, she was aware of the door slamming and all locks being turned.

"Now they have the keys," she said out loud. "That's not going to help."

She got up from the floor and sat herself upon the bench. Nausea swept over her and she felt her legs go wobbly and weak. She bent over. Remembering to keep her head lower than her feet, she touched her head on the floor and that just made her feel worse.

Then she remembered that she was sitting on a bench and didn't need to keep her head that low, she raised it until she was resting it on her knees. Soon she felt better.

So now would be the time to open the door at the rear of the shed, which would take her to the tunnel. But without her set of keys, there would be no way that she could get in there. So here she was, stuck in a small shed unable to get in or out and would now have to wait and see what transpired.

She was beginning to wish that Treen had built a bigger shed.

Gran had almost nodded off when she heard voices outside. As the door handle was tried one way and then the other, Gran jumped up and shouted at the window, but the girls walked away. It was dark outside and almost midnight, it had been a very long day.

The twins, after searching the woods and plenty of shouting, had arrived at the large stone where Michaelmas, Sadie and Lydia had been found.

"It seems like ages ago."

"I know."

They both stood there, focussing for a while.

"I'm going to ask Michaelmas for help," said Alice.

"Good idea," said Janey.

The girls jumped up onto the stone and sat side by side, quietly asking. The clearing became darker until it was almost impossible to see.

The moon rose and cast a spotlight at the edge of the trees. In the spotlight was a man.

"That's not Shudder again is it?"

"I shouldn't think so. We didn't ask him for help did we?"

Janey could not argue with this excellent logic and understood the rules about praying. The spotlight moved towards them, bringing the man with it.

"Michaelmas!" the girls said together.

"Hello girls!" he answered.

"You do look well!" Alice informed him.

"Thanks sis! That's a lovely thing to say!"

"Dead is not that bad then?" asked Janey.

318

"No it's not bad. Don't be scared about it, but don't try and get here too quick!"

"Tell us something about being dead."

"Well for a start, you should stop calling it dead. That makes it sound like a full stop. I'm not in a full stop, so don't worry about that."

"We asked for help Michaelmas. Can you help us?"

"Of course I can help. I've been trying to help you for ages, but no response!"

"What do you mean?"

"I have been jumping up and down in front of you shouting Hellooooo! Look at me! And so on."

"We didn't hear you. Why didn't you make yourself more clear?" they answered indignantly, all three of them back to childhood.

"Blah blah blah! You need to slow your mind down and listen to stuff. Everyone keeps their mind running way too fast."

"Well you don't have much else to think about do you?"

"I do! Anyway, I am supposed to be helping you. I can only do so much, but I can give you some advice."

"This isn't going to be one of those vague, but supposedly meaningful messages is it?" Both had experience of people who could contact the dead.

"Might be. The messages are only as good as the conditions at the time of giving them."

"You've started doing it already!" The girls laughed.

"Well, for a start you had better go back and rescue Gran. She's stuck in the shed, you'll need to get her out. Then she will be able to sort you out with the Old Peoples' Club. They will be able to do loads now."

"The Old Peoples' Club?" asked Janey with surprise.

"Yes. Go and get Gran. I'll see what I can do from here."

The moon went behind a cloud and he was gone. Dawn was breaking and a lot needed to be done before sleep or food could be thought about. The girls raced back to the shed and after using the spare keys which the chough relinquished grudgingly, they managed to free their Gran.

"Michaelmas says we have to ask you what to do next!"

Gran brushed herself down and made her way back to the cottage with the twins following her.

"Tell me what has happened."

This they did, including Mrs Ladywoman stopping them on Wide Lane.

"Right. Get the cart and we'll go round to her house."

Janey chose the golden pony, Nicky. He was her favourite pony and would never be sold. He happily allowed himself to be attached to the cart. Janey kissed him on the nose and he nuzzled her back.

On the trip to the old sweet shop, the girls got no further than the shop front before they were met for the second time by Mrs Ladywoman, who was standing on her steps.

"Girls, girls you must get to the Doctor's house immediately. Lydia is in terrible danger."

The girls went cold. "How do you know? What kind of danger?"

"They are trying to kill her. You must go there and try and get into his house. Drug is evil and must be stopped. There will be others there who are trouble too. It's all

320

coming to a head and we are all in danger." She looked at Gran who gave her a conspiratorial look.

"You must relax, Necessity," Gran said to her friend. "Where is Cal?"

"Probably with Drug, I should think, being badly influenced and encouraged to act shamefully."

The others looked at her, a little surprised at her attitude.

"You come with me Seren and we will bring our meeting forward to this morning. I think we only have tonight. The dark is here."

The twins trotted the pony along the busy street with the refurbished brass lamps from Treen's goat cart swinging happily at the four corners of their own brightly painted cart.

After a splendid trot along Wide Lane and up Mill Lane, they turned swiftly into the drive of the old familiar house. Soon they were hammering upon the door and shouting to be let in.

After the door had been answered and the discourse unsatisfactorily concluded, the door was slammed firmly in their faces.

"We have either got to break in or find some other way of seeing where Lydia is."

Janey said, "Let's go back to the keepers' house and leave the pony and cart there. If we come back over without it, we stand a better chance."

This they did.

When Nicky had been instructed to stay where he was and the girls went around the side of the cottage and into the kitchen, they saw their keepers sat at the table. They didn't seem too surprised to see their youngest daughters.

"Hello."

"Hello, have you come to see Lydia?"

That question came as a shock to the twins.

"Yes, well, no. Why, is she here?"

"Not now, you just missed her."

David came into the kitchen.

"Have you come to see Lydia?" he asked.

"So Lydia has just been here then?" Alice asked the obvious question, "Why are you here David?"

"There are a lot of things to sort out because a lot of stuff is happening at the moment."

"Don't we know it."

"Lydia has gone back into the tunnel," said David.

"The tunnel? You know about the tunnel?" Janey asked.

"Of course I do."

"Cup of tea everyone? Rhubarb mousse?" Their mother keeper was busying herself about the kitchen, not exactly enjoying the visitors' presence, but accepting it.

"Sit down girls," said David, "and I shall tell you what I know."

It took a while to tell them about him being a brother and his undercover role with the Council. The keeper Prixs merely listened and didn't appear too concerned, even when David told the girls about what really had happened that night at the mill so many years ago.

"How come Lydia doesn't trust you then?" asked Alice reasonably.

"Because she's paranoid like that," he answered. "She doesn't believe anything unless she has proved it for herself."

Janey was uncomfortable. "How come you two have never been bothered about what has happened to us?" she asked her keepers.

"What was there to be bothered about? Everything is natural and follows the normal course of events," their mother reasoned.

"Normal? What's normal about what Cal and the others do to children? What about all the missing children?"

"It must be normal if it happens a lot. It's hardly out of the ordinary is it girls? Anyway, none of it ever seemed to do any of you any harm!"

"No harm!" Janey was incredulous.

"You are all alright aren't you? You always seemed to want to go down and visit your uncle happily enough!"

"But we didn't! Can't you remember forcing us and we kept screaming and begging not to be sent and crying and saying we didn't want to go and would do anything not to be sent?"

"Oh that was just you being silly and naughty! You all acted naughty. That's what children do!" Mother was unfazed by the argument.

Janey was interrupted from making any further protestations by a knock at the door. David got up to answer it and was surprised to see a stranger there. The girls were interested to see a very handsome, tall stranger, who smiled beautifully in their direction.

"Can I help you?" asked David coldly.

"Well yes, I'm looking for Lydia. I think she lives here doesn't she?"

"Come on in and sit down," said father keeper. He would not like to admit that he felt a little unnerved with the way the conversation had been progressing up to that point.

"How do you know Lydia?" asked Alice.

"I am the coastguard from Seaside where she used to live. I came back from a sea trip and discovered that she had left. Her husband didn't seem too worried about her and said she had gone back to Mill Village and was divorcing him. So I came to look for her."

The twins grinned at each other and smiled back at the man. Yes, they could see why their sister had become friends with him. David didn't look so pleased, while the keepers remained detached.

"Is Lydia here?" he asked.

"Not at the moment. We are looking for her to be honest. There is quite a drama going on," Alice informed him.

The coastguard sipped his tea gratefully.

"Is it anything to do with all the people going up towards the Town?" he asked.

"What do you mean?"

He had everyone's attention now.

"I've been waiting outside for a long time," he informed them. "Plucking up courage to come in and I heard screaming and shouting in the distance. There were loads of lights too, like a fire. Is it a special occasion or something?"

"No, but I'm going to see if the pony is alright," said Janey.

"Oh he's fine," said the coastguard. "We've made great friends together out there."

"Well I'm going out anyway."

They all trooped out to the front of the cottage. But even before they got there, they could hear the screaming from the direction of the Town and could see orange lights reaching far into the sky.

"It's a fire," said father.

"It's coming from the park I think," said mother.

"It's an execution," said David.

CHAPTER TWENTY-TWO *THE OPC*

As Lydia entered the mill, she was confused to see how many old people were standing in the corridor of the new development. She recognised a lot of them from her childhood and others from the time she had spent in the Town during the past week.

The past week. Was that all it was?

She was met by Necessity Ladywoman, who hugged her and said, "So glad to see that you are alright Lydia. We need you to come with us now. We have a lot of work to do."

The group of people moved to the sides of the corridor in response to a wave from Necessity. As Lydia walked along, she saw her Gran in the line and they hugged.

"Gran! What's going on? Are you some sort of underground warrior?"

The women laughed and Seren said, "Well that's an interesting take on it Lydia. Come on girl, we don't have time for niceties. There are things going on outside now, as we speak and we have to defend ourselves and others against this terrible evil."

Lydia smiled at her Gran but now she felt like a colleague, not a granddaughter. She followed the people down the corridor thinking how she had always considered that all these older people were a bit insignificant. Not deliberately so and if she had been asked outright whether or not someone was worth listening to because they were a certain age, she would have said no. But of course she patronised them as much as anyone else did.

However at the moment, Lydia was completely under the influence of these previously unconsidered ladies and gents. She followed them through the doors at the end of the corridor and eventually they came out onto the courtyard which had once been the loading bay and was now intended as a communal area for residents of the apartments.

They were heading towards the huge chimney. This had a set of stone steps leading to a large wooden door halfway up the chimney. The beautifully crafted metal railings followed the steps up and surrounded the chimney itself. Lydia stopped walking for a moment to take in the spectacle of the phenomenal structure. It was rumoured that the chimney was built on top of an ancient hermitage and subsequently the mill was a particularly likely place for spectacular events to take place.

The group arrived at the chimney and apparently no one had a notion of how they were going to get in.

"Who has the key?" asked Necessity.

"Not me," said Seren.

Everyone patted their pockets and looked in their bags, even though they all knew that there was no key to the chimney about their persons. Lydia didn't pat anywhere, just watched the group from her viewpoint at the back of the crowd.

She recognised Necessity's sister from her day at the Lawyer's. There was the couple who she remembered walking past the end of the mill that night many years ago.

There was Mrs Snailwort, the old lady who lived in the house at the rear of the surgery and whose kitchens she and Sadie had trespassed through the other day. Had she been surrounded by these activists her whole life?

"Someone must hold the key," said Goggyeye Ladywoman. "Isn't it you Pixie?"

"No, I don't think so. I've never been to the chimney before."

"But you have some keys, you know you have."

Lydia patted her pockets in the style of her contemporaries and felt of course, the two keys which she had picked up during the week.

"What about these?"

Seren took hold of the keys and skipped up the steps in defiance of her great age. Finally the club no longer needed to play the feeble characters that were expected of them within the community.

She tried first one key and then the other and soon discovered that neither was any good. That was a blow

"Are you sure that these are the only keys you have?" she shouted down.

"Yes!" came the firm reply.

"What about the one I gave you in the Lawyer's office?" asked Goggyeye gently.

"Gran's got that one."

"Where did you find the other?" Goggyeye insisted.

"At the flat stone."

"Oh. Come on down Seren. We shall have to find another way."

328

Lydia thought that Goggyeye seemed quite cross that the keys did not fit and she suspected that the old woman thought she was holding back on them. But she wasn't. She looked around and realised that Tamson was nowhere to be seen. That was odd.

"What's in the chimney?" Lydia asked.

"All sorts of things are in the chimney," said the man she had often seen driving a goat cart late at night. Lydia stared at him. "I've been watching you all," he added.

"Oh," said Lydia, "What kind of things?"

"All sorts of important stuff," he answered.

"You've no idea, have you?" She looked at them all. These lovely people might be in a club, but she instinctively knew that they were capable only of protection and spying and noticing. To know what to do with any information they collected and then act upon it, was beyond their remit.

"Have you kept a record of the information you have collected?" Lydia asked speculatively.

"Well, I can tell you in two words exactly," answered Necessity.

This number, she had vastly underestimated and proceeded for a full three minutes to tell Lydia of the difficulty they had all had recording the information and the weekly meetings where everything was discussed. Discussions appeared to happen over and over again and no conclusion reached.

"Of course, it was all written down in the book," she finished.

Lydia pricked up her ears at this comment.

"The book? There's a book?"

"Oh yes. Spawg Lally keeps the town records, as you well know and he keeps all our records too. Spawg, Spawg, come here!"

Spawg, a man of at least 200 years old, pushed his way to the front of the group. He was a tall, dark haired man with very green eyes, supposedly because the Lally ancestors had arrived from the green island across the sea, many years ago. It was said that his ancestors were amongst the original settlers here, having come as hermits and sages. They kept stories alive from the early days and when the stories became too long to remember to pass on, they began to write them down.

Having remembered all who had died and been born, they quite naturally became record keepers. Spawg had taken over from his father, Sparkle, when he had decided to take the last cart after an argument with one of the old Turncoats about responsibility. He said that he had had enough.

The Scriber family checked and made some entries and passed copies to Spawg.

Spawg wore the record keeper's uniform of long, green diaphanous material which swirled about his body. It was intertwined with crystals and stars. It appeared to have a life of its own and was never removed from the record keeper's body.

"Hello Lydia!" he said cheerfully.

"Hello Mr Lally!" she answered. She liked him.

"I can call you Pixie now can't I? We all know that is who you really are!"

"Of course you can, Mr Lally. It is who I really am and it's about time I started acted like it," she said with resolve.

330

"Now everyone," she said with authority. "We need to move quickly and decisively. Firstly, we shall get ourselves into this chimney and then Spawg will take me to the records office. There is something I need to sort out."

She surveyed the group of people standing in the yard. They looked up to her with admiration and some adoration it had to be noted.

"Right, now think of something. Empty your mind. There must be a simple solution. There is always a simple solution. Why don't the keys fit?" Pixie stared at the crowd again, who were all still smiling, but shifting restlessly from foot to foot. Necessity smiled and Goggyeye waved. Seren put her hand around her neck and then pointed to Pixie.

"The necklace." She pulled the necklace from her shoulder bag and put it around her neck. Then she took the keys and put first one in the top lock and the second one in the bottom lock. The door opened smoothly and she went in.

"Where's she gone?" asked Mrs Ava Banana, the greengrocer's wife. "She's vanished!"

"Just go through the door and follow Pixie. She knows what she is doing," Seren instructed them. Fifty-four elderly people, ranging in age from 167 to 343 years of age marched magnificently up the stone steps and through the large wooden doors. Some temporarily halted their progress as unusual sounds carried across the darkness from the direction of the Town and strange lights appeared in the sky, but the queue were soon all inside the chimney.

Pixie moved swiftly along the room in which they all found themselves. The necklace had not rendered her invisible, but ensured that she exuded a bright aura which radiated in the darkness of the room. At the same time that the lamps were lit, she touched the necklace and stood in front of the group. She was their leader.

"Where to now, Pixie?" was the inevitable question.

Pixie surveyed the scene around them all. The room was a magnificent hallway with columns stretching high and beyond their vision. The floor was made from a shiny stone and everywhere was bathed in a golden light. Hidden in the dark recesses behind the columns, were several tall statues of seated and cloaked men. They were all painted in bright and beautiful colours.

Hanging from the ceiling were long strands of multi-coloured materials, swaying gently and emitting wonderful perfumes. The sound of tinkling bells came from nowhere and everywhere.

"Home," whispered Pixie.

The atmosphere was broken for the moment, because of the talking and mumbling among the group.

"Stay here everyone please," she instructed and walked towards the rear of the room. There was another set of huge red doors, so tall that it was not possible to see the tops of them. But, they opened easily and silently when pushed gently by Pixie.

As she became accustomed to the gloom in the room beyond, her eyes went up and up. She needed to take in the biggest statue she had ever seen. It was similar to the sitting statues outside, but more brightly coloured and wider and taller. She looked up beyond the brightly coloured cloaks and the resting hands of the form and then to the many strings of stones which hung about his neck. His face was almost impossible to see, so high was it, but she felt safe and warm and at home standing here in front of him. Like he knew her and she knew him.

Again the moment was broken and she heard voices from the main room.

"Pixie! We need to start moving and doing things! We can't all hang around here and waste time!"

"Alright," she answered and turned back to the statue.

She noticed a glow coming from the statue's resting hand and felt the need to climb and look. As the hand was several times higher than her height, it took a minute or two to scramble up the stone plinth, the stone cushion and folded feet. Then she could climb into the hands of the statue.

This felt so comfortable that she sat down there for a while, next to a small group of objects. There was a bottle containing light, a jar in which there was powder resembling snowflakes and a tiny dagger. She put them carefully into her leather shoulder bag, knowing that they would be required later. She looked out from her seat into the room, noticing the smells and the sounds and the colours. All so beautiful.

She closed her eyes and was transported to Beyond and beyond. She opened her eyes again and clambered down the statue. Turning round to give him a last look and a wave, she stepped lightly out of the anteroom and into the main room where the others waited, somewhat impatiently.

She smiled at them, knowing that now, she really was calm and at peace. For a while, at least. "Well I thought this place would be full of smoke and coal dust!" said old Mrs Kaleidoscope, who kept the toy shop on Town Street.

"You thought right then didn't you Mrs Kaleidoscope?" said Ava.

"I did, so can we leave here now? There is nothing to see save for years of old soot."

"Is that all you can see here everyone?" asked Pixie.

"Yes, of course," chorused the audience.

"Why, what can you see Pixie?" asked Spawg.

"Beauty and peace," she answered. "You will all see it one day, but perhaps you are not yet ready."

She walked out of the chimney and onto the stone steps outside. Looking over to the main town up the hill, there was still an orange light and a strange smell.

"I can smell that rotten chimney out here now," said Goggyeye. "Better get that door shut."

"That smell is not coming from the chimney. It's fresh smoke."

"Smells like a barbeque or something."

Pixie looked above the orange lights and saw dark spirits. Thousands of them. They surrounded the light and every so often dived down. Eventually they appeared to get what they wanted and triumphantly pulled up a screaming and terrified man. Cal was receiving his just desserts it seemed.

"He must have been dying at the same time I was released from my fears," she murmured to herself.

"What next Pixie?" asked Spawg.

"I want you to take me to the Records Office. Seren, Necessity, Goggyeye and Mr T Bacco come with us."

Mr Bacco, who kept the shop which specialised in pipes and their accoutrements, smiled pleasurably at the inclusion. He was generally kept out of things, his family constantly being accused of ruining the health of the village people.

334

"Everyone else split into groups and find out where any members of the Council are now. Try and persuade them to meet us at Finders Hospital at midday tomorrow. Tell them anything to get them there. Tell them I am to die there or something."

"What about Shudder?" someone asked.

"I will deal with Shudder," said Pixie.

The group split up, leaving the yard in their own particular direction. Pixie and her team left by the south exit, which took them around the back of the mill and up a ginnel running parallel with Bell Lane and Mill Lane and joining with Town Street near the market place. The smell of smoke and burning was getting stronger as they neared the Town.

Pixie remembered this ginnel from her childhood. They ran through the area that had been used hundreds of years ago by their ancestors. Some said that these were the original tracks and others said that this was where people escaped from trouble. The latter explanation was reasonable as the walls of stone were high and in some areas topped by hedges.

The floor was stone and earth and during heavy rainstorms the extra water made walking down there very slippery and dangerous. There was no delay tonight and the group made quick work of the journey.

The Record Office was situated next to the Lawyer's and opposite the park and the Dragon Inn. As they crossed the end of Mill Lane, they noticed another group of people walking and running up the hill.

It was a group led by David. Following were Pixie's keepers, her young sisters and another man bringing up the rear. In the darkness, Pixie could not make him out until he got closer to her.

Upon seeing him, she almost stopped breathing and her face broke into a smile which her family had never seen before.

"Teg Morlin," she said. "What are you doing here?"

"What do you think silly?" He waved a book at her.

"That's my journal."

"I know, you thought you had burnt it, but hubby found it when he got back and rescued it from the fire. Don't worry though, I was with him and managed to get it away." Teg carried on grinning.

"Thanks. How did you manage to do that?"

"He was reading your goodbye letter and got distracted."

"Was he upset?"

"Not really. He went to tell the woman who sells the fish on the quayside. I don't expect he will be upset for long."

David did not appear to be too pleased about these friendly and intimate exchanges. The twins on the other hand, were riveted.

"We heard noises and saw a fire or something at the park," the twins said.

"So did we," said Spawg. "We were just coming to investigate."

At that moment, some townspeople ran towards them. They reached the group at the crossroads of Mill Lane and Town Street.

"Oh it's terrible, it's terrible. The bad old days are back!"

"What do you mean?" asked Goggyeye.

336

"Anarchy! The witches are in control again! I knew this day would come. It was foretold!"

The woman fell to the ground sobbing and crying.

"What has happened?" asked Necessity.

"There was one of those silly Council meetings at the Dragon Inn. You know the stuff. Mr Turncoat, you're usually there aren't you? You weren't there tonight were you?" The scrap man looked at David strangely.

He wasn't the only one.

"We thought we saw a fire or something up there," said Alice.

"A fire! Oh yes there was a fire," said one.

"Yes, if it weren't for the Inspector being involved it would have been called murder. It should be called murder now, except I don't suppose many people will miss the old trout. Perhaps his wife might. She is the only one bothered about him."

"Murder! Who has been killed!" asked Necessity with alarm.

"That old Cal," said the scrap man.

"Invention is dead?" screamed Necessity, "He's dead! Why? How?"

"They executed him. They took him onto the fire of treason and burnt him. He didn't like it much. He screamed and cried for ages before he died."

Necessity was prostrate on the road, screaming and crying uncontrollably. Her sister Goggyeye had her arms around her and was trying to comfort her. It wasn't working.

"Why is she so upset?" Janey asked.

Goggyeye replied, "Because he was her son."

CHAPTER TWENTY-THREE *RECORDS*

To say that this revelation came as a surprise was an understatement. Because this meant that Necessity must not only be the mother of Invention, but also of Doctor Catapult, and Goggyeye was their aunt.

How was it that she had separated from old Calico Catapult and joined the Old Peoples' Club? But, most importantly, whose side was she on?

These thoughts flashed through the minds of most of the people there. But the sight of the old lady weeping and wailing on the pavement and then the screaming and running townspeople and the smoking bonfire in the near distance, created too many extra excitements to their minds.

"Can you manage with your sister Miss Goggyeye? We really ought to go and investigate the Dragon Inn and see what is going on there," said Lydia.

"My poor dear Cal, he was such a good boy!" wailed Necessity.

Even Goggyeye, with her arms around her sister, had to raise eyebrows at this plainly ridiculous comment. She must be the only person in the world who could have made that statement and meant it. It must be the shock.

Goggyeye waved them away and the group left her. Lydia's mother stayed with the two women, but it could not be said whether this was because of concern for Necessity or because she was scared of going any nearer the Dragon Inn.

Mr Bacco went home to fetch his pipe.

The nearer to Dragon Inn they got, the thicker the smell and atmosphere. The twins started to cry.

"Why are you crying?" asked Teg.

"I feel so out of control. I feel like it's too much to take in. I mean I'm glad Cal is dead, really glad he's dead ..." Alice couldn't finish, so Janey helped her.

"Executions aren't right. I didn't think they were done these days. We heard about them in the olden days, but not in our lifetime."

"I've heard about them when I was a lad," said father Prix.

Lydia looked at her keeper. She couldn't remember when she had heard him bring up a memory or an opinion.

"They burned that old teacher we had once. But I can't remember why it was. I expect there was a good reason," he ruminated.

"There has never been a good reason to execute anyone. Even if they've killed someone, it just makes the executioners as bad as the killers. Except they think they have right on their side. And the version of what's right changes through the years."

Spawg Lally had studied all the records ever made, so it was reasonable to assume he knew what he was talking about.

They had arrived at the front of the Dragon Inn. They were not the only people there. Some of the Council

339

members stood outside, staring at the flames. They were too scared to see the fire from the rear. Other people stood alongside them, hands to their mouths and eyes as if this would remove the terrible event from their experience.

The yard behind the inn and the park was lit still with the orange light. The sound was horrible, crackling wood and a rushing sound as the flames leapt to the sky. There was a smell of an ordinary bonfire, but with an added something that no one wanted to put into words.

"Is this how life is in Mill Town?" Teg asked of David.

"It's bad enough, but this is another step into the darkness. I don't know how they expect to step back from this. Will you help me with something?"

"Yes, will do," answered Teg.

"Come with me inside here."

The two men went into the inn. Lydia watched them and felt a desire to follow, but a tap on her arm from Spawg reminded her that there were more important jobs to complete.

"Come on Pixie, we've got to stop this."

"I know. Let's go."

They walked past the inn, crossed the lane and onto the Records Office. This building was made of stone taken from the old castle, which at one time stood at the top of the hill, where the park now was. The rest of the stone had been used to build various homes and farmsteads. The Turncoat farm was built from it, as was Finders.

Spawg moved his tunic to one side and pulled out a long golden chain. Along this chain were several gold keys and he fiddled with them all until he came across one he liked. This, he used in the glossy red door and unlocked it.

"Come on Pixie. Work to do."

Lydia, who had been looking back at the inn, turned round again and smiled at Spawg. She followed him in and before long they were walking through dim corridors lined with bookcases which in turn overflowed with books.

"Doctor Catapult has a lot of books," Lydia commented.

"His family liked to keep books too. But we've kept more!" he winked. "Our family always believed in seeing all sides of the argument. That way the truth can be discovered eventually."

"Yes, I expect so. Mr Lally," she began slowly. "Did you know about Necessity and Cal?"

Spawg stopped his progress and smiled again.

"Because we keep every record here, is that what you mean?"

"Of course, you must have known about it. You know about everything."

"I do know about everything. It's because I know about everything to do with everyone that I never tell anyone anything. I know all the secrets." He tapped his nose and grinned.

"Will you tell me the relevant ones?"

"I can't do that Pixie, I have taken the vow." He smiled at her again. He smiled a lot.

"I see."

They had arrived at the door with a sign on it stating that inside was a restricted area and should not be entered.

They went into the inner records room. It was huge. No. Huge was too small a word for it. It was colossal.

Every inch of the walls was sectioned into family names and sectioned again into headings as follows:

Births

Marriages

Deaths

Divorces

Adoptions

Rental Agreements

And so on.

"There's a lot of stuff here Mr Lally!" she said with understatement.

"Everything is in here Pixie. Absolutely everything."

"Let's find the information about Necessity and Cal first. Then I need anything you have about Shudder."

Spawg thought for a moment. He had taken a vow never to reveal any of the records or secrets, but lately he had begun to think that these records had to be of use to someone. He had received more than one request for sight of at least some of the records so that a family could establish their own story. Spawg had sympathy with their desires and was working out where his duties really lay. He had been in discussions with the lawyer about that.

Tonight was different. The world did not feel secure any more. He made an immediate decision to show Pixie whatever she needed to see.

He beckoned her to follow him and they moved through the miles of bookshelves and their accompanying books and paperwork. A, B, C, D and so on until they arrived at the letter N.

"All records are cross referenced here. If you look up a name, you get their birth, marriage and death records and anything that they may have needed to see a lawyer about. Divorces and such. If you look up any of the legal records separately, you will need to know a date."

"If you give me the books on Necessity and Cal," Lydia asked, then as an afterthought, "Probably all the Catapults I should think."

Spawg gave her the leather volume entitled 'Necessity' and placed it on the long heavy wooden table which stood in the middle of the room. He walked back to the shelves and Lydia sat at the table and opened the cover. At various times, Spawg returned with the bound volumes of Cal, Drug, the sisters and Calico Catapult. Eventually he put next to her hand, a small leather notebook and pen.

She looked up to him and smiled, then opened the book and began to write notes. As she read and wrote, she learned a lot.

Lydia leaned back in her chair and was so preoccupied that she did not notice Spawg returning with Teg.

"Oh hello!" she said, pleased that she would now have someone to tell her discoveries to. She trusted Teg.

"Pixie, I just had a record arrive from Seaside and went to fetch your friend to tell him."

"I didn't realise you kept records for Seaside too. Perhaps you could let me see my file?"

"I will let you see that when we have this mess under control. I don't think you should take on too many projects at once, you will get distracted," said Mr Lally, then added, "I will leave you two here and make some tea."

Teg sat down next to his friend and smiled.

"That's a funny smile Teg."

"Perhaps because I have something to tell you and I'm wondering how to broach the subject."

Lydia put down her pen and said, "Just tell me Teg. So much has happened this past week I am totally hardened!"

"Your husband is dead. Mr Lally was told and he came to fetch me because he thought that I would be the best one to let you know."

"Oh no! What happened?"

Lydia was not too upset about the news, he hadn't been much of a husband and she could not pretend that her heart was broken in any way with the news of his death. She wasn't happy about it, but not sad. Enough said.

"They had been trying to get his signature because of your divorce and that is how they found out so quickly that he was dead. Even I'm surprised how quickly the news arrived here, usually it would take weeks. Wrinkles fell into the harbour after he had seen the fish lady. There is some suspicion that she pushed him in because he said that he wouldn't marry her. The Inspector there will investigate it and let us know. But the records show that he is dead."

"Right. Was I still married to him when he died?"

Lydia had no idea whether or not any divorce had gone through.

Spawg said that he could check it with his records and wandered off. Soon he returned with some papers and the confirmation that without the signature, the divorce papers had not yet been submitted and so Lydia was now a widow and not a divorcee.

"That means you get his boat, the cottage and all the fishing rights," said the still smiling Teg.

"That is something to be pleased about!" she answered.

"Better not think about it just yet, there is a long way to go with the mess you got yourself involved in here. Do you think you could do with some help?"

"Yes please!"

They learned that Necessity had been married to old Mr Catapult for years and together they fetched ten children from Finders Hospital, of whom only four were known in the town. They had separated, but never divorced before the old man eventually died. That had been eighty years ago and from that point Necessity ran the sweet shop.

"So does that mean that she didn't approve of the Catapult secrets or that she was an undercover Council mole?" asked Teg.

"Undercover Council mole?" giggled Lydia.

Mr Lally noted how he had heard Pixie giggle more during this past hour than he ever had. What could that possibly mean?

"There is one way to find out if she was a mole," he said. "We can take a look in the other records."

"Which other ones?"

"The records which detail everything that a person has ever said, done or had said or done to them. These records show a person's whole life and are used by Beyond after the last cart ride."

"Goodness, that's quite specific."

"Yes and it's very revealing. To learn what people think and say about you and to know the effect of every word and action can be disturbing."

"Does everything really matter that much?" asked Teg as he leaned back in his chair and put a comforting hand on Lydia's shoulder.

"Yes it does."

"I should have thought that it was the motivation behind the deed that made the most difference," observed Lydia. "You know, whether the intention is to hurt or to gain. I hope that's it anyway."

345

Mr Lally took less than five minutes to put several other ledgers on the table. They belonged to Necessity, Lydia, David, Inspector Water Glees and finally, a large black ledger, entitled:

Shudder

Lydia flicked through them all, but decided that the one on Shudder must be read last.

"It seems that when Necessity was a young girl, she was in love with Grandfather, I mean Treen Prix and they were going to marry, but her keepers stopped it because Calico Catapult had decided he wanted to marry her."

"And a Doctor was a much better prospect than a woodworker in a mill, I should think," said Teg.

"I would rather have my Granddad than him," Lydia noted.

"You did as you were told, just the same as she did," Teg pointed out.

Lydia dropped her head as she felt her face burn. That was exactly what she had done. But presumably her match had been planned in order to get her out of the way.

"Anyway, they fetched all those children, but only the first four grew up to adulthood. The others were recorded as being born and adopted, but no deaths were ever recorded. That seems wrong Mr Lally."

"They weren't the only children that vanished. There have been hundreds over the years," he said.

"Why didn't anyone investigate? Why didn't you investigate? It must have made you curious?"

"What point was there in being curious? I couldn't have done anything about it. Most people in any sort of authority were involved in the disappearances of the children. You needn't worry, they all went back to Beyond, they are all safe now."

"But they didn't go back. They are stuck here still. They can't get back to Beyond, I think it is Shudder who is keeping them here. I have to do something about it. Pass me David Turncoat's file."

This was done and she read it quickly. She put it down and picked up the next file.

"David and I were picked up from Finders at the same time by my keepers, so they weren't lying about that. There is nothing here about him being adopted by Turncoats though. Wow, he does seem to have infiltrated the Council, because he has been giving information to Spawg for years.

"All this information has been waiting for someone to do something about it. Oh! It seems Mr Scriber is a goody too, he has been trying to use the law against Inspector Glees, but hasn't been getting very far."

Lydia compared Glees' file with David's.

"So Glees' father was brother to Calico Catapult. They like to keep it in the family. He hasn't done anything good for anyone as far as I can see. Not even for Michaelmas. He made sure that Emtee Oreful got rid of his body pretty quickly. Seems even he has been getting worried about how far things have gone sometimes. He hides behind the Shudder knows best, idea."

"Says here that Necessity left Calico when the children were quite small. It looks as though she was scared of them, that's what she told Seren anyway. They had been through so much that they decided to bond with Calico and deal with it that way," Teg informed her. "I see from your file that you've come across Shudder quite a bit, David has too."

347

Lydia took the file from him and shut it.

"That is nothing to do with you Teg. Let me keep my own secrets."

"Fine Pixie. Now open this file Lydia."

Lydia opened it and read.

"Shudder came from Finders apparently, from a different section to the others. I've seen that section, those children often grow into the people who do the terrible things to other children. I think that they are the ones who never go back to Beyond and just come straight back. There can be no hope for them until they reach Beyond. But to do that, they must behave and be kind to others or they have no chance. Crikey, Shudder is over nine hundred years old and the stuff he has done is horrible. He's been involved in every disappearance and every murder ever recorded."

"That'll be why he looks like he does. All that evil has transformed him," said Teg.

"In the same way that goodness makes you beautiful?"

"Might make you beautiful if you are lucky."

"Thanks," she laughed.

"He can't take any last cart. All those children have to be released first. While they are trapped, so is he. It's a vicious circle."

"So do we have to kill Shudder or release the children first?"

"What do you mean, we?"

"Lydia Pollack, I'm not letting you do it on your own."

"It's Prix, Lydia Prix."

Spawg broke the moment by dumping a pile of files on the table.

"What are these Mr Lally?" asked Lydia.

348

"Missing children Pixie. They are all missing children."

She looked at the pile of books and saw them as young girls and boys, leaving Finders in the hopes of a lovely simple life and ending it frightened and shamed at the hands of one of those disgusting people.

Flicking open a few of the children's files, she noted that most had worked at the mill prior to their disappearance. After the mill was closed, children then began to disappear from the streets or school or the woods. Tamson's file told of a young girl with loving parents who vanished and was never found.

"No one has ever done anything about it," she murmured.

"I don't suppose anyone put it all together. The ones that are suspicious have tried to form groups in opposition, but haven't done anything except make records and wait."

"For what?"

"For a leader, Pixie, for you!" Mr Lally was standing in front of them.

"Why me?"

"You know why. That's why you came back this time, to put a stop to it. It's in the records. In your records."

Spawg opened her file at page 222 and showed her.

She read:

Lydia is really Pixie and has great power and foresight and will kill Shudder and free the children and then everything will be alright. The End.

"That all makes sense then," said Teg.

"Well if I've got foresight, I'd better get out of here and sort out Shudder."

"We can start at the Dragon Inn. It was on Shudder's orders that Cal was executed. He accused him of treason and the whole Council agreed and then they took him out and burned him. Cal was denying it right to the end."

"Who actually did the burning?"

"The Inspector and Doctor Catapult. But Oreful and Burgess helped drag him to the fire and tied him to it."

"Why did they burn him?" Lydia asked the question, but could personally think of loads of reasons to burn him.

"Treason was the accusation. But I think it was because he let you escape instead of dying."

"Nice."

They left the records office and Spawg accompanied them. He gave her a hug.

"Look after yourself," he said.

"I'm sorry it took so long to come back," Lydia whispered to him.

"Better late than never Pixie," he whispered back.

Teg and Pixie walked into the smoky street and headed to the rear of Dragon Inn.

"I want to see it for myself," she said.

CHAPTER TWENTY-FOUR *SHUDDER*

It was now almost dawn, but Town Street was as busy as any market day. News of the execution had travelled almost as fast as the smoke. Most had arrived for a good look and gossip. There was plenty to talk about.

Only two people were apparently devastated by the passing of nasty Invention Cal, his mother Necessity and his wife Tatty.

Tatty had initially started walking up the steep slope of Mill Lane when her husband did not return from his meeting. She suspected him of some more 'funny business' as she referred to his peccadilloes. It wasn't that she disapproved of his actions, just that she didn't want him spending too much time away from home. Then she had met Necessity and Goggyeye at the junction with Town Street and been given the news.

She screamed and cried almost as much as Cal had in his final moments, but the sorrow was mainly to do with her future prospects. She was highly unlikely to find another man to take her on unless she had a serious makeover. She enjoyed having a husband to boss about and she still had a desire for a baby from Finders.

"Perhaps now they will let me have a proper baby instead of one of those freaky babies," she said to Goggyeye, brightening considerably.

"Yeeees," answered the old woman. "That's an interesting if slightly inappropriate take on the situation."

"Perhaps I shall pop over to Finders later on today, no point in wasting time here crying when I have the rest of my life to plan!"

The women walked to the scene of the execution, with everyone much calmer now. They saw Lydia and Teg walking towards them.

"I hear that we have something in common now Lydia!" she said jauntily.

"What could that possibly be?"

"We are both widows. Perhaps we should go to the inns together and start looking for new husbands!"

Lydia said nothing and pulled the chuckling Teg away.

The innkeeper at the Dragon was enjoying himself. He had been serving drinks and meals all through the night, Inspector Glees being preoccupied elsewhere. He might be able to buy a new outfit for his demanding wife at this rate.

Teg ordered them a drink each and some food. Neither had eaten or drunk for quite a time. They were served quickly and Teg insisted that they first ate in the inn before going out into the back yard.

"I've already been here with David. You'll need a settled stomach," he informed her as they left the inn by the back door.

The yard was hung about with a grey mist, which hit them both with the smell and taste of smoke and ash.

Walking towards the great pile of still smouldering wood, Lydia realised that her eyes were stinging. She rubbed them.

"Are you alright?" asked Teg gently.

"I'm not crying!" she answered indignantly.

"Fine. Come on closer and have a look."

They moved nearer, feet crunching against the grit and ash on the yard. The pole which had been in the middle of the fire was only a couple of feet tall, but still visible was the chain which had held her uncle there. The damp air of the morning was making the ash spit and steam.

"There's nothing left of him."

"Unless you count the stuff you are standing on."

She looked down at her feet, stained with clumps of pale grit. She was standing in his bones and teeth, burned beyond recognition.

"Oh," was all she could say in answer.

They retraced their steps to the front of the inn, Lydia's feet still crunching. Then she said. "Tonight at Finders, I will kill Shudder. I want you all there to see it." She walked down Town Street in the direction of Mill Street. The Doctor, Inspector and other members of the Council watched them go. There were many 'ooohs' and 'aaahs' and 'who is Shudder?' depending on the particular experience of the chatterer.

As they walked past the shops and cottages which lined the streets, Lydia noticed that the enterprising townspeople had opened each of their businesses in order to make money out of this drama.

"Just like my Granddad's time. When they had executions back then, it was like a party," said one.

"There should be more of them, then we'd make some money," said another.

"I can think of a few more that need burning," was another opinion.

Lydia saw old familiar shops that had remained exactly the same since she was a girl and felt as though she were a ghost visiting a place for the last time.

Teg, noticing her change of mood asked, "Are you really going to kill Shudder? I know you said he was horrible, but I thought that murder was beyond you. And I thought that you didn't approve of killing?"

"You have no idea what I am capable of Teg. Shudder deserves everything he gets."

The twins arrived in a cart pulled by two ponies.

"For speed," they explained.

The two Scriber boys were standing on the pavement outside the Lawyer's office.

"We saw everything and want to help," they said.

Lydia saw the way the wind was blowing and suggested that the Lawyer boys watched and took note of anything suspicious and useful around the town for the next few hours. Then they were to come to Gran's cottage in the early evening.

She told the twins to drive down to the air raid shelters and drop her and Teg there and then go and make sure that her sisters and their families were safe and out of the way.

"They are to stay in their own places until all this is over. Particularly Marjoram and her family, I don't want the baby hurt."

"What exactly do you think is going to happen?" This all seemed wrong to Teg.

"A lot," she answered.

The girls dropped them off at the entrance to the old mill, where the air raid shelters were located. Lydia jumped down and then unusually, reached up and hugged her sisters.

"Wooaahh Lydia. You are not going to die you know!"

"Hopefully not!" she answered, but inside she wasn't so sure.

She waved them goodbye and walked towards the entrance of the air raid shelters with the same feeling of unreality that she had on Town Street. This feeling had been growing since... when?

Since Cal died. Now she was free to just be Lydia. Her abuser was dead and could never, ever hurt her or her family again. He was dead. Good.

"I'm just not used to feeling free," she said to Teg.

"Well you are free now Lydia."

But he was thinking about Wrinkles Pollack.

They reached the entrance and Lydia pushed on the door. It didn't move, so she knocked on it.

It was opened by Tamson.

"Come on in Pixie and... Ooohhhh I see you have a friend with you!"

Lydia blushed and pushed her way in.

"Tamson, I need to see the other children again. Then I have to get to Finders and sort Shudder out once and for all. I need your help."

"Who are you talking to Lydia?" asked Teg.

"Can't you see or hear her?"

"No."

"Don't know what use you are going to be to me then."

"Thanks." Teg's face fell. It mattered to him a great deal what Lydia thought of him. He had expected a much bigger reaction from her upon his arrival. He knew that she

355

was pleased to see him, but she seemed to be very wrapped up in this adventure she had fallen into.

There was no way he was going to let her know that he had been aware of the death of her husband when he arrived that evening. He had been waiting for a good time to tell her, but events had overtaken him.

He didn't know whether he would ever tell her that he had been present at Wrinkle's death.

"Well, I shall be as useful as I can, where I can."

"Just follow me then, I shall let you know what to do."

Teg followed her meekly.

Tamson took them back to the corridor where all the lost children now lived. Even down here they had heard about the execution and no one seemed unduly upset. Cal was involved in the sadness and loss of many of the souls in the tunnel rooms.

Lydia duly told Teg everything that Tamson said. It was very annoying.

"You've said you will kill Shudder. That won't be as easy as you think you know."

"I don't expect it to be easy."

"How are you going to do it?"

"No idea," she announced. "The best way will be to deal with whatever happens, when it happens."

They stood at the end of the corridor in silence. The atmosphere here was depressive and soul destroying.

"Is everyone here very sad?" Lydia asked suddenly.

"I think so, but then so would you if you were condemned forever as they are," said Tamson. "I've been condemned too. I know how they feel."

"I know how they feel too, and I've been depressed, but the best way to become free is to free yourself."

356

"Like with a key or a bribe or something?" asked Teg.

"With your mind," answered Lydia.

The others looked at her puzzled.

"With my mind?" said Tamson. "I've been thinking about leaving here ever since I arrived. I have missed seeing my family, they are dead and I can't see them ever again!" She was getting upset.

"When you understand things a bit better, and you will, you will understand that letting go of bad experiences frees you and makes you stronger. It's always how you deal with your life story. The path you have always depends on how you think and then as a result, what you choose to do."

"That is irritating rubbish, Lydia. Please don't treat me like an idiot."

"I'm not! I wouldn't do such a thing! I'm just trying to help you. That's all."

Nothing else was said as they did not wish to lower the energy level any more. The depressive state of the corridor was bad enough as it was. Besides, the others really didn't understand what Lydia was talking about.

It is best to keep your opinions to yourself. Everyone has their own ideas and don't want to listen to anybody else. Who is to judge who is correct?

Rattle and pester, her mind never left her alone.

Shut up Lydia!

"How can we speak to all the children? It's very important."

"They meet for prayers at the church every evening."

"Which church?"

"The church at the cemetery."

"I didn't think that they could leave the tunnel."

357

"Certain places, like the cellar and the church. They can't go outside of the perimeters of those places. Oh and the Snooty Family place."

Lydia perked up at that news.

"Their place? How do they get there? The family are Council people aren't they?"

"Well yes they are. But they don't know about us going there, we travel through the water system. It's easy to travel through water."

"I thought that ghosts couldn't pass over water?" asked Teg.

"They can't, but this is technically passing along the edge of the water."

"Oh."

"So what will we do now?"

Lydia said nothing and opened the first cell door. Inside it was tiny and despite the fact there were no windows, it was perfectly possible to see clearly in there. There was a scent, which brought back to mind the statue room in the chimney.

The room was quiet, but there was a fog of sadness. On a table at one end were pictures of people in family groups, drawn on card and nestled in between little ornaments and keepsakes.

Lydia walked towards the table, passing a tiny bed on the way. She noticed how similar this room was to the bare cells in the house of the Doctor. The children had created for eternity, their last memories before their examinations.

"Are all of the rooms like this, Tamson?"

"Yes they are. Mine is too," she added solemnly. "Everything we can remember about our old lives we try and recreate so that we don't forget. It's like trying to hang on to the past."

Lydia totally understood this. She had quietly kept many small items her keepers had wanted to throw away and copied in her house at Seaside, the rooms at home or Gran's. She knew that many of her contemporaries wanted to progress and change and although she had no real problem with that, she always wanted to mentally and physically recreate what life was like before that night at the mill.

"I wanted to go back to being small and have all my family around the kitchen table laughing and smiling."

"And safe," added Tamson.

"I still want life to be like that," said Lydia. "I get cross inside when people want to change. It's like if I can keep everyone and everything as it was, then nothing bad has happened."

"But you can't in life, any more than we can in death. We are all stuck here in the belief that if we keep our lives as they were, then our keepers will find us and all will be back to normal."

"Does Shudder ever come here?" asked Lydia.

"He can't come. He can send others though, but they can't affect us anymore. We can affect them because every time they feel us, the effects of their crimes touch their mind. Then they begin to turn in on themselves."

"So, if Shudder comes into contact with all of you, he will be in bigger trouble?"

"Oh yes, but up to now, we have not had a chance for that to happen. You can make it alright again, Pixie." Tamson looked at her in hope.

"Because I've been through it all once, before this life as Lydia?"

"And you came back to help us."

"I was called Pixie last time then?"

"Yes, just a mill girl called Pixie Prix. A young mill girl who lived in a cottage with her keepers many, many years ago and one day vanished."

"I had been chosen by the mill manager for special treatment." It was coming back to her.

"The family liked young girls and young boys. They said we were untouched and pure." Tamson began to shake at the memory.

Lydia sat down on the tiny little bed and touched with tenderness the dolly and the lacy cushion embroidered with the words:

I love my mummy

She started to cry.

"The mill manager was the son of Snooty. His keepers built the mill for him in order to keep him occupied. He used to torture goats and then pick on other children at the school. When he grew up he got worse, so they thought the mill would keep him busy."

"And all that did was allow him to have a permanent supply of children. That's sick," said Teg.

"His name was Shudder. Shudder Snooty. He never died, but his appearance altered, the more evil he committed."

"So he's still alive?"

"Yes, he recruited more as he corrupted them through the years."

"That's horrible."

"That's why I've got to kill him tonight."

Teg sat next to her and put his arm around her. He was rewarded with Lydia resting her head on his shoulder and sobbing. He stroked her hair and kissed her head.

She liked the feeling, but decided that this was not an appropriate moment to like anything. Lydia got up. She gave one last look around the room and pushed Teg into the corridor.

Tamson travelled through the wall and they were met by hundreds of young girls and boys floating in the corridor. Many held a picture or a keepsake and every single one of them looked in Pixie's direction.

"They want you to help them. You must help them," Tamson said.

"I will help you all," promised Pixie.

"Do I have to help them all too?" enquired Teg.

"Yes you do," she instructed.

"Everyone listen to me!" Pixie shouted to the gathering.

"Here, stand on this table," said Teg as he dragged it out of a room.

She stood on it and he held her secure as she spoke.

"I want you to go to the church as usual tonight and pray. You must wait in the church until you hear my instructions. Then you must all come together and face him. He is your biggest fear and you must face him."

The children looked terrified at the prospect.

"I will be there with you. I promise that you will be safe. I promise." She emphasised the last word.

The children looked at each other and then back at Pixie. Tamson smiled at her and began to clap her hands. The other children slowly began to join in and soon the whole group clapped in unison.

"I can see them and hear them!" announced Teg in surprise.

Somewhere else, somewhere outside, they heard a long, loud howl.

"That's Shudder," said Lydia. "The children are getting stronger and he's getting weaker. He knows it."

The children clapped still, as Pixie and Teg pushed their way through the crowd towards the main tunnel.

"We must get back into the mill and find the water course."

Tamson floated in front and led them to the tunnel door into the mill. There they entered the reception area and the caretaker's desk and cupboard and went through a door.

A huge turbine, the workings of which none of them understood, stood silent and imposing. They walked around the edge of it and were now by a canal with lock gates at intervals along its length. The levels in each lock were higher than the one prior and were used as a system to bring water up from the river at the bottom of the hill.

"I bet they are going to charge the inhabitants of the mill apartments a lot for this water system," noted Teg.

"The Snootys think they own everything," said Pixie.

Soon, they were at the bottom of the canal and walked out into the light through a large opening at the end of the tunnel. They were now in the woods at the edge of the Snooty estate and on the other side of the wall from the lane. The river tumbled over rocks and through the trees as it made its merry way from the Moors and onwards to Prix land. This sharp bend in its course ensured there was increased water pressure at this point.

"I've just realised that when all this water system starts up, the Prixs will have no water and most of the village won't be able to use their wells!" said Pixie.

"I don't imagine that they care too much about that," answered Teg.

They walked through the trees noting how perfectly silent the place was.

"Not a bird or a bat or an eagle or anything," Tamson said. "This place is evil. There is evil everywhere."

"Usually are evil people in authority!" Teg said.

"Not always," Pixie answered. "Some in authority are good and kind."

"Where's that then?"

She wasn't going to get into this familiar argument at the moment.

"Move on!" she instructed. And he did.

The river passed in front of Snooty Manor. Pixie shivered. Over the far wall lay her Gran's cottage and on many occasions they had stared at the wall from there and wondered what the Manor would look like close up.

Now she knew. It was magnificent and spectacular and ginormous. And evil.

CHAPTER TWENTY-FIVE *THE MANOR*

Pixie went to the manor door and stood, hand poised and ready to knock. She thought better of it and put her hand down by her side.

There was the possibility that Shudder would answer the door, grab her and slam the door behind her. Why think of that all of a sudden?

The truth was that the place was very quiet, disturbingly quiet. There was no one about and there were no lights on.

Pixie looked through the windows and saw beautiful furniture and paintings. It was luxury like she had never seen. Moving along to the next window she saw the same again, luxurious curtains, furniture and lamps.

On the wall by the window was a huge oil painting, picturing the Snooty family. Mr Snooty held his son in front of him and Mrs Snooty with several more children stood next to them both, looking left out. Pixie assumed that the handsome little boy, dressed in some blue velvety outfit may well have been Shudder. He was blonde haired and angelic looking, but even Pixie could see at a quick glance that Shudder appeared to be holding his little toy bear very firmly in an inappropriate way.

It made her cross to think that they had made their money to the detriment of all those young people. All those mill workers turning up day after day to work hard and earn a pittance, so that this family could buy anything and everything they wanted.

Then when they saw an opportunity to make more money with the mill conversion, the workers were sacked.

Pixie felt sad and angry.

A dark shadow passed swiftly past the window glass she was looking through and caused her to step back. She almost fell into some stone urns, but was saved by Teg. He was always happy to grab hold of her.

The shadow had gone and the room empty again.

"Are we going in?"

"Not sure that would help us," Pixie answered. "Although, I would really like to have a good look round. I bet the bedrooms and bathrooms would be worth viewing."

"Let's go in then!"

Pixie thought. "If we wait until I've killed Shudder, then I can come here and take control of the place. They are bound to want to sell it and then I can bring my family and friends round for a look. We won't be disturbed."

"You are confident and inventive Pixie, I'll give you that."

Pixie smiled. She was feeling young and free again. The moment altered when Teg reminded her that they still had to go and kill the aforementioned Shudder.

"I will show you how to get to Seren's, I mean your Gran's, and then I'll go back and collect the children for this evening. What time are we to be there?"

365

"Well," she answered slowly, "the usual time I suppose. How do you get from these grounds to the church?"

"You get there with the necklace, we can get there because we are dead."

"Ok fine."

"How am I supposed to get there then?" asked Teg.

"We will work something out."

Tamson floated back along the river bank towards the tunnel opening and Teg and Pixie walked towards the woods.

"The girls and everyone else should be at the cottage by now. What are we going to get them to do?"

"Nothing," answered Pixie. "I just told them to make sure the others were secure and wait there. If they stay there, then they will be safe from trouble."

"So we are not going to fetch them then?"

"No."

Teg thought again. "What about food? We haven't eaten for ages."

"Here's a biscuit," she said, reaching into her bag. "Drink some water from the spring and you will be fine."

Pixie ate a biscuit and had a drink to keep him company.

"Hang on a minute," she said and scampered back to the house.

She looked at the urns and then moved her hands around the base.

"What are you doing?"

"The pattern on the side is the same as my necklace. That must mean something. I just don't know what yet."

She carried on touching and was rewarded with a loud jingling sound as another key fell to the pavement.

"Wonder who keeps leaving all this stuff around the village?"

It was a good question, but unlikely to be answered.

Pixie dropped the key into her bag to join the things she had collected at the chimney altar. She hoped that when any item was needed, she would be able to extract it easily and not have to rummage about in there.

Yeah.

They continued walking by the river, through the low hanging trees and enjoying the scent of wild garlic and flowers and the sound of rushing water. Pixie knew that so long as they followed the flow of the water, they would reach their destination. The river flowed beneath a stone bridge as it travelled out of Snooty Land and towards the woods. They walked under the bridge and at the far side of it, climbed onto the road above. This road would lead them to Finders Hospital. The daylight was fading rapidly and the pair walked in silence. They saw no one else.

Pixie felt pretty calm considering where she was going. She still had no idea what she was going to do, but as she seemed to have coped well these past few days, she wasn't too worried.

They trudged on, listening to the branches of the trees serenade their journey. The gates reached and recognised, were entered. This was the first time in the journey that they had a suspicion that they were being followed. Pixie hated that sensation and kept looking behind, but saw no one.

It was almost dark now and so if anyone were hiding in the tree line, it would be impossible to see them. All they could see were trees waving in the increasing breeze and a road disappearing into the dark distance.

"The church is through there." Pixie pointed to the woods on their right.

"Shall we go and see it?"

"No, not yet. Hardly anyone knows it's there. We need to keep going to the hospital." There was another noise behind them.

"Blimey. I feel really scared Pixie," shivered Teg.

"Move faster then."

Soon, they stood in front of the doors of the hospital. The noises got louder and lights were appearing in the distance. Chanting and singing accompanied the lights. The inhabitants of Mill Town and Village were on their way for another evening of fun and jollity.

Another execution.

They arrived on goat carts and on foot. They carried torches and hampers. Children, grandparents and friends accompanied each family group. They made their way down the drive and upon seeing Pixie and her, as yet unidentified friend, they cheered.

"Miss Prix, Miss Prix! Is it true that you are to kill the evil Shudder tonight? What time is it happening?"

Pixie looked embarrassed.

"I have no idea when it is happening, I don't have an itinerary. Keep well away."

She turned back to the entrance and pulled Teg through the doors. At the same moment she felt a restraining hand on her arm. She pulled away sharply and said, "Please don't do that."

"I'm sorry Miss Prix. It's just that I wanted to speak to you personally." The words came from the mouth of a sad looking woman whom Pixie recognised from the bakery on Town Street. Mrs Barabun's husband stood next to her, looking equally humble.

"Can you help us find our little boy? He disappeared years ago and we have no idea where he is."

"I'm sorry to hear that," Pixie said simply.

"Have you seen him anywhere? He has blue eyes and red hair and a very sweet disposition. He went to play in the field at the back of the cottages where you lived. Sometimes he used to go into your aunt's house for sweets and then he vanished. Mrs Cal said that he had left their cottage that day and said he was coming back home. She had even sent him with an order for us to deliver the next day."

"But he never came home," said Mr Barabun sadly.

"He never came home," sniffed Mrs Barabun.

Pixie felt sick.

At that exact moment she heard a familiar screeching.

"Liddy, Liddy! Have you come to fetch a baby too?"

Her Aunt Cal was running towards her. The fat on her frame wobbled horribly.

"No I haven't," answered Pixie.

She took hold of the hand of the baker's wife and said, "I will do my best for you."

Pixie grabbed Teg again and went into the hospital, slamming the doors behind them.

"Lock them Teg," she instructed.

Teg shut the heavy doors and pulled the metal bar across.

"Don't think anyone will get in through there," he said.

There was no one at the reception desk, so the pair went directly into the corridor.

"Where exactly are we going?"

369

"There is a ward of special babies in here. If we go there Shudder should come to see what I am doing. He already knows I am going to kill him and he will want to protect his protégés."

"Protégés eh! I bet they will be very interesting!"

"Very. All I have to do is remember where they are."

She headed out of the reception area closely followed by her friend and strode out along the shiny corridor. After passing through a few swing doors, Nurse Hickson stood directly in front of them.

"Mrs Pollack, what are you doing here again?"

"I've come to kill Shudder."

"I see."

"I need to see the babies please."

"You are not seeing any of the babies, only the new keepers can see the babies when they are ready to be collected."

"I don't mean the nice babies. I mean the Shudder babies."

Nurse Hickson's face darkened.

"How do you make your face do that?" asked Teg.

Nurse Hickson ignored him, but said to Lydia, "Any baby in this hospital is under my protection, no matter where they came from and who they belong to."

"Why do you let him keep those babies here? I know he hasn't brought them into Mill Town yet, because no one has noticed them. He's still at the stage of corrupting Beyond babies."

"How do you know about that?"

"Because every baby he has corrupted has either grown up a confused victim or an abuser. The victims go back to Beyond eventually and the others go to… well a place we don't really want to think about. Horrible thingamajigs take them there."

She stared at the nurse, who stared back and began to fidget nervously.

"Look, I've been doing this job for a long time and took over from my mother and my grandmother. I don't want to lose my job and so I do whatever is necessary to keep it."

"Even if that involves being cruel?"

"I am never cruel," snapped the nurse. "I protect the wanted babies."

"By allowing Shudder to do what he wants?"

"I don't. I stop him touching the others by allowing him to use that ward. It's a good deal."

"You made a deal with Shudder?" asked Teg, almost in admiration.

"I made a deal with Shudder. I knew him when I was a girl and I am quite aware of what he is capable."

Pixie looked at the nurse's face for the familiar expression a victim would have. She owned the expression.

"It was either letting him use the ward or losing all babies from Beyond. What do you suggest I should have done?"

"I think that you should help us now. It will finish tonight."

"How can you be sure of that?"

Pixie changed tack. "Mr Lally must get some of his records from you, Nurse Hickson. That means that you know about me coming back. Did you tell Shudder I was back?"

"Naturally. He has kept a special watch on you and your family. He's been waiting for you."

"Fabulous."

Teg looked confused about this quick fire conversation he was witness to.

"So do we get to see the naughty babies then?" he asked.

Nurse Hickson looked from one to the other, then turned on her heel and said, "Follow me."

They did.

The nurse clicked along the corridor, upstairs, then downstairs, then upstairs again. Everywhere smelt very clean indeed.

She stopped eventually and turned back to them.

"Put on your necklace now Pixie," she instructed. "You can borrow mine," she said to Teg.

As soon as the necklaces were donned, a set of wooden ward doors materialized in front of them. Three quarters of the way up each door was a circular window. Above the doors on the wall was a sign which read:

Troll Ward
Back up Babies

Teg laughed. Pixie didn't. She pushed the door open and saw the cribs lining both sides of the ward. Glancing to one side of her, she saw a bell on the wall. It was the old emergency bell. She pulled it hard. The sound was dreadful and loud. Teg put his hands on his ears.

"What are you doing that for girl? It's horrible!"

"Watch," was all she said.

There was another sound which accompanied the bell. A screaming noise that gradually became louder than the bell ringing.

Pixie stopped ringing, but the babies didn't stop crying. Teg took his hands from his ears for a very short time before he put them back.

"I don't want children Pixie!" he shouted.

"I do," she answered.

The babies were all sitting up in the cribs. They appeared to be unchanged from her last visit all those weeks ago. No a few days ago, that's all. They stared at the two people invading their space.

The babies screamed and screamed as Pixie moved towards the first baby. She wanted to know if he remembered her. The baby reached up to her throat and tried to grab hold of the necklace. She put her hand over it protectively and the baby started to cry again.

"Do babies act like this all the time?" asked Teg.

"No, not really, but these babies are pretty horrible. Shudder wants to bring them into the Town."

"How is he going to do that?"

"By shutting down the gate from Beyond and making sure the babies given to people here were these. That way he could start to control the whole area through the children."

"How do you know all of this?"

"I'm not really sure," she said truthfully. "I think I might be remembering it."

She looked at the screaming babies, with their screwed up eyes and screwed up fists.

"Why are they screaming all the time?" she said, almost to herself.

"To irritate us?"

"It's more than that." She looked about the room and noticed a hole in the wall with a grille over it.

Putting her ear to it she listened carefully.

"I understand now," she said. "Shudder talks to them through this. They are trying to drown out the noise, so we don't hear him too."

"Are you sure about that?" asked Teg. "I think it's more like they are calling him here."

Pixie thought about that and had to agree that was a distinct possibility.

"If they are calling him by crying…"

"Yes …"

"That means that he is on his way now!" she announced.

"Oh heck," said Teg.

"It's great news! It's what we want!"

"It's what you want."

"Don't you want it?"

"I don't want to get killed, if that's what you mean. And I certainly don't want to get shuddered."

"He won't be in the mood for that Teg. He will be worried and he only wants to, you know, when he feels in control. He likes to get other people to do any killing, he's too much of a coward."

Pixie was shouting this through the grille.

"So he won't kill us then?"

"Course not. He is incapable of killing. But I'm not." She was still shouting.

"Ssshhh!"

"Don't ssshhh me Mr Morlin. If you have a problem about my plan, you can't even get back without me now."

"I could take off this necklace and then the ward would vanish."

"No it wouldn't. You would vanish from my view and I would still be left to deal with it. You would be stuck in the hospital corridor and wouldn't be able to get out of the front door. The Town are waiting for another execution out there. They may pick you!"

"I wouldn't leave you anyway."

"Why? I would leave you."

"Would you?"

"When you tell me the truth about Wrinkle's death, I will listen," she said unexpectedly. Teg said nothing.

The babies suddenly stopped screaming and turned to look at the intruders. Each ugly little baby with bright dark eyes and their lips set in firm thin lines.

The lamps in the ward went out and they were aware of noises out in the corridor.

"Is that him?"

"Probably."

Pixie moved towards the doors, trying not to notice the babies whose eyes followed their every move. Teg followed her.

They crouched under the round window, against the wooden doors. The noise of slapping and creaking could be heard along the corridor. Pixie stood up carefully and peeped through the window. Although only able to see the shiny white wall opposite the door, she could see the glow of a lamp from around the corner, which Pixie knew would be preceding Shudder.

"He thinks he's really important," muttered Pixie.

"He's pretty good at promoting fear though isn't he? You have to give him that. I mean the creepy noises and the lamps and all that."

He had succeeded in making her smile.

Now, the glow of the lamp got bigger until shadows could also be seen.

"There are three shadows!" whispered Teg.

Pixie put a finger to her lips and tiptoed back to the rear of the ward and Teg tiptoed alongside her. The babies followed their progress and as soon as the lamplight reached the door, their complete attention was shifted there.

The round glass lit up brightly, almost blindingly.

Then, at each window was a face, staring inside the ward, trying to accustom their eyes to the gloom. Teg and Pixie could see the faces quite clearly from their vantage point.

Inspector Glees and Doctor Catapult appeared satisfied with what they saw, or did not see and moved their faces away from the windows.

"Are they going away?" asked Teg.

Before she could answer, there was another face at the window. Shudder Snooty may have been a good looking little boy, but the brown, leathery, face and sticky chattering at the window was most definitely not nice.

His jaw moved up and down so quickly that the sound of chattering teeth was audible through the closed doors. His nose twitched and saliva dripped from his mouth. Pixie shook involuntarily.

"He has to die," whispered Pixie.

Shudder moved away from the window and the lamplight followed him. For a moment it was dark again. But, only for a moment.

The doors burst open and in came Glees and Catapult followed by Shudder. They stood in the doorway and Shudder sniffed the air. He poked the Doctor with a sticky hand and Catapult said, "Lydia, we know you here. Come out and let us see you."

At this order, every baby turned from the front of the ward where they had been fully concentrating on their master and faced the rear of the ward. They tried to shrink further behind the crib, but it was no use. Catapult and Glees ran to the back of the ward and grabbed them.

Teg struggled a lot, but was overpowered by the Inspector. Pixie and Teg had their arms tied behind their back by the Doctor and both of them were dragged in front of Shudder.

For the first time, Pixie did not feel scared of Shudder. She was more worried about how she was going to get out of the situation. There was a way. There had to be.

"Where are we going to take her?" asked Glees.

"I don't actually think we are taking her anywhere. Are we Boss?"

Shudder shook his head.

"We are just killing her here, now." Catapult took a knife from his pocket.

Pixie began to struggle. Inspector Glees held her tightly as she jumped about. Doctor Catapult raised his knife and brought it down on Teg's back.

"No! Don't do that!" she shouted.

CHAPTER TWENTY-SIX *HE'S DEAD*

The shock of seeing the knife make contact with her old friend shook her to the core. What happened after that shocked her even more.

"There you are Teg my friend, you are free now," said Doctor Catapult as he cut the rest of the ties that bound him, allowing Teg to shake his arms.

"Why did you tie me up anyway?"

"Didn't know how long we needed to keep up the charade. Doesn't matter anymore," said Glees. Shudder chattered and shook and dribbled. He put out his arms and patted Teg on the head with the palms of both hands. He was pleased.

"How could you?" asked Pixie.

"Sorry old girl. I've been watching you ever since you arrived at Seaside with Wrinkles. I've reported back here on your every move. I'm afraid it was necessary."

"Necessary! Why?"

"You are trying to upset the way the Town has been running. We had a plan, which would give us complete power at last. You have been trying to ruin it for us."

"I still don't understand why!" she said.

Shudder poked Teg and encouraged him on with his speech.

"Our leader Shudder is a valued member of the Snooty family, the most ancient of all the witch families and we are descendants of their followers. You are descended from the hermits. We are natural enemies."

"I thought we were friends?"

Shudder chattered away again.

"She has to die now Teg," said Glees. "You go on, I will do it."

"I would very much like to do it," said Teg. "There are one or two things I would like to do to her first."

Glees nudged Teg and winked. "Understood!"

Doctor Catapult said, "We need to hide and protect Shudder. To do that, we need to clear the crowds from the front."

"How are we going to do that?" asked Glees.

"Tell them that Lydia is being kept here for her own safety as she has gone a bit mad," reasoned the Doctor.

"Go on then! Leave me to it," said Teg.

Catapult handed his knife to Teg. The men helped Shudder shuffle out of the ward and closed the door behind them.

"Just us two now, Pixie."

"And all these babies."

The babies, still silent and staring, sat up in their cots.

"I killed Wrinkles for you Lydia. You are back to being Pixie, I'm confused. But you are free now."

"Hardly."

Teg took the knife and put it against Pixie's face, then ran the blade down her chest. He looked into her eyes and cut her ties.

"If you go and kill him, then I shall be really free. I can't come with you, I must stay here."

"Are you a traitor? I believed you."

"I suppose I am a victim. Spying for them kept my little sisters and brothers safe. I did what I had to do."

"The babies will tell Shudder."

"I will deal with the babies. They won't tell anyone."

"You can't kill babies."

"I said they won't tell anyone. That's different. Go."

As she left the ward, she noticed Teg going towards the grille in the wall. She was now standing back in the corridor, wondering whether or not to remove the necklace. In the distance she saw a lamp moving away from the ward.

Pixie rummaged through her bag and looked at the keys, the bottle of light, the snowflake jar and the dagger.

"No idea how to use these," she muttered to herself.

She sat down in the corridor and brought her knees to her face with her hands.

"Being someone who sorts things out is very tiring," she said quietly to herself. Brushing down her dress, she noticed suddenly how dirty she looked. It had been a while now since she had washed and dressed back at Gran's. She tried to see her reflection in the shiny white tiles, but that offered no clues to how she was presenting herself to others.

Teg being one of Shudder's men came to her mind, as if just realised. But then he had let her go. It's like David. She had no real clue about whose side he was on. She could accept that David had gone undercover in a misguided attempt to sort stuff out, but he was never one for an exit strategy on anything. He froze and thought that he would think just a little longer instead of acting. Teg, on the other hand was an adventurer, a risk taker, both traits attractive to any woman.

But he was one of Shudder's men, even if he had set her free. What was he going to do to the babies? Best not think about that anymore. She had liked Teg though, but he had killed Wrinkles. She thought they were friends. Mind you, none of them knew who she really was. Sometimes, she was anxious Lydia and sometimes she played calm Pixie.

She rummaged around in her bag again. A tiny dagger was soon tucked behind her bracelet, so that she could reach for it easily next time she was tied up.

The bottle of light. Maybe that would be to see something in the dark? Or see something that others couldn't see? No, the necklace did that.

The keys so far had helped her get into places that she wouldn't have otherwise been able to enter.

Jar of snowflakes? That was mad. Perhaps they would mask something from prying eyes. It was a pity there wasn't a bath and a new outfit in there too.

Suddenly the sound of shouting and running took her mind away from the contents of her bag. There was lamplight at the corner of the corridor closely followed by shadows. The shadows grew in size as the owners got closer to the corner. It was mesmerising.

"Lydia! Lydia! Where are you?"

The sound of her young sisters almost made her cry with pleasure.

"I'm here!" she answered, "I'm here!"

The girls ran towards her, followed by Gran and Marjoram and Sadie and their families. The two Scriber boys closely followed her younger sisters.

"Why didn't you come home you idiot? We had a plan to help!" said Janey.

"We only knew where you were when there were villagers walking past the cottage and they told us where they were going," said Gran

"We had to run here! All the way from Gran's and my feet are killing me!" said Sadie.

"I've had to leave Dotty with Mr Chariot's father and I don't want to leave her there for too long," said Marjoram.

"Michaelmas would like to be here," said Alice.

"Yes he would, but I intend to avenge his death." announced Lydia.

"Looking like that?" asked Sadie.

"I know. I was just thinking that. I look a mess."

"Good job we brought this then," said Janey bringing a red lace dress from her bag.

"It was my mother keeper's," said Gran. "She wore it at her initiation many years ago."

"It's beautiful," said Lydia. "I will go and put it on."

"We've already found the bathroom. You can have a wash and do your hair too." Alice handed over another bag.

"We will all help. You can't kill Shudder and be written in the Town's history for ever, when you look like a forest dweller. Because you do," Sadie informed her.

The sisters and their Gran went into the wonderfully clean bathroom, and prepared Lydia for her upcoming stage appearance.

The men stood outside in the corridor, now seemingly unable to speak to each other while the women were involved in women things behind a closed door. They paced about, hands in pockets and smiled at regular intervals to each other.

Soon the women appeared and the men had to admit that Pixie looked beautiful.

"Just like my mother," said Gran. "There is a painting at the club I will show you when it's all over, where she is wearing this dress. You look the same."

After the admiration, which even Lydia took part in, they decided to leave the hospital.

"We have to get to the church now, all the children will be praying there. Shudder will be trying to find it too. They want to seal the children off and prevent them from ever confronting Shudder. I need to ensure that they all meet him."

"Did you see anyone when you came in?"

"We saw the Doctor and the Inspector moving amongst the crowds. I think they were trying to persuade them to go home, but they weren't having much luck," said Mr Chariot.

"They know that something exciting is going to happen and Glees won't prevent them from seeing that," said Gran.

"Shudder is still in the building. We need to persuade him to follow us," Pixie told them.

She began walking and the others followed. They walked up and down stairs and eventually arrived at the reception area, where there was no sign of Shudder. Standing there, Pixie wondered what to do next. She looked about her and noticed a grille in the wall. Could this be connected to the ward? If so, was it connected to Shudder in another place? She decided to risk it.

With her mouth at the grille she shouted, "Shudder, we are going to the church, you must come with us. This is your final chance to stop all those children ever confronting you. You have to stop me getting there."

"Are you sure you know what you are doing Lydia?" asked Alice.

"She knows," said Gran.

"So, Shudder Snooty, you big coward, we are going to the church. We are going through the crowds, follow if you dare."

She walked to the front door and turned to Mr Chariot nodding to him to open it. Outside they could hear shouting and chanting and, as she stood there, she checked her appearance in the glass and took a deep breath.

The door was opened and Pixie was hit by the sound of her name being screamed at her by the crowds on the lawn. Hundreds of lamps lit the night and this alteration from the gloom of the reception area, caused her to screw up her eyes. Blinking a couple of times helped her eyes adjust and she walked down the stone steps, closely followed by her family.

She made her way across the lawn and amazingly, the crowd parted as she walked. She went towards the woods and upon reaching its edge, turned back to the crowd. Was it imagination that she saw a large shadowy figure cross the lawn at the rear of the hospital where there was no crowd?

She saw Glees and Catapult and David with other members of the Council. The Snooty family were in their sedan chairs alongside keepers of missing children. David Turncoat waved to her, but she didn't wave back.

Pixie put her hand into her bag and brought out the jar of snowflakes. She knew suddenly that this was not to obscure anything, it was to reveal.

As she opened it, the snowflakes swirled slowly out and reached up into the night. She put the jar onto the grass and silence fell on the crowd as thousands and thousands of snowflakes left the jar. A column of snow flowed into the sky and soon began to fall all over the area.

There was much ooohhhing and aaahing and if a survey were to be taken amongst the crowd at that particular moment, it would be fair to say that the majority would say that tonight was the best night of their lives. And it wasn't over yet!

As the snow fell, the church appeared in view. Firstly, in a misty incomplete form and then gradually solidified into the recognisable structure. The stone church rose up against the backdrop of the night sky and falling snow. Lights inside shone through the coloured glass. The graves and memorials were gradually being covered in snow, as far as the eye could see.

Pixie was aware that the crowd were slowly moving towards the church.

"What are all those stones on the lawn?" asked one.

"They've got writing and names on them," noticed another.

"They are all your prayers," explained Pixie. "Everything you have asked and prayed will remain here on record until granted. The stones will not vanish until the prayers are answered."

"How do the prayers get answered?"

"They are all listened to and all will be answered eventually. That's why you should be careful what you wish for." She turned to the questioner and grinned.

He didn't appreciate the joke and merely scowled at her. She may be some sort of celebrity at this moment, but she was still an arrogant idiot, he thought.

She smiled again and again noticed the shadow crossing the edge of the cemetery and standing alongside the monument to Gladys Ailwood. She said nothing.

As they all neared the church, the sound of music and singing reached their ears. It was calming and beautiful. David looked at Lydia moving across the white lawn in a beautiful long red dress. He had never seen her looking like that before. She moved to the door of the church, before looking back at the crowd and waving to them. He saw her family follow her through the door. She didn't ask him to follow.

As the Prixs filed in through the door, David noticed a large shape follow them in and shut the door behind them.

It was Shudder.

The sight which met her eyes as she stepped into the church was ethereal. Hundreds of ghost children sat in the pews and the choir stalls. Tamson was at the organ and some others took care of the doors. The bell tower was guarded by a little red haired boy and Pixie knew instantly that he was the son of the baker.

Without thinking, she made her way to the pulpit and climbed the stairs. The effect of the tall confident woman, dressed richly in red and looking down on the congregation was stunning.

"Tonight we shall remove Shudder from our lives so that we can carry on travelling on the path we want and not the path he has decided for us. I know he is very close now. But he is unable to face us. That is not possible for him. In fact, I want you all to promise that you will never let him know, that if he gets as far as ringing the bells in the tower, we are lost. The ringing of the bell is the only way he can escape us and banish us to permanent incapacity."

The children murmured and nodded their heads vigorously. They had no intention of betraying the woman who had promised faithfully to free them.

"You are only trapped in the darkness of the tunnel, neither living a life in the Town nor living with your loved ones in Beyond, because of what he has done to you. The way you died was terrible. But I want you to know that Beyond has not forgotten you and has never stopped listening to the prayers of those who wanted to help you. You must understand that the only way to complete the path to freedom is to face the terror you want to avoid. Everything must eventually be faced and then dealt with. By accepting responsibility you will gain power and will no longer be lost. Tonight, if we work together, you will be free. We shall all be free."

A round of applause acknowledged their acceptance of her words. Her family clapped while looking at each other wondering how Lydia ever got to be like this.

The applause stopped. The bell was ringing.

"I was wondering why she was saying that about the bell, when she knew that Shudder might be about," said Sadie.

The ghost children were moving from their seats, scared and bewildered. Pixie raised her hand.

"Sit, sit! Everything is going to plan!"

She stepped down from the pulpit and made her stately progress along the aisle in the direction of the tower. The bell was now ringing violently, with neither tune nor rhythm. Pixie was unfazed and everyone else was worried.

She arrived at the tower door, opened it with her key and looked inside. Smiling, she turned back to the congregation and asked them to come.

They saw Shudder ringing the bell. As far as he was concerned, the bell ringing had not met his expectations. Upon learning that ringing the bell would save him, he was now discovering two things. Firstly, ringing the bell was having absolutely no effect on the ghost children or Pixie. Therefore she had been lying from the pulpit, which he wasn't sure was allowed.

Secondly, he was not a good campanologist. Hanging upside down, one leg caught in the rope and swinging wildly from side to side, proved that fact beyond any reasonable doubt.

Pixie stood in front of him. Shudder looked pathetic and helpless. He was chattering wildly and his saliva dripped steadily in an arc onto the floor of the tower. Upside down, his twiggy protuberances scraped the floor and appeared to be causing him pain. His pointy head swung only a few inches higher than the floor and he tried to lift it up on each swing so that he did not hit it. His long brown cloak was partly wrapped around the rope and half covered his body, trapping his arms and only just covering his private areas.

"Shudder, you do realise that tonight is the last night of your life here, don't you? There won't be another morning or another night. There will be no more child experiments and no killings. Do you want to say sorry or ask for mercy?"

She took out the tiny dagger from her bracelet. "I could use this. It will be quicker for you?"

At this, Shudder tried to escape. His shaking and wiggling caused the rope to swing again as a pendulum. He was in mental and physical torment. He let out a noise, a cross between a howl and a scream.

There was hammering on the outside door and shouting from Glees and Catapult.

"Let us in! What are you doing to him?" and other pointless phrases.

Pixie went out into the main body of the church.

"Everyone, this is the time I was telling you about. You need to be really brave now."

Some of the children looked scared and tearful and one or two were holding hands.

"I know that you are scared. But you are also tired of living in the dark, without your family. Sometimes it seems easier to stay somewhere you don't like, than make a move to somewhere that's better."

"What if it's not better?" asked Tamson.

"Don't you think it will be better? I'm not asking you to do anything that will hurt you. All you need to do is face him. It won't be easy and it won't be nice, but looking at him, really looking, will free you forever."

"I'm scared to see him. Will you come with me?" said the baker's boy.

"Of course I will. I'll come with you all, you don't have to be alone. Besides, I have seen Beyond and it is beautiful there."

"Do you know anyone there?" asked a young girl.

Tears came to her eyes as she said, "Oh yes, my Granddad and my brother. You will find your families and be happy and safe. You will be amongst friends."

The boy held one hand and the little girl the other and they went into the tower together. When the children saw Shudder they tightened their grip and trembled.

When Shudder saw the children he screamed and trembled and swung from side to side. Helplessly, upside down and trapped by the rope from a church bell.

When the children came back into the church, they were smiling and confident. This gave hope to the others and two by two, holding hands with Pixie they went into the tower room. They faced the one who had ensured they died in terror and pain and been consigned to the darkness for so many years.

With each visit, Shudder struggled less and his chattering became weaker. By the time Pixie had taken the last few in, she almost felt sorry for him. But her desire to free all the children stopped her changing her mind.

The banging on the outside door stopped and there were no more demands to be let in.

Tamson was the last ghost child she took in to the tower. When Tamson saw him, she walked to the weak thing hanging and went over to touch him lightly. "He's scared Pixie."

"I know," she answered.

Shudder stopped wriggling and emitted a low moan.

Pixie took Tamson out into the church and then asked everyone to follow her outside. What a spectacle, the red dress preceding a long line of ghost children out into the snow covered graveyard. As they all came into view of the crowds, some children recognised keepers and some keepers recognised children. Many recognised no one because they had been dead for too long.

Another blood curdling howl came from inside the church.

"He's dead," said Pixie.

Then something miraculous happened. The ghost children floated up through the still falling snow and as each child flew, a memorial from the graveyard vanished. The ghosts swirled over the crowds, saying goodbye where appropriate.

Pixie reached into the bag for the bottle of light and opened it. The light followed the spirits and surrounded them all. It was as if there was a huge comet in the sky.

The snow fell on the lawn as it cleared of its monuments, each stone prayer vanishing behind the ghost as the prayer was answered.

The ugly babies floated up too, forming a red crackling comet across the sky.

"So Teg sorted that out for us at the end."

"Who did?" asked Gran.

She smiled and hugged her Gran. "It's over now."

Gran hugged her back.

CHAPTER TWENTY-SEVEN *EPILOGUE*

"Oh look at her enjoying the cake!" said Marjoram.

It was Dotty's first birthday party and everyone was there. Alice and Janey were present with their new husbands, Jot and Mark Scriber. After a ten month courtship there had been a joint wedding. They were in the process of building a new cottage each at the edge of the woods at Gran's. In the meantime they were all living with Lydia at Snooty Manor.

The Snootys sold the place to Lydia and moved to their Snooty Shooting Moorland Manor. They didn't want to remain in Mill Town and so put in a manager at their Old Mill apartment complex.

Marjoram and Mr Chariot, Bobby and Dotty enjoyed an increase in income. Mr Chariot had taken over the funeral business in Town from Emtee Oreful. He had the brilliant idea of putting bodies in boxes under engraved stones, which would be looked after by their relatives. This stopped the necessity of dumping or burning the bodies. There was a lot of money in that.

Sadie and her husband continued to farm and Sadie often visited the market to meet her friends. Mr Prince appeared neither to know nor care who she met there.

Ginger took over as Inspector from Glees. The Doctor, now banished from practising had sold the family home and was moving away to Seaside accompanied by his sisters. He said he wanted to retire.

A new doctor from City was coming to take over the practice and the hospital. He told the Council that he was tired of all the dramas and business of City and wanted a quiet life in a rural town. His name was Doctor Lumberkins Parasol.

David Turncoat worked on his family farm and was rarely seen in the town. It had not helped when an early attempt at reconciliation with Lydia had met with a sharp rebuff. He suspected that she had held a torch for the traitor Teg and of that he did not approve. He found himself in the position of being neither brother nor good friend.

Teg went with the Snooty family to the City, apparently he and the youngest daughter were to be married. He had wanted to marry Lydia, but she suspected that his real interest was in her money and property and refused his offer.

The old Council was disbanded and a new Council elected by the townspeople. Now an election must be held every five years. Lydia was asked to be Council leader but refused to stand for any position. Most of the new members were from the Old Peoples' Club, because they had a lot of experience between them. Seren Prix took on a major role and wished that Treen could have been there with her to share the honour.

Spawg Lally was now head of the Council and announced a complete change in the way it was run. He said that a limited number of records would be made available to anyone who could prove a desire to track their ancestry. But so far there had been less interest than he had anticipated.

"I know who my keepers are, we keep it in a book at home," said one.

"I hope no one else is allowed to see our family secrets," was a common answer.

"I never liked my dad anyway, I don't want to look at his records," was another.

An inflammatory law he introduced was the list of anyone who had taken part in any of the examinations.

The 'List of Nasty and Offensive Examinations' as it became known, was very effective during its early stages. It ensured that all those who had suffered in silence and felt unable to receive a sympathetic response from Glees, could now make statements. But as time went on, old arguments began to play their part and some accusations were perhaps not as honest as they could have been.

Once a name was added to the list and nailed to the board in front of the Police Office, no one would deal with that man in any way. Soon he could no longer pay his bills and so far eighteen properties had been bought by wily property collectors. These were already rich men and they were becoming richer. The accused men and their families were forced to leave Mill Town and Mill Village and seek a new life elsewhere.

The Scriber family were inundated with legal requests for defence and prosecution and it was natural that the firm put those claiming abuse on the top of their case lists. Most of the cases were still being assessed and evidence collected. The problem here was, the Scribers were supposed to represent both defendant and accuser. There was talk about the necessity of an alternative firm of lawyers. The Scriber brothers had talked about splitting up and earning money from both sides.

The Council were to act as judge and jury.

The penalty was death.

This new freedom from fear was creating other problems never considered before.

"We ought to have somewhere to lock people up after they have been accused and keep us all safe," said Mrs Banana and others.

It was not yet known when consideration would be given to people who were losing everything while trying to prove their innocence.

"Better that, than the guilty go free," said a self-righteous Council member.

These reasons and similar were why Lydia had no desire to be in any position of authority.

Aunt Cal was not at the party. She tried to order a baby from Finders the day after Shudder died and was refused.

"Your husband only just died and it has to be said that your record as an aunt has not been the best. So no, I am not letting any of our babies come to you," Nurse Hickson told her.

And as soon as Auntie Cal's name appeared on the list, her landlord took back her cottage and she left on one of the carts going to the City one rainy Saturday. She had not been heard of since.

Mother and father Prix began to see their children more often and enjoyed spending time at Snooty Manor. Father loved working in the garden and he helped convert the buildings next to the old stone coach house into stables for the pony business.

Although the twins were also building houses next to the woods, the space at the manor ensured that the business could expand as they wanted. Plus the animals were safer.

Lydia Prix entered the room and looked at her guests. Dotty's party was taking place in the grand ballroom at the Manor. It was the best room in the house.

Lydia smiled at Marjoram and tickled Dotty under the chin, who giggled in appreciation. The party was going well, all the family and all of their friends were there. There was music and food and games. Everybody was enjoying themselves.

It had not taken her long to persuade the Snooty family to sell. She called there the morning following the last adventure, to talk about Shudder and discuss what was to be done with his remains. Snooty family remains were kept in a crypt on the Manor property which the family had owned for many generations. They were buried in separate stone boxes.

Eventually it was agreed that Shudder could be kept in his box in the crypt and Lydia would purchase the Manor. She promised to keep the crypt safe and allow any future dead Snooty to be buried there.

As the price agreed was cheap, Lydia had plenty of gold left over and decided to invest in property in addition to helping her family. Two apartments at the old mill were now owned by her. The one by the reception door, where she first met Shudder, held a particular fascination. She intended to rent it out eventually, but as she often went there on her own and just sat, she did not feel that now would be appropriate. Lydia felt that she needed to have one part of her in the past, in order to be able to cope with the future.

Another acquisition had been the chimney. The salesman had been most surprised when she asked whether or not it were for sale. After that, she spent many hours visiting the hidden chambers in the chimney. She told no one what she saw there and they assumed that she just liked spending time on her own.

"She needs a lot of quiet time," said Janey.

"A lot happened to her in such a short time," mused Gran.

"It could take her years to get over it," her mother pointed out. Mother Prix had often noticed her daughter standing at the window of her apartment, looking sad and lost. The feeling which rose within Mother Prix may have been recognised by another as guilt. That recognition was not made by Mrs Prix however.

Lydia also began acquiring land around the town, through old Mr Scriber. He agreed to keep her identity secret, whilst enjoying the benefit of fees and commissions.

"You look lost in your thoughts, Lydia," said Gran, as she poured a drink for her granddaughter. "Are you enjoying living here now?"

"I am Gran. I am. It's nice to be surrounded by so many nice things."

"I am not so sure that keeping all of the Snooty paintings and furniture and stuff is a good idea, Lydia. They are such bad people and I don't want the energy to rub off on you."

"It won't Gran. It can't." Lydia smiled and wandered around her room, surveying her family and friends.

She enjoyed the feeling of security from property owning and all the gold in her safe. After inheriting everything that Wrinkles possessed, she rented out the cottage in Seaside and sold his boat and fishing stuff. It would have also greatly surprised her family to know that she had bought Cal's cottage.

Her thoughts were interrupted by Alice. Her thoughts were always being interrupted and that was why she liked her times of meditation.

"Lydia, we were thinking of ordering some more ponies. We have heard of a really good line of rainbow ones and want to be first in there."

"And that means we will need those other stone buildings near the tunnel entrance for stables," said Janey.

"Do whatever you want girls. I honestly don't mind. I want you to succeed."

The girls scampered off, deep in conversation.

Mr Chariot called everyone over to the table to watch Dotty blow out her candles.

During this excitement, Jot Scriber said, "Oh, have you heard that a new club has been started up at that church?"

"New club? What new club?" asked Lydia.

"Something about seeing the golden light when the children all went up into the sky. Because there was also a dark light and creatures when Cal died, they have decided to start meeting at the church once a week and ask the golden light for help and security. They think that if they worship the golden light, then all their wishes will be carved in stone outside the church and granted straight away."

"I'm not so sure that it works if the wishes are purely for selfish reasons," commented Lydia.

"Well they have already starting writing up a set of rules to make it work."

Lydia shook her head. Some people shouldn't be allowed out, she thought.

After the party, everyone returned to their homes or their rooms at the Manor. Lydia went outside and walked down by the river. She sat down on a log on the path by the riverside. The river rushed around the rocks and pulled down the tree branches so that they trailed in the water this way and that. The moon reflected on the surface of the water, splitting into a thousand fragments as it did so.

Lydia felt as though this picture mirrored her mind, which had been very unsettled since last year. She held her chin in her hands and fell into her familiar meditative state. She still found it difficult to make sense of all that had happened and where her place was now.

Often feeling deserted and lonely, treated differently by her neighbours and no longer required to solve their problems she recognised that her fame had been a short lived thing. She had insisted on keeping hold of the keys to all the entrances to the tunnel and telling no one where they were. Just in case …

There it was again, the feeling that she was being watched. She looked around quickly, but could see nothing. For a few days now, Lydia had been sure that someone was following her.

During her quiet times at the chimney, sitting in the hand of the statue she had asked for help from her friends from Beyond. There had been no answer.

"Lydia! Are you there?"

"I'm here!" she answered.

She saw a man walking towards her wearing a white uniform. It was Doctor Parasol.

"Come with me Lydia, we need to talk," he said.

She followed him.

"Must be some sort of emergency," she said.

"It's not really an emergency Mrs Pollack, but the Inspector at Seaside has told us that you are wanted for questioning in connection with the murder of your husband."

"But, he died after I arrived here! Why have you waited over a year to come and talk to me?"

A man grabbed hold of her arms and pulled them behind her back. Lydia saw Teg standing behind him.

"I had to tell them Lydia, I couldn't keep it quiet any longer."

"What are you talking about? His death was an accident," she cried.

"Your hair was found at the murder scene and you wrote in your journal that you wanted to see him dead. Everyone knows that you are unstable Lydia, thinking that you are a pixie and bossing everyone about. You need to spend some time in hospital again until we have everything sorted out," said the Doctor.

Teg was waving the journal in his hand.

"Don't worry Lydia, I shall take care of your estates, just as you asked me to. I have shown the documents to my City lawyers and they agree that it is all legal and binding." He smiled at her.

As she was dragged away, Teg winked and said in a whisper to her, "There is no such thing as happy ever after. We always win in the end Lydia.

Always."

Lydia stood up straight and laughed at them all. She could see what was at the tunnel entrance, ready to help her.

"I will bet you right here and now that I shall be free again tomorrow. There is such a thing as happy ever after. It's guaranteed!"

PROBABLY TO BE CONTINUED ...

A SELECTION OF PUBLICATIONS

Of

PAGANUS PUBLISHING

The Specials by A A Prideaux is a murder mystery set in 2012.

An old man is found dead in his home and DCI Revie and DS Jackson face the task of discovering who murdered him.

At first, it appears that there is no reason the quiet widower should have been killed. But the investigation soon reveals that the gentle old man had been a long term and particularly deviant paedophile. As the story unfolds throughout the year and the body count rises, the police discover more people who have been living an apparently normal life while successfully hiding their past. The lives of all the people involved can never be the same again. The Specials reaches its dramatic conclusion in Snowdonia.

A Ghost Story by A A Prideaux. John Prideaux (1505-1568) lived in Stowford and had a wife and two children. He had lots of friends and great connections and lived in one of the largest houses in Stowford.

One evening in 1547, he and his family and friends were at their usual Tuesday night dinner. They took weekly turns as to which house the dinner and entertainment were held. This night was the turn of the Prideaux family at Stowford Manor. They ate their meal and as they settled down, John told the gathering a ghost story. He told them of a stranger he once befriended and the mysterious path the meeting led him along. Present at the dinner were Parson William Hele, Robert and Sybil Fox, Thomas and Joan Rogers and John and Ann Prideaux. Before the evening ended, the friends are on a mysterious quest of their own, leading to a remarkable conclusion at St Petrocs church on snowy Dartmoor.

A Christmas Story by A A Prideaux is about Clifford Prideaux (1902-1963).The story begins in a modest home in early Edwardian Leeds, where the Prideaux family await a surprise event on Christmas Day 1902. The story takes the reader from 1902 to 1993 in a short story and gives a flavour of what Christmas meant to Clifford and his family. A Christmas Story gives a flavour of the times prior to the Great War for those with no money and no property. What the family had, was their love for each other and that love cannot be exaggerated.

A A Prideaux has written about each of her Prideaux ancestors from 1040 to the present day. She has traced every one of them through research and discovered where and how they lived. A A Prideaux has travelled miles in this search. She has old books, family documents and stories which have helped her in the conclusions drawn. Clifford Prideaux and her mother were responsible for setting the fire in her soul that turned into a Prideaux obsession. A Christmas Story is one of her fictionalised tales which draw on known facts. In this case, the story is written with personal experience of the author. This Clifford Prideaux (1902-1963) story takes us to Leeds and a tiny stone cottage full of love and warmth. These stories bring the Prideauxs to life, giving them personalities and allowing the reader to know them as people, not just names.

"A Christmas Story is about my grandma and grandad. Christmas was always a special time for Grandad Clifford. It's magic ran through his veins from the first day. Clifford was a kind man, but also a mystical one. Even after his death, he has visited his family on many occasions. I think of him as a hermit character, cloaked and walking with a long staff. He appeared in his role of Clifford for only 60 years before he returned to being the hermit." **A A Prideaux.**

The story of **'The Bishop and the Witch'** by **A A Prideaux** takes place between 1596 and 1608.John Prideaux was born near Dartmoor in 1578 and eventually became Bishop of Worcester. He spent most of his adult life at Exeter College, Oxford as Regius Professor and Vice Chancellor.

He was involved in many of the important events which took place in England during the reigns of Elizabeth I, James I and Charles I.

When John Prideaux gave evidence in 1606 at the Star Chamber about Anne Gunter, he did so as a well-known and respected Oxford academic. At the 1604 Witch Trial at Abingdon her alleged tormentors, Elizabeth Gregory, Agnes and Mary Pepwell were ultimately found to be innocent. Anne was sent to stay with Henry Cotton, the Bishop of Salisbury until her father confronted the King and asked him to intervene in the bewitching case. King James took a personal interest in Anne's troubles and put her under the control of Richard Bancroft, the Archbishop of Canterbury.

Anne later confessed to King James that her symptoms were faked on the instructions of her father, Brian Gunter. He was arrested and faced his accusers at the Star Chamber in 1606.

Anne Gunter was given a dowry by King James and she disappeared from the history books. History does not tell us what happened to Anne Gunter, but A A Prideaux provides us with a potential solution.

A A Prideaux tells the story of the possible meeting of John Prideaux and Anne Gunter at a much earlier time and how that meeting could have had a bearing on the outcome of the trial. Most of the characters playing a part in this story actually existed, making her version of events a possible one.

"John and Anne become friends and allies and we find that the story was not such a simple one. We discover who the real witches were and how John struggled with his faith during his involvement with the Gunter family. The reader must draw their own conclusions whether the events were caused by demons or drugs.

This is an alternative tale based on historical facts and a lot of artistic license."

A A Prideaux

Thank you. Do call again.

www.ingramcontent.com/pod-product-compliance
Lightning Source LLC
Chambersburg PA
CBHW051313250626
47155CB00007B/2301